Volle
by Kyell Gold

VOLLE

Copyright © 2005 by Kyell Gold

Published by Sofawolf Press, Inc
St. Paul, Minnesota
http://www.sofawolf.com

ISBN 978-0-9712670-8-4

Printed in the United States of America
First trade paperback edition: January 2005

Third Printing: July 2021

Cover and interior art by Sara Palmer

For my mother,
who taught me to write
and instilled in me the fierce desire to do so,
even though (or perhaps because)
she could not have known how I would use it.

I love you, Mom.
Please stop reading now.

Author's Note

"If you're going to write a quarter of a million words, why on Earth would you choose the unknown and unlikely genre of anthropomorphic gay erotica?"

Sometimes my inner voice chimes in just a bit too late.

The truth is, I never set out to write one novel, let alone two. I had been kicking around a story idea about a prisoner with some information, and a guard sent to seduce him into giving up that information, and how they eventually fell in love. When I sat down to write it, I took the path of least resistance and made the main character a gay fox, in keeping with my own predilections.

"The Prisoner's Release" was a fluffy little story that nonetheless kept nagging at me. What information did this fox have that was so valuable? What happened after the story ended?

You hold the answer to the first question in your hands right now.

The novel grew organically from my thoughts about this fox and where he'd come from. Because the short story had included some explicit erotica, that framework naturally extended itself to the novel. I've always felt that it should be possible to include some erotica in a story that would enhance the story more than it distracted from it (I'm not sure it's possible or desirable to write non-distracting erotica).

I'm not sure whether I proved that point with "Volle," but I gave it a try. I hope you enjoy the result.

"Volle" precedes "The Prisoner's Release" (published in two installments in Sofawolf Press's adult magazine "Heat"). The other bookend is "Pendant of Fortune," a novel of similar length, which takes place afterwards. It is forthcoming from Sofawolf Press.

And for reference, "Volle" is pronounced to rhyme with "wall," not with "holy" or "whole."

Kyell Gold
December 2004

Prologue

In the city of Divalia, the capital of Tephos, the walled palace sits beside the river, long and low. Inside the walls, the palace is surrounded by three gardens on the north and south. The one on the south side, onto which the main gates open, is the pride of the king. A crew of ten gardeners has no other job but to tend the garden, and nobles and servants alike roam through its lovely flower displays and shaded gazebos that run the length of the palace.

On the north side of the palace are the other two gardens, the rear gardens. They are less frequented and less tended; only two gardeners look after each one. The doors from the palace into these gardens are rarely used.

If you were to wander through the western rear garden, you might eventually come across an old statue of a lion warrior. He stands boldly facing the outer wall of the palace, sword raised, lips curled in a fierce snarl. His mane is richly detailed, though much of the detail has been lost to time. There are nicks and blemishes in the bronze, and it has turned mostly green with age. There is no plaque to identify the origin of the statue, nor any dedication to explain its presence.

It looks like any of the other statues in the gardens. Perhaps it is older and more worn, and certainly it is not in the front garden with the rest of the statues. In your wanderings, having seen the other statues that commemorate valiant generals and glorious battles, you might only be momentarily confused by the lion's mane—there are no maned lions in Tephos. After a moment, you might wander past the statue, deciding in your own mind that it was dedicated to the lost memory of a long-ago warrior, or a battle the king had fought against the southerners.

But you would be wrong.

Book 1: The Palace of Divalia

Chapter 1

The Hungry Bull, in the lower part of Caril, capital of Ferrenis, was a noisy place even in the early afternoon. Little sun made it through the dirt-clouded windows, and that's how the patrons liked it. Mostly congregating in couples, they tended to stay for a while and keep ordering drinks, and that's how the bartender liked it. Some of the patrons' wives didn't like it quite as much, so it wasn't unheard of for a female voice to shout a name over the din.

"VOLLE!"

The slender fox in a back booth flicked his ears and turned his muzzle instinctively. The wolf who was occupying his attention saw the movement and grinned. "That for you?"

Volle nodded. It was Seir, of course, come to fetch him to his Very Important Meeting. He could see the suddenly quiet patrons of the tavern craning their necks to see where he was, though because Seir was a mouse, they would be looking for a male mouse.

He'd half-expected this to happen. He was sick of hearing about how lucky he was, that it was unheard of for someone his age to get such an important assignment. Lucky or not, he would be gone for years, and because Volle believed strongly in taking advantage of opportunities while he could, he was determined to get every little bit of playtime in before he left the city of Caril. It had taken him longer to meet up with a suitable playmate than he'd counted on, true, but this was his meeting and they would not—could not—start it without him. It was the most revenge he could muster against the strict and officious Duke of Westermarch, who was the king's Minister of Intelligence. Duke Avery had taught a class in politics at the Academy which Volle had nearly failed, his stubborn resistance to being confined clashing with the Duke's insistence on nearly military attendance and participation in the class. They disliked each other, but Volle was sure the Duke wasn't as afraid of him as he was of the large, fierce wolf. If Duke Avery had come looking for him, he would have been out the back door without a second word to his companion.

Just the thought made him crane his neck around the edge of the booth slightly to look towards the bar. The bartender, a portly boar, was leaning across the counter to talk down to someone. If the Duke were here, the boar wouldn't be looking down, that was for sure. Volle was sure that Seir had come alone, just as sure as he was that the bartender wouldn't give away his location. Rolli was an expert at plausible misdirection, allowing his clients to get out the back door if they had the wits to use the time he gave them.

"Want to go upstairs?" Volle whispered. He could tell the wolf was ready to adjourn to a more private setting, though another five minutes of petting would have been polite.

"Uh, sure." The wolf's light grey ears flicked. "You won't get in trouble?"

"I might." Volle laid on the charm, giving the wolf his best wide-eyed smile. "But you're worth it."

It worked, of course. The wolf was a year younger than Volle, probably an apprentice to some merchant. Volle hadn't bothered to check because that wasn't what interested him. He liked the wolf's build, and his brown eyes and pretty smile, which he got to see again. "Okay. You first?"

"Yeah." He nuzzled the wolf, slid across the booth, and bumped into someone he hadn't noticed standing at the end.

"Come on," Seir said. She stood four feet high, still below his eye level even when he was seated. That had nothing to do with why he hadn't noticed her. She had a peculiar talent for being quiet and unnoticeable that he hated when she used it against him. No matter how many times he told himself to keep an eye out for her, she always managed to sneak up on him. It wasn't anything she'd learned at the Academy, his professors said. She'd just always had that talent.

She wore a simple linen dress and a leather vest, similar to the one Volle wore over his linen tunic. Her arms were folded and she was tapping one paw. He turned his charm on her. "Oh, hi, Seir."

"Didn't you hear me calling you? Volle, this isn't one of your Academy tests you can just walk into late and do barely enough to pass. This is real."

"I was kind of in the middle of something."

The wolf leaned forward. "Wait a minute. You're married outside your House?"

Seir laughed. "He's not the marrying type. I keep an eye out for him. Otherwise he'd end up doing something stupid, like keeping Prince Gennic waiting."

Volle blinked. "The Prince?"

Behind him, the wolf echoed his words, and added, "You really do work for the royal family?"

"Well, 'work' in the loosest sense of the word," Seir snorted. "Yes, the Prince is coming to your briefing. I told Reese to tell you."

"He didn't, the bastard." Volle cursed under his breath. "Fox take him! Do I have time to get back and change?"

"If you hurry." Seir grinned. "Come on."

With a quick wave to the perplexed wolf, Volle slid out of the booth and followed Seir out of the tavern. "Why is the prince coming?" he asked as they hurried through the streets to Eagle Bridge.

Seir shrugged. "He's taking an interest in military matters, I suppose. He doesn't have to give reasons. This morning, he told Duke Avery he wanted to know more about this operation, and Duke Avery invited him to the briefing. I suspect that he was hoping you would be late. I couldn't find you, so I told Reese. I didn't figure you'd be gone all day."

"Things to do," Volle muttered. "Who knows how long it'll be before I get back here."

"There's a Hungry Bull in every city," Seir said. "I'd hoped that by this point you would realize that there are more important things."

"Sorry to disappoint you," Volle said sullenly. Just because she was a couple years older than he was and had graduated from the Academy with honors, she thought she could boss him around.

The annoying thing was that a lot of the time, she was right.

"Listen," she said as they walked beneath the carved eagles into the Nobles' Quarter. "I may be one of two people in this whole city who knows your potential. I talked Avery into going ahead with this mission. He wanted to wait another year or two to see if another fox came up through the school."

"Why do they need a fox anyway?"

"I assume we'll find out today." They paused to let a carriage go by. In the Nobles' Quarter, the buildings had room to stretch their splendid marble limbs, looking down on their crowded neighbors across the river. Above them, the palace walls and towers stood watch, promising security.

The Academy lay just inside the Nobles' Quarter, because most of the students were nobility. Volle, like Seir and Reese, had been admitted despite his House because he showed particular intelligence and aptitude, and because his mother had sold her house to pay his admission. The house had been one of three things his father had left her: the other two were a fox cub growing in her belly and a gold pendant, which Volle had worn all his life.

He left the pendant on and changed everything else, slipping into his best cotton shirt and velvet doublet, with almost-matching trousers scrounged from the tailor's castoffs. Reese, a hare whose eleven-inch advantage in height over Volle was entirely due to his ears, came into the room they shared as Volle was finishing his wardrobe.

"Hey, Volle," he said as the fox came in. "Seir asked me to tell you that Prince Gennic will be at your briefing." He winked at the mouse.

"Thanks," Volle said. "It is a great comfort to me that the two of you care so much."

"Hey," Reese said with a shrug and a grin, "it's our mission too."

"Thanks to me," Volle said.

"Who else would they pick to keep an eye on you?" Seir asked as they walked out into the sunlight.

"That's what I mean," Volle grinned.

He always felt a shiver when he walked up to the palace. He'd gazed at it often as a cub on the streets, imagining the wonders that lay within, the beautiful people and the elegance of the royal family of cougars. He'd been in the palace several times during his Academy career, and still felt that same prickling all through his fur and tail every time he stood at the gate, with the southern tower looking down on him.

They met in the northern tower, out of the way of the normal traffic of the castle. It was stuffy even with three windows open to the outside, and Volle thought it was fortunate that he'd left the pub unsatisfied, otherwise he'd be asleep in minutes.

The room was more or less circular; the underside of the stairs formed part of the ceiling to the left, and the door was set into a flat wall, but the rest of the room conformed to the shape of the tower. Six wooden chairs sat around a table, and an upholstered chair sat off to one side. In the upholstered chair, tail tucked quietly underneath it, sat Prince Gennic.

The eldest of the three princes was a short cougar, with a broad tawny muzzle and round black ears, white-striped like all his family. At this meeting, he wore very simple royal clothes: a green tunic that matched the upholstery in the chair, a fancy blue velvet vest over it, and short cotton trousers. He kept his paws folded in his lap, and his ears forward, listening intently.

Seir, Reese, and Volle sat in three of the wooden chairs. Across from them, a large, grizzled wolf sat next to a small female raccoon. The wolf was dressed simply, in a leather vest over a plain tunic, but the vest bore three medals of valor and numerous scars that were as significant as the medals. The raccoon was dressed elegantly, in a long pink silk dress. She wore a simple gold necklace and a silver headpiece to go along with it.

Volle knew the raccoon well. Madame Ferich had been tutoring him in comportment and fashion for the past month—one of the reasons he relished the opportunity to sneak down to the pub and abandon all her lessons. The wolf he remembered from the Academy, and the charged look he got when their eyes met showed that the Duke of Westermarch had not forgotten any of their previous encounters.

He started the meeting without preamble. "This is the last time I will talk to any of you for several years, perhaps the last time ever." He pushed a sheaf of papers across the table to Volle. "These are your papers. Your history, your pedigree, and a summary of information about your family's holdings. Learn that last one and burn it; keep the rest. The Tephossians are big on paperwork and you'll have to carry papers around with you most of the time.

"There is also a letter of reference from Lord Tistunish, which you will need to present to the court. Lord Tistunish is a sympathizer, but he will not know your true identity. He thinks you really are the inheritor of the Vinton estate, as well as a Ferrenian sympathizer, and that's why he's helping us place you in the palace. Be sure you do not tell him differently, nor lean on him too much. Let him guide you." Volle nodded.

"The letter is very important. Do not lose it." He glared at Volle, and the fox's ears drooped a bit.

"I won't."

"You'll have plenty of time to read and study the documents on the week-long ride to Divalia."

"Week long?"

"You're going to your 'family estates' first, so your carriage approaches from the proper direction. In addition, it would do you good to meet some of the people you're supposedly ruling. In effect, you *will* be their lord."

Volle sighed, audibly. The Duke flicked his ears forward and then growled. "Believe me, Volle, if there were another fox available or another peerage we could impersonate, I would go for it and leave you to f—sleep your way through Caril." He altered his words at the last minute, glancing at Madame Ferich, who wore an amused grin. "This mission demands someone who is dedicated, intelligent, quick-witted, and patient, and as far as I have been able to tell, you are none of those things. But we're stuck with each other. Just remember that there are a hundred students in your academy who would gladly switch places with you if they could."

But they can't. Volle said the words in his head as the Duke talked, looking down at the table. He didn't bother pointing out that there were only twenty-four students in the academy at present.

"I don't know—" Why you even joined, Volle finished in his head, but the Duke sat back without finishing. After a moment, he resumed the briefing as if nothing had happened.

"We are especially interested in any military movements, of course, and those around the Reysfields are of paramount importance. But any information you can get for us will be useful. Most important is that you not get caught. You will be holding this position for a long time, hopefully, and will be a key component of our intelligence in Tephos."

While he was talking, Volle let his gaze wander over to the Prince. The handsome cougar was watching the wolf speak, but his eyes flicked over to Volle and stayed there when he saw the fox watching him. He smiled, and Volle saw his tail tip twitch under the chair. He was handsome, and well built, and Volle immediately found himself wondering how that compact, firm body would feel on top of him...

He jerked his attention back to the Duke even as his sheath started to push against the leather of his trousers. Fantasizing about the Prince was bad enough, but if Duke Avery noticed, he couldn't fail to mock Volle for it, and he would delight in doing that in front of the prince. Volle's ears drooped as he looked up cautiously, but the Duke was looking at Seir and Reese, and didn't seem to have noticed Volle's wandering attention.

"...the team already in place. Seir, you know Tella and Sherr already. There's also a rat who's coming home, name of Jenner. Reese, you're his replacement. Derrik is coming home as well—he's our expert on the palace, so he'll stay for the first few weeks while you get settled, Volle. Don't be seen with him, though. We think he may be compromised. They won't do anything about him as long as he stays away from the palace, but if you were seen with him it would end the operation. There are a couple safe places to meet; make sure you stick to them.

"Clothing will be handled by Madame Ferich here. You will bring nothing Ferrenian with you. Volle, that includes that pendant you wear."

"This?" Volle's paw went to his throat. "My mother..."

"We'll keep it safe." Madame Ferich spoke for the first time. "In Tephos, you might be asked to explain it."

"The less you have to explain, the better." Duke Avery growled. "I cannot overstate the importance of this mission. Our last contact in the Tephos palace was exposed six months ago and had only been a servant. She didn't learn anything useful, but the rumors she brought back indicate that there is a very serious threat against our country in the works. This is not a training exercise or a child's game. If you are caught you may delay our response to their plans and cause irreparable harm to your country."

"And you might be killed," Madame Ferich added.

"Yes, that too." The Duke waved a paw dismissively. "Any other questions, any of you?"

Seir spoke up. "How much am I taking back for our funding?"

"See the Exchequer for that. He'll give you a couple hundred gold pieces. That should be enough to last you through the year." When nobody else spoke up, the wolf turned to the Prince. "Your Highness, is there anything you would like to add or ask?"

The Prince stood, and smiled. "Good luck to all of you. You are performing an inestimable service to my family and to the country."

Volle stood and bowed in return, as the others did. Was it his imagination, or did the prince's gaze linger on him, and his smile widen slightly? He must be imagining. The prince wouldn't be flirting in a meeting like this. Just the thought aroused him further, so he was quite glad when the Prince left the room, even though the arousal didn't follow immediately.

"All right, then. You leave tomorrow morning at first light. The carriage will take you from the back of the castle. As his Highness said, good luck." The Duke grasped each of their paws as they walked out the door, shaking it firmly, but when he took Volle's, he held it tightly and didn't let go.

"If you screw this up," he whispered close to Volle's ear, "I will personally shove your tail so far up your ass you will be coughing up fur. And then I'll bite your balls off." He showed his imposing fangs in a mirthless grin. "And don't think I don't mean it." He drew his muzzle back.

"Yes, sir." Volle would be annoyed later, but at the moment the Duke really looked as though he'd like nothing better than a mouthful of fox, and not in the way Volle usually liked to think of it. He flattened his ears back and slipped his paw out of the wolf's viselike grip.

Outside the room, Madame Ferich took his paw and smiled up at him. "Do not worry," she said softly. "You are smart and capable. You will do fine. Just try to keep him inside some of the time, okay?" She inclined her muzzle towards Volle's sheath.

"I will, Madame," he said, though he was still too apprehensive to return her smile, and lowered his muzzle to touch his nose to hers.

"I'll bring your clothes by later," she said. "Go on and learn your history now."

Seir had taken all his papers, so Volle followed her down the stairs, with Reese close behind. They remained quiet all the way back to the room Volle and Reese shared, where Seir closed the door behind them and sat on Volle's bed.

"That went better than I expected," Volle said, more lightly than he felt.

Reese chuckled, but Seir gave him a severe look. "This isn't going to be easy, Volle. You have a lot to learn and remember."

"I can manage it, Seir. Let me see that stuff." He took the papers from her and shuffled through them. "Wow. There is a lot. But I know a lot of this already. History of Tephos, geography..."

"We'll have time," Seir said. "We wouldn't be leaving now if I weren't confident that you could do it. Or at least, pretty confident. We'll have a good team there backing us up. Reese, you've got some stuff to learn too. Maps of the city and the palace, important locations, and drop points."

"I've got most of the maps already. I'll look at the rest of the stuff on the trip."

"Right." Seir nodded approvingly. "Now pack up and get some sleep, you two. We leave at first light."

Chapter 2

Volle found it hard to get to sleep. He tossed and turned, while Reese lay silent in the other bed. Finally he lay back on his back and closed his eyes, hoping that would do it.

A familiar scent wafted to his nose. He blinked, and opened his eyes. Prince Gennic stood over him, wearing a robe tied around his waist.

Volle tried to sit up, but the prince shook his head and put a finger to his muzzle, smiling. "I would not normally intrude," he whispered, "but I felt I had to say goodbye to such a handsome fox personally." He untied the robe and shrugged it off his shoulders, revealing nothing but his clean, sleek fur underneath.

Volle stared at the prince's stocky form. He could see the rippling of muscle under the tawny fur of the prince's arms, and the slow rise and fall of his broad chest and slender stomach, bright white in the moonlight.

"Let's see how you greet your prince," the cougar purred, sliding the sheets slowly down. Volle, helpless to resist, watched as the prince uncovered his nakedness.

"Excellent. I like that in a subject." The prince smiled at him and rested a broad paw on the fox's sheath. Volle moaned with the sensations. "I think this will be quite enjoyable."

Then the prince was astride him, powerful legs squeezing his sides. The moonlight lit his stomach and stiff length, but his muzzle was hidden in shadow. "Now," he breathed softly, "let us enjoy the night."

He moved his hips and Volle moaned again, resting his paw on the prince's legs. The prince leaned over and held his shoulder with one paw. Heat radiated from his paw pads.

"Volle." He heard Reese's voice from the other bed.

The prince's rear was warm too. Volle squeezed the thickly muscled leg with his paw and moaned, "Not now, Reese."

"Volle." Reese's voice was more insistent. The prince was gripping his shoulder tightly, shaking him as he moved back and forth.

"No," Volle moaned, and slowly became aware that he was sitting back in the corner of the carriage. Reese was leaning over him, shaking him by the shoulder.

"Volle, you're dreaming. Wake up."

Volle opened his eyes. Sunlight, streaming into the carriage, explained the warmth on his shoulder and lap. He looked at Seir, who wore a familiar smirk, and Reese, who was just grinning. "Dammit," he muttered, "why couldn't you just let me sleep?"

"Your moaning was getting annoying," Reese said, and sat back down. He glanced at Volle's trousers. "You know, it's going to be another week or so on the road. If you keep having these dreams, you're going to pay for your own room at the inns."

Volle sat up and yawned. "If you'd get over your thing with girls, maybe we could share my dreams as well as a room." He winked at the hare.

"Ha. Dream on. Anyway, you're not my type. I prefer someone who can think about something other than sex once in a while."

"I'm not thinking about it now." Reese looked steadily at Volle until the fox grinned. "Okay, I'm lying, I was." He enjoyed the byplay with the hare, even though Reese thought his sex drive was dangerous and self-indulgent. Volle had never been able to make him see that it wasn't just the physical that he was after. So he played the game with Reese and tried not to make too big a deal out of his sex life.

Reese rolled his eyes, and Seir chuckled softly. "Here, read some of your papers. That'll take your mind off sex." She handed over a few of the sheets.

"More studying? I thought I was done with that." Volle groaned, but good-naturedly, and he took the sheets.

The carriage was still moving smoothly over the road, so Volle had little trouble reading the papers. They detailed the Vinton family holdings, a small estate in a mountainous valley. It was one of the three smallest holdings in the country ("size isn't everything," Reese remarked when Volle told him), and produced mainly wheat and other grains. Because it was small and remote, the passing of the Vinton family line had been of little consequence. The castle was inhabited by the Governor, who took the place of the lord in matters of internal law, economic trade, and political dealings with the capital.

The last of the Vintons had been killed some twenty years ago in a battle. They were red foxes, of course, one of twelve noble fox families in Tephos—but one of only two to hold land and a title. Geri Vinton had been granted the estate by King Telas IV as a reward for valiant service over a lifetime in three different wars. His descendants had held the valley for a hundred and fifty years, against Ferrenians and raiders.

The battle in which the last Vinton had died had been with the neighboring Ferrenian barony. The conflict was not sanctioned by either Tephos or Ferrenis; it was a private matter between the principalities. Volle found only vague references to the origin—some woman, or child, or perhaps herd of cattle, had been stolen from one side to the other, and it sounded as though it were part of a cycle of ever-increasing thefts and raids that inevitably ended in a pitched battle every ten or fifteen years.

He skimmed the geography of the valley—it was really very simple—and then got distracted watching the Kell Lake in the sinking sun's light, which streaked it with fire and made the red mountains beyond it glow. For the first time, it occurred to him to wonder when he would ever see them again.

They stopped soon after, and he was able to watch the sun set from their window at the pub. While he nursed one tankard of ale, Reese drained three of mead, and was soon in quite a jolly mood. Seir retired early for bed after their meal, and Volle considered joining her, but he wasn't quite tired enough. Automatically, he'd been scanning the bar for cute young males, before he remembered that he'd be sharing a room with Reese and Seir.

Reese noticed, of course. "Say, that badger over there looks lonely. Maybe you should buy him a drink." The badger was old and grizzled, and had twice yelled at the ferret who'd brought him his dinner.

"Looks more your type," Volle said, but Reese ignored him.

"Hey, that wolf's making eyes at you." He leaned across the table. "No, really. Look!"

Volle couldn't help glancing at the wolf, who was a farmer of some sort. His brown fur was pretty enough, and he had some nice muscles on him. He also had a mate at his table, a plain but pleasant-looking bitch who ate in silence.

"I know you like wolves. Maybe his wife would want to watch." Reese was swaying a little bit, and Volle chuckled finally. He hadn't realized it until now, but when they went on the job, Reese wouldn't be able to get drunk any more. Volle himself liked the odd glass of ale or mead, but rarely to excess. He always held out hope that the evening would end in more pleasant circumstances than a drunken stupor.

"Maybe so. Or maybe you could keep her entertained."

Again, Reese ignored him. "I can just see you goin' at it with him." He made a crude pantomime that involved his muzzle and tongue.

Volle grinned, and then noticed that the wolf and his mate *were* looking at them. "Hey, Reese, cut it out."

"What? Can't take a little fun? You don' usually mind attention. Hi!" He waved to the wolf, pointed at Volle, and made a kissy-face, then started licking the air with his tongue. The wolf frowned, and turned back to his mate.

"Reese!" Volle was torn between laughter and anger.

"Come on, tell me you weren't thinking about it, you horny fox."

"Not with *him*!" Volle kept his voice low. "I have some standards."

Reese laughed. "First I've heard of that. Remember th-the mangy coyote in the bar at the academy?"

"Reese." Volle glared at him.

"He wasn't even a student!"

"All right, finish your mead. I'm going to go to bed." Volle stood up and stretched, suddenly tired of the conversation. Reese usually didn't bring up the coyote any more, but he'd obviously had a bit too much to drink. That had been before Volle had learned discretion, one of his first liaisons at the Academy. He still held fond memories of the coyote (though it was true he'd gotten fleas from him), but he'd long since given up trying to explain that to Reese.

"I'm gonna h-have another one." Reese tried signaling to one of the ferrets, but they were all busy.

Volle watched them scurrying about with drinks, and had an idea. "I'll send one over with your drink. Don't fall asleep here."

"Hey, I can h-handle my mead."

"I know you can." He left Reese at the table and intercepted one of the ferrets.

"Hi. My friend would like another tankard of mead."

"Sure. I'll get to it in a second." She had stopped only long enough to get drinks at the bar, and was about to scurry off again.

"Here." He put a silver piece on her tray. "This is for you and the other barmaids if you'll do me a little favor."

She stopped cold, and glanced at the silver piece, then up at Volle. "What? We don't sleep with the customers."

He shook his head. "I don't want that. Just want you to flirt with him and tease him. Get him all worked up."

Her eyes sparkled, but she raised an eyebrow. "Why?"

"Oh, I just want to have some fun with him. He's drunk and he's been annoying all night."

She gave him a sultry wink and dropped her voice. "Oh, sir, we'd have done it for free. But we'll put a little extra into it, to give you your money's worth."

"Thanks." He admired her sultry curves and the sleek sheen of her fur, and the grace with which she threaded her way through the tables, balancing the tankards. But her scent didn't arouse him at all, and the thought of taking her in his arms stirred no reaction in his sheath. The way Fox made me, he thought, and walked up the stairs and down the hall to their bedroom.

Seir was in bed, but not quite asleep; she turned over as he came in. "Huh. I would've expected Reese to be the first one back."

"He's still drinking." Volle stripped his tunic and trousers off, stretched, and crawled into his bed. It was stuffed with hay and lumpy, but not completely uncomfortable. He sighed, and pressed his muzzle into the rough fabric.

"Yes. I hope that's not a problem as well." Seir's tone was more thoughtful than worried.

"I know we're young, but we're not stupid." Volle turned over. It wasn't enough that he was leaving his home behind for who knows how long, and he was going to bed alone, but Seir had to pick on him all day? Or pick on Reese, which amounted to nearly the same thing: they were too young and undisciplined to succeed as spies, they couldn't control their desires, they would screw up everything. Yeah, they'd gotten into trouble at the Academy, but that was all small stuff— late for classes or missing at bed check. Well, except for that report he'd lost. And the time Reese had shown up drunk to an inspection.

Seir said his name gently, then again more insistently. He turned over and looked at her.

"If we had serious doubts about you two, you wouldn't be going. Fox or no fox. I just worry about everything. That's my job. So get some sleep, okay? Don't want you dozing off and moaning in the carriage again."

She was smiling, so Volle smiled back. "Okay, Seir. Good night."

The next morning, Reese was slow to get up and held his head a lot. He moaned when they walked out into the bright sun, winced when the driver yelled to the horses to giyyap, and closed his eyes with every bounce of the carriage. Volle enjoyed it, though he tried to keep his voice down. He couldn't resist teasing the hare once they were on the road.

"Trouble sleeping last night, Reese?" The hare just glared at him. "Visions of ferret girls dancing in your head? Or elsewhere?"

"You can laugh, but they were all over me, Volle. Couldn't get enough. As soon as you left."

"You didn't bring one back to the room, did you?" Volle was finding it harder and harder to keep from laughing.

"Uhhh… I don't think so." Reese looked genuinely confused. "Did I make some noise? I'm sorry."

"Oh, we understand, Reese. For someone as irresistible as you are."

"Oh, shut up." The hare closed his eyes and held his head miserably, then cracked an eye open. "Wait a minute. How did you know about them? Oh, you didn't…"

Volle tried to look innocent, but it was difficult when he couldn't keep the wide grin off his muzzle. Reese slumped back in his seat. "You put them up to it. You bastard."

"Well, I guess I'm not the only one who thinks about sex." Volle folded his arms smugly.

"All right, Volle. Enough." Seir smiled. "Let's go over some of the things you need to listen for. First of all, the Reysfields. Our negotiations with the Wachsen Lands probably have the Tephossians worried about us attacking, and they may attempt a pre-emptive strike. Now, the officials who would be involved in this are …"

They talked for most of the day about the various people in the palace, and the various issues that King Barris was concerned about. Reese recovered around midday and listened to the discussion, putting in a couple words here and there. By the end of the day, Volle had left most of his homesickness behind. The terrain they were entering was wooded and sparsely populated, and for the next two nights they had to make camp in the woods. The driver of the carriage, an old badger whose name Volle learned was Brock, was also a skilled woodsman; his only concern was that they might meet bandits, but their luck held and they saw none.

As they emerged from the woods late in the third day, they saw the land rise up ahead of them, and got their first view of the land of Tephos. The mountains rolled gently across the landscape, lower, softer, and greener than the Red Mountains of Ferrenis. This was the northern edge of the range; to their left, the mountains stretched away southward. To the north, they subsided into rolling hills and then flatter farmland.

The open area the carriage was now entering sloped down to a river valley across a grassy plain. The river wound in tight curves through the plain, but to the north, where it fed the farmland, it widened and ran straighter. Volle studied the river with indifference. He could see a building where the road met the river, and supposed that would be the inn where they were staying, and the border post into Tephos.

"The Otrine," Seir said, leaning past him to look at the river.

"I know. And those are the Ancient Hundred." He indicated the mountains with his muzzle. "How closely guarded is the border?"

"Here? Not much. We're still going to use the disguise for you, though."

Volle stuck out his tongue. "I hate that stuff. My fur feels sticky for days."

"I'd think you'd be used to that," Reese said with a smirk.

"Not at all the right kind of sticky," Volle returned, but that just reminded him that he hadn't been sticky—the right kind—in days.

"Well, I am sorry, but it's necessary. We don't want reports of a red fox crossing the border here to have any chance of reaching the palace." She took a large ceramic pot out of her pack and carefully placed it on the seat beside Volle. "Here. We'll sit up with the driver if you want some privacy."

"Privacy?" Volle's ears flattened. "You mean it has to go everywhere?"

"'Fraid so." Seir spread her paws. "We just have to prepare for every eventuality."

"Great." He opened the pot and wrinkled his nose at the slight tarry scent. "It smells," he objected. "That won't fool them."

"Oh, we have some scent for you to put on over it. You'll claim to be a woodworker, using pitch to seal the wood, and that explains the smell." Seir hustled Reese out onto the running board. "Come on, climb up with the driver."

"Do I have to?"

"Yes. Now go." She followed him and disappeared, but left the door latched open.

"I don't care," Volle said, but too late. He looked out the door at the grassy fields rushing by, and sighed. Then he took off his tunic and trousers and sat naked on the seat next to the pot.

It was almost arousing, if he thought of it that way: sitting here where he was exposed to the world. In his fantasies, a lithe highway-wolf would leap into the carriage. He'd have his sword out and a cocky smile on his muzzle, but the demands for money would die on his lips when he saw the naked fox. He'd lower his sword, walk forward, and take Volle's paws in his own...

His fantasy provoked a reaction in his sheath, and his paw strayed down to brush up and down it, becoming in his mind the velvety paw of the highway-wolf. He brushed along the fur, and the quickly showing skin, and started to breathe a little harder. Eyes closed, he fell deeper into the fantasy, paw completely circling his length now, his body shivering with every stroke.

Something bumped the carriage above his head. The noise startled him and drove the highway-wolf from his mind. As he moved, he bumped the ceramic pot to the edge of the seat, and barely caught it before it toppled to the floor. For a few heartbeats he held it, panting, and then set it back on the seat. With a sigh, he got to work.

The pot contained a black salve, which coated his fur and turned it black. It felt heavy, but it would dry without leaving much residue on his fur. A casual brush, even a longer touch, would be fooled, though a close examination would probably reveal the secret. Seir carried the white salve that was necessary to dissolve the black one and restore the fur's true color.

It was something the Ferrenians had worked hard to perfect. They were justly proud of their alchemical works, and in theory, Volle too was proud of them. In practice, he despised them. The black salve dried normally, but the white left a sticky residue on his skin that had lingered for days, the one time he'd used the salve last year in a training exercise. And that had been only on his back and shoulders! He couldn't imagine using it over his whole body.

Well, use it he had to. He dipped a paw into the pot and drew out a glop of the salve, smearing it into his chest fur. As he did, he looked down and noticed that his arousal was fading somewhat. Mischievously, he took his black-coated paw and gave himself a few more strokes to renew it. He was rewarded with the odd sight of a black member streaked with pink in a couple places he'd missed. He grinned to himself and coated it more thoroughly with another pawful, then took care of the rest of his groin, until his sheath and sac were completely blackened. The sight made him grin, and put him in better spirits as he reached for the pot again.

He left his tail tip white, and left a white patch at his throat. When Reese climbed down from the driver's seat, Volle was standing at the door, watching the river and the mountains, and letting the wind ruffle through his fur. He smiled at Reese and stepped aside to let him in.

"Put some clothes on, why don't you?" Reese made a show of averting his eyes as he scrambled into the carriage.

"Got to wait for it to dry. What's the matter? Tempted?" He posed alluringly against the door, angling his hips toward Reese.

Reese snorted and picked up the pot. "Turn around."

"Good heavens! After five years you've decided you like my tail?" Volle grinned, turning around to face the door and giving his tail a little lift.

"You wish. Though it'd be almost worth it just to see if you put the coloring...there." Reese grinned, and a moment later Volle felt the hare's strong paws on his back. "Seir sent me to make sure you got your back done. You missed a couple spots."

"Mmm. If I'd known you were coming, I'd have left other spots undone." Volle brushed Reese with his tail, chuckling.

"And you'd have done those yourself."

"Oh, so you like to watch?"

Reese snorted again. "I set myself up for that one." He stepped back. "Okay, I think you're good from behind."

"So I've been told." Volle grinned and turned around. He brushed his paws down his stomach and chest. "I think I'm mostly dry now. I can at least put the trousers on, if it'd make you feel better."

"Please." But Reese smiled as he held the trousers out to Volle, and Volle was smiling as he put them on. "You look really different. I wouldn't know it was you. Even the scent is different."

"This is good stuff. I forgot that I don't mind putting it on." Volle brought his tail around and brushed it with his claws. "It does look good, doesn't it? Mysterious?"

Reese laughed. "You can't have sex with that stuff on. They couldn't help but notice."

Volle winked. "How innocent you are. There is always a way."

"Well, maybe not in Tephos." Reese's expression became more serious.

"What do you mean?"

"You know they're mostly Panbestian Orthodox, right?"

Volle nodded. "Of course. You've already teased me about being lumped in with wolves and coyotes under the god "Canis." What does that have to do with anything?"

"The Orthodox Church frowns on recreational sex, but they don't really bother the straight couples because they can't prove they're not trying to have cubs. But the same-sex couples are...shall we say, discouraged."

Volle stared at him. "Really? But that's...they can't do that."

Reese shrugged, and the hint of a smile played around the corners of his muzzle. "I'm sure there are places where it goes on. But those would be seedy, grimy joints frequented by dangerous lowlifes. Not suitable for a peer of the realm."

"But...that wasn't mentioned in any of the texts."

"Did they say that it wasn't true?"

"No." Volle stared glumly down at his paws. So his little adventure in the pub would be the last of its kind for quite some time.

"Your paws will be good friends, yes," Reese said, and Volle shot him a dirty look. "Unless you decide to try out ladies."

Seir swung down into the carriage and closed the door behind her. She saw Volle's expression and looked over at Reese. "What?"

"I was telling him about the Panbestian Orthodox Church's attitude toward some of his favorite activities."

"Ah, yes." Seir sat beside Volle and patted his knee. "You wouldn't have had time for such distractions anyway."

"I'd have made time." Volle managed a smile. "I made time at the Academy."

Seir shook her head, and grinned. "You probably would have, at that." She lifted his arms, checking the fur all over. "You look good. I like the white patches. Nice touch."

"Thanks."

"Reese, you checked all the other areas?"

"Not as closely as he'd have liked me to, but yeah."

Volle snorted. "You don't trust me? I know how to cover *that* area."

Seir chuckled. "I know you do, but a second pair of eyes is always better. So get your shirt on. We'll be there in another hour. Everybody have their paperwork?"

Reese studied his. "I am Marik, returning home to Tephos after selling my wares to the peasants in southern Ferrenis. Why aren't you the merchant and us your assistants?"

"This is Tephos. Females are treated somewhat differently here. Even me being an assistant might be a stretch if you were married. As it is, they'll probably assume we're sleeping together."

Reese put on a look of mock indignance. "They'll think I can't do better?"

Seir swatted at him. "You don't have to do anything, just don't contradict them if they make assumptions. Volle, you have your papers? They're huge on papers."

Volle waved his papers desultorily. Seir nodded. "And Reese, we were selling in southern Ferrenis because…"

Reese shrugged, transforming something in his expression. "That is where the money is. I bring the money home to my motherland, at least."

"Excellent. We'll have no troubles."

And they did not. The Ferrenian guard, a bored-looking marmot, asked Reese a couple questions, barely glancing at Volle and Seir before waving them across the bridge. On the other side, the Tephossian guard, an equally bored-looking weasel, glanced at all three papers, then waved them through without a single question.

They pulled into the stable at the inn, where Reese ordered the stable boy, a young badger, to look after their horses. He made a big deal of breathing in the air and bellowing, "Ah, Tephos! I am home!" His overacting was so amusing that even in his black mood, Volle couldn't keep from smiling.

The pub was empty save for a dirty goat with matted fur sitting at the bar. He didn't move when they entered, even when Reese called out loudly, "Innkeeper! A round of mead, if you please, and make it Vellenland mead if you have it."

"No Vellenland," the bear behind the counter replied. "We have Cauter mead, regular and blackberry; we have Forest mead, and we have Holtan's ginger spiced cider. And Royal mead, of course."

"Cauter regular, then," Reese said. He chose a table, and Volle and Seir joined him at it.

"Cauter?"

Reese grinned at Volle. "Cauter's second best to Vellenland. A distant second, but still ahead of third."

Volle shook his head. "Who would've thought your drinking would be so useful?"

"Wait 'til you taste it. In the palace I bet you'll get Vellenland mead, too. Pity they don't make very much of it."

The bear plunked three mugs down on their table. "Six copper."

Reese rummaged in a pouch and handed him six coins. The bear pocketed them, then stood by the table watching Reese.

The hare sniffed his mug, then touched it to his lips and took a sip. "Mmm. Excellent." He smiled up at the bear. "Thank you very much."

The bear smiled and nodded. "Pleasure, sir. Enjoy."

Volle sipped his mead. It was good, but it couldn't quite dispel his thoughts. He turned to Seir. "Why didn't anyone tell me?"

"About what?"

"About the Tephossians being…" he lowered his voice. "Panbestian Orthodox."

"I thought you knew that. It was covered." Seir had an amused expression on her muzzle as she sipped the mead. "This is very good, Reese. Nice choice."

"I did, but I didn't know how…I mean, their feelings about…" Volle sputtered and looked back and forth between the two of them.

"What, did you think this was going to be some kind of pleasure holiday? This is work, Volle. Whether or not you can indulge your personal tastes should be beside the point."

"Someone still should have told me." He took another drink from his tankard, but his mood was souring the taste.

Seir touched his arm gently with a paw. "Maybe they were afraid you'd react exactly this way."

Volle was torn between resentment and self-pity. Did they really think he would have shunned his duty just because he would have to essentially take a vow of chastity? He had half a mind to do just that. He breathed in the scent of his mead and listened to Reese ask something innocuous of Seir, only half paying attention. The fatigue of the journey, the salve in his fur, and Reese's news that afternoon were mounting to make him irritable, as much as he tried not to be. He reminded himself that he was here because he was the best qualified in his class, that a kingdom was depending on him, and that he should be honored.

But they needed a fox, and I'm the only one. And if I'm going to act petty and self-involved, I only have a few more days to do it. Fox knows they never allowed that at the Academy.

"I'm tired," he announced, and stood up. "I'm going to go lie down."

"All right. We'll wait for you for dinner." Seir spoke quietly. "You'll feel better after a nap."

"Hope so." Volle left the table and walked over to the bartender. The bear, polishing a glass, had been watching him.

"Help you, sir?"

"Could you show me where our room will be tonight?"

"Certainly, sir. Right this way." The bear led him out of the bar and around to a staircase in the back. Volle took a moment to look at the sunset and savor the slight chill in the air. The river burbled to itself as it moved along behind him, and in the distance he could hear wild beasts howling. Crickets chirped nearby, and he flicked his ear at the drone of a mosquito.

"I didn't catch your name," he said to the bear as they walked down a short hallway.

"Gord, sir. Gord Stoutheart."

"Ah. A pleasure, Gord. I'm Yarrin. Yarrin Fletcher."

"Hope you enjoy your stay, Mr. Fletcher. Here's your room." He opened the door onto a small room with two bunk beds and a dresser. On the far wall, there were two closed windows. Besides a small rug in the middle of the floor, the room was otherwise featureless. The beds looked comfortable enough, well-stuffed with hay and down, and the sheets were crisply arranged on them.

"I'm sure it will be fine." He tried to remember what alias Reese was using. "I'm sure Mr. Senom will approve."

"Thank you, sir. We'll see you for supper then?"

"Yes, I'll be down in an hour or so. I just need to rest from the road."

"If there's anything else you might need, sir, let me know. Washroom is down the hall. I put the hot water in at sunrise and after dinner." Gord stepped back into the hallway and prepared to leave.

Volle breathed in, and thought he caught the scent of a female on Gord. "Are you married, Gord?"

"Sir? Yes, five years."

"Ah. Good for you, Gord."

"Thank you, sir." The bear looked faintly puzzled as he walked back down the hallway.

Volle checked for a lock on the door, and was pleased to find a deadbolt. He closed the door and locked it, then walked over to a window and opened it. The room was a bit stuffy and warm from receiving the afternoon sunlight, but the air outside was fresh and cool. He breathed it in, then went to lie down on one of the beds.

Time at the Academy was regimented and packed full of activities, and he had probably not been in a room alone for more than ten minutes at a time in his five years there. Savoring the privacy and the free time, he leaned back and put his arms behind his head. He let Seir and Reese melt away, and brooded again on how he would cope, going to live in a land where the one thing he loved most was denied him.

His tunic felt a little warm, so he took it off to relax. His eyes drifted downward, pulled by the hours of studying and the weariness of sitting in the carriage all day. In his half-dozing state, his paw slid down almost unconsciously to his trousers, trailing claws up and down his sheath. He imagined the highway-wolf crawling through the window and finding him in bed, not even on the pretense of robbery any more. He could feel the wolf's paws guiding his own up and down the bulge on his trousers, loosening the ties at the front and sliding his paws down inside.

"It is forbidden, you know," the wolf whispered to him. "But you are too lovely for me not to risk it." Volle moaned softly, feeling his arousal grow as his erection slid out from his sheath under his paw. "All in black. How exotic," the wolf said, sliding Volle's paw along the fox's deep black length. The coloration didn't rub off on his paw as the soft pads slid up and down, even when they began to press more firmly. Volle gasped, and though his eyes were closed he could see the wolf leaning over him, dark brown eyes focused intently on his paw above a hungry smile. He could smell the wolf's musk in the dusty room and hear his soft breathing over Volle's own panting moans.

"If they catch us," the wolf whispered in his ear, "we will be in terrible danger." His paw impelled Volle's to move faster still, in time with the trembling sensations that were overwhelming him.

"Mustn't...get...caught...then," Volle said, his whole body shaking with repressed desire. Only four days or so, but it seemed so long, and he hadn't had a moment alone since then. His paw worked faster and faster, and his erection was so hard and so hot he could barely touch it. His back arched on the bed and he moaned a series of short, staccato gasps as warmth sprayed over his stomach and chest. His paw kept sliding up and down, getting slicker, until finally he was too sensitive to continue. He fell back onto the bed, panting heavily, keeping his paw curled around himself.

Of course, the wolf was not there when he opened his eyes. The only scent in the room, apart from the strong musk of his activity, was the damp scent from the river wafting in through the open window. He smiled and listened to the quiet sounds of the night, gazing out the still-closed window by the bed. When he did glance down at himself, he blinked and sat up, nearly cracking his skull on the frame of the top bunk.

There were streaks of white on his belly and sheath, and the blackness of his erection was mostly gone. Only a few patches of black remained on what looked like dirty pink skin. It didn't take long for him to determine what had caused the coloration to lift, and he cursed softly. Fortunately, his paws were black, and as long as he kept his clothes on, nobody would notice the streaks, or his much more odd than exotic member.

In the dresser, he found a couple cloths that were meant for towels. He used one to clean himself up, trying to minimize the area he had to wipe. He was nevertheless left with a large white patch at his groin and several white streaks down his front.

As he put his tunic back on and lay down, yawning, a thought struck him, and he chuckled. "I wonder what *is* in that removal salve," he mused as he drifted into sleep.

Chapter 3

The three-day trip through the mountains was cold, but otherwise uneventful. Seir insisted that Volle wash off the coloring in a remote mountain stream where he would have no chance of being seen, and as a result he was still shivering and slightly damp when they arrived at the inn on the outskirts of town, late at night.

Volle introduced himself to the innkeeper as "Volle of Vinton," as though it were no big deal, and the slender, nervous-looking wolf dropped the glass he was drying. He showed Volle to a private room, ushering Seir and Reese to another, and drew a hot water bath when he saw how Volle was shivering. The bath felt wonderful, though it still didn't clean all of the sticky residue off Volle's fur.

In the morning, Seir and the driver slipped off to the capital, and Volle awoke to find the governor waiting for him downstairs, a pudgy raccoon by the name of Anton. He took a liking to the raccoon after only half an hour of talking, and agreed to take a walk with him through the town. With obvious pride, Anton pointed out the progress the town had made in the last twenty years—a wall repaired, a new mill—and then stopped, flustered, as he realized he might be bragging that the town didn't need a lord.

Volle reassured him that he didn't intend to stay, that the town was in very capable paws, and that he saw no need to change the arrangement the people had become used to. He would represent the town to the king, and he would rely on the governor to keep an eye on things at home. Anton was visibly relieved, and from then on he made a point of introducing Volle to all the citizens of the town. By the end of the day, Volle was more exhausted than he'd been in a long time, and he sank into his bed at the inn gratefully. He'd turned down offers from two different vixens to share the bed with him. There had been a black wolf who'd caught his eye, but he remembered the Church and didn't dare ask.

He spent one more day walking around the town with Anton, meeting the elders of the village, the craftsmen, and the farmers. The land's small army assembled and presented arms for him—such arms as they had, which were largely bent or battle-damaged. He tried to remember all the names, as he would be their representative for an indeterminate period of time and would have to act accordingly. By the following morning, though, he was ruefully telling Anton that he would need reminders in the updates.

The role absorbed him so thoroughly that for the first day of the trip to the capital, Volle pored over the papers and names and ignored Reese, who sat across from him in the hired carriage. The hare watched him with amusement at first, then boredom, and finally annoyance.

As the sun was sinking, he leaned across the carriage and said quietly, "Don't forget why you're here."

Volle looked up and swiveled his ears backwards. He was sitting below the driver's seat, and though the carriage was closed, he could still hear the driver humming to himself. The young marmot who'd volunteered to drive them was eager and helpful, but of course had not been taken into their confidence. He gauged the volume he could speak at without being overheard, and said, "I know. But I am their lord now. I need to be able to carry out that function too."

"I'm just saying, don't forget the main reason."

Volle smiled. "I won't. You just worry about the streets and drops."

Reese snorted. "I know those cold."

"Fine. I don't know this cold yet, so let me study."

The hare threw up his paws. "Whatever."

They shared dinner with their driver, who wanted to know everything about Volle's past—where he'd grown up, how he and Reese had met, how long they'd known each other, if he remembered his father at all, and so on. Volle humored him; it was a good chance to practice his story. Reese chimed in once or twice, but mostly stayed silent until the driver went to bed. Then he and Volle discussed the story quietly between themselves, making minor adjustments and additions.

Midway through the fourth day, as Volle was studying his original mission papers again and Reese was napping, the driver rapped on the carriage. Volle put the papers into his leather pouch and opened the door. "Yes, Ben?"

The marmot smiled and pointed. "We can see the palace. Thought you might like to take a look."

Volle climbed up onto the riding board and looked ahead. They had crested a hill and were starting down its gentle slope, and spread out before them was Sophasol, the great plain of Tephos. The Reysfields were the eastern plains, Volle remembered, rich with maize and wheat. The Lurine River wound its way through the fields, a shimmering snake in the golden expanse. They had crossed the Lurine far to the south, where it was wide, brown, and sluggish. Here it was bright and quick, more narrow and lithe. Volle traced its curves northward until they brought him to Divalia.

The capital city's most visible feature from this distance was the large stone wall that encircled it. As they were looking down into it, Volle could see the buildings inside the walls. It looked very much like the jumble of buildings that made up Caril, and the sight gave him a pang of homesickness. Although, of course, Caril's defense was the Carilla River, the wide blue river whose fertile plain had kept settlers near it, and whose accommodating bend had provided the crèche for the city to grow. Caril had no need of walls, and to Volle, they made Divalia seem old and provincial.

In the midst of the jumble of buildings, a large grey structure arose. Glints of gold caught the sun atop the three towers; otherwise it was the same grey as the walls. The "palace" was actually a fortress, and might be more appropriately called a castle; where Caril's palace was of white marble, low and long and a part of the city, this palace looked like a smaller replica of the city itself. Each of the three towers anchored a section of wall, giving it the appearance of an island in the sea of houses that was Divalia.

"It's beautiful," Ben breathed reverently.

"Very impressive," Volle said, not wanting to openly disagree. "How long until we arrive?"

Ben looked at the road ahead of them. "Probably we could get there late tonight. If your lordship wishes to hurry."

Volle checked the weather. There were a few clouds in the sky, but there didn't seem to be any threat of rain that they needed to outpace. "No need for that. Let's find an inn and arrive at the city in the morning."

"I'll keep my eyes open, my lord."

Volle grinned, still getting used to the honorific, and patted the marmot on the back. "Thank you, Ben." He caught a glimpse of the youngster's happy grin as he climbed back into the carriage.

Reese cracked an eye open. "How long?"

"We'll stop somewhere tonight and then arrive tomorrow morning." Volle took his papers out and shuffled through them again.

"Kay." Reese stretched out on the seat.

They pulled up to the south gate just as the sun was reaching its zenith. Three other vehicles were ahead of them, all farmers' carts. Volle took the opportunity to get out of the carriage and stretch. Reese had just stepped out onto the running board when Ben called, "Hey, there's a Lord here! Move aside!"

Everyone on the three carts ahead of them turned to look: a family of raccoons, a family of goats, and a solitary antelope. They stared at Ben, then looked down to Volle. None of them moved otherwise.

Volle scrambled quickly up onto the riding board. He held his paws up. "Don't worry. No need to move. We'll wait until you're done." Their eyes searched him, and then they turned back around and started to murmur amongst themselves.

Ben looked confused, and a little bit hurt. Volle patted his shoulder. "I appreciate it, Ben, but a lord must remember that he owes his people his service, as well as exacting from them their loyalty. We aren't in a hurry. No need to put out these people just because we could."

"Okay." The smile returned to the young marmot's muzzle. "I'm sorry." He urged the horses forward as the antelope's cart went through the gate and the line moved up.

"That's all right. I know you had good intentions." Volle looked down and saw Reese smirking at him, so he elected to stay on the cart until they reached the gate, with Reese walking alongside. The day was sunny and pleasantly cool, so he leaned back and let the breeze off the wall ruffle his fur.

"Have you been to the city before, Ben?"

"No, my lord. This is my first time." Ben looked up at the walls. "It's huge."

Volle remembered that he was supposed to be from a small village, and nodded. "It is indeed. And the walls look impressive." In truth, he wasn't impressed with the walls, which were pockmarked and cracked near the gate. Along the top, it was crumbling in several places, and the guard posts at the top were not only unmanned, they looked unsafe. Volle filed the information away, with a glance at Reese to see that he was doing the same.

Only two guards stood at the gate. Volle watched one inspect the papers of the raccoon family while the second inspected the cart half-heartedly. As they were waved through, the guards were already eying Volle and his carriage.

Both guards were wolves. The one checking papers had more brown on his muzzle and ears, while the one that opened the carriage door and looked inside was a uniform grey with white on the lower muzzle and throat. He sniffed at the inside of the carriage while the brown one examined the papers Reese handed him.

"Lord Vinton, eh? Welcome to Divalia, sir. And who are these?"

Volle patted Ben on the shoulder. "Ben Woodson, my driver, and Reese Pawfast, my personal assistant."

Ben only had a certificate of birth from the church in the village, but the guards didn't seem to care. "Just follow Market Street to the river, and turn right. Cross at the next bridge, not the Market bridge. Shorter and less crowded. Once you're across, you'll see the palace on your right."

"Thank you," Volle said. The other wolf had taken a cursory sniff inside the carriage and now gave the brown wolf a hand signal that Volle assumed meant 'all clear,' because they were waved into the gate.

He watched the city with eyes as eager as Ben's as they drove slowly down the street. Every city has its own feel, and though the closeness of the houses was similar to the crowded neighborhoods of Caril, the scents and colors were different. Caril seemed brighter to Volle, full of light-colored houses and gaily-dressed people, but maybe he was just in a poor part of Divalia. The paint on the houses was peeling, and many of the people in the street walked with drooping tails. The smells were not worse, just different. He smelled cooking, and washing, and the cooking had different spices and the washing had different soaps. The wood even smelled different, though it was similar to the oak that made up most of the wood in Caril. For Volle, Divalia had just enough familiar sights and scents to make him acutely aware of the absence of others.

He was wearing his traveling clothes, but even those were fine enough to make people look twice as he drove past. They looked away again quickly enough, so Volle guessed that lords and nobles were not an unusual sight in the city, if perhaps not a common one. He had to admit that he liked the attention he was attracting.

The Lurine River in the city was murky where they reached it, in contrast to the bright blue it had been down in the plains. They drove along it for a short way, long enough for Volle to see branches and other debris floating in it. The bridge they crossed was in good repair, though, and fairly empty of people. And on the other side, the grey walls of the palace rose in front of them.

As they turned towards the main gate, Volle saw across from the palace a large stone building surmounted by seven ornate spires, six surrounding a higher central one. The top of the tallest spire was decorated with a golden ornament in the shape of a sunburst: the symbol of the Panbestian Church. Volle was familiar with the Great Cathedral in Caril, a large, open building with three towers and beautiful stained glass windows. This building, by contrast, looked austere and forbidding, covered in ancient reliefs and grey stone. There were stained glass windows, but only in a few narrow strips down the side and in a rosette above the large wooden doors. The rosette was also in the sunburst design, so Volle would have known even if he hadn't already that the church was of the Orthodox branch.

He already knew that he would not be able to remain celibate for any length of time. On the trip to Divalia, he had twice locked himself in his room to disappear into sticky fantasies, once of the bandit wolf again, and once of Prince Gennic. Fantasies and his paw weren't enough, though. There had to be some outlet for him here in the city. He'd reasoned that there must be some nobles facing his dilemma, and he had only to find them and discover their solution. Probably there was a very discreet place nearby—a bath house, maybe, where you could be anonymous without royal finery, your scent hidden in the strongly perfumed powders and soaps.

As they went down the streets in front of the palace, which spanned several long blocks, he searched the buildings on the right hand side to see if he could spot such an establishment. He couldn't, but that relieved him rather than discouraging him. If it were discreet, obviously it wouldn't be spotted. Imagining the hot water and steamy rooms filled with young, handsome males, he felt his sheath stir, and quickly turned to look at the other side of the street.

The palace walls had windows in them, narrow ones that looked more recent than the wall itself, as they were lined with a darker stone. Volle supposed they'd been added after the city walls were put up, when the palace no longer needed unbreachable walls to maintain its security.

The arch of the gate was much older than the metal bars which spanned it. The sentry, a large boar, looked more alert than the wolves at the front gate had. He checked their papers, then bowed to Volle and waved them through.

Ben drew in a gasp as the carriage entered the front garden. It was immense and, Volle had to admit, beautiful. Trellises lined the path, overgrown with purple and red flowers. Bushes of lilac had been sculpted into a sweet-smelling topiary to the left; to the right, small paths meandered through patches of red, white, and yellow roses. An enormous gazebo occupied the center of the gardens, with a field of bright yellow flowers on its low roof and bright orange flowers surrounding it on the ground. Volle had no doubt that the gazebo, viewed from above, would form the shape of a sunburst.

Ben's jaw remained open as they pulled up to the main entrance of the castle. The steps were of white marble, but the archway and walls were of the same grey stone that made up the outer walls. A royal crest adorned into the keystone, but Volle didn't have time to examine it. As soon as they pulled up, a liveried footmarten helped him down from the carriage.

"This way, my lord," he said, and escorted Volle inside, leaving another footmarten to help Reese and Ben with the luggage.

To one side of the gates, Volle noticed a small wooden hutch, and heard the cooing of pigeons from inside. The footmarten, he noticed, was referring to a small scroll of paper, on which Volle saw the words, "Lord Vinton – new to the castle – show him to Steward." So they used pigeons to communicate between the gate and the palace.

"Where are we going?" he asked. "I'm new here, you see."

"Yes, Lord Vinton. The Steward greets all new arrivals to the palace and assigns them quarters. He'll direct me and I'll return to show your bags and servants to your quarters."

"Thank you. And your name is?"

The marten ducked his head. "Renaldo, my lord."

"Thank you, Renaldo." Renaldo led him quickly down a large main hallway lined with tapestries and portraits, broken up by elaborate sconces that Volle expected would hold torches at night. The carpet they walked on felt soft and comfortable under his bare paws; thick wool, he suspected from the scent. He tried to keep track of where they were going, but after Renaldo led him up a staircase adorned with lion heads at the base, and around two bends in quick succession, he was no longer sure he could get back to the main hall.

Renaldo showed him to a waiting room that featured several plush-looking couches. Behind a desk, an alert-looking young red fox sat. He smiled at Volle when he saw him, a smile of familiarity that someone who misses his family wears when he sees another of his species. Volle answered the smile warmly, and waited politely while Renaldo announced him to the fox.

"The Steward is in," the fox said, standing, "and I'm certain he will have time for Lord Vinton." He walked close to Volle on his way to the other door in the room, and Volle caught a whiff of his scent. It was fresh and clean, like the forest on a spring day, and he thought that under it he detected the subtle scent of arousal. Interesting. The fox wore a subdued blue cotton outfit of tunic and trousers; not a uniform, but still a cut above the clothes Volle had seen on the people in the streets. He watched the fox's tail as he stepped through the doorway, then back a moment later.

"The Steward will see you, Lord Vinton."

"Thank you. I'm sorry, I didn't catch your name."

"Arrin." The fox extended a paw shyly. Volle reached out to grasp it, but to his surprise, the fox took his paw and bowed, touching his muzzle to it. "Honored to serve your lordship."

"Thank you, Arrin." Volle smiled. The fox was very cute, with his wide eyes and big ears and elaborate etiquette. Volle was sure that Arrin could smell his modest arousal as well as he could now smell Arrin's, and he smiled. Maybe life at the palace wouldn't be so bad after all. At worst, he might be able to talk to Arrin about where a discreet liaison could be found.

Renaldo clearly did not quite gather what was going on. He stayed standing where he was, paws clasped behind his back, waiting for Volle to go in. When finally Volle did, Renaldo stayed a step behind him.

The Steward's office was nearly twice as large as the waiting room. Dark wood paneling lined the walls, here and there enhanced with a relief of the royal crest. The two large windows had a view of the river and the city beyond that was at the moment rather grey and gloomy. One portrait hung on the wall behind the desk, depicting a glowering bear dressed in robes the color of wine. Volle had seen the same portrait in the main hall, but hadn't noticed the gold circlet. Now he realized this must be King Barris.

The Steward himself was a small, harried-looking coyote who wore a red velvet sash across his chest over a light green doublet. He was filing some papers and muttering to himself when Volle entered, but as soon as he noticed the fox, he stood and waved Volle to the chair in front of his desk. "Come in, Lord Vinton, have a seat."

Volle sat down and arranged his tail behind the chair. Arrin and Renaldo remained standing. "Please call me Volle."

"Volle, then. Pleasure. I'm Alister, the Royal Steward, and I'm sorry I'm going to have to be brusque and rush you out of here, but there is simply too much going on today. Load of wine arriving for the banquet tonight, or supposed to have, but nobody knows where it's got to, and—not your problem, I'm sorry. Welcome to the Jewel of Tephos, but everybody calls it the palace, and yes I know it's more like a fortress, can't be helped. Call it the palace and it seems like more of one. You've got papers?"

Volle handed him the papers he had. "Right here. I was raised in—"

"Merinland, I see. Where's that?"

"It's a small province in southwest Ferrenis. My father, um, met my mother there while on duty in a minor skirmish on the border, and she lived there after he left. We never knew what happened to him, but I guess he was killed, because the people in Vinton didn't know—"

"Killed twenty years ago, yes. Got the report right here. Ferrenis, eh?" He looked sharply at Volle, ears forward, golden eyes slitted narrowly. "You understand your loyalties, eh, lad? Lord Tistunish thinks you do, but he doesn't say what he bases that on."

"I bear no love for the Ferrenians," Volle said stiffly, entirely in character now. "They barely lifted a finger to defend us when my father's troops were attacking. My mother always said the Tephossians treated us better than our lord ever did. She died cursing Ferrenis after our lord's men turned us out of our farm."

"Sorry, lad. Did you ever meet your father?"

"No. He didn't stay around to see me born. My mother said he wanted to, but..."

"Yes, I see." Apparently satisfied, Alister consulted his documents. "The old lord Vinton never occupied quarters in the palace. He liked to be out on the road, as I guess you know." He glanced up at Volle and then back down. "The quarters his father used are now occupied by Lord Fardew, and we won't be turning him and his whole brood out. We've got half a dozen empty ones...ah." He chuckled. "Renaldo, Lord Vinton will be staying on the first floor in the south wing, in the chambers next to Lady Gervis. You know the ones?"

"Yes, sir. I'll see to it that the chambers are prepared and his lordship's luggage taken there." Renaldo turned sharply and left the room.

"Now, for staff. Most of the lords just have a personal servant. The palace has housekeepers to clean the room. You have a personal servant?" Volle shook his head. "Want one?"

"Yes." They would trust him more readily if he had a native servant. If he brought his own servant, it would be easier to be suspicious.

"All right. I'll have Arrin select someone and send him down. If he's not satisfactory, just let us know. The Exchequer will take care of the fee if you like. You'll have to see him anyway to sort out the taxes. Twenty years is a long time."

"Taxes?" Volle hadn't thought of that, and neither, apparently, had Seir or the others.

"Yes. You'll have an income from Vinton, but part of that is owed to the palace." He held up a paw. "Take it up with Minister Ullik, the exchequer. Arrin, can you see if Minister Ullik is free?"

"Certainly, sir." Arrin looked at Volle before leaving, but turned his muzzle quickly when he saw Volle was looking at him. He hurried out of the room, tail waving.

"Banquet tonight, not in your honor of course, but you've come on a good night. There will be good food and a show. These things happen about once a month. Your personal servant will be told about them, or you can send Renaldo or any of the others to find out from my office when they are. The King holds audience once a week in the morning for commoners, afternoon for Lords, we can tell you when that is too. You won't be on his Council yet—maybe ever—but there are a number of things you can sit in on. The Secretary administers all the governance meetings. I'll have Arrin send him a note announcing your arrival. Arrin! Arrin!"

"He went to the Exchequer," Volle said.

"Ah, right. Good lad. Anyway, tell him that when he gets back. Oh, and have him get you a certificate of residence. You'll need that to get into and out of the palace regularly."

"I got in just now without one."

"And Renaldo brought you here to me immediately. You need the certificate to prove you live here. Oh, no guests without papers, and you have to get papers for guests from either this office or the Minister of Defense." He looked up at Volle. "Five years ago there were some incidents with palace guests. Vandalism and such. So now all guests have to have papers. A few bad apples…" He sighed.

"I know how it is," Volle said, but he was a bit shocked. That was stricter than at the Academy, even.

"Well, we carry on. Now, if you haven't any other questions, might I trouble you to wait in the waiting room?" The coyote had already sat back down behind his desk and pulled his papers in front of him. His eyes remained on Volle, but Volle could see his eagerness to get back to his work.

"I'm fine. Thank you very much for your help." Volle smiled, stood, and bowed.

"Pleasure. Call on me if you need anything. Welcome to the palace." With that, Alister bent his head over his papers.

Volle wandered out into the waiting room, closing the door behind him, and smiled to himself. Alister reminded him of the Steward back in Caril. Maybe the harried look and twitchiness came with the job. He hummed softly as he examined the portraits in the waiting room. None of King Barris there, but there were several other portraits of bears in royal finery. And near one of the sconces…

He examined the wall, still humming softly. The torch had left a sooty halo on the wall, but to the left there was a patch on the edge of the halo that was markedly lighter than the rest, about a foot from the edge of the portrait. Obviously another portrait had hung there in the past and been taken down in favor of this one. The painting that hung there now was an old one, showing a grizzled female bear with spectacles. Her clothes indicated that the portrait had been painted some sixty years ago or so, if his fashion knowledge was reliable.

"That's a nice song. What is it?"

Arrin had padded up behind him while he was distracted. Startled, he bristled and then calmed down. "A lullaby. My mother used to sing it to me."

Arrin's expression softened, and he looked up at the portrait Volle was examining. "That's Lady Althea Barris. Great-grandmother of the king."

Volle smiled. "She looks pretty fearsome."

"Legend has it she killed her own daughter because she tried to run off with a commoner," Arrin whispered. He lowered his whisper even further. "Some say it was a common *woman!*"

Volle blinked. He looked at Arrin. The fox was smiling, and Volle thought he was only joking. He smiled back. "Well, my mother's dead," he said, "so I've nothing to worry about on that account, anyway."

"I'm sorry to hear that." Arrin's expression changed immediately from amusement to sympathy. He lowered his ears respectfully.

"It's all right. She died in her sleep." His mother had, in fact, died in her sleep the previous year. He'd gotten a letter about it from his aunt.

Arrin nodded, and slowly brought his ears up. "The Exchequer is free in two hours, just before dinner. His office is just one floor above this one." He pointed up.

"Thank you. Oh, the Steward told me to ask you to leave a note with the Secretary about me?"

"I already did." Arrin flashed white teeth in a broad smile. "He's available to discuss your involvement in the government at any time tomorrow or the day after. And here's your certificate of residency, all filled out and stamped."

"Thank you again." Volle took the paper and bowed his head, and Arrin's ears flicked in embarrassment.

"Just doing my job, my lord," he said. "Um…since Renaldo isn't back yet, may I show your lordship to his chambers?"

Volle smiled. Was Arrin flirting with him? He couldn't be. The Orthodox Church…well, maybe when he was more sure of his position here, he would be able to tell how to respond. "I'd like that. Thank you."

"Let me just tell the Steward where I'm going." Arrin walked quickly across the room to the Steward's office, and Volle noticed his tail wagging jerkily from side to side, as if he were trying to stop it and not succeeding.

"My Lord." Renaldo entered the waiting room and bowed. He was panting slightly. "Please forgive my tardiness in returning. Your lordship's chambers are being prepared and will be ready for you within fifteen minutes. In the meantime, I will show you some of the other rooms of the palace. If your lordship has finished here?"

Volle looked at Arrin, who had just turned around and was looking blankly at Renaldo, then to Volle. He smiled, but it was less broad than his previous smile. "Thank you, Renaldo. His lordship is done. It was a pleasure to meet you, Lord Vinton. Please don't hesitate to come see me if there's anything you want."

The phrasing…it *had* to be flirting. Anything he *wanted*? Like a cute young fox in his bed? Volle still didn't know whether to flirt back. Unsure of his situation, he just bowed his head and said, "Thank you for all the help, Arrin. I'm sure I'll be seeing you again."

He hoped he was just imagining the look of disappointment that flashed across Arrin's muzzle before he composed himself and sat down. Or maybe he hoped he wasn't imagining it. Renaldo hustled him out of the office before he could say another word or sort out his thoughts.

"The Exchequer is up these stairs and to the left." Renaldo pointed up as they walked down the stairs. Volle had to walk fast to keep up with him. He bounded through the palace with a marten's energy, barely able to keep to a walking pace, and Volle was glad he'd had the morning to rest in the carriage. "This is the main dining hall. Formal banquets and dinners of state are held here." Volle poked his head in and saw a raccoon and two wolves scurrying around tidying a huge room, with a large crystal chandelier and windows scattered throughout the ceiling. Portraits adorned the walls and the three fireplaces were edged in gold. The long table was made of beautiful glossy mahogany.

"The King's audience chamber is through there. It's closed now. It's actually not too difficult to find your way around the palace. The main hall runs from the main gate to the back gate, straight through. Every corridor eventually ends up there." Renaldo kept up a running commentary as they walked. "There are six staircases and each one has a different statue at the base. Bear, wolf, weasel, rat, lion, goat. You noticed the Steward was up the Lion stair?"

"I did."

"Your apartments are on the first level but by the Wolf stair. The corridor is actually around behind the stair. See, here's the Wolf stair." They were approaching another staircase, this one with carved wolf heads on the balustrade. The wolf heads were whiter than the rest of the stair, though, and Volle distinctly remembered the lion heads being the same color.

"Are these newer?" he asked as they passed.

"I guess so." Renaldo shrugged. "There's a clock at the base of every stair. They toll the hour and half hour." He waved to the large standing clock as they passed it, then turned right down a narrow passageway. He passed three doors on the left—none on the right—and at the fourth, he stopped. It stood ajar, and Volle could hear sounds of activity within.

Renaldo signaled to Volle to wait, and stepped inside. He reappeared almost immediately. "They're just finishing up," he said. "Your lordship can come into the parlor while they finish the bedroom."

Volle stepped into a room about the size of the Steward's waiting room. A threadbare carpet lay in the center of the floor, and the walls were paneled wood, bare except for a small version of the portrait of the King. There were three chairs in the room, one occupied by Reese and one by Ben; the third was in front of a nice wooden desk. A door stood partly open in the middle of the wall to his left, and two narrow windows, barely wide enough for him to get his head through, looked out onto the front gardens.

Reese waved a paw. "So there you are. Sir." He only added the honorific at Renaldo's sharp look. "Ben and I were discussing where we should spend the night. Is there a tavern nearby?" This last was to the marten.

"Outside the main gate and to your right, the Prancing Unicorn. Excellent hospitality."

Reese nodded. "Thank you."

Two youngsters in aprons, a coyote and a badger, came through the door and bowed to Renaldo. "All finished, sir," they panted.

"Good." He clapped his paws. "Back to the kitchen with you, then." They scurried out.

"Your lordship, the rest of your quarters…" Renaldo pulled the door open and waited for Volle to walk in. "This is the sitting room. We will bring some more furnishings down tomorrow." The room was bare except for a single couch. One narrow window looked out onto the street, and a single door led out in the opposite wall.

Renaldo crossed to the door. "Your bedroom."

Inside, Volle saw a lovely four-poster bed, with what looked like a down mattress and linen sheets, bright white. A small table stood beside it, and a wardrobe, newly polished, gleamed in the corner. The window was just as narrow here, but there was a fireplace in the wall beside it. Renaldo gestured towards this with a paw. "None in the parlor, unfortunately, but there is one in the bedroom. The chimneys run through the wall to a vent in the tower. These are all in good working order, though they're used infrequently. It does get quite cold in winter. My lord is from the south, so it may be quite a shock. Many of our southern lords return home for the winters. As for bathing, your lordship will have to use the public baths just down the corridor. Only five other lords use it, and there is always a servant on duty. There used to be a bath, private, through there, but it was walled in and a door broken through to the apartment next door. Lady Gervis insisted." He indicated the wall opposite the window, which had a doorway in it that had been filled up with bricks. "I'm sorry about the unsightliness of it, my lord. We'll get a tapestry to cover that up."

"Quite all right," Volle said, studying the room. "Thank you very much, Renaldo. You're a great help."

The marten bowed. "Your lordship is too kind. I do my best." He retreated from the room.

When Volle returned to the parlor, only Reese and Ben were there. Ben was standing by the door, and he bowed as Volle entered. "I thought I would take the carriage to the tavern, my lord. Reese said he would join me there later."

Volle looked at Reese, who had a serious expression. No doubt he wanted to lecture Volle again on not forgetting why he was here. Well, that wasn't necessary, he thought. "You don't have to wait here, Reese. Go ahead with Ben." Reese started to protest, but Volle cut him off, unable to resist a pre-emptive jibe of his own. "Really, I can manage. I know how long it's been since you were in a tavern."

A shadow of anger passed over Reese's muzzle, but then he smiled, shrugged, and got up. "All right. You know, I am a bit thirsty. And hungry, too. I hope you find something to satisfy your appetite here."

Volle glared at Reese as Ben chirped, "Oh, I'm sure they'll provide food for your lordship here. They have to!"

"Mmm, yes," Reese said, joining Ben at the door. "My mouth's watering just thinking of all that young, fresh meat." He smirked at Volle, who had to grin back.

"Take care of yourself. I'll be in touch."

"You too, Volle." Then they were gone, and he was alone.

He sat down in the chair at the desk and watched the view out of his window. The crowd in the street outside was rather light, perhaps because it was approaching the dinner hour for many of the people. Or maybe it was always light. None of the buildings were familiar, and he had no idea what to expect when he looked up and down the street.

It began to sink in, slowly, that this was his home for the next several years. Maybe longer, if he did his job. As long as the palace accepted him as Lord Vinton, he would be expected to remain here, gathering information. He would have nobody to talk to except one contact in the palace, and that as sparingly as possible. Occasionally he would be able to slip away to see Seir and Reese, but that too would have to be sparing. He would have to inhabit the role of Lord Vinton.

He had known his work would be hard. Until now, he had not realized it would also be so lonely.

Chapter 4

The Exchequer saw him about an hour before the banquet. Volle paused on the staircase as he passed the Steward's office. He'd be lonely for company tonight, he knew, and the impulse to go ask Arrin to join him was very strong. But he'd have to hold back, until he knew how strong the Church's influence was in the palace. His first impression was not heartening.

He was shown into an office where an old fat squirrel sat behind a desk. The ubiquitous King's portrait hung behind him, but where the Steward's office had been more spartan, Minister Ullik had a portrait of himself hung next to that of the King. On the other side was a portrait of him with a female squirrel and two children.

Volle had to guess that the portraits were of the Minister, because he little resembled the handsome squirrel they showed. Either they had been done a long time ago, or the portrait artist had been very generous. Ullik's front teeth were gone, and one of his ears was notched. He had gained at least fifty or sixty pounds since the portraits, and his fur was not quite as sleek any more. The one constant was the calculating expression. Even in the portrait with his wife and children, he had an annoyed, distant expression as he gazed at the viewer, as if figuring how much this would cost him.

Ullik coughed and waved Volle to a chair. "Close the door. Have a seat. You're the new Lord Vinton, eh?" His voice was low and raspy, and as Volle got closer, he could smell something bad in the squirrel's scent. The dry, dusty scent held also a hint of decay and dirt; perhaps he hadn't washed in a while. Volle sat down, feeling a bit more worried.

"Thank you," he said cautiously. "Sir. I'm supposed to see you about the taxes and about a wage for a personal servant."

Ullik's eyes gleamed. "Yes," he chattered, eyeing Volle up and down. "The taxes. The Vinton seat has been unoccupied for twenty years, yes? And in that time, the taxes on your income have gone unpaid, yes? Vinton is a small province, but still, over twenty years, the amount due is, I'm afraid, substantial."

"Substantial?" Volle couldn't keep his tail from twitching nervously. He could get the money if he needed it, but he wasn't supposed to touch it. They'd assured him that his income would be taken care of by his property.

"Quite." The squirrel pushed a piece of paper across the desk at him. Volle picked it up and scanned it quickly. In a spidery hand, a column of numbers had been added and then multiplied by twenty, with a figuring of interest.

"Eight hundred and forty-three Royals?" Volle almost squeaked. "I can't…I don't…" He looked up at the Exchequer helplessly.

"Terribly sorry, my lord, but until the amount is paid, you will not be welcome at the palace." Ullik was looking at him with a slight smile, but it was a shrewd one.

Relief: he would have to leave. He could go back home. Panic: he couldn't leave. He couldn't fail his mission. "Can't I pay a bit at a time? I can maybe ride back to the province, see what they have there? I don't think they'll have all that, but I can try..." He was talking faster than he should, and he just trailed off, looking at the squirrel, who was shaking his head. "Isn't there any other way? I mean, I don't want to leave the palace."

As soon as he'd said that, the smile on the squirrel's face told him that that's what he'd been waiting for. "Well, Lord Vinton, I don't know. Do you have any other...talents... you could offer?"

"Talents? I..." Volle knew suddenly what he was getting at. His eyes flicked up to the family portrait.

Ullik followed his gaze. "Oh, yes, I'm married," he said. His tail twitched behind him. "But a wife doesn't always take care of all her husband's needs, you know? Of course you don't. Not married. And you're still *young* and *handsome*. No problem getting the pretty vixens to do what you want."

Volle just stared at him numbly. "You'd forgive eight hundred forty-three Royals?"

The squirrel's smile widened. He raised his eyebrows and shrugged. "I can make the balance come out. If I am convincingly persuaded." He said the last two words in almost a hiss, which turned into a whistle through the gap in his front teeth.

"But what about...I mean, what if someone..."

Ullik leaned back and put his arms behind his head. He pushed the chair back from his desk and smiled. "Yes, well. Lock the door before you start."

"But...the Church!"

Ullik frowned. "Lord Vinton, if you would prefer to go home, we can end this meeting right now."

"No. No, I..." He stood up, numbly, and walked to the door. The bolt slid across simply and easily, but he still stood staring at it for a moment. He couldn't believe he was about to do this. He'd hoped for relief from chastity, but not like this. Even at the thought of what he was about to do (whatever it might be; he had a good idea), his sheath wasn't stirring.

He turned and walked back towards the desk. Ullik had already undone his pants and lifted his tunic, revealing a small sheath and a huge sac below it, the biggest Volle had ever seen. He'd never been with a squirrel before; maybe it was a rodent thing. He walked around the desk, tail curled down between his legs.

Ullik's face was set in a gleeful expression of anticipation. He actually licked his lips as Volle approached, and slid forward on the chair more. He was already quite aroused; Volle could see a drop of clear fluid trickling down his hard maleness.

Volle took a breath and then knelt beside the chair. He reached out and took the stiff length in his paw. It was warm to the touch, but if he blocked out the smells, it wasn't all that different from others. He could pretend he was somewhere else, pretend that the fur pressing against his paw was from a lover doubled over and not from an obscenely distended belly. He stroked up and down, thinking, please let this be all. Let this be over soon.

"Mmmm." The squirrel's expression of pleasure was a deep, rough rumble. Volle knew he was imagining things, but to him it sounded like the rumblings of an upset stomach, a wet, roiling sound. He moved his paw more quickly, trying not to listen and trying not to smell the dry, dusty smell that was quickly being overpowered by the squirrel's arousal and his breath. He obviously took snuff, a practice that Volle found revolting.

"That's very nice, my lord." Ullik said the last two words with a mocking undertone. "But I'm sure you will agree that a debt such as yours must be worked off with a more skilled instrument than your admittedly capable paw."

Volle stopped, and then lifted his paw away. He swallowed, working his tongue in his muzzle. It took a moment for him to steel himself sufficiently, and once he had done that, he had to work himself into a better position. He ended up crouching half under the minister's desk, his head between Ullik's knees. He could see patches of grey in the fur and he was sure he could hear fleas scratching around. The smell was too strong to ignore now, and while the arousal itself wasn't completely unpleasant, the dirt and accumulated oils in the yellowish white fur between Ullik's legs made Volle's nose wrinkle. He almost sneezed, but held it back, and gingerly touched his tongue to the minister's length.

The sooner he comes, the sooner I go. The sooner he comes, the sooner I go. He held the short member in his paw and slid his muzzle up and down it, chanting that refrain silently to himself. It was fairly hard to pull the shaft away from the flabby stomach so his muzzle could work on it, and he found to his surprise that his paw was getting tired. He worked his muzzle and tongue faster still, ears alert for the phlegmy, raspy moans of the minister as his body tensed and shifted.

Soon now, he told himself, and quickened his muzzle's licks and suckling as he heard the squirrel gasp shortly. He felt a familiar shiver in the shaft he held, and four strokes of his muzzle later, warmth spurted out into his muzzle in time with a series of grunts from above.

When he was sure the minister had finished, he slid his head back, still holding the fluid in his muzzle. It tasted sour and bad, and since he hadn't swallowed immediately, he was finding it hard to work himself up to it. He looked back and forth behind the minister's desk for somewhere to spit it out.

Ullik was panting. "Oh, that was good. Yes." He saw Volle's muzzle moving and reached out with a paw to brush under his chin. "What's the matter there, my lord? You know, when you make a deposit with me, I don't just spit it back on your desk. I put it in my vault and keep it safe." The paw reached up, holding Volle's muzzle closed.

Volle's eyes searched Ullik's, but found nothing there but cruel pleasure. He took a couple breaths and then swallowed.

The paw released his muzzle, and he banged his head on the desk as he recoiled backwards. The taste lingered in his mouth, reminding him of waking up after a night at the tavern. He wiped his muzzle and then got up unsteadily.

Ullik had pulled his trousers back up and was arranging his shirt. "I assume I will see you at the banquet tonight?"

Volle nodded. "So...I'm all right, then?" He edged slowly back around the desk.

"Yes, you may stay in the palace." Ullik smiled at him. "I think that was well worth forgiving one year of your debt."

"One..." Volle steadied himself on the desk with a paw.

"You surely didn't think that would make up for all twenty? We can discuss the regular payment of the rest of your debt in the next few days. Once you get settled in." His smile was smug and confident. "Now you'd best run along. Not much time to change before the banquet."

Volle unbolted the door and fairly ran for his quarters. His muzzle still felt disgusting, no matter how many times he opened it to pant and let the cool air in.

He checked the large clock at the base of the stairs. Half an hour 'til the banquet. He didn't think he'd have time for a bath, but he definitely had to wash his muzzle and get the taste out of his mouth.

The baths were easy to find; the smell of scented powder wafted down the corridor a good thirty feet away. He followed it to a white stone archway, inside which a plump female raccoon stood. She straightened when she saw him and favored him with a warm smile.

"Evening, sir. Freshen up for the banquet?" She reached behind her for a small stack of towels and handed him one.

Volle took the towel and leaned over a basin of water. He dabbed at it with the towel. It was lukewarm and only lightly scented. "Thank you. Is there some water I could wash out my muzzle with?" He cleaned his muzzle with the damp towel and then rubbed the fur dry while she answered.

"Oooh. I think...let me see, sir." She disappeared into a small doorway, leaving Volle to look around the room. The two ceramic basins had a few small cracks, but were otherwise in excellent condition, and he could now tell that the water they held was scented differently. The one he'd used was roses, and the other was jasmine. To his nose, the scents were moderately strong; to non-canids, he suspected they would be very light and subtle. More scents like those emanated from the curtains to his left; through there, he suspected, were the powder baths, large basins full of scented powder for a person to roll in.

Those were luxurious enough, but then he noticed a curtained archway in the back of the room that billowed gently with steam, and Volle could smell the soaps. Warm water baths! He was sorely tempted to immerse himself in one, but he would never have time to dry off before the banquet.

He had just put the towel down and started smoothing his muzzle fur when the raccoon returned with a pewter mug. She handed it to him. "Here, sir. Clean water."

"Thank you." He rinsed his muzzle out and spit the water into the drain. The water was cool and refreshing, and got rid of some of the taste. He emptied the mug, swallowing the water this time, and handed it back to the raccoon. "Again, thank you."

She curtsied and smiled. "At your service, sir."

Back in his rooms, he examined his wardrobe. The only fancy thing he had to wear was the doublet he'd worn to the meeting, on his last day in Ferrenis. He took it down and fingered it softly, feeling again very lonely. Banquet, he told himself, great place to meet people. Except, of course, he would be meeting them in the hopes of finding out whatever information they had, always with that in the back of his mind. Not just to be social, just to make friends.

He sighed and pulled the doublet on, adjusting it. There was a full-length mirror inside the wardrobe, which he used to check his appearance. He wished he had more formal pants than the soft cowhide ones he was wearing, but that would be something to take care of in the coming weeks.

After five minutes spent brushing his tail, he felt calm enough and presentable enough to attend the banquet. He found the dining hall easily, because as soon as he got to the main hall, he could hear and see the crowd of nobles milling around outside it.

They were of all different species, but he did notice a preponderance of bears. Wolves, raccoons, and weasels were all well represented, and of course there were several rodents: two squirrels, a beaver, and a dignified-looking white rat. The Exchequer, to his relief, was nowhere to be seen. He only saw two other foxes, and neither of them was a noble: the first was a footfox, walking around jotting names on a list, and the second was a personal servant attending a foppish-looking weasel who kept adjusting his lace collar. Volle's glance through the crowd failed to turn up a single other pair of leather pants. Some males were wearing colorful cotton short pants cinched just above the knee, and some were wearing what looked like a knee-length skirt. The females, of course, were wearing long, loose robes. They all tended toward the heavy side, especially the males, but only a few were as excessively overweight as the Exchequer had been.

"Lord Vinton?" He turned to see a large black wolf glowering at him from under white bushy eyebrows. He was dressed in charcoal grey: a lighter grey vest over a darker shirt, and short pants that matched the shirt. The shirt stretched out slightly over the pants, but the wolf carried the extra weight well. A black paw was extended towards Volle, and he saw a bit of grey fur both on the paw and on the muzzle.

He reached out and grasped the paw. "Yes, but I don't believe I've had the pleasure."

The white eyebrows lifted, and the light blue eyes sparkled as the wolf smiled. "Lord Tistunish of Hallenford. Even if Lord Dewanne weren't on vacation, you'd be easy to pick out." He glanced at the leather trousers. "Did you just arrive today?"

Volle nodded. "It's been a long trip." His ears flicked, and he smiled. "These are the nicest clothes I have."

"Plenty of time to remedy that. See that you do. The palace tailor is a good old goat, he'll find something for you." Lord Tistunish cocked an ear to the footmarten who was announcing that the King had entered the banquet hall. "You'll need to go down to eat, soon. Junior nobles are announced first and you're about as junior as they come. Your personal servant..." He looked around behind Volle.

"Haven't been assigned one yet."

"Ah. Never mind, then. Come along. I'll ask them to arrange the seating." He took Volle's arm in a surprisingly strong grip and steered him towards the nearest footman, which happened to be the fox.

The fox met Volle's eyes and gave a quick smile of species familiarity, then turned to Lord Tistunish. "Yes, my lord?"

"Lord Vinton is to be seated next to me at dinner."

The fox looked again at Volle, and inclined his head. "I'm sorry, my lord. I didn't realize who you were." He made a note on his scroll and looked back at the wolf. "Yes, my lord. I'll see to it. Lord Vinton, you'll be in the first group called. I believe they are getting ready to announce them now. If you would follow me, your lordship?"

Lord Tistunish shook his paw again. "Go ahead. I'll see you at dinner."

"Thank you." Volle smiled, shook the wolf's paw, and set off behind the fox.

The fox and marten conferred, and only a minute later, the marten announced, "Welcome to the Royal Banquet in honor of the Festival of the Renewal. My lords and ladies, it is my honor to invite you to join their Majesties at this sumptuous feast."

He opened the door and stood in the doorway to one side, facing the other side, and called out a list of about ten names. Volle heard his among them, but hung back to let some of the others go in first so he could follow their lead. He ended up eighth in line, behind a chubby young wolf with grey fur and in front of a raccoon and his wife. The foppish weasel was near the front of the line.

The wolf glanced at his trousers and gave him a rather condescending look before facing forward. Volle frowned at his tail, then chuckled to himself. "Short tail, small tool," he muttered under his breath, and the childish words made him feel better.

The line of nobles proceeded to the two chairs at the head of the table where the King and Queen were sitting. They were imposing in person, as most bears were, but they did have a noble carriage and alert, if not kind, eyes. Each noble bowed deeply to both and kissed the Queen's paw, then met a servant on the other side of the royalty and were escorted to their seats.

Volle heard the wolf in front of him say "All honor to their gracious majesties," as he bowed, so when it came his turn, he repeated the phrase. The Queen smiled at him and moved her gaze to the raccoon and his wife behind him, but the King's eyes lingered on Volle. The next servant, a badger, was about to take Volle's arm when the King held up a large paw.

"Lord Vinton?"

Volle looked back into the clear brown eyes. "Yes, your Majesty." Unsure what to do, he bowed again.

"We have heard news of your coming. We are pleased to see the Vinton seat occupied again. Please feel free to visit us if the Vinton lands have any pressing needs." Formality prevented the words from being as pleasant as they might have been, but Volle didn't know whether that was the King's doing or the fault of the circumstances.

"Thank you, your Majesty."

The King looked down at his trousers and then lowered his paw, turning to look at the raccoon behind Volle. "Hello, Lord Black," Volle heard him say as the badger led him around the table.

He was seated about halfway down, closer than all of the junior nobles except the weasel. The next group had been announced and was moving into the room as Volle sat down. The badger pushed his chair in gently, then left to escort another noble to his chair, and Volle could study the room, thankful that his trousers were hidden from view.

The place settings were silver, or at least looked like it. There were five pieces in front of him: two forks, two spoons, one knife. He also had a goblet that proved to be crystal; he ran his claws over it to check. Very fancy. Of course, he'd never been invited to dinners of state in Caril, so he had no basis for comparison.

There were, by his quick count, about a hundred place settings at the table. They were filling in rapidly, as each guest entered, paid his or her respects to the royal couple, and were seated. He looked curiously to see whether the herbivores had their own section. At the Academy, they'd been seated at a separate table, because the smell of meat made some of them ill. Here, he noticed deer and goats sitting beside bobcats and wolves. Either it didn't bother the nobles here, or they had gotten used to it.

Once the table was about two-third filled, the groups entering became smaller, until the last seven nobles—the most important, Volle presumed—were introduced individually with their wives. "Lord and Lady Quirn." A pair of bears entered. "Lord and Lady Wallen." A pair of deer entered, the male turning his head so his antlers would clear the doorway. "Lord and Lady Fardew." A pair of wolves entered. "Lord and Lady Ullik." The Exchequer and a plump female squirrel entered.

He wore a fancy silk shirt that strained across his chest and stomach, and a skirt that didn't quite conceal the shape of his thigh. His wife was wearing a shorter dress than most of the other ladies, and she had curled her long headfur. It looked rather dreadful, but Volle didn't see any more, because at that moment the Exchequer glanced in his direction, and Volle looked quickly down at his paws on the table.

Lord Tistunish had been facing his wife, an ample bitch who was nearly as tall as he was, though her fur was a more standard grey and white. He noticed Volle's movement and glanced at the Exchequer, but didn't say anything. The room remained almost totally silent as the nobles walked by and took their seats, all at the head of the table.

"Lord and Lady Barclaw." Volle didn't look up until he was sure the squirrels were in their seats. He saw the backs of two bears as they approached the king.

"Lord and Lady Villutian." Two more bears entered.

"Lord and Lady Alacris." A third pair of bears entered, and when they had been seated, the murmur of conversation filled the hall. The great wooden doors were swung shut, and four smaller doors at the sides of the room opened. Raccoons bearing small silver platters marched stiffly around the room serving, from the head of the table down.

"Already had a run-in with Ullik?" Lord Tistunish asked quietly as they waited for their meal to be served.

Volle nodded. "I have to collect some back taxes."

"Back taxes…" The wolf was silent while the raccoon placed a platter in front of him, then in front of Volle. The appetizer was an entire game hen, roasted and steaming, with the head still on. Volle could smell orange and honey in the sauce as well as two spices he didn't recognize. His stomach reminded him loudly that he hadn't eaten since breakfast, and Lord Tistunish grinned and elbowed him.

"Go ahead and eat, Lord Vinton. The King's started." Indeed, Volle saw, the King had already made his way through half of one of the two birds on his plate. The Queen was delicately picking apart the other with precise motions of her fork and large claws.

Volle picked at his bird with a fork and found that the meat peeled easily away from the bone. He took a bite and chewed quickly, reaching for another as soon as he felt he could politely do so.

"Oh, about Ullik." Lord Tistunish was chewing thoughtfully. "He'd sell his mother to the merchants if he thought he could get a fair price for her. In fact, he might have—nobody's seen her in years." The wolf chuckled, and Volle joined in. "What I mean to say is, check your land's records. Just to be sure that the amount he told you is correct. He's a powerful lord, and not one you want to be on the wrong side of, but you don't want to let him get a hold on you, either, and he's not above mishandling the numbers if it works to his advantage."

"Thank you. I will have the records checked." If he lied, Volle thought furiously, if I went through that for nothing ... but he couldn't think of anything he could do except walk away from Ullik. He absolutely did not want to make enemies in the palace.

"So tell me about yourself," Lord Tistunish said, and Volle spent the next three courses talking about his childhood, mixing in a few strategic falsehoods. He didn't remember his father (which was true), but his mother had told him that he was the lord of a small valley in Tephos (not true). That story took him through the salad course, which was a small bowl of greens with berries he was familiar with and a vinaigrette dressing. Wine was served with that course, but Volle only sipped at it; he didn't want to drink too much. He noted that most of the nobles, including Lord Tistunish, did not share his concern.

By the time the roasted goose with apple stuffing had been dispatched, the conversation in the room was considerably louder. Lord Tistunish had heard Volle's story and was giving him pointers on palace etiquette, with his wife Tika chiming in from time to time. She had a nice smile and kind eyes, and Volle liked her immediately.

Dessert was a plum pudding garnished with cleverly crafted marzipan birds. Volle had three on his plate, but he saw that some of the lords closer to the King had at least ten, and he marveled at the kitchen staff's industriousness and creativity in creating so many colorful, lovely birds. He was so full by that point that he didn't eat them, but he certainly enjoyed looking at them.

"My lords!" A great bellow sounded throughout the hall, and everyone fell silent. The bear standing to the right of the King—Lord Alacris?—was standing and had raised his wine goblet. "We have eaten at the King's table and drunk of his wine. Please join me in drinking to his continued health and fortune. To the King!"

"To the King!" The roar swept the hall. Goblets were drained and refilled.

The King himself stood, and Alacris sat. "Thank you, my friends. The Festival of the Renewal is a time of joy and celebration, a time to celebrate fertility and life." He was enunciating enough that Volle suspected he was a bit tipsy. "A toast to the Mother of us all, and to all of our mothers!"

"To Mothers!" Once again, the wine flowed. Volle joined in the toast, but contented himself with a sip each time. Lord Tistunish and

"Ullik? He'd sell his own mother to the merchants if he thought he could get a good price for her."

his wife both followed the example of the other lords and drained their goblets.

"And in celebration of life, you will find in the theater immediately following dinner a performance of the Ermine Dancers, specially commissioned to appear here. Drink up, and enjoy the show!"

More wine was downed and poured. People started to get up, and after a couple minutes, Lord Tistunish and his wife followed suit. Volle stood along with them, waiting for a break in the crowd as the nobles strolled by. "Ermine Dancers?"

"Beautiful ladies from the northern mountains. They travel throughout the country every few years. Quite, um, engaging, the last time I saw them."

His wife smiled and kissed him on the nose. "You two go ahead, dear. I'll be waiting for you when it's over." The look that passed between them was unmistakable, and made Volle smile.

"You're very lucky," Volle said, and felt confident enough to add, with a sly grin, "Nice to see you're not into your dotage yet."

Lord Tistunish roared and clapped him on the back. "You young whelp! No, I haven't quite got your youthful stamina, but I have energy and experience. And besides, these Ermines would get a rise out of even old Alacris here!"

The bear and his wife happened to be passing them at the time. Lord Alacris swiped at the wolf, and grinned. "Get on with you, Tish. Not all of us can be as wolfish as you."

"Might ruin your noble bearing!" Tistunish shot back.

Alacris's wife tittered behind a paw, and the bear rolled his eyes good-naturedly. "See you at the dance, Tish."

"He's a good sort," Tistunish muttered to Volle as they made their way through the emptying hall. "King's advisor, but not nearly as stuck up as most of the high nobles. So you're not married, are you?"

Volle shook his head. "No."

"Vixen back home?" He shook his head again. "We'll have to find you someone, then. Don't want to risk the Vinton line dying out again." The wolf chuckled. "Maybe you shouldn't attend the dance. Wouldn't want you to be all worked up with nowhere to…go."

Volle chuckled. "I can handle myself," he said, which set off another roaring laugh from the wolf.

They walked outside of the palace proper, to an outdoor amphitheater with an open stage and sheltered seats. Several private boxes sat along the sides, but Tistunish led Volle down to the common seats. The center was already filling up, so they took a pair of seats at the edge. "The view is just as good from anywhere for this show," the wolf said with a grin as they sat.

Volle nodded. He didn't mind the seats; from this vantage point, he could watch about half the audience without seeming too obvious about it. He couldn't see Ullik or Alacris—in a private box, most likely. He did recognize the foppish weasel, and the wolf who'd been in front of him in the line. He thought he saw the Steward as well, though he was fairly sure the coyote hadn't been at the dinner. He tried sniffing the air for familiar scents, but the only one that came in clearly was Tistunish. The rest of the scents merged into a fluid background that he didn't have the knowledge to sort out.

He was just craning his neck around behind him to see if he could spot Arrin anywhere when a cheer from the crowd brought his attention back to the stage. A single slender figure stood there, wearing only a green silk tunic tied around the waist. What he could see of her fur was snowy white, except for the very tip of her tail, which was coal black. Her slender musteline muzzle surveyed the crowd but remained expressionless, Her shiny black eyes catching gleams of torchlight as they turned this way and that. She looked right at Volle, and then at one of the private boxes above him. Closing her eyes, she executed a deep curtsy, but instead of keeping the back leg on the ground for support, she lifted it off the stage and held that position for a good twenty seconds.

The crowd applauded politely, as a line of five more ermines, dressed in different colored tunics, trooped out behind the first one, their paws making almost no noise on the wooden stage. They each imitated the curtsy of the first one in sequence: the third one started when the second was halfway down, and so on. After a moment, the first one began to rise, and then the second, and so on until they were all standing in a line on the stage. And then the dance began.

They were not just dancers, but acrobats, and their lithe movements across the stage were amazing to behold. Volle was fascinated, though not with the tongue-hanging-out absorption of much of the crowd. They moved fluidly, gracefully, each step blending into the next and complementing the steps of the others at the same time. They seemed to be part of an intricate flowing clockwork rather than six individuals.

He leaned back in his seat to watch, enjoying the show, but not seeing quite what Tistunish found so arousing about it. He looked at the wolf and saw that his expression was more one of anticipation than fascination. Looking around, he noticed the same tension in many of the nobles around him. They were enjoying the show, but also waiting.

The ermines went through two dance numbers before Volle found out what the crowd was waiting for. One by one, they slipped out of their tunics, tossing them to the side of the stage. Tistunish, and indeed most of the crowd, leaned forward eagerly. The ermines each spun slowly on the stage, showing off the gentle slopes of their chests, the supple curves of their rumps, and the touch of pink between their legs. They broke off into pairs and began a slower dance number in which they pressed close together, running their small paws over each other.

Volle could smell the increased arousal from the crowd. He was sure that any canid could smell it; five minutes later he was sure it was obvious to everyone, and that the crowd was feeding off of itself. He shifted as he felt his sheath bulge, though it was more in response to the musky aroma of the wolf next to him than the erotic dance on the stage.

The ermines were moving more quickly now, tongues flicking as they brushed past each other. The dance was still technically lovely to watch as they slid around and past each other, now and then changing partners, but always in perfect synchronicity. They used their black tails to highlight patterns on each other, small black patches moving along soft white curves in shapes as graceful as the rest of their movements.

Nevertheless, Volle grew slightly bored with the show. The eroticism had been thrust to the fore, and as lovely as he thought the ermines were, he didn't find them exciting. He leaned forward and scanned the rest of the crowd.

Every other male, it seemed, was leaning forward, intent on the show. Volle spotted only two who seemed as disinterested as himself. One, the foppish weasel, turned and looked back just as Volle was looking at him. Their eyes met, and Volle thought he saw the weasel smile before he touched the beret he wore and turned back to the show.

Volle continued to watch him, thoughtfully. Was he just affecting boredom? He was sitting alone, with no wife that Volle could see. He filed the weasel away as potentially an interesting contact for later.

The other bored male noble, a bear, was more sleepy than anything else. His eyes were half-shut the first time Volle looked at him. Five minutes later they were almost completely shut. His wife turned to look at him but didn't make any move to wake him up.

The ermines were now rubbing against each other quite enthusiastically. Volle suspected this had to be the last number; any further and they would need to bring beds out onto the stage. Fortunately, the ermines concluded that number with several bows, and Volle stood with the rest of the crowd to give them an ovation and several curtain calls.

"Well!" Tistunish said, composing himself somewhat as the nobles hurried to the exits. "I must be getting back. Yes." He clapped Volle on the shoulder. "We must find you a vixen, dear boy. Next week, you will come dine with us in our chambers. Tika knows many families in Divalia. She'll find a suitable consort for you."

"All right," Volle said. What harm could a dinner do? And at least it would allow him to talk to Tistunish about palace politics.

"And I have some other…friends. You should meet them sometime. All in due time, though." His eyes were already looking towards the upper windows of the palace.

Volle smiled. "Get to your duty, sir. Thank you for the dinner company."

The wolf waved a paw. "My pleasure. Oh, and none of that 'sir' rubbish. Call me Tish. Everyone does."

Volle bowed. "Then I insist you call me Volle."

"I'll do that. Good night, Volle." The wolf moved off with the crowd. Volle followed his progress for a few minutes, then lost him.

When the crowd had thinned out, Volle ambled towards the exit at the top of the amphitheater and turned towards the garden. He wanted to go by the inn where Ben and Reese were staying, to tell Ben to ask the governor for any records of taxes paid during the last twenty years. He thought he knew his way around well enough to get there and back, and he could use the walk; his sheath was still hard from the scents of the show. No chance of release tonight unless he used his paw, but maybe he could relax a bit. To drink, though, he'd need money. He started to turn back to the palace to get money, but then remembered he'd worn his purse out of habit.

A paw on his shoulder stopped him. He turned and saw the weasel, wearing the beret at a jaunty angle. The weasel was smiling, and his bright eyes were sparkling.

"You're new here, aren't you?" he said without preamble.

Volle nodded, and bowed. "Lord Vinton. Volle."

The weasel stuck his paw out. "Lord Helfer Ikling. No need to bow to me. Vinton-Volle, was it?"

Volle laughed. "Just Volle." He shook the weasel's paw. "Pleased to meet you."

"The honor and pleasure are mine. There, now that's out of the way…I noticed you didn't seem to appreciate the sensual portion of tonight's program." Helfer looked at him intently.

Volle's ears flicked. "Ah, well, technically it was quite impressive. I—"

"But it would've been more interesting with some young male ermines instead?"

"Uh…I…" Volle stammered.

Helfer laughed. "That's answer enough. Well, if you were as affected by all the pheromones as I was—and with that nose of yours, I'm guessing you were hit harder—would you like to join me for a little indulgence more suited to our tastes?"

Volle blinked. He looked to either side, but there were only a few stragglers left and nobody seemed to be paying attention to them. Looking back at Helfer, he considered him. He was attractive, if about a foot shorter than Volle, but Volle had never been attracted to the musteline set. They tended to get excitable and lash out with claws and such, and they came quickly and often. If not for that, he might have just said, damn the Church. "Well, I have an errand to run outside the walls…"

"Perfect! That's where I'm going." The weasel started down the path, then looked back at Volle. "Coming?"

"Listen." Volle caught up with him and stopped him. "You seem very nice, but…wait, why do we have to go outside?"

"Because that's where the place is," Helfer explained patiently. Light sparked in his eyes. "Oh, you thought I meant…ha! I'm sorry,

Volle, nothing against you, but I don't ride in the palace stables, so to speak. Leads to complications and all sorts of other things. I prefer to get a nice mount down the street, have a good ride, and send him on his way." He grinned. "Better?"

He was still talking as if he didn't care who heard them. But he was offering to show Volle to one of those secret places where he could find an erotic performance more to his tastes, and Volle just couldn't pass that opportunity up, not if he were going to survive years in this palace. He'd have to trust that Helfer had been doing this long enough to know how not to get caught.

He smiled broadly. "Yes, that's fine. I'm terribly sorry."

Helfer shook his head. "I can see how you might have thought that. You must get a lot of offers. New noble, young and good-looking as you are..."

"I've only been here a day," Volle said, avoiding the question. He wasn't quite sure how to respond to it, and Helfer didn't press.

They kept walking towards the gate. By this time, the moon was high in the sky and most of the torches in the garden had been extinguished. Volle could see nearly as clearly as if the sun were up, but the world had a grayer cast to it. Plants glowed silver where the moon touched them, and the shadows under them were blacker than pitch. It had an ethereal beauty to it; everything seemed slightly less real in the softer light of the moon.

He hadn't brought his certificate, but Helfer had. "This is Lord Vinton," he told the guard. "He's with me."

The guard nodded and let them through, handing Volle a small purple piece of paper. "This'll get you back in as long as you come in with Lord Ikling, sir," he said. "I'd remember you, but I go off duty in an hour."

"Thank you," Volle said as they started off down the surprisingly active street. They walked on the sidewalk, avoiding the filthy cobblestones, and smiled at the people hurrying around them.

"Late to his mistress," Helfer said, pointing at one. "Late to his ale. Oh! Late for an appointment with me!" That one was a slender white rabbit, whose ears turned at Helfer's words. He didn't slow down, though, and soon was lost. Volle laughed.

"Thank you," Helfer said with a smile. "I can't tell you how refreshing it is to be in the company of someone who finds me amusing but not attractive."

"Oh, you're attractive enough," Volle said. "This is the inn I need to stop at." They were underneath a gently swaying sign that bore a picture of a unicorn dancing.

"You really have an errand to do? I thought that was just to get rid of me." Helfer grinned teasingly at Volle. "I'll wait out here."

"Would it have worked?" Volle shot back as he walked in.

"Not if I was determined!" Helfer called after him.

He shook his head, smiling, as he let his eyes adjust to the slightly darker interior. Ben and Reese were nowhere to be seen in the main room of the pub, so he walked up to the bar and waited for the beaver behind it to get over to him.

He did so, and eyed Volle's clothes before speaking. "Evenin', sir," he said amiably. "Pint of Vellenland?"

"No, thanks. I'm looking for a marmot and a hare who are staying here? I need to give them a message to deliver for me."

"Ah. They went up to the room about an hour ago. Said they were leaving at first light. If you leave the message with me, I'll see they get it."

Volle nodded. "Have a quill and paper?"

"In the office. I'll fetch some." The beaver waddled through a small door behind the bar, and returned with a quill, an inkpot, and two sheets of paper.

"Thank you. I'm much obliged." Volle scrawled a hasty message to the governor asking him to send all tax receipts from the past twenty years to him at the palace by personal messenger. He sealed it, and wrote a second note to Ben asking him to deliver the first note personally to the governor. As he was writing it, he realized that he didn't know whether Ben could read, so he added "or Reese" to the address.

He gave it to the bartender, who promised to deliver it, and dug in his pouch for a silver coin. "This for your trouble, good sir."

The beaver bowed. "Your lordship is too gracious."

Volle smiled at his promotion in status. "I appreciate the trouble you're taking. Good night, sir."

He didn't see Helfer at first when he walked back into the street, and he thought the weasel might have gotten bored or left him behind. But Helfer appeared behind him a moment later. "All done? Good. The place is just down here."

He led Volle back past the front of the palace, past a noisy pub with a cup and a crown on its sign, then down an alley that was darker than the street, but no less traveled. It was harder to avoid the press of people, and the scents started to combine into one big crowd-scent again, making Volle a little nervous. He stuck close to Helfer until the weasel stopped and said with a grin, "Here we are."

Above them, a wooden sign creaked gently. On it, a golden-brown canid with an enormous erection was grasping it and leering out of the painting. "The Jackal's Staff," said Helfer, and put a paw on the door handle.

"It's right out in the open," Volle said. "Is there a password or something?" Helfer looked at him blankly. "The Church…don't they…I mean, why do they let this operate?"

Helfer's expression cleared. "Oh, you poor thing. You must have been raised strict Orthodox. No, the Church here is Orthodox Third Council. They don't care who you love." He took Volle's paw and pulled him gently toward the door. "Come on. Really, it's okay. You won't get in trouble. Unless you really believe—er, unless you're strict Orthodox, too. But no, you don't act like it."

"No, I'm not." Volle looked up at the sign again, and at the entrance. "I was just told that Divalia was." His tail twitched back and forth. All this time he'd been steeling himself for a chaste life, for sneaking around in the shadows not only for information, but for pleasure, and it was just a joke on Reese's part. No doubt he'd thought it would be funny, to tell the sex-crazed fox he couldn't indulge in his 'hobby.' It just underscored to Volle that Reese and Seir and everyone else didn't understand what intimacy meant to him. It was more than just a hobby; it was a *need*, and not just for the physical aspect of it. It was a need to be close to another person, to earn their trust and give his in return, and every part of the physical act that he enjoyed stemmed from that. Otherwise he could just stay in his room and make love to his paw.

Helfer laughed. "You wouldn't catch me here if that were true! Whoever told you that?"

Volle flexed his claws. "A 'friend' told me. I'll have to correct him when I see him again." He made his paws relax and shook his head. Whatever the motivation for the joke—if it had indeed been intentional—it was over now, and he was on the threshold of what promised to be a very enjoyable close to the evening. "Okay, let's go in."

The inside of the Jackal's Staff looked small for the size of the building. The first thing Volle noticed wasn't the décor, but the powerful scent of lust that permeated everything. He took a moment to catch his breath, feeling his sheath bulge again at the intoxicating aroma. This wasn't a natural smell, like the one produced by the crowd at the show, but was no less enjoyable for that.

Helfer grinned at him and inhaled deeply. "Mmm. Hits you hard, doesn't it? So to speak." He chuckled and made his way to a small table. There were perhaps a dozen of them arranged on the floor. To the left of the door was a small stage where two raccoons played a violin and a cello. The melody was nice, if not particularly artful. Three other patrons occupied a table each, and a pink-robed cougar wandered between them. Her fur was dyed white, with pink highlights around the muzzle and light blue ears.

Volle sank into the plush chair beside Helfer's and watched the scene. The cougar was talking animatedly to one of the patrons, a black bear, but broke off her conversation when she saw Helfer. She patted the bear's shoulder and hurried over, and it was only when he caught her scent that Volle realized she was male.

"Helfer, darling!" he squealed. "So lovely to see you again. Are you just renting a room tonight?" He eyed Volle. "I must say, I wouldn't blame you."

"Tally, this is Lord Vinton," Helfer said, grinning.

Volle half rose and extended a paw, but the cougar swept around the table and engulfed him in a hug. "Lord Vinton! Welcome to the Jackal's Staff. I'm Tally, and my job is to get you whatever you want." Volle laughed and patted Tally back. "You can call me Volle," he said, and Tally beamed at him.

"Volle it is! What's your pleasure tonight, darlings?"

Helfer was eying the patrons. "Who's the rabbit over there?"

"Yefi Whetwood. He's a paper maker. He hasn't found anyone he likes yet. I asked him to wait until Mario was available, but...you think?" Tally smiled down at Helfer. "Yes, I think he might like you. And I know you'd like him. Here." He handed Helfer a piece of paper and a quill. "It's okay, he can read."

Helfer scratched a few words in a loose, spidery hand, folded the note, and gave it back to Tally, who tucked it into a pouch in his robe. "And what about you, Lord Volle? What is your fancy tonight?"

Volle spread his paws. "Wolf, or a cat." He gave Tally a broad smile.

The cougar giggled and batted his nose gently with a velvety paw. "Oh, Helfer, he's a flirt! I'm not available, sugar. But I'll send out Jonas and Richy. If you don't like either of them, then Celann should be free in about twenty minutes. I know you'll like him." He gathered his robe and glided back to the rabbit's table.

"How do we pay?" Volle asked Helfer, who was watching Tally hand his note to the rabbit, who looked over.

Helfer waved a paw and smiled. The rabbit looked uncertain, then smiled back. "Pay in advance, and you always pay Tally, never anyone else. If you want to give a little extra for a good performance, give it to him afterwards. It varies from three to five silver, depending on who you get and what you want him to do. Don't worry, I'll cover you this time." He turned to Volle and grinned. "Think of it as a welcome-to-Divalia gift. And now, I think I have a rendez-vous."

He got up from the table just as Volle said, "Will I meet you back here?"

"Oh. Right, we'll meet here and then go back." He tipped his beret. "Enjoy! I know I will." He sauntered over to the table, sat down with the rabbit, and started talking.

Tally, meanwhile, had vanished behind the middle of the three doors in the back wall. He emerged with a young wolf and a young puma and returned to the black bear, while the wolf and puma came over to Volle's table.

Both wore nothing but a linen loincloth, and that was pulled tightly across their waists to highlight the bulges underneath. The wolf was a standard grey, with a creamy white chest and stomach. Volle could just see the lower edges of the white fur between his legs below the edge of the loincloth. His sheath tightened further at the sight.

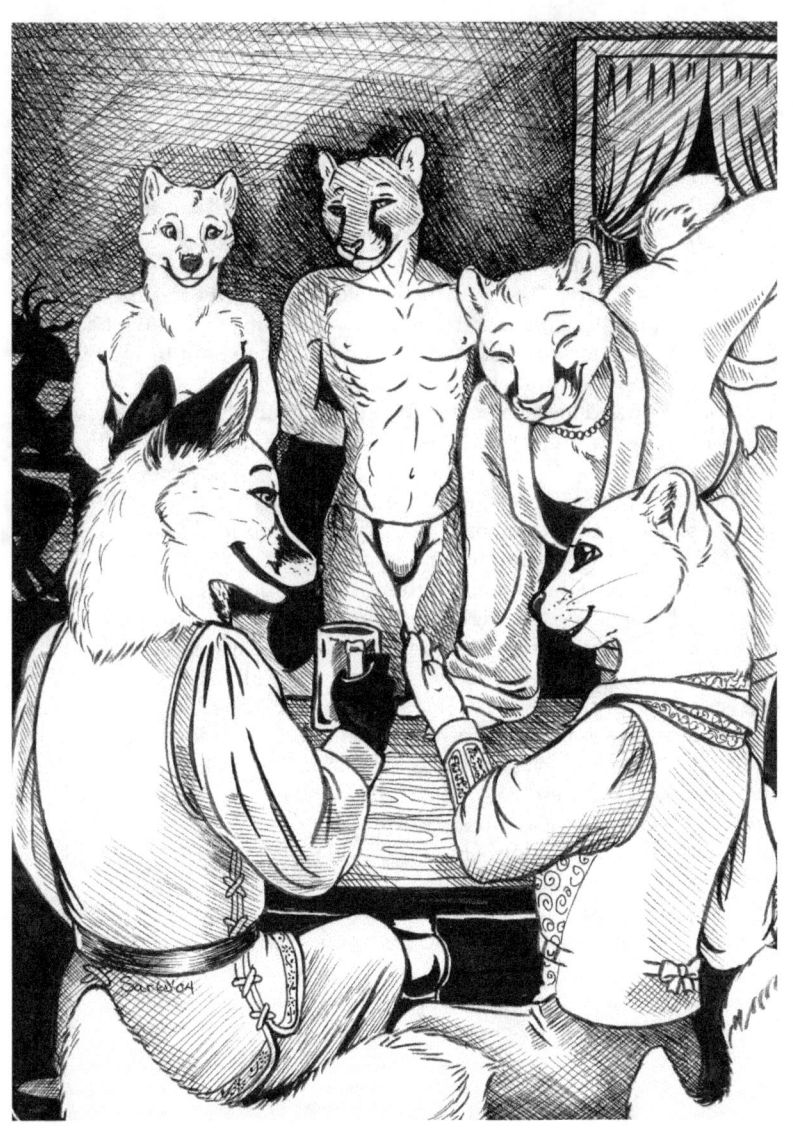

"Think of it as a welcome-to-Divalia gift."

The puma's fur was tawny on his well-muscled arms and legs, and his slender tail lashed behind him. His fur was trimmed shorter than the wolf's, so his muscles were more visible. There was a line of white fur on his right shoulder that Volle supposed was a scar, not dyed, and for a moment Volle was tempted to choose him just so he could ask about the scar.

Both wore enticing smiles and kept their ears perked forward. They gave him a chance to look them over, and then spoke.

"I'm Jonas," said the puma with a slight purr.

"And I'm Richy." The wolf turned slowly in front of the table, showing off his back and rump and letting his fluffy tail swing back and forth. The puma followed suit, and when they were both facing him again, Volle pointed at Richy.

Jonas nodded and walked back without losing his smile. Richy held out a paw to Volle. "Shall we go, sir? Or would you prefer to sit here?"

Volle's trousers were almost painfully tight. He shook his head and stood up, taking the wolf's paw. "Lead on." He noticed as they walked out that Helfer and his paramour had already left.

Richy led him through the rightmost door, down a wood-paneled corridor that bent left and right three times. He stopped in front of a door and opened it, letting Volle precede him into a small room.

The room was decorated sparsely, but tastefully. The main item, of course, was a large bed with white linen sheets. A small chest sat in one corner, and two chairs in the other. There was no window in the room, but Volle did notice a vent in the ceiling above the small table that held two candlesticks. There was red patterned wallpaper that extended from the floor to halfway up the wall.

Richy closed the door behind him and turned the lock. "Would you like the candles lit, sir?"

"No, I can see okay." Volle walked around to the other side of the bed and then back, examining the room. Richy walked straight to the bed and sat down, looking up at Volle as the fox approached him. When Volle didn't move to sit down on the bed, Richy smiled.

"What does his lordship wish to do tonight?"

Volle smiled. "Please, just call me Volle." His paw wandered up to his doublet, slowly unfastening one button.

"I can help with that, if you like, sir." When Volle nodded, Richy stood up and walked around behind him. His paws were quick, soft, and sure as they undid the fastenings and then tugged the doublet free. Volle unfastened his belt and lifted his tunic off, and set it on the table where he saw Richy had put the doublet. He turned to face the wolf, who smiled and reached for his trousers. Volle placed his paws on Richy's shoulders as the wolf's deft paws slid his trousers down his waist, easing them over his erection. The feel of the wolf's shoulders under his paws, the feel of the wolf's paws against his fur, and the slow uncovering that left him fully revealed all combined to give him a fur-tingling thrill. It never got old, that feeling. He was opening himself to the wolf and the wolf was accepting his paws. His fingers dug through new fur, and new eyes looked at his body for the first time and wanted him (even if the eyes were being paid to want him).

Richy placed Volle's trousers with his other clothes. Volle stretched in front of him, his erection throbbing so much it nearly hurt. Richy nodded approvingly and started to unfasten his loincloth, but Volle said. "Let me do that," and the wolf lifted his paws with a smile. Volle easily undid the knot and pulled the cloth away, slowly, drawing out the moment.

The wolf's sheath was plump, and though he wasn't as aroused as Volle was, he was showing a bit. Volle could see he was nicely proportioned, and his white fur was immaculate, from the tip of his sheath down to the bottom of his small sac. In fact, he was very sleekly groomed all over, and he smelled of wolf musk and pine, a pleasant combination.

"Why don't you sit down, sir?" He knew how to put a soft, caring tone in his voice. Whether it was real or not, Volle didn't know, but he felt as thought it was, so he let himself enjoy that feeling.

"Volle," he reminded Richy as he sat down on the bed. He leaned back, and felt himself relax. He hadn't realized until then how much the day's events had weighed on him. Had it really been just that morning that he'd woken up outside Divalia in a small pub that smelled of sheep and grass? And since then he'd been accepted into the palace, been taken advantage of by a fat squirrel, attended a sumptuous banquet and a delightful show, and made two friends.

"Volle?" Richy was kneeling in front of him, earnest green eyes looking up into his.

Volle smiled. "I'm sorry. It's been a very long day." He caressed the wolf's ears and let his paw slide down to the grey shoulder. The fur was smooth and warm.

"We needn't do anything if you'd rather just cuddle." Richy smiled. "Though it looks like you're up for more than that." His paw slid up gently between Volle's legs.

"Oh, yes," Volle breathed, closing his eyes. "I want to, very much."

"Would you prefer top or bottom?" Richy's soft paw had restored to Volle's member what little stiffness it might have lost during his reflection on his day, and it continued to brush gently up and down, making Volle shiver.

"Ohhhhh." Volle opened his eyes and looked at the wolf. "I think I'd like you to sit in my lap."

Richy's smile broadened. He leaned over and gave Volle's member a quick lick, and then rummaged in the small chest. He rubbed something under his tail, then came back over to Volle and curled the same paw around the fox's shaft. Volle felt the coolness of something slick and the warmth of the paw behind it, and gasped, shivering, as it slid up and down. Richy wiped his paw off on a small towel, which he tossed onto the chest, and then he climbed up onto the bed, straddling Volle on his knees. Slowly, he worked his feet around Volle's back until he was sitting on the fox's thighs, their sheaths pressed together.

Volle smiled up at him, and touched noses. He slipped his arms around the wolf's back and held the lithe body against his chest.

"Ready?" Richy said quietly, nuzzling Volle's ears. Volle nodded eagerly, his tail thumping the bed. Richy lifted his hips and pressed forward until his tail was just above Volle's shaft. Slowly, he lowered himself onto it, easing it into himself.

The warmth around his member, the furry body against him, and the musky desire in his muzzle brought a moan from Volle's muzzle. He licked at the wolf's chest as he slid further into him, panting. When he was buried deep under Richy's tail, he looked up again and rubbed his muzzle against Richy's.

"Okay?" The wolf had a playful smile on his muzzle.

"Wonderful," Volle replied, and brought his paw between them to rub his pads up the wolf's growing erection.

Richy breathed into his ear. "Don't worry too much about me, Volle. Just focus on you." He started to shift his hips expertly back and forth, sliding the fox's length in and out, stroking the sensitive skin with his muscles.

"Just…want to feel you…" Volle murmured, already panting hard. He closed his paw around the wolf's warm shaft.

"That's fine," Richy breathed, still moving. "Just don't worry about me. How are you doing?"

"Oh, that's so good," Volle whimpered softly, pressing his muzzle into the wolf's chest. His legs tightened against the bed and his tail wagged more vigorously. "Just like that…"

Richy's feet pressed against Volle's back as he lifted his hips, rubbing at the base of his tail. They relaxed as he let himself slide back down the fox's shaft, then pressed in again with the next stroke. Volle held the wolf's member in his paw, enjoying the warm stiff feel of it, but not stroking, and with his other arm he held the wolf against him. The coupling seemed to go on and on, and he thought for a moment that his excitement would keep growing without end. His blood was racing, his fur tingling, and his paws clenched and released with every warm stroke. He let the cares of the day drift away, forgot Ullik and Reese's joke and everything else, and lost himself in the warm rump of the wolf in his lap.

When his knot was swollen, Richy pressed himself down on it, and Volle clutched him tightly as his muscles seemed to want to contract all at once. He moaned into the wolf's fur and pushed off the bed slightly as his hips thrust up. He felt the tension through his whole body, and when his climax came, he felt the pulses of his release through his whole body as well. Richy's legs tightened around him as he gasped out his pleasure in stuttering moans.

It ended too soon. He sank back onto the bed, panting, and gave Richy's chest a lick before looking up at the wolf, who was smiling back down at him. "That felt good."

"It was," Volle said. He couldn't keep the smile off his muzzle even if he wanted to. "Oh, I needed that. You were wonderful."

Richy kissed his nose. "You were a delightful customer. If you want to lay back, you can."

"Mm. I think I do." Volle licked Richy's muzzle and then lay back, supporting his head with one paw. With the other, he teased Richy's erection, which had remained dry throughout. "You've got a very nice...shape there. I wouldn't mind having that in me someday."

Richy chuckled softly. "I'm here four days a week. I'd be delighted and honored if you asked for me again."

"I think I just might. You're a beautiful young wolf."

He felt Richy's tail wag against his legs. The wolf's paw stroked his chest. "And you are a very handsome fox."

He filed away the understanding that Richy was just saying what-ever it took to get a better tip and repeat business, and let himself enjoy the compliment. "Thank you," he murmured. His black paws traced Richy's curves through the white and grey fur, lazily enjoying the feel of the wolf around him as his knot slowly shrank. Richy's grey paws ca-ressed his chest and muzzle at the same time, and the warm hazy glow almost sent Volle to sleep. The caresses were beautiful and tender, and they made Volle want to bury his muzzle in the wolf's thick chest ruff and stay there all night.

Richy sliding off his knot sent a shiver through him and brought him back to full wakefulness. He grinned up at the wolf, who reached for the towel and cleaned Volle off before wiping off his own fur. When he'd done, he dropped the towel back on the chest and lay down on the bed next to Volle. One grey paw stroked Volle's stomach fur gently.

"How long do I have?" Volle said, smiling at the green eyes that were so close.

"As long as you want." Richy nuzzled him.

Volle lifted a paw to return the strokes, and sighed. "Probably not too much longer. I'm supposed to meet my friend downstairs."

"All right." Richy smiled and touched his nose to Volle's again.

Volle pushed his paw through the soft white fur, yawned, and closed his eyes. "A few more minutes..."

It was actually close to twenty minutes later that he padded back out into the main room. Business had picked up with the later hour, but Helfer was nowhere to be seen. The raccoon band was gone, and the only noise in the room was the buzzing of conversation. Volle made his way to one of the three empty tables and sat down, stifling another yawn.

Tally spotted him a few minutes later and walked over. "Volle, darling, how was everything?"

He smiled. "Wonderful. Oh." He fished in his purse and found two silver pieces. He handed them to the cougar. "Please tell Richy I had a delightful time."

Tally beamed. "He's an adorable little thing, isn't he?" He leaned over and lowered his voice. "You know, for a slightly higher price, we can arrange for him—or anyone else here—to be available to you on a regular schedule."

Volle laughed softly. "It's only my first day here. I don't know if I'm ready to be scheduling my paramours yet. But thank you for the information."

"Oh, no need to make a decision now, darling. I'm just telling you. Our staff likes repeat customers, too. That way they know what they're getting."

"As long as it's something good."

Tally giggled and waved a paw. "Oh, you're a good one. I can tell just looking at you. You keep yourself neat and you have a nice scent. I'm sure Richy had a good time too."

"Hope so." Volle smiled.

"Oh, he did. Don't worry your red little head about that." Tally patted between his ears. "I have to run off, dear, but do have a drink on the house. We have a barrel of wine and a barrel of water back there. Help yourself." And then Tally was off to talk to another customer.

The raccoon combo had returned, and Volle had finished a cup of rather watery wine, by the time Helfer returned. He wore a wide smile and there was a little bounce in his step as Volle joined him at the door. They waved to Tally and walked out into the street.

Helfer looked Volle up and down, and grinned. "So you had a good time."

"Oh, yeah." Volle smiled. He was tired and wanted nothing more than to crawl into bed, but his tail apparently had plenty of energy. It seemed to be wagging of its own volition. "How often do you go there?"

"About once a week. Want me to bring you along next time? I'm not paying again, I'll warn you."

Volle laughed. "That's okay. I'll pay my own way. Just as soon as I get my money situation straightened out."

"What situation?"

He told Helfer the story of his meeting with the Exchequer. For a moment, he considered telling him the whole story, but the thought of reliving the experience made his fur prickle. Besides, what if Helfer thought badly of him for giving in so easily? Already he was feeling ashamed, but he'd been so unsure about his position at the palace that he hadn't felt he had another choice.

"I can't believe he would've let Vinton slide for twenty years without taxes. Not Ullik. He probably just wanted to scare you."

"I sure hope so." Volle sighed and looked around as they turned onto the main street to head back to the palace gate. It was, if anything, a little more crowded, mostly with nocturnal species like foxes, raccoons, and weasels.

"Stay alert," Helfer warned in a low voice. "This time of night there are cutpurses about."

Volle let a paw rest on his purse. "Thanks."

"That's another pub I visit sometimes." Helfer had turned around and was pointing further down the street, beyond where they'd turned. Volle could just make out a sign painted with a picture of a rooster. "The Lonely Cock."

He was grinning, so Volle was sure the innuendo was intentional. "Is it the same kind of place?"

"No, it's a real pub, but you can be sure when you approach someone that they're at least interested in your gender."

"I don't have much trouble with that."

"Really? I'm never sure. Is it something you can smell?"

"I guess so. I'd never really thought about it." Volle touched his muzzle. "It's just sort of a feeling."

Helfer shook his head. "Now I have another reason to envy you canids your long muzzles."

Volle laughed. "Aww. But hey, don't tell me your flexible back doesn't come in handy. I've seen some weasel contortionists."

"If you don't practice, though, you get kind of stiff. Actually, that happens even when you do practice."

They both laughed as they approached the palace gate. The sentry on duty took Helfer's papers and accepted his vouching for Volle. They strolled into an even more deserted garden.

"I would've thought there'd be just as much activity inside the palace as out," Volle mused.

"It's the bears," Helfer said. "They like using daylight, so everybody else has to be up and about in daylight too. Nocturnals are out of luck."

"What do you do with the government?"

"As little as possible." He chuckled. "Really. Getting involved in politics and government just leads to trouble. Get people mad at you and you put all this in jeopardy." He waved a paw at the palace. "I'm afraid I like my life a bit too much for that. So I lay low and try to remain unimportant."

"How long have you been here?"

"Lived in the palace for ten years. Only been Lord Ikling for two."

"Oh." Volle was going to ask what had happened to make him Lord, but Helfer cut him off.

"Say, I usually go for a nice run through the gardens in the morning. Want to join me?"

"Sure. When?"

"I'll send Caresh—that's my valet—down to your chambers when I'm ready. Where are you staying?"

"First floor, south, next to Lady Gervis."

"Oh, I know the place. Caresh could find you anyway, but I might as well make it easier on him. It's a date, then." He eyed Volle's trousers. "Do you have shorts? Loose ones?"

"You mean like skirts? I don't, no."

"I'll send down a pair. Hm. Maybe we should visit my tailor, too."

"I was going to see the palace tailor…"

"Wexlin? Good Weasel, no. He's always two years behind the times and he refuses to catch up. Didn't you wonder why everyone at the banquet looked so hideous?"

"No, I was more worried that people were staring at me."

"Well, good point. They probably were."

Volle snorted and felt his ears flick self-consciously. "Thanks."

"Glad to help. Oh, don't worry about it. Wouldn't you rather be noticed?" They'd reached the palace and Volle turned to go to his room. Helfer was preparing to go another way.

"I'd rather be noticed for something good." Volle extended a paw. "Thanks so much for the night out. I really needed it."

"My pleasure," Helfer said. "Nice to meet someone my age who shares my tastes." He shook Volle's paw and smiled brightly. "See you in the afternoon."

"Morning, you mean?"

The weasel grinned and waved as he turned around. "I wouldn't bet on it." He scurried up the stairs and down a corridor.

Volle was still grinning as he found his way to his chambers. Not only was life going to be considerably more pleasant than he'd hoped, but he'd made a friend who had nothing to do with the government, a friend he would not have to get information out of, a friend he could relax with and just be Volle. He determined that he would not miss running with Helfer in the morning. Something would have to replace his exercise regimen from the Academy, and it might as well be running.

He managed to get his shirt and trousers off, and fell into bed dreaming he could feel the young wolf pressed up against him.

Chapter 5

He woke early in the morning out of habit, even though his body told him he needed another couple hours of sleep at least. Apparently late risers were the norm in the palace, because the corridor and baths were empty, save for the bath attendant. Perfect, he thought, and headed for the warm water baths.

When Volle returned to his chambers, drying himself with a fluffy towel, there was a short skunk standing smartly at attention outside his door. He wore a white linen tunic with a blue vest over it, and blue cotton trousers, and at his side he carried a large satchel.

Volle held the towel in front of himself. "May I help you?"

"Lord Vinton?"

"Yes."

The skunk bowed. "My name is Welcis, sir. I am to be your personal servant."

"Oh. Well, come in, then." Volle opened the door to the parlor, and the skunk followed him in.

"I am led to understand, sir, that these chambers do not have separate quarters for a personal servant."

Volle looked around the parlor, and then thought about the sitting room and the bedroom. "No, I suppose not. Would you be willing to sleep in the sitting room?"

The skunk bowed. "I was going to suggest that I could use the servants' quarters down the hall, but if Lord Vinton wishes me to remain close by, I would be honored to take those accommodations. I can assure his lordship that his sitting room will remain functional."

"Thank you, Welcis." Volle stood awkwardly for a moment.

The skunk reached into the satchel and pulled out a brush with a leather strap across the back of it. He slipped his broad paw through the strap. "Would his lordship like his fur brushed?"

"I...thank you." Volle led Welcis into the bedroom. "I'm afraid we're rather short on furniture…"

The skunk smiled. "If his lordship would sit on the edge of the bed?"

Volle did so, and the skunk sat behind him, brushing down his fur in smooth, firm strokes. Volle closed his eyes in pleasure. He and Reese had once treated themselves to a full wash and brush at a salon frequented by nobles, and had never forgotten how good it felt. I can have this every day if I want, he thought with a grin. Wait 'til I tell Reese.

His damp fur did not dominate the skunk's smell. Volle had known only one skunk, growing up in Caril, and so he took a moment to acquaint himself with Welcis's natural scent. It was strong, but not objectionable; rather like a fox's smell, but slightly more sulphuric. Volle found it harder to read Welcis's mood than he would with a less musky person, but other than that the smell didn't bother him.

"Stand up please, sir?"

Volle stood, and let the towel fall to the floor. He didn't feel aroused, just relaxed, and his tail waved slowly back and forth to show this, until Welcis took it gently in his paws and brushed it smooth.

"Oh," Volle said as the skunk was brushing down his legs, having delicately avoided his sheath. "I'm supposed to go running with Helfer—Lord Ikling—today. I'd hate to think this was all for nothing."

Welcis smiled. "Sir, you have an appointment with the Secretary in an hour. Lord Ikling will be along after that. The rest of the day is free, for the moment, but if his lordship desires another bath after running, I am at his disposal."

"All right." Volle smiled. His stomach growled at the same time, making Welcis's ears perk. "I haven't had any breakfast. I'm not sure where to go."

"It is the custom for breakfast to be delivered by the personal servants. I do apologize for not bringing it this morning, but I was not sure whether—his lordship had eaten." The pause in his sentence was minute, but Volle heard it.

"Please don't apologize. I'm not used to having a servant, so I think I'll have to rely on you to teach me about that."

"I will be happy to help his lordship enjoy the full benefits of his station. Luncheon is served informally in the smaller dining rooms. The Lords often gather there to take lunch, though some take it in their rooms as well."

"I'll probably lunch after my run with Helfer. Did you say something about the Secretary?"

"Yes, sir. When the Steward's assistant sent me down, he told me that he'd made an appointment with the Secretary for you."

"Was that Arrin?"

"Yes, sir."

Volle thought about the cute young fox for a moment. Now that he knew that Reese's warning about the customs had been wrong (intentional or not), he thought he might try to follow up on what he'd thought was Arrin's interest. If the fox were still interested, that is, after his apparent brush-off. He emerged from those thoughts with the realization that he was still naked and starting to show where his mind was wandering. He went instinctively to the wardrobe, but of course he hadn't put his clothes away yet and it was empty.

"Allow me, sir." Welcis walked smoothly out and returned a moment later with Volle's bags. He opened them and lifted out a pair of informal cotton trousers. "I think these would be suitable for an appointment with the Secretary, sir."

"Thank you, Welcis." Volle slipped the trousers on, then put on the tunic Welcis handed to him.

"With your lordship's permission, I will arrange a visit from the palace tailor." Welcis was arranging Volle's clothes in the wardrobe, a job that took him all of five minutes. Volle hadn't brought many outfits.

"I believe Lord Ikling is going to take me to a tailor outside the palace," Volle said. "And besides, until I resolve my money situation, I'm not sure I should be buying clothes."

"As his lordship wishes," Welcis said, "though if I may offer an opinion, I should say that the money will be taken care of, and his lordship should not wait to present an appearance in accordance with his station. I only offer this because I understand that his lordship may not be acclimated to his current situation."

"Why do you think the money will be taken care of?"

"Arrin informed me that his lordship visited the Exchequer. Since my own expenses are being paid, and his lordship was allowed to remain in the castle, I can only assume that his lordship's credit is good."

"But I can't pay a tailor in credit." And to get credit he would have to visit Ullik again. He was hoping to put that off as long as possible. At least until he got an answer from Anton, and that would probably take over a week.

"The palace tailor will be paid directly by the palace from your lordship's account."

"Oh. I see. Well, then, by all means, arrange a visit. I suppose Lord Ikling's tailor can wait."

"Yes, sir. Would his lordship like a breakfast before his appointment?"

Volle nodded. "Yes, that would be wonderful." He had only just stopped himself from saying 'yes, please.'

He ate breakfast in the parlor when Welcis brought it back; it was an egg-and-tomato dish that he found very tasty. Welcis informed him when he had to leave for his appointment with the Secretary and how to get there.

On his way up the Goat stair, he reflected that having a personal servant was probably the only way he would be able to manage life at the palace. He'd only been there a day and already someone had scheduled him for an appointment he hadn't requested, not to mention the several he had. He felt rather like it was his first day at the Academy again, when he'd shown up not knowing where he would be going or what he'd be doing, and by the end of the first day his week was planned out; by the end of the week his first year had been planned out.

The Secretary's office was more luxurious than the Steward's or the Exchequer's, and he had two assistants, both bears. They waved Volle in as soon as he arrived, so he had very little time to look around at the velvet wall coverings and the many paintings. These, in contrast to most of the others he'd seen, were not of people but of events: great battles and coronations and voyages.

In the Secretary's office, the theme continued. The only exception was the portrait of the King that hung behind the large desk. The Secretary was also a bear, larger than his two assistants both in height and girth. His fur was more honey-golden than brown, and his eyes, when he looked up at Volle, were also golden. He wore an elegant yellow vest over a linen shirt, and he had a warm smile.

"Welcome, Lord Vinton. Have a seat." Volle smiled and sat down. "Welcome to Divalia. This is where the country's future is shaped, her destiny molded, and as a peer of the realm, you have the honor of being a part of that. I understand you arrived here from southern Ferrenis. How was the trip?"

"It was pleasant," Volle said. "I enjoyed seeing so much of Tephos. It's a beautiful country."

"Ah, you've only seen part of it." The Secretary beamed. "You will have seen the plains of Sophasol, but not the mountains of Gerrenland to the north, nor the orchards of Vellenland to the east. The mountains are my favorite, though."

"The ones we can see from the walls?"

"Yes! I miss them. I try to get away at least twice a year, but you know, it's so difficult. The minute I leave, there's a page running after me with a message." He chuckled. "My name is Prewitt. Please call me that. I hate being called 'Mister Secretary.'"

"I'm Volle."

"A pleasure to meet you. So how did you come to learn of your ancestry?" The tone remained affable, but Volle was conscious of the scrutiny of those golden eyes.

"My mother died last year. She said she had hidden it from me, but that it was no longer her secret to hide."

"So she and the former Lord Vinton met in…"

"Merinland. There was some fighting there."

"I remember." He scratched his chin thoughtfully. "I thought Lord Vinton was killed elsewhere, though."

Volle spread his paws. "The people in Vinton didn't know. He just never came back. The Steward said he was killed in the fighting, but didn't say whether it was in Merinland or elsewhere."

The golden eyes searched him for a moment, then looked back down at the desk. "Indeed. Well, I didn't know him personally, but I understand he was not a resident at the palace. Preferred to keep to his part of the world." He looked back up. "I'm glad to see you don't follow in his paws. This country needs more young lords involved in her governance."

"I'm pleased and honored to help in any way I can. How involved can I be?"

"You know that the king is the absolute authority, right? Well, he assembles small councils, five to seven nobles, to be his advisors on certain important subjects. The ministers each chair the councils and take the recommendations to the king." Volle nodded. "Now, obviously you won't be placed on any of the councils for a while, but I'm sure we can find something for you to do. You can sit on one of the tribunals if you like."

"Tribunals?"

"The King hears cases once a week. Usually those are cases brought forward by the wealthy or the peerage. Any other cases are heard by tribunals made up of five nobles. We have three of them and they each meet once a week. I could place you on the Feliday one. I believe Lord Creane mentioned that he would like to be replaced. You'll meet for two weeks as an observer and then take his place."

He was already scratching on his paper with a quill, but Volle said, "All right" anyway.

"Excellent. See how you like that. In a while, when you've gotten more accustomed to life here, you can sit in on some of the councils—the Agricultural or the Taxation council, perhaps—and eventually you'll be given a seat on them."

"How will I know when I'm accustomed enough?" Volle grinned slightly.

"You'll know." Prewitt smiled. "If you want an audience with the king for any reason, of course, Ursiday is the day he holds court. It isn't formal, but do have your valet add you to the list."

Volle nodded. "Is there anything else I should know?"

Prewitt leaned back. The chair creaked under his weight. "Banquets like last night's will be announced at the dinners. If you don't take dinners here, the Steward has a list. That's for palace-wide events. Some are smaller and for those, invitations will be issued. If you have any questions about the workings of the palace or your responsibilities here, just come see me. And I think that's all I have to tell you."

He rose, and Volle stood with him. The bear's enormous paw enfolded Volle's gently, shook briefly, and then released it. "Pleasure to meet you. I look forward to seeing you about the palace."

"Thanks for your help." Volle smiled, and left, spending no more time in the anteroom than he had on the way in.

Once in the corridor, though, he paused. He'd walked through the palace several times now, and had begun to think he could find his way around. As a test, he decided he would look for the Steward's office and Arrin, though he had no idea yet what he would say to him. He was near the Goat stair now, he knew, and he'd passed the Weasel stair on the way over, so if he were correct, then the Lion stair would be to his right. He decided to try navigating the corridors without returning to the main hall, trusting to his sense of direction.

The corridors didn't run straight, but bent and divided. He tried to follow his sense of direction, but all the doors looked and smelled the same, and he ended up back at the Goat stair. He had passed some nobles and servants in the corridors, but didn't want to ask directions just yet. He could always go down to the main hall if he got lost.

On his second try, he found the Rat stair. Sculptures of rats stood against both posts, and a rat design was woven into the fabric that covered the stairs. He noted that none of the other stairs had had carpeting, but also remembered that he hadn't seen the Bear stair yet. Most likely the king was in that area, and he was sure there would be carpeting for the heavier bears' paws.

Moving on past the Rat stair, he was gratified to find that, as he'd expected, the Lion stair was the next one. He was on the right floor, and he thought he remembered which door was the Steward's. Approaching it, he found it slightly ajar, and caught the scent of a fox from inside. Tail wagging at his achievement, he pushed the door open.

Arrin was sitting at his desk talking to the Steward, who was pointing to some things on a paper. They both looked up as Volle entered, and Arrin flashed a surprised smile.

"Ah, good morning, Lord Vinton," the Steward said. "If you'll give me just a moment, I can see you."

"Oh, I don't need to take up your time," Volle said. "I can just talk to Arrin."

"It's no trouble, I assure you."

Volle paused, awkwardly. "Actually, I was rather hoping to talk to Arrin."

Arrin's ears flicked, and he tried to hide his wide smile. The Steward merely looked puzzled. "Well, you can speak to him when I've finished, then."

"Thank you." Volle sat down. He had realized when pressed by the Steward that he hadn't actually thought of anything to say to Arrin when he did talk to him, so he focused on that while the Steward was talking. He did notice that Arrin kept glancing at him, but the Steward seemed oblivious.

"All right, Lord Vinton, I'm finished." The Steward was scurrying towards the corridor.

"Thank you," Volle called, standing, but the Steward was gone before he got the second word out.

"He's very busy," Arrin said apologetically. "We really could use another assistant."

"Maybe I can find someone," Volle said without thinking, then hurriedly added, "when I've gotten to know a few more people here."

Arrin smiled. "It's just hard to find someone reliable that the Steward trusts. Half the time he's so busy because he's checking up on tasks he's assigned to other people. I tell him he should just trust them, but…" He spread his paws. "So what can I do for you, Lord Vinton?"

Volle smiled. "Well, as I was saying, I don't really know anyone yet. And you were very friendly yesterday, so I wondered if you would like to join me for dinner, perhaps tomorrow night."

"Really?" Arrin smiled. "I would be delighted and honored, Lord Vinton. Tomorrow night would be fine. At eight?"

"That sounds perfect." Volle smiled. "I do appreciate it."

Arrin's ears flicked back in embarrassment and he smiled. "I hope I will be pleasant enough company."

"I'm sure you will. Now, if you'll excuse me, I have an engagement for lunch."

"Of course, Lord Vinton."

As he stepped back from the desk, Volle noticed that Arrin's tail was wagging. He chuckled. "I'll see you tomorrow night, then." He felt his own tail wagging slightly as he stepped back into the corridor.

It was an easy matter to find his rooms now. He found Welcis talking to Renaldo in his parlor when he returned. There were some items of new furniture, including a dinner table that could seat four, and four chairs. The whole set was made of a dark wood and was beautifully carved, but it was weathered and chipped in several places. Next to it was a small cot and a neat little valise.

"Ah, my lord." Welcis indicated the table and chairs. "Your furnishings. I presume you will want them in the sitting room?"

"There doesn't seem to be enough room in the parlor. Yes, the sitting room will be fine."

"Are these suitable?" Welcis looked anxious. "They are not in the best condition."

Renaldo put a paw on the table. "They have been used, certainly, but they are very finely crafted. I assure his lordship there are none better available now."

"They'll be fine, Welcis. Thank you for asking. As a matter of fact, I will be entertaining tomorrow night. Could you procure a cloth and perhaps some candles?"

"Certainly, sir. The only matter remaining is of my own arrangements."

"Is that your cot?"

"Yes, sir."

"That and the valise are all you have?"

"Yes, sir."

Volle considered. "Renaldo, is there a sort of screen we could use to set off part of the sitting room, so the cot could go behind it?"

The marten nodded. "I believe we could find something, my lord."

"And if there's any other furniture that Welcis would like—a small table, perhaps, and a chair—then bring it along as well."

"Yes, my lord."

"Thank you, sir," Welcis said. "I believe a small desk and chair would be pleasant, if they're available."

"I'm certain we can find something." Renaldo made a small note on his scroll. "We will have it here later today or tomorrow. Certainly before his lordship's dinner."

"Thank you, Renaldo."

The marten bowed. "Pleasure to be of service, sir." He turned to Welcis. "Let's move all this into the sitting room." They moved the table together, then moved the chairs and the cot while Volle watched, seated in one of the upholstered chairs. He couldn't help grinning. To go from the Academy, where he had to do nearly everything himself, and come to this place, where people argued about the best way to wait on him, was positively intoxicating.

When Renaldo had left, Welcis came to stand in front of him and to one side. "My Lord, Lord Tistunish called while you were out. He will call again this afternoon. I apprised him of your schedule and he said he would find you here after your run."

"Thank you, Welcis." He wondered if it were too late to get out of Lord Tistunish's plan to set him up with a mate, and how he would present that request to the old wolf. While he was putting together a reasonable-sounding request, there was a knock at the door.

Welcis sprang to answer it, and admitted a tall fox holding a small cloth bundle. He and Welcis greeted each other familiarly, and then he walked over to Volle.

"Lord Vinton. My name is Caresh, and I have the honor to be the personal servant to Lord Ikling. He requested that I deliver these to you, and inform you that he will be awaiting your company down at the front entrance."

Volle took the bundle, which proved to be a green skirt with a crest sewn into the side. The crest showed a weasel head over two crossed stalks, one that Volle thought might be wheat, and one that was a branch of grapes.

"Thank you, Caresh," he said, and the fox bowed to him, turned smartly on his heel, and walked back out, tail waving.

The palace was busier than it had been when he'd taken his bath. Dressed only in the shorts, he felt a little exposed walking through the main hall, but none of the people he passed gave him a second glance. He found his way to the garden and Helfer was there waiting for him, clad in a similar pair of shorts. He waved a paw. "Sleep okay?"

"Just fine. Been up for hours." Volle grinned, jogging in place.

"All right, all right." Helfer waved him down the path. "I'll show you the route I usually take. Twice around the palace. There's one point when we have to stop and climb over a wall, but otherwise it's smooth."

"Lead on." Volle matched Helfer's pace as he ran through the garden. They ran steadily, not sprinting, so Volle had a chance to admire the sights and smells of the different gardens as they passed through them. There were three large gardens, of which the front gardens were the most elaborate. Wild profusions of color were artfully arranged to create a brilliant harmony, and although the smells were a bit strong and sweet, they were harmonious as well. The trellises Volle had seen upon entering stood in the middle of the gardens, but smaller ones decorated the borders. As he ran past one, Volle noticed that the wood was elaborately carved, and that there were small benches hidden below the tangle of vines.

The other gardens were tamer, but Volle found them just as beautiful. They featured the same winding paths, but the bushes were sculpted into near-geometric shapes and were simply green, rather than being allowed to grow and blossom. The scents were subtler, because the flowers were placed more sparingly, at the centers of the green areas between the paths. Every so often, a statue or fountain appeared around a bend in the path.

It only took them about fifteen minutes to make a complete circuit of the palace. Although the gardens didn't completely circle the palace, the front garden was connected to the first rear garden by a large tunnel obviously intended to drive carriages through. The stables were somewhere behind the first rear garden, and a six-foot-high wall separated the two rear gardens. The second rear garden connected back to the front garden through a smaller sunken passageway that smelled of garbage and was obviously used by the kitchens to dispose of their waste.

Stopping to climb the wall between the two rear gardens was a nice break. Volle used the time to relax and think about life at the palace so far. Helfer would not be much use in discovering information around the palace, but Volle didn't care. He liked the little weasel, who seemed to have boundless reserves of energy and humor, and he refused to immerse himself in serious work without some kind of outlet. He'd had a hard enough time getting time away from his studies at the Academy, and he was determined to relax more now that he had the chance. This was a long-term position, and he had to behave naturally, he reasoned.

Besides, he was enjoying himself. Even the run, which he'd dreaded at the Academy, was pleasant, what with the flowers and the soft dirt path and the half-naked weasel trotting at his side. The pace was slower than he was used to, the run was more leisurely, and the breeze was cooler. It seemed impossible that any plot against Ferrenis could be brewing here, on such a bright and beautiful day.

All in all, he thought as they came to a stop, this was nowhere near as bad as he'd been thinking it might be. He'd envisioned himself locked in a dreary castle, sneaking around corridors, risking his life to get information back to his country. The reality was much simpler, much quieter, and much more easy to get around. The only thing he didn't know yet was how he would remain in touch with Seir and the others, and he was confident Seir would figure that out.

He was hardly panting, and Helfer didn't look too winded either. He grinned at Volle. "Country stamina, eh? Most of the lords in this place couldn't keep up with me after one go-round. You're in good shape. Best to stay that way. Life here favors the fat, if you hadn't noticed from the banquet."

"I didn't think it was that bad."

"Not even after the banquet? The mass waddle down to the theater?"

Volle laughed. "I guess I didn't notice."

Helfer snorted. "Oh, come on. You can tell me. Don't worry about sugarcoating—" They had entered the palace and turned towards Volle's quarters, which were closest. As they turned a corner, Helfer abruptly stopped talking and patted Volle on the shoulder. "Well, I'm going to run up for a bath. I'll see you tomorrow?"

"Sure," Volle said to the weasel's retreating back and tail. He paused, puzzled, and looked down the corridor. A badger, a raccoon, and a rat were walking towards him, the rat at a quick pace, but none of them seemed frightening. The rat was looking right at him, though, and moving purposefully. Volle walked to the baths and waited there for the rat.

He was slightly shorter than Volle, wearing a black vest and black trousers with a silver belt. He wore nothing under the vest, leaving his skinny chest exposed. The fur there was a grayish-white, decently groomed, and the rest of him was brown. His beady eyes scanned Volle up and down, and Volle didn't need to smell him to sense his interest.

The rat was holding his paws together in front of him. "Lord Vinton?" he asked finally.

"Yes."

"My name is Dereath Talison. I'm the assistant to Lord Fardew. He's the Minister of Defense." He spoke quickly, as though he were afraid Volle would run away.

"Yes?"

"Lord Fardew asked me to interview you and I was wondering if this would be a convenient time." The words were rushed out in the span of time it took him to drop his head, looking from Volle's muzzle down at his groin. It could have been a deferential bowing, but Volle didn't think so.

"I've just been running..."

"I know. I waited until you got back."

"...so I would like to bathe. Then I will be at your disposal." He continued as if the rat hadn't interrupted him.

"Oh, very well. So I'll just wait here for your lordship." He made a more courteous bow then, actually bending at the waist.

"All right." Volle sighed. "I'll be right out."

While he rolled in the scented powder, he wondered what the defense minister could want with him. Probably the same thing everyone else did: to know what his leanings were and where he stood. Even if he hadn't had time to figure it out yet. He took an extra long time rubbing the powder into his fur, half hoping the rat would be gone when he emerged, but Dereath was waiting right there, standing in the corridor with his tail fairly quivering in anticipation.

Volle supposed the scent from the powder bath was strong enough to let Dereath know when he was coming. Still, the rat was making him nervous, and seeing him go straight to Volle's door and open it for him didn't help. He tightened the towel around his waist and walked inside. Welcis took the skirt from his paw silently. He glanced at Dereath, who was closing the door, and then inquiringly at Volle.

"Dereath is here from Lord Fardew. He just wished to ask me a few questions after I get dressed. He'll wait here." Volle indicated a chair, and Dereath slid into it.

Welcis nodded. "Very good, sir." He followed Volle into the bedroom.

Ten minutes later, brushed and dressed, Volle walked back into the parlor and sat across from the rat. "So, Dereath, what can I do for you?"

"Listen," the rat said, "if Lord Ikling has been talking about me, really, I apologized for that and he still holds a grudge. I just want—I don't want you to think anything of me until I have a chance to make an impression." He looked anxiously at Volle.

Volle relaxed a little, but not much. The truth was that the rat had already made an impression on him, and not a good one. He was willing to give him the benefit of the doubt, though he also wanted to hear what Helfer had to say about Dereath. "All right." He smiled. "Go ahead."

Dereath smiled back, and nodded. "We had heard that your lordship grew up in Ferrenis, so of course we wanted to find out what you could tell us about them. Any information will be useful."

Volle shook his head. They'd expected this kind of questioning and had given him a list of things he could tell the Tephossians. He recited the list as though he were recalling old memories. "Well, I don't know what I can tell you. We paid our taxes to the king regularly every year, and never had much doings with the capital. Once a noble came through town, but I had to work in the fields and I didn't see him. I know that they're pretty quick to take your farm when you fall behind on your taxes." He tried to put real anger in his voice.

"You speak very well, for a farmer." Dereath meant it as a compliment, no doubt, but Volle took it initially as an accusation.

"My mother insisted on it," he said quickly. "Wouldn't have me talking like the badgers—family of badgers lived down the road." This was actually true. He'd been friends with the badger cub nearest his age, but his mother had said they weren't the 'right sort' and had ended that friendship. "I guess it was because she wanted me to be worthy of my father, but I didn't know that then."

"Very noble." Dereath smiled. "So you have no love for the Ferrenians."

Volle shook his head. "I've been treated better in one day here than in twenty years in that country." He smiled, and stretched his shoulders briefly; they were still stiff from the run.

"Oh, let me help with that," Dereath said, although the motion had been very slight. Before Volle could say anything, the rat had scampered around behind him and pressed his paws down on the fox's shoulders.

He had strong paws, and the rubbing was not entirely pleasant. Volle was more aware of his scent, which was arousal mingled with earnestness and the strong smell of rat. He couldn't help squirming a bit under the paws.

"No, it's okay," Dereath said, misinterpreting his movements. "I can still ask questions from here. So you would have no compunction about going to war with Ferrenis?"

"War?" Volle twisted around to try to look at him, forcing him to stop rubbing.

"It's just a hypothetical. I mean in the worst case." Dereath patted his shoulders, but Volle stayed facing him.

"If it were warranted, I guess I would have no trouble," he said slowly.

"Oh, of course, if it were warranted. Just relax." Dereath tried to force him to face forward, and after a moment he complied, gritting his teeth through the rubbing. "Where did you come into Tephos?" he said conversationally.

Volle almost gave it away right there. His mind was on the paws on his shoulders, not on his cover story, and he almost blurted out the name of the inn. He caught himself with a quick cough, and then said, "I'm not sure. I was just trekking across the mountains and I fell in with a merchant on his way to Vinton, so I hopped a ride."

"I see." Dereath fell silent. Volle hoped desperately that the interview was over, but the rat was just preparing to speak again. "If…if you're not busy, Lord Vinton, I would be honored if you would join me for dinner in my humble quarters."

Oh, no. "Tonight?"

Welcis, who had returned quietly a few minutes before, coughed. "I believe Lord Vinton has a dinner engagement tonight."

"No, he doesn't." Dereath's tone had taken on a sharp edge.

"Sir, Lord Ikling issued an invitation to dinner. I accepted on your behalf."

"I didn't see anyone come in."

"I brought the skirt up to return it to him. He issued the invitation at that time."

Dereath was silent. "Maybe later in the week, then."

"Maybe," Volle said agreeably, resolving to fill his dinner schedule as quickly as possible.

The rat lifted his paws from Volle's shoulders and dropped them to his sides. "I suppose there's nothing more I need to ask you." He walked slowly toward the door, then turned back to Volle. His expression was worried again. "You will remember what I said? About Lord Ikling? Tell him I'm sorry, would you?"

Volle nodded. "I will." He watched the rat leave, and then sank into his chair with a sigh of relief.

Welcis coughed. "I fear, sir, that I must confess to a minor infraction of protocol."

"Oh? What would that be, Welcis?"

"I may have inadvertently invited your lordship to dinner with Lord Ikling before Lord Ikling was aware of it."

Volle grinned widely. "You lied to get me out of dinner with the rat?"

"I sensed that his lordship was not enthusiastic about the prospect of dining with the gentlerat in question."

"No, I wasn't. Though I suppose I should. I need to make friends around the palace." He sighed. "Do you think it would be a breach of protocol to arrange a dinner with him and some other people? I just don't want to be alone with him."

"Is your lordship suggesting a dinner party?"

"I don't think I want anything as large as a party."

"By 'party,' sir, I merely meant a gathering of people. Four is an acceptable number."

Volle chuckled. "I'm not sure I know four people. I can't invite Helfer, not if he has some problem with the rat."

"If your lordship wishes, I would be happy to select two more people who would be of appropriate station."

"Welcis, that would be wonderful. Thank you." He paused and flicked his ears. "What is the appropriate station?"

The skunk smiled in recognition of the thanks, but the smile only lasted a moment. "Since your lordship is a noble, and Mister Talison is not, that does present some difficulty. However, Mister Talison is a part of one of the ministries, which elevates his standing somewhat. I believe another ministry functionary and another noble of your lordship's seniority would round out the dinner nicely."

"Thank you again, Welcis. I will leave it in your paws."

"Thank you, sir."

Volle had a thought. "One more thing, Welcis."

"Sir?"

"Minister Ullik is not welcome, nor do I wish to accept any invitations from him. Just for the record."

"Very good, sir."

Welcis left to investigate arrangements for the dinner, and presumably to inform Helfer that he'd invited Volle to dinner. Volle scarcely had time to realize that he hadn't eaten lunch before Lord Tistunish had knocked on his door and let himself in.

"Afternoon, Volle!" Volle had stood when the wolf walked in, and now received a forceful pat on the back as Tistunish grasped his paw.

The wolf looked around. "So they put you here, did they? Isn't that interesting. At least, I think…it's been so long."

"What?"

"I'll see if I'm right and then tell you later. Hope you had a good evening after the show. I know I did." He winked broadly.

"I had a fine evening, yes." Volle waved the wolf to a seat, a little puzzled but willing to let it go. "I met Lord Ikling and he took me out for a…drink."

"Hmm." The wolf's brow furrowed. "Ikling. He's harmless enough, but a bit frivolous. Not exactly the best companion."

Volle suppressed a twinge of irritation. "He seems nice enough, and we hit it off rather well."

"Well, that's fine, that's fine. Just don't model your behavior on his. His father was well-respected, you know. Served as the Minister of Agriculture for years. Young Ikling never picked up on that sense of duty."

"How did his father die?" Volle asked quietly.

There was a lengthy pause. "Bandits. He was returning home to Vellenland when the carriage was attacked by brigands. He tried to fight them and they killed him."

"Oh. Poor Helfer."

Tistunish grunted. "It's a dangerous world. But let's not dwell on that. I came by to invite you to dinner in a week's time. Tika has a vixen she would like you to meet."

"Oh." Volle shifted in his seat. "About that, Lord Tistunish—"

"I told you, boy, call me Tish."

"Tish, then. You see, I, uh…don't like females."

"Don't like them? What's wrong with them?" Tish seemed half-angry, half-amused.

"No, no, I mean…I prefer males."

The wolf shrugged. "I rather figured that, given you've taken to Ikling. So what?"

"Well, it seems to have a rather direct bearing on whether I should be introduced to vixens."

"Listen, boy, you're not going to father any future Vintons in some other boy's ass, are you?" He coughed. "Sorry. But you have a duty to your people to keep your name and blood alive, and for that, unless the laws of nature have recently changed, you need a vixen. And one of good breeding. As for what you prefer…" He shrugged again, but his expression was one of resignation. "You can't always have what you want. You have a duty to your people, and to your country. That's the life of a noble."

"Regardless…" Volle began, but Tish cut him off.

"Oh, don't get that stubborn set to your muzzle, boy. You don't have to stop screwing around with boys. In fact, I suspect that once you have a cub or two, your wife will be glad to be—"

"Wife?!" Volle yelped.

"Well, you can't have a cub without a wife? Yes, yes, I know you can, but not a legitimate one."

"Look," Volle said, "I appreciate this, but it's all a bit too much. I've only been here for two days and already you have me married with cubs and...why so much interest in my life?"

Tish grinned widely. "Blame Tika. She loves to meddle, and I suppose it just rubs off on me. Volle, nobody's going to force you to get married tomorrow. There's courtship and engagement periods, though I suspect you won't be too interested in the courtship. But one of the duties of a lord is the continuation of his line, and as that's a pleasurable duty, usually, we thought we'd bring that up first. You saw what happened to Vinton without a lord."

"Seemed to get on pretty well," Volle said, but the number of improvements the town had wanted came back to him now. They'd done a lot themselves, but that meant that either they'd paid their taxes and seen nothing for it, or that they hadn't paid and were now in a lot of financial trouble.

"No representation here leaves them vulnerable. If the neighboring lord decided to walk over and take possession, nobody would come to their aid."

"Who is my neighbor?"

"Hm." Tish scratched his muzzle. "You know, I don't know that. I'll look it up. In any case, Volle, you will attend dinners and meet my wife's vixen friends. If for no other reason than that it will make my wife happy."

Volle grinned slyly. "You seemed to do a good job of keeping her happy."

Tish laughed. "Ah, but I'm old and can't keep her as happy as I used to, at least in that way. So I have to find other ways to do it."

Volle chuckled back. "You're not that old," he said politely, and Tish waved a paw. "You said you had other friends to introduce me to?"

The wolf nodded. "And some things to talk to you about. We meet on fairly short notice, because we're not sure of the popularity of our position and it wouldn't do to have someone listening."

"Is there...any urgency?" Volle wasn't sure how to ask the question. He'd been told not to lean too much on Tistunish, but the wolf hadn't mentioned anything about an imminent plot against Ferrenis.

"There is always urgency, in that preparation now saves action later. But I don't believe there is any need for action immediately."

"All right." Volle rested his muzzle in his paw. Either Tish was unaware of the plot, or it wasn't as imminent as he'd been led to believe. Or it didn't exist.

"There's not much action we can take anyway," Tish said. "We can only suggest and advise. But perhaps I should start with a history lesson." He leaned back in his chair. "How much do you know of Tephos's history?"

"Not much," Volle replied, which was true. "I've heard of Bucher, of course. And wasn't Gerreld king before him?"

"He was. But that was before my time. I knew King Bucher somewhat—I was just a cub at the time and my father was Lord Tistunish. I didn't quite understand what was going on at the time. Not many did, I think.

"King Bucher started the Reys Wars. Oh, some of the younger lords here will have you think the Ferrenians started it, but that isn't true. Bucher managed the whole thing, and managed it well. And after that, he sent the army to the west and annexed the entire country of Delford. When he tried to go still further west, the army was too spread out. They were beaten at Firalitz and at Gerdan, and then the Delford people, meek herbivores that they mostly are, rose up and massacred most of the remainder of the army in one bloody day and night.

"The campaigns were glorious and brutal, both in success and in failure. Not everyone agreed with him. The Gaiavox here in Divalia was jailed for trying to criticize him from the Church, and another Gaiavox was installed who was a supporter. Bucher built a new prison, excavating a park and building four floors of dank, horrible cells where the people who opposed him were kept, and often died.

"He expelled all the foreign embassies." Volle knew that; it was why his knowledge of Tephos' recent history was incomplete. "The luckier ambassadors were sent home, sometimes with all their appendages intact. The rest…" He waved out the window with a paw. "Prison."

"Why did the people put up with it? Jailing an official of the church? Imprisoning those who disagreed?"

Tish smiled without humor. "The church was weaker then, but it's not so different now. Do you think anyone would stand up outside of Council and criticize the king in public? This is what I'm getting at. But about Bucher—you don't remember your father, do you?" Volle shook his head. "It may be difficult for you to understand this, then. Imagine that you knew your father growing up. Imagine that he was a great fox, maybe a fierce warrior in battle, or a brilliant politician or tactician. You admire him and want to be like him, and yet he beats you, sometimes brutally. You tell yourself that it is because you aren't worthy of him, that you deserve the beatings, and that you should try to be better so that all the things he does for you will be worthwhile. That is how Tephos felt about Bucher. Some still do.

"But after the army was massacred, he had fewer soldiers to maintain order. He withdrew them all into the palace and tried to rule from there, never leaving. Word of the massacre filtered slowly into the country, and the people began to adore and fear him less. And love turns so easily to hate, Volle." The wolf sighed wearily.

"What happened?"

"They stormed the palace and killed him. Hung his body on the gate. Some say he was still alive when they strung him up, but after the stones were thrown and the people's claws were bared…there was not much left. The guards saved some remains, and he is buried in the chapel as befits one who was king, even if he was a brutal one.

"And that, by the way, in case you were wondering, is why there aren't more foxes in the peerage here."

"What did Bucher have against foxes?"

Tish shook his head gently. "Nothing, Volle. He was a fox. A red fox, like you. And when the mob stormed the palace, anything with a red coat was torn to pieces."

Volle looked down at his tail, numbly trying to imagine the horror of the scene. Tish let him absorb that before continuing. "They wanted to follow the Panbestian circle in choosing the next ruler, but Bucher had been cunning. One of the things he did was jail and kill all the bears of noble descent, so there were none to succeed him. He planned to break the circle and install his son after him."

"What happened?"

Tish shrugged. "They broke the circle anyway, the ones who unseated him. They had no choice. Lord Fardew, the one who held the title then, was a noble wolf—the current one is just a wolf—and rather than skip the Ursina and select a Herbivoran, they decided that Bucher had been an aberration, and a true Canida king was needed to erase his memory. A lot of paw-waving, but it satisfied people. So he took the throne, became King Halloran, and did his best to mend the kingdom while still keeping it safe from attack by Delford and Ferrenis. He did as well as could be expected, though there were always those who expected more. And seven years ago, he stepped down when King Barris was of age, and the circle was repaired. So they say."

Volle absorbed this. "What happened to King Halloran?"

"He retired to his estate in Reys and lives there still. Fardew is a landless peerage, so it doesn't pass hereditarily as the landholder peerages do. As is the custom, King Barris installed many of his friends into the landless peerages. Fardew was one, but I don't think they are as close as they once were. But that is not entirely relevant. This also I want you to understand." He leaned forward. "Under each house, as you know, the kingdom moves with the traits of the king. The Herbivora excel at defense; the Mustela at attack. The Canida bring unity and harmony; the Felida bring individual glory, but also discord. The Rodenta destroy and rebuild; the Ursina maintain the status quo."

"It doesn't sound like King Bucher was much for unity."

"Unity, my lad, is neither good nor bad, but it can be achieved by good or bad means. Bucher's method was harmful in the long run, but in the short run he gathered a mightier army than this kingdom has ever seen. Halloran's method was different: he sought to include everyone in the kingdom, thinking that exclusion would perpetuate the wound inflicted by Bucher's reign. And perhaps he was right; still there are those who argued that all of Bucher's surviving lieutenants should be put to death, or at least imprisoned."

"They weren't?"

Tish shook his head. "Indeed not, though most of them have died of natural causes by now. Three of them had children who now sit in the peerage. Ikinna, Whassel, and Ryshko are all the children of nobles who were part of Bucher's reign. And this brings me around once again to the point of your presence here."

Volle sat up straighter and perked his ears forward. Tish rested his muzzle on his paws. "The Ursina, as I said, are known for times of peace and maintaining the status quo in the kingdom. Any changes that take place are slow and plodding. However, they also have a good deal of momentum, and once an Ursin king is pushed in or decides upon a direction, it is very difficult to change the course. Over the last three years, I have become aware that within the palace, there is a faction that is trying to nudge Tephos into a war with Ferrenis, under the pretext that the land taken from us after Bucher's fall is ours by right. Their real motive, I believe, is to attempt to restore to Tephos the glory attained under Bucher. But they ignore the blood and bones on which that glory was built." He shook his head slowly. "I am too old and too well-known to do more than recruit a defense against them. My leanings are well known and the ones I suspect do not trust me with any of their plans or confidences. I have been watching the younger Lords and hoping there would be one in whom I could place my trust. Can you bear that burden?" He looked up at Volle, and the joking and laughter that Volle was used to seeing in his eyes were gone. In their place was an earnest pleading, which only partially concealed his worry. His ears were partly back, and his tail lay limp at his side.

Volle nodded. "My Lord, I would be honored."

He didn't know if the title was appropriate, but it seemed so, given the seriousness of the moment. Tish sighed, and leaned back with a smile. "Thank you. It is nothing we need act upon quickly, but I believe there will be a chance to act within the next year. Keep your ears open, and gain the confidence of the Lords I mentioned, if you can."

"I will try my best."

"And I will help you where I can. One last thing, Volle. Lest you think Bucher was an aberration and war now is unlikely, consider this: Nothing symbolizes Bucher's reign more than the prison he built. And though his reliefs and statues have been removed from it, the prison still stands, and is still used. The ones who tore him down and reviled his name still kept his gold, and still use his prison. Remember that."

Volle wasn't quite sure what to make of that, but he nodded. "I will."

"Good." Tish leaned back and relaxed, the seriousness slipping away from his muzzle. "Now, have you a personal servant yet?"

"Yes. He left just a little bit ago. I'm already being flooded with social engagements."

The wolf grinned. "Good. Get to know people quickly, especially the ones I mentioned, and make a good impression. Go to lunch in the common dining room when you can. You'll see people and there's always a lot of informal discussion that takes place over lunch."

"I'll try to make it there. Thanks."

"It looks like you're fitting in pretty well here. Seen the Secretary yet?"

Volle nodded. "He put me on a tribunal. Feliday, I think."

"Good, good. Tribunals are wonderful experience. Also not usually very busy, so you can usually get a nap in if you need one." He winked. "Seriously, that's where I first met the old Lord Mafitte…" He launched into a story of a case he'd heard years before, and how Lord Mafitte, a northern puma, had helped solve it. Welcis returned in the middle of the story with a plate of lunch for Volle and an official invitation to dinner from Helfer. Volle thanked him and reflected again as he ate on what he'd been missing by not having a personal servant in the past.

Tish finished up his story and stood, apologizing for leaving. "Dinner tonight," he said. "Have to help the wife with a couple things." His ears flicked in what Volle thought was a very cute, embarrassed way, but the fox spared him any teasing. They shook paws, and Tish left after reminding Volle (and Welcis) of his dinner engagement.

Volle filled in the few hours remaining before dinner with a nap. Welcis woke him gently and helped him get dressed, informally, then guided him to Helfer's chambers, where Caresh received him. "This way, sir," he said, opening the main door. Welcis bowed and walked away, down the corridor.

"Thank you," Volle said, looking around. He was in a small bare foyer, with a plain wooden door leading to the left and a more ornate one straight ahead of him. Caresh opened the ornate one and ushered him into a parlor, about the size of his own.

The first thing he noticed that was different, though, was that this one had a fireplace. A small fire was set in it, crackling merrily—small enough that it was obviously more for ambience than for heat, especially as the weather was only starting to get chilly, and the palace was quite bearable. Like him, Helfer had a desk over near the window, but his desk was slightly smaller and less ornate. In front of the fire, a small intimate table had been arranged, with a white cloth over it and two goblets. Volle also noticed that Helfer didn't have a door leading into the inner rooms, but a green curtain patterned with the weasel crest he'd noticed on the skirt.

Caresh cleared his throat. "Lord Vinton," he announced.

A moment later, Helfer swept the curtain aside. Volle had a glimpse of brightly colored fabric before it fell into place again. "Volle!" He smiled and strode forward. "Glad you could make it for dinner."

Volle flicked his ears back, grinning abashedly. "Well, I'm glad you could invite me."

Helfer waved a paw, and Volle caught a faint scent of jasmine from him that he didn't remember smelling previously. "It's much better than dining alone, and I saved you from Dereath, I understand. Please, have a seat. Caresh, some mead please?"

While Caresh was fetching the mead, Volle sat down across from the weasel. "What is the problem with Dereath, anyway?"

"You seem to have figured it out without me telling you."

"Yes, but he said there was some problem between he and you and he was worried you'd already mentioned it to me."

Helfer tapped the goblet as Caresh returned and filled it. "It was a year ago," he said. "Really, I'm not that upset about it. I just don't want anything to do with the little sneak."

"Can't you tell me?"

"I don't know if I should. I mean, maybe he's changed since then."

"Oh, come on." Volle grinned. "Pushy, clingy, stubborn…"

"All right, all right." Helfer laughed. "He hasn't changed that much. But first, to your health." He raised his glass.

"Your health as well." Volle followed suit, and took a drink of mead. It was surprisingly smooth, and warmed him more than the fire had.

Caresh left to bring dinner, and Helfer leaned back in his chair. "The whole thing with Dereath was pretty simple, really, but just totally soured me on him. Like I said, it was about a year ago, and he'd just started chasing males. He says that he'd just figured out that he liked males, but I suspect it was because he'd had no luck with the females."

Volle chuckled and took another sip of mead. Helfer went on. "Everyone pretty much knows what I like. I don't make a big secret about it. There aren't many young nobles period, much less gay ones, so of course he came right after me like an arrow from a bow. At first I tried to be patient, you know, teach him about the etiquette, and where to go, and try to tell him not to be quite so pushy. As you noticed, he really didn't get that lesson at all.

"But the real problem was that I found out after about a month that he'd been using his position—you know he works for Fardew, right? In Defense? Well, they're also in charge of intelligence, inside Tephos and out. So he was using his information to find out where I went and what I did. I think he actually put one of the palace spies on me."

"Good Fox. Er, Canis. Sorry. Ferrenian habit." Volle flicked his ears. "He did say a couple things that sounded like he knew what my schedule was already."

"He works fast. Probably found out that you went to the Jackal's Staff with me last night. Hmm, I wonder if that means he's still tailing me." Helfer sighed. "I hope not."

"I hope not too." The sense of well-being the mead had fostered in him was rapidly dissipating. Although he'd been sent to spy on the Tephossians, it hadn't occurred to him that they in turn might be spying on him. And that it was for personal reasons made it seem even more creepy. "Welcis—my personal servant—is trying to arrange a dinner party so he doesn't get the idea I'm putting off his dinner invitation."

"Which you are." Helfer grinned. "Who's coming?"

"I don't know. I told Welcis to leave you out. He said he would find another young noble and some other palace functionary. I just want there to be other people there."

"Smart move. And thanks for leaving me out." Helfer grinned. "I knew you were a trustworthy friend."

Volle laughed. "How? You've only known me a day."

"Oh, you're polite and reserved, but you have a sense of humor. You're attractive but you don't call attention to it. And you know how to have a good time."

Volle flattened his ears and smiled. "I appreciate that. I'm really glad I met you."

"All right, enough with that." Helfer grinned. "Has the Secretary tried to stick you on a tribunal yet?"

"Yeah. Feliday."

"Tch. I'm sorry you didn't know to avoid it. It's the most deadly dull duty you can imagine. If there's anything worse than listening to other people's petty problems, it's sitting around that room not listening to people's petty problems. And they expect you to be an instant expert in everything. Oh, they've tried to convince me to serve on one for a couple years now, but I keep putting it off."

Volle shrugged. "I don't mind. It sounds interesting." But he was less sure of that now than he had been after Tish's visit.

Helfer chuckled. "Better you than me." He took another drink.

"Say…what are the rules for marriage for us?"

Helfer gave him a look of mock surprise. "Why, Lord Vinton, is that a proposal? After only one day?"

Volle sputtered. "I didn't mean that…" Helfer's grin was contagious, and he couldn't help laughing.

"I know what you meant. Sadly, that's one of the drawbacks of being a noble. There's no law against it, but it is strongly encouraged that you have offspring, and that means marrying a female. Now, if something happens to her, and your pup survives, then you're free and clear. Like Lord Barclaw, lucky devil. His wife died of cholera. Oh, don't give me that look, you know what I mean. Anyway, he's got another bear, I think his name's Chellon, and they're very happy together. Didn't you notice them at the banquet?"

"The banquet…" Volle searched his memory. "I don't remember any couples that weren't Lord and Lady."

"Oh, well, that's the nobility. Any companion of a Lord is a Lady, even if the Lady is male. And vice versa, I suppose, though there aren't any female couples at the moment. Only five or six Ladies in the peerage right now."

Volle laughed. "Really? Oh, that's interesting. I think I like that."

"So why the interest in marriage?"

"Mmm. Well, Lord Tistunish has it in his mind that I need to continue the line."

"Old Tish? How did you fall in with him?"

There was a question Volle didn't have an answer for. His mind raced. "I guess he saw me wandering around outside the banquet last night and took me under his wing," he improvised.

That seemed to ring true enough. Helfer just chuckled. "He's a good wolf, but thinks he knows what's best for everyone. He had a couple talks with me to try to convince me to take on some duties, and so forth..." He affected a bored tone. "I explained that I appreciated it, but that I was managing very well. Really, I grew up in the palace. I know what goes on here, and I can make my own decisions."

Caresh returned with a plate of appetizers, grape leaves wrapped around a rice and chicken mixture that smelled of honey, lemon, and a couple other spices. He placed it in the center of the table and then left the room again.

"That smells good..." Volle looked at Helfer. "Is there some etiquette I should know about?"

The weasel grinned. "As host, I'm supposed to let my guest serve himself first. Then when we're both served, I take the first bite. After that, it's every grape leaf for himself."

Volle picked up one of the cylindrical leaf packages and held it near his nose. Whatever else he might have to say about the palace, the quality of the food was far better than he was used to at the Academy. He waited for Helfer to choose a leaf package and take a bite, and then he slid the whole thing into his muzzle at once.

"Mmm." It tasted better than it smelled, even. The chicken was cooked evenly and was very juicy. He chewed happily.

Helfer was chuckling. "Mm, nice to see how much you can fit in your muzzle." He winked. "Now I know Richy had a good time too."

Volle laughed and looked pointedly at the half Helfer was still holding. "Given how you're eating them, I don't know if you want to make that comparison."

Helfer chuckled and finished his. "I can adapt my eating habits to the dish very easily." He picked up another and ran his tongue over it before sliding half of it into his muzzle and biting down.

Volle pretended to cringe, picked up another, and ate it more slowly. "So if you don't mind me asking, why do you avoid the tribunals?"

"Just can't be bothered with it." Helfer shrugged. "Once you get into that political stuff, you make enemies and then you end up spending your life just doing politics instead of the job you're supposed to be doing. I don't want to do the job, and I hate politics even more, so I figure why bother?"

"But don't you feel a responsibility to your people?"

"We have a very capable governor named Burren who sends me, from time to time, petitions to take to the king. I take them to the king, he invariably grants them, and my work is done. Burren manages the rest and I don't worry about it. Get yourself a good governor, Volle, that's my advice."

"Why do they need you at all, then?" Volle grinned as he ate one more grape leaf.

"Oh, they don't," Helfer replied cheerfully. "But it's a matter of prestige to have someone in the palace with access to the king. It means they don't have to worry about sending someone who can present to the king every time they want something—they can just send the paper and they're sure the king will see it soon. I think Burren hopes I'll make something of myself, and perhaps I will. But not just now." He finished one more of the appetizers and licked his lips. "Life's too short."

"I can certainly see that. Still, I think I won't mind helping with the tribunals. The people seemed so excited to have a lord again, I feel like I should do something to help them if I can." He tilted his head. "How often do you see your people?"

"I go to our Vellenland estate about once a year. Burren sits down with me and tells me very seriously all the issues facing the land, and I try to stay awake. Then we go out and see the lush orchards and vineyards and the happy farmers and I wave to them. After that, I usually drink a lot and spend a lot of time in bed with whatever lucky fellow I happen to have brought with me." He smiled. "It's not that I don't care; I do. But when the issues are things like 'Farmer Jones wants to call his apples 'Sweetwater' but Farmer Smith already calls his oranges "Sweetwater"' … well, I usually tell Burren I trust his judgment, and that's the end of it."

Caresh reappeared then, clearing off the table to make room for the main course. A raccoon wearing an apron had helped him carry a tray of food up, which proved to contain a small tureen of rice and two plates of a fish he couldn't identify in a sweet lemon sauce that had a salty undertone to it. Conversation halted while they dug into the fish and rice, and then the small sugar cakes Caresh had brought along as a dessert. Finally, when Volle felt as stuffed as one of the grape leaf appetizers, they leaned back. Helfer had dismissed Caresh for the night, so they left the plates where they were. "He'll get them in the morning before I'm up," Helfer said with a grin. "He's really a terrific servant. Was my father's for as long as I can remember."

"Welcis is pretty good, too."

"All the servants here are first-rate. They have to be—this is the premier job. They get paid very well, from what I understand."

"I'd imagine. I thought the banquet must have been the best food available, but this was pretty good. Is it this good every night?"

"Just about. The cooks here are good too. Bears like good food." Helfer grinned. "That's one benefit of having a bear on the throne."

Volle grinned back. The meal had made him languid, and he was finding it difficult to keep his eyes open. Even the nap he took hadn't made up for the activity that afternoon and last night. Helfer was still energetic, though, tapping his paw on the floor.

"Say, Volle, do you read much?" he asked after a moment.

"When I can." Tracts and tomes and dissertations at the Academy, he thought, but little else.

"Ever read anything by P. Zinsky?"

Volle shook his head. "Who's that?"

"Only the best author in Tephos!" Helfer sprang out of his chair and rummaged in his desk until he emerged with a couple string-bound books. "Here, look. You can borrow these if you want."

"Thanks." Volle looked them over. The first had a picture of two very obviously male foxes embracing. The title was "A Brush With Love." The prominent position of the foxes' tails made the pun clear. He chuckled and looked at the next, titled "The Ringing of the Belle." The cover showed a handsome, muscular raccoon dipping a slender, effeminate wolf, their muzzles just touching.

"I've read those a bunch of times, ever since I was thirteen." The weasel flicked his ears, smiling. "Got me through a lot of nights. 'Brush With Love' isn't one of his best, but I thought you'd like the foxes. The other one is my favorite."

"I'll read through them. They look like fun. Thanks again."

"No problem. Hey, feel like going to the pub?"

Volle grinned and shook his head. "No. I'm kinda tired. I'll meet you for a run tomorrow, though. A little earlier, maybe?"

"Yeah, I shouldn't be out too late, unless there's a cute bunny I just can't pass up."

"You like rabbits, huh?"

Helfer nodded enthusiastically. "They've got that whole herbivore thing going, and they have great stamina. Plus I have to admit I love the ears."

Volle chuckled. "Big ears never did anything for me." Reese would've been in trouble otherwise, he thought. "But what about the teeth? I'd never let those teeth near my…"

"Oh, I don't let them do *that*. But they're good for lots of other things." He winked. "Now you're getting me all excited."

Volle stood up, grinning. "I'll let you get going, then. Thanks for the dinner."

"Oh, thank you! I enjoyed it. We'll have to do it again."

"Definitely." Volle's tail wagged as he shook Helfer's paw and headed for the door. "See you tomorrow!"

Out in the corridor, he started paging through the books as he walked. *The black mask that lay like a swath of night across his face hinted at deep secrets, but the ebon depths of his eyes promised that all those secrets would be revealed and shared, one by one. A gentle brown finger pressed into the whiteness of Kris's fur, the lightest feathery touch, and the warmth of the fingertip seemed to sear him with passion wherever it landed. Slowly, it traveled downward, while the muscular arms held him securely...*

A piece of paper fluttered out of the book as Volle turned the pages, amused. He bent to the floor and picked it up. It bore Helfer's name and official seal and had some amounts of money listed on it, with Ullik's signature at the bottom. Volle initially shuffled it behind the book, not wanting to intrude on his friend's personal life, then remembered that he was a spy, and intruding was what he was supposed to be doing.

It was not very revealing, as it happened. It was a receipt for taxes from Vellenland, from which Ullik had deducted the costs of a personal servant and the replacement for a tapestry in the main hall that had been "damaged." The paper must have been sent back and forth, because underneath that, Helfer had scribbled "why replace? those stains come right out," and Ullik had written, "the smell will not." Helfer's reply had been, "rubbish!" and Ullik had answered, "your lordship owns the tapestry now and may hang it in your chambers if you wish." To this, Helfer had not replied.

Volle grinned and shook his head, and walked back to Helfer's door. The paper was official and he thought Helfer might not want it roaming about the castle. He opened the door into the foyer, and then walked into the parlor. "Helfer?"

The room was silent. "Helfer?" he called, a bit louder. Still no answer.

He frowned. He hadn't left the corridor outside the door, and he was sure he hadn't heard the door open and close. Could Helfer have changed his mind and gone to sleep? He decided to risk poking his nose into the sitting room.

What he saw beyond the curtain startled him. The room was covered in large and small plush pillows. Two couches sat at one end, framing a medium sized chest that sat against the wall. Two doors in the wall to his left were firmly closed, and opposite him was another doorway with a curtain. The lingering scent in the room left little doubt what Helfer used this room for. "Helfer?" he called tentatively, but there was still no reply.

The boundaries of their still-new friendship warred with his instinctive curiosity and the compulsion of his mission. He looked back at the parlor door, which he'd closed behind him, and then stepped into the sitting room. Just a quick look around, he promised himself.

Making his way cautiously through the pillows, he tried the first door, which led to a private bathroom. The scents of the bath salts were mingled with a basket of some herbs that sat on the edge of the tub.

Currently the tub was filled with powder, but it was deep enough to hold water as well, and a bucket nearby confirmed his suspicion that it occasionally did. He could smell jasmine, and realized where Helfer had gotten that scent. The weasel, though, was nowhere to be seen.

Nor was he behind the other door, which led to an expansive wardrobe. Volle gawked at the assortment of clothes that hung from racks or lay folded on shelves. Helfer must have an outfit for every day of the year, he thought. Green and yellow were the predominant colors, and the family crest adorned fully half the garments Volle could see.

"Luxurious," he muttered, closing the door as quietly as he could. He padded over to the other curtain and gently drew it aside with a paw.

Behind it was Helfer's bedroom. There was a fireplace here, and a large canopy bed with pale green silk sheets. The bed was carved of fine mahogany, with weasel totems scampering up the posts, and the headboard had flaking gold leaf on it. A small table stood nearby, and a small wardrobe (*more clothes??*), but like the other rooms, it was empty.

Puzzled, Volle withdrew his muzzle and walked slowly back to the parlor. He was certain Helfer hadn't gone out his front door. The corridor had been very quiet, and nobody had walked over it in either direction. Either Helfer was much stealthier than Volle had given him credit for, and had snuck out without saying hello or asking how Volle liked the book, or else he was hiding somewhere in his apartments for some reason.

He set the piece of paper down on Helfer's desk, and stood looking out the window for a moment. It looked out onto a busy street, and from the second story, the window could be opened. Volle did so, and breathed in the night air for a moment. To his right, he could see the Lonely Cock, and just as he was grinning again at the name, he could have sworn he saw Helfer walking down the street towards it.

"Hey..." But he didn't want to yell, and now he wasn't sure it was the weasel after all. He'd been wearing the same green tunic, but several people in the street were wearing green. The scents floating up to him all jumbled, and he couldn't sort them out to pick out Helfer's.

Behind him, the parlor door opened. He turned and came face to face with Caresh, who looked impassively at him.

"Oh. Good evening, Caresh."

"Good evening, Lord Vinton."

"Helfer—Lord Ikling had loaned me these books, and one of them had a personal document in it, so I just wanted to return it." He couldn't stop his ears from flicking nervously. "I just set it on the desk there. I hope he won't mind."

Caresh shook his head. "I imagine he will not, though I expect he would appreciate being told at your lordship's earliest convenience."

"Of course," Volle nodded. "Er, is Lord Ikling out?"

Caresh looked at him and then glanced at the curtain leading to the sitting room. "Lord Ikling was addressing some matters with me in my quarters," he said smoothly. "He has only just now left."

"Oh, I see. Thank you, Caresh." Volle walked past the other fox as he started clearing the dinner dishes. "Goodnight."

"Goodnight, sir."

He paused in the foyer and closed the parlor door behind him. He lifted his nose and inhaled deeply. There was Helfer's scent, but it was old, and there was definitely no scent of jasmine. Nor, when he inhaled again outside, was there any in the corridor. He closed the door and walked thoughtfully back to his rooms, holding the books in his paw. He didn't know why, but Caresh had definitely been lying.

Chapter 6

In the morning, the palace tailor Wexlin came by. The old goat had brought his measuring tape and some fabric swatches, and after taking Volle's measurements, he let Volle choose some fabrics. Volle liked the feel of the linen, and asked for it in an orange-red.

"That'll do fine," Wexlin said. "What do you need, and how many?"

"Well,"Volle said sheepishly, "I don't really have anything. So I need some casual outfits and a couple formal ones, and whatever else I might need. Oh, and some skirts for running."

Wexlin nodded again. "I'll make the formal outfits with the lace and velvet, if that's okay. It's traditional for them." Volle nodded his agreement. "Do you have a family crest to embroider onto your clothes?"

"I do. Hold on." Volle rummaged through his papers and found a drawing of the Vinton crest, a fox's head with the Panbestian Canis symbol on a diagonal striped background.

The goat examined it. "Rather simple. I can start right away; we're not very busy. We can have four or five shirts, some skirts, some formal pants, a couple doublets…" He did the tallies in his head. "I'll have them sent down as they're ready. Probably a month for the lot."

"That'll be fine, thank you." Volle smiled, and the goat bowed and left.

Caresh brought down another skirt for him, or perhaps it was the same one. He dressed, and met Helfer in the same spot again. The weasel seemed to be in good spirits. "All ready?"

Volle nodded, and they set off. "Oh, did you find the paper I left on your desk?"

"No, haven't looked at it. What is it?"

"It was just one of your papers that was stuck in one of the books you loaned me. I brought it back because it looked personal—it had figures on it and your seal, and I figured you'd want it."

"I appreciate that. Thanks."

"I had to go back into your parlor to leave it, and you weren't there. I hope you don't mind."

"No, not at all."

They continued on through a particularly fragrant patch of flowers while Volle wrestled with his conscience. Staying on good terms with Helfer was important to him, but he realized that the weasel was about the least important contact in terms of his work. Chances are he would never find out what Volle had done, but what if Caresh had told him? With his keen nose, Caresh could have detected Volle's scent in the sitting room, at least, even though he'd been careful not to touch very much. He'd been in there long enough.

He was also curious about where Helfer had gone and how he'd gotten out. But he couldn't ask that straight out, so coming clean wouldn't satisfy that curiosity. But on the other paw, Helfer was the best friend he had so far, and if Caresh *had* told him...

As they rounded the corner of the palace, coming to the edge of the main garden, he said, "You left pretty quickly last night. I...I kinda looked through the curtain to see if you were in there, and I didn't see you."

Helfer chuckled. "I was talking to Caresh in his quarters," he said. "But you're free to roam through the chambers if you like."

"Interesting sitting room."

Helfer laughed. "Laying room, I call it. I don't do much sitting in there."

Volle grinned. "Lot of doors off it." He'd decided to compromise. He'd seen the doors, but there was nothing secret about them, so he hoped Helfer would volunteer to tell him what was behind them, and he did.

"Private bathroom, and the room that used to be mine growing up. I just keep my clothes there now. And of course the bedroom."

"Private bath? Lucky. My private bath was taken away."

"Oh, yes, Lady Gervis. Well, my father served for many years and when I was old enough he applied for larger chambers. Those happened to be empty at the time and so we moved in. I'm spoiled now, I admit it, but I'm not going to move."

"I wouldn't either." They paused to climb the wall separating the two rear gardens, and then set off again.

For the rest of the run they remained silent. When they got back to the gates, Helfer patted Volle on the back. "Thanks! See you tomorrow? I'll probably stay in tonight, but I'll let you know if I change my mind."

"Sure. I've got a dinner date tonight anyway."

"Oh? With who?"

"Assistant to the Steward. He's pretty cute and I think he was flirting with me."

"Arrin? Oh, he's a good fox." Helfer squinted at Volle speculatively. "I think you two might hit it off. You looking for something serious?"

"Not really. Why?"

He shrugged and grinned. "Lot of the functionaries are. But he knows the situation. Have fun. Oh, and go ahead and keep the skirt 'til you get your own."

"Okay, thanks. I saw Wexlin this morning." Helfer rolled his eyes. "Well, I can't afford to see your tailor until I get my money straightened out."

"I guess. See you tomorrow, then." The weasel jogged away up the stairs.

Volle had decided to take lunch with the other lords, following Tish's advice, so after a quick bath and some help with his wardrobe from Welcis, he headed for the dining rooms. Perhaps, he thought, he could locate one of the lords that Tish had mentioned. A few tables were set up at which some lords were sitting, while uniformed staff brought them food and carried it away. Volle sat down at a table with four other lords, who turned politely to acknowledge his presence.

The first, a middle-aged wolf, was sitting beside two younger bears. Apart from them, separated by a place from both their group and Volle, sat an older squirrel. He muttered "Shenio" when introductions were being made, but Volle didn't know if that was his name or a regional curse of some kind. None of the other names were ones Volle knew.

As the staff came and went, bringing bread, honey, and the rich chicken pastries that were the main lunch dish, the lords chatted amiably about the weather, the conditions at the palace, and the price of various foods and liquors and what was to be done about it. This led into a political discussion, to which Volle listened avidly.

"Back when we owned the mango groves, the mead was cheap! One copper for a mug!" This was "Shenio" talking. Mangoes, Volle knew, were grown in southern Ferrenis and in Delford, the country on Tephos's western border. Tephos's southern lands were too mountainous for mangoes to grow.

"So what are we going to do, invade them again?"

"That's what old Blood'n'Guts would like, isn't it?"

"Well, you'll never hear him say it out loud, but it's there all right."

"Lord Vinton?" A paw on his shoulder interrupted the conversation. Volle turned, fuming inwardly, and met the blue eyes of a young grey fox in a peach-colored silk shirt. "I'm sorry to interrupt, but you are Lord Vinton, right?"

Volle nodded, and the fox held out his paw. "I'm Lord Vanadi. I understand I'm to attend a dinner at your chambers tomorrow night." The others at the table, after looking up briefly, returned to their conversation. Volle listened to them with one ear, but they'd stopped talking politics and started talking about the next Church service.

"Yes, that's right. I'm new at the palace and I'm trying to meet people." He smiled broadly. "My personal servant said he would invite a few people, just for a quiet evening, since I don't know anyone."

"Oh, I'm glad to join you." Vanadi smiled. "I just wanted to ask, how familiar are you with the Panbestian Screed? Because I have a couple books that really helped me come to terms with my place in the hierarchy of life, and I'd be delighted to share them if you're interested."

"Well. I'm not sure…"

"Oh, they're really wonderful. Tell you what. I'll just bring the one."

Volle forced a smile. "Okay."

Vanadi's return smile was obviously not forced. "Great! I'll see you tomorrow night, then." His tail was wagging as he headed off.

By the time Volle returned to the conversation, some of the original lords had left and new ones arrived. They were now talking about the ladies of the court. It was the younger ones who drove this conversation; "Shenio" had his head down in his arms. Volle did learn that there was to be a cotillion in a couple weeks' time, but other than that, he learned nothing of use. Frustrated, he wished he could ask them to go back to talking about politics, but realized that that probably wouldn't work too well. So when he had finished his food, he bid them good day and left.

That left him the rest of the afternoon to prepare for his dinner with Arrin. He honestly didn't know what to expect, so he decided not to worry about it. Welcis would no doubt take care of the arrangements. After some time spent examining his papers, Volle curled up in bed with "A Brush With Love."

...russet fur caught fire in the light of the sunset. Jorehn gasped, a look of stunned surprise on his muzzle. The stranger approaching him was a fox like himself, tall and well-formed, with a confident stride and a cocky tilt to his ears. He drew closer, and closer still, so that Jorehn could see the highlights in his fur, a red the color of the sunset, a yellow as bright as a daffodil, the whole pattern looking like autumn leaves spun into threads and woven to form a perfect tapestry wrapped around the divine image of the vulpine form. As his eyes traveled lower, he saw that the stranger was wearing a simple skirt of yellow cloth, and the shape of the cloth at his waist reminded Jorehn of nothing so much as a plump, hard lemon...

At first, Volle just giggled at the elaborate prose. But as he read on, he found himself more and more engaged with the characters, and more and more aroused by their exploits. He closed the bedroom door and took off his trousers so that he could brush a paw back and forth over his swollen sheath.

Mychal's muzzle came close to Jorehn's ear, so that Jorehn could feel his warm breath against the soft fur inside. 'They may separate us in body, but they can never pry our spirits from our embrace of love. A part of you will always be in me, and a part of me will forever be in you.' Jorehn sighed at the words and nodded, as his body's senses sang in an ecstatic harmony with the part of Mychal that was physically in him. His lover's passion moved as easily into Jorehn as his words had done, and both stirred a fire in him, one in his heart and one in his loins. The two danced together through his blood...

Volle's own blood had surged to his sheath, bringing him fully erect. He was panting as he read, barely aware that his paw had closed firmly around himself and was stroking quickly. At the climax of the story, he closed his eyes and lay back, paw working until his back arched and he moaned in pleasure. Warm spatters fell on his tunic as he finished himself, and finally he lay back on the bed, panting.

The bedroom door opened, and Volle suddenly found the energy to scramble with his tunic to cover himself. Welcis's head poked inside.

"Sir, is anything wrong? I heard…" He assessed the situation quickly and bowed his head. "Terribly sorry, sir." He made to shut the door.

"Wait! Welcis…how much longer until dinner?"

"Two hours, sir."

"Is the table set?"

"Not yet, but I have sent for a cloth and some settings. They should be here within the hour."

"Excellent." Volle fingered his tunic. "Would you be able to find me some nice dinner clothes? I don't think the tailor will be quite done with mine."

"Yes, sir."

"And…I think I will need this laundered." He grinned sheepishly.

Welcis's expression didn't change. "Sir, I will be pleased to take care of that." He waited expectantly.

"I'll leave it by the wardrobe here when I change later." He was still erect, though his legs and tunic were hiding that well enough. His ears flicked a bit self-consciously. "Also, if you can find a scent to put in this room and the sitting room…something subtle, maybe a sage or lavender smell?"

"Very good, sir." Welcis retreated, closing the bedroom door behind him.

Volle sighed and lay back to finish the book.

A single tear trickled down the fur of Jorehn's cheek, blurring the image of the harbor and the departing ship. He clutched the railing as the vortex of despair and anguish threatened to engulf him, but then he remembered Mychal's strong, assured voice telling him to be strong. The sweet baritone would remain forever in his memory even if he never heard it with his ears again, and every word that voice had spoken would remain etched like traceries of frost upon the fragile glass of his soul. Mychal's arms seemed to lift him, to give him the strength to stand defiantly upright. In the saffron and vermilion of the sunset he saw his love's fur, and so he lifted his muzzle to the heavens as though his lover dwelt there and said, 'I love you still, and forever will.'

And although the ship was no more than a black blur on a turquoise canvas, he knew without knowing how that Mychal stood on the deck looking back at him, his golden eyes shining, repeating the same words back to him. And then his sadness was tempered with the joy that is ever-present when two hearts are joined, for he knew that time and distance no longer mattered; as Mychal had said, their bodies were apart, but their spirits were one.

To his surprise, Volle found a tear in his own eye as he set the book aside. He lay back and enjoyed the wash of emotions for a moment. The characters had appealed to him, and as he reflected on them, he wondered if Arrin would be his Jorehn, then chuckled to himself. "Romance," he said aloud as he stripped off his tunic, "is best left in books."

Welcis found him a very nice silk shirt and a pair of dressy short pants to go with it, and had even remembered Volle's color preferences;

both were a soft lemon yellow. To offset the similarity, Welcis had found a wide cloth belt that was a deep reddish-orange, and he helped Volle tie it around his waist.

Volle studied the end result in the wardrobe mirror. "This looks very nice. Thank you, Welcis."

"I only regret, sir, that I was not able to locate a suitable cravat to complete the ensemble. For a private dinner, I believe this will be more than adequate, however."

"I'm sure it will be fine." He admired himself again. "Let me know when Arrin arrives?"

"As a matter of fact, sir, Mister Villencort is already here. He arrived just as I was returning with your lordship's clothes. I instructed him to wait in the parlor."

"Oh! Well, send him in. No, I'll go out."

"Yes, sir. I will bring the dinner in fifteen minutes?"

"Excellent."

"In the meantime, sir, I have taken the liberty of bringing a carafe of wine up from the palace cellars. The occasion seemed to call for wine rather than mead, although as a precaution, I did also bring up a bottle of blackberry mead, which I would be delighted to pour if his lordship wishes."

"No, no, wine will be perfect, thank you." He walked past Welcis, through the sitting room where the table had been very nicely set and a subtle hint of lavender filled the air, and into the parlor.

Arrin was sitting in one of the chairs, dressed in his blue tunic and trousers. The tunic looked neat and clean, though, so it was obvious he hadn't come straight from his office. He stood when Volle entered and bowed, but Volle extended a paw to him.

"None of that, please. This is just a friendly dinner. I don't want to be a Lord all the time. I find it rather tiring."

Arrin grinned back and clasped his paw, humor sparkling in his eyes. "It's a fatigue I wouldn't mind, to be honest. As you wish, though. Thank you so much for inviting me to dinner."

"Thank you for accepting." Volle smiled and sat down. "Dinner will be served soon. In the meantime, can I offer you some wine?" Welcis had entered the room with the carafe of wine and two goblets on a tray.

"Oh, yes. Thank you!" Arrin took a goblet, and Volle took the other. Arrin lifted his. "To my gracious host."

They drank, and then Volle lifted his goblet. "To my handsome guest."

Arrin's ears flicked all the way back, and he smiled shyly before lifting his goblet and drinking. "So, how do you like it here so far, my — host?"

Volle smiled broadly at the other fox. "I'm enjoying myself quite a bit. The people I've met have all been very helpful and very friendly. Well, not all…but most."

Arrin looked as though he wanted to ask who hadn't been helpful, but he refrained. "I'm glad to hear that."

"How long have you worked for Lord Alister?"

"Two years now. I like him. He's a good person to work for."

"Did you grow up here?"

The fox nodded. "Well, not in the palace. I grew up in Divalia. But my mother worked in the palace laundry, so I was here a lot, and I got a job with the staff when I was fourteen. I served Lord Alister several times, and after he got to know me, he asked for me personally when his old assistant left." He sat a bit straighter and his ears perked with pride.

"You must be a great help to him."

"I like to think so." Arrin tilted his muzzle. "What about you? How did you spend your childhood?"

Volle told him the story about his farm, his embittered mother, his absent father, and the discovery of his birthright. By the time he finished, Welcis had left and returned with a young badger and two trays heaped with platters. They disappeared into the sitting room and returned empty-pawed. The badger left, while Welcis announced grandly, "Dinner is served."

Volle ushered Arrin into the sitting room before him. The appetizer was several squares of raw fish with a dark sweet glaze and a leafy garnish. Volle found the taste, as usual, lovely.

Arrin looked around the sitting room while taking his first bite. "It looks like you're making yourself at home here." He sniffed the air and smiled. "I love the scents you have."

"Welcis has helped immensely with that. I don't know what I'd do without him. And he's only been here two days."

"Lavender's one of my favorites." Arrin smiled shyly again and bent to his appetizer.

"I've always liked it." Volle smiled. Arrin's shyness was very cute. He ate very delicately, and very properly, too. "So tell me a bit more about yourself. What do you do for fun?"

"Oh, well, I don't know what there is to tell. I used to play an old beat-up trumpet with a street band, growing up, but I don't do that anymore. I like going down to the pub, or just spending a quiet evening in the garden talking." He looked down. "I know that's not very exciting."

Volle chuckled softly. "I never knew anyone who played music."

"Oh, everyone here plays something. The lords, anyway. It's part of their education."

"Interesting. I didn't know that."

"Most of them don't do anything with it. There's a conservatory if you want to play with some of the instruments."

Volle shook his head. "I'd be afraid of breaking them."

"Oh, I'd be happy to show you sometime." Arrin stopped suddenly, and the shyness returned. "That is, I mean, if you'd want."

"I'll see how much time I have, but I think I would like that." Volle smiled. It was probably too early to tell whether there would be much romance, but he thought there would be at least be friendship there, once Arrin got over his nervousness. He enjoyed talking to the other fox and so far was finding him interesting enough to want to hear more of.

"What about you? What do you do for fun?"

Caught off guard, Volle flicked his ears. "Well, I like an evening down at the pub, too…I mostly just like spending time with friends. I play darts sometimes, but not very well." He thought it was probably better not to mention the Jackal's Staff and like places.

"I could never get the hang of it either." Arrin smiled as Welcis took their plates away and presented the main course, a long strip of beef with rice and sautéed vegetables.

Volle nodded, and started eating. "So what sort of work do you do for Lord Alister?"

"Oh, I do a lot of filing and paperwork for him. I run around and deliver messages, and help him coordinate palace functions, and help administer palace functions…"

"So you had something to do with the Ermine Dancers?"

Arrin giggled. "Aren't they tacky? Oh, I'm sorry. They're really lovely, and good, but they just pander so much. But the King loves them, and the lords won't say no to an aphrodisiac like that, so…" He chuckled. "They're popular up north and very hard to get, even for the King. They cost a fortune."

"Wouldn't be so bad if they were male," Volle said lightly.

"Oh, well." Arrin ducked his head. "I suppose not. There are some groups in the city like that. Not as good, but…" He shrugged. "I guess I never really wanted to see that in public." He looked up at Volle with some apprehension, as though waiting for approval.

Volle smiled. "Hey, I can understand that. I don't mind, myself, but private performances are much more enjoyable."

Arrin's ears flicked again, and he gave that shy grin that Volle found so cute. "Yeah, I…I think so, too."

Volle chewed and thought. Probably it was too early to ask if he were a virgin. He was sure Arrin was inexperienced, though. Best to change the subject. "What's the hardest part of working for Lord Alister?"

"Oh, trying to keep everybody happy." He replied instantly, ears coming up. "I mean, when it's the king asking us to set up a banquet, well, that's easy, everything else gets moved around it. But when there are two lords who both want the services of the kitchen staff on a certain night, or when Lord Tallio wants to hold a fete for his family, visiting for a week, on the same day that Lord Busse wants to assemble the castle to admire some painter he's discovered, well, it gets delicate."

"But you manage?"

Arrin nodded. "Lord Alister takes on the really hard cases. Everybody's always wanting something, but he trusts me more now, so I can take some of that off his paws." He took another bite, and looked up at Volle. "So what about you? Tell me about the trip here from Ferrenis. I've never been out of the city."

Volle told him about the mountains, about the town of Vinton and what the people were like there, and then about the long journey through the southern plains. Remembering the flowery prose of the book he'd just read, he tried to paint the scenery with the same blush, describing the snow on the mountains ("already?" Arrin asked, "but it's only fall") and the silvery track of the river through the plains. He tried to remember what the city had looked like from afar. So much had happened in the last three days that he felt that journey already receding into the past, and was glad to have the chance to relive it with a captive audience.

He finished the story as they were eating dessert, a small golden cake with fruit and a light cream topping. Arrin sighed. "You describe it so beautifully, I could almost see it."

Volle's ears slid back, caught off guard by the compliment. "Thanks." He smiled. "It really is a beautiful country."

"I'd love to see the mountains sometime."

"Maybe that can be arranged." Volle smiled and leaned back, allowing Welcis to clear the last of the plates. "Shall we go back to the parlor? There's no fire there, but the chairs are a bit more comfortable." He'd intentionally mentioned the fire so that Arrin could ask where he did have a fire, and having mentioned the bedroom, Volle could invite Arrin in there. Of course, it was still too warm for a heat fire, but a small romantic one would set a nice mood.

Arrin didn't take the opportunity, though. He just nodded and said, "Certainly."

They took their wine back into the parlor and relaxed in the upholstered chairs. Volle made a mental note to attempt to get a loveseat in here. Or maybe in the bedroom, by the fire. For a little while longer, they made small talk, and then Arrin set aside his goblet.

"I should leave," he said apologetically, getting up. "I do have to be up early tomorrow."

Volle rose as well, trying to keep the disappointment off his muzzle and tail. He walked Arrin to the door, where he grasped one of his paws. "Thank you for coming. I had a lovely time."

"Oh, I did too." Their eyes met, and their muzzles were already close. Volle could feel the other fox's warm breath on his whiskers, and he deliberately brushed his muzzle against Arrin's. Arrin responded with a nuzzle of his own, and then Volle gave the side of his muzzle a short lick, and Arrin opened his muzzle willingly to Volle's.

They kissed for a long time, sliding into each other's arms, and Volle could feel the warmth in Arrin's chest and the desire, full like his own, pressed into his hip. But when he tried to lead the other fox to his bedroom, Arrin resisted.

"Lord—Volle. I really want to…to take this slow. I like you a lot and I think there could be something between us, but I want a little more romance. I know us males in general just hop into bed with each other, but I think that makes it less special." He traced a finger along Volle's cheek ruff, eyes pleading softly. "I'd like to see you again. Would that be okay, still?"

Volle smiled, nodded, and kissed Arrin's nose. "Certainly. Thanks for telling me. I would love to see you again." He squeezed the fox's paw and then let it go.

Arrin smiled back, and his ears perked up. "Maybe in a couple days. Come by and let me know when you're free."

"I will. Good night, Arrin."

"Good night, Volle. And thanks again." His tail was up and wagging slowly as he left.

Volle grinned and closed the door, heading back to his bedroom. A romantic! Who would've thought? All he'd really expected from the evening had been a good lay, but it had turned out to be less than that, and also more. He didn't feel so bad now about having pleasured himself earlier. Though that kiss had gotten him more than a bit worked up. He didn't mind so much, though. It was fun to have an interest that didn't immediately become sexual, and he was looking forward with much anticipation to the next visit from Arrin. He would have to do something nice for him.

In the meantime, there was always "The Ringing Of The Belle." He dismissed Welcis for the night, stripped his clothes off, and crawled into bed. But he hadn't gotten through more than the first three pages when he fell asleep, paw on his sheath, a smile on his muzzle.

Chapter 7

Volle went running the next morning with Helfer again, and told him about the date. He came in for a good deal of teasing about the romanticism, as well as the impending dinner with Dereath and the other two. Helfer didn't know Vanadi, but "he sounds like a real fun time," he said sarcastically upon hearing of Volle's meeting him at lunch.

When Volle returned to his chambers after a bath, Welcis informed him that Lord Ullik had been asking him to schedule another appointment. "He seemed most eager, sir."

I bet he did, Volle thought. "Put him off until next week if you can," he said. "I'm going to be busy with the tribunal and with other duties, and I don't know when I'll be able to see him." He sighed. "I just need enough time for Ben to get back with those receipts. Hopefully that'll straighten everything out."

"I see, sir. Will there be anything else?"

"No thank you, Welcis. I'll return this evening for the dinner party. Seven, was it?"

"Yes, sir."

"I'll see you then." He finished dressing and walked quickly through the palace to the main gate, and out into the town. The mention of Ullik had brought a sour taste back to his muzzle, and he suddenly felt confined in the grey stone walls of the palace.

The afternoon was cool and overcast, and not many people wandered the streets. Volle walked in the other direction from the Lonely Cock and Jackal's Staff; he wanted to explore a bit. The smells of the city reminded him again of Caril and he sighed, a surge of homesickness rising again in him.

From one alley, he caught the whiff of a fried pastry, and his stomach reminded him that he'd skipped lunch. He and Reese had often gone for the fried pastries sold by the small shop outside the Academy and eaten them in the park nearby, which was about all they could do in the half hour break they had for lunch. The memory made him lonely for his friend's company.

He found the shop, which was run by a small mouse couple, and bought a pastry. "Two coppers, sir." They weren't sure of his standing. It was obvious he had money, but his clothes were dirtier than they were accustomed to from the lords of the palace.

As he paid them, he looked around the area. "Is there a park near here?"

"Yes, sir. Just down the alley, take a right on Dragon, left on Walnut, and it'll be on your right in half a mile."

"Thanks." He smiled, waved to them, and walked down the alley.

Many of the shops were familiar to him, but some of the goods they sold were not. He stopped in a store that sold thick wool rugs that he assumed were made from sheep, but when he felt them, the texture was different. Some of the fruit in the fruit stalls was unfamiliar too. But even though some of the smells were different, the texture of the city felt similar enough to that of Caril that his homesickness began to abate somewhat. It helped that the fried pastry smelled very similar to those he was used to.

He found the park and sat down on an empty bench, finished the pastry in a few bites, and leaned back to let the wind ruffle his fur and the scents of the park fill his nose. The grass, the flowers, the trees—the smells weren't as rich as in the palace garden, but felt somehow more real to him.

"Hello, Volle."

He snapped upright and almost fell off the bench. Seir was sitting next to him, looking away from him. Downwind, of course.

"Seir!"

"Shh. We shouldn't be seen together. I just wanted to tell you we've set up a regular meeting place and time." She was whispering, counting on his sharp ears to catch her words.

He sat back, carefully looking in the other direction. He knew her ears were as sharp as his, so he whispered too. "When and where?"

"Every other Rodenday, starting a week from tomorrow. At the Jackal's Staff."

He coughed, hiding an exclamation. "How did you know…?"

"Volle, we need a place to meet outside the palace where we can have privacy and where it won't look suspicious if you go there frequently. I must say, I hope your job is progressing as well as your hobby."

He remembered then that Seir had been complicit in Reese's joke, and growled. "You went along with him. I'd have thought you'd be honest with me, at least."

She chuckled. "Aw, Volle, don't take it so hard. No harm done. We knew you'd figure it out eventually, though I admit not even Sherr thought you would figure it out as quickly as you have. I guess he just didn't know your drive."

"Hmph. Where is Reese, anyway?"

"He went with Ben back to Vinton. Isn't that what your note said? He figured it was important enough that you wanted him to go along. Wasn't too happy about it, either."

"Well, maybe we're even then. When does he get back?"

He felt her shrug. "Three days there, three back if they hurry. Next Caniday, maybe."

"Have Ben deliver the note to me personally at the palace, okay? Don't go to the Exchequer. He's a slime."

"That's a useful bit of information, anyway. All right, I'm going to go. Remember, a week from this Rodenday, at the Jackal's Staff. Tally will tell you that that wolf you had last time is waiting for you in back. Just go along with it."

"Tally? Is he one of us?"

Seir snorted. "No, but he knows the value of a gold coin and a closed muzzle. Sherr's used him before. I think he thinks we're into some kind of group thing that you don't want talked about."

Volle rolled his eyes. "If only. Good to see you, Seir." When he looked over again, she was gone.

He felt considerably lighter of spirit as he watched the clouds swirl and move over the park, and the people go by beneath them. The feeling was relaxing after the press of people and activity over the last couple days, and it was with some regret that he noticed the gradual darkening of the sky. He got to his feet, stretched, and returned to the palace.

His feeling of well-being lasted exactly as long as it took him to reach his chambers, where Dereath greeted him.

"Oh, I'm glad you're back!" The rat sprang to his feet and rushed over to Volle. He was wearing the same black vest, black pants, and silver belt as the last time Volle had seen him, and Volle thought, doesn't he ever change? "I wanted a bit of time alone with you before the dinner."

Volle tried to step back, but the rat kept pressing forward. "Er… why?"

"See, I know you don't know the other two people here really well, so I thought I could brief you on them and you'd feel more comfortable with them that way."

"Oh. Okay." Volle didn't know what to say.

"Lord Vanadi, first. He's a grey fox, just became a Lord a year and a half ago when his father died of whitemouth, so don't mention diseases. His mother died in the same epidemic, and that's actually how his father died, he went home to be with her and caught it himself. All very sad. Now, he's very religious, goes to church every day, not just on Gaiaday. So don't speak ill of the church. I don't know if you would, but you probably shouldn't. He's got a prospective wife back home and a mistress here in town. Her name is Charmaine and she's a goat." He snorted. "Takes all kinds, I guess. I don't think that'll come up, but you know it in case it does."

"Wait, wait, what is this?" Volle backed away, paws out.

"Information. Just from Lord Fardew's files. Now, the functionary is a young coyote. Her name is Llana. Don't have as much on her. She's not a Lord, you know. But she does have a *bit* of a weight problem, and her father works in the stables here in the palace, so…"

"Hold on, hold on! I don't need to know this."

Dereath looked hurt, but shrugged. "I just thought it'd help."

An idea occurred to Volle. "What's in those files on me?"

"Nothing much...yet. Your father was killed in a border skirmish, you grew up in Merinland, you like males, wine, and yellow clothes. And you have a great body." He grinned. "Okay, that last part is just in my files."

Volle eyed the rat. "And what's in your file?"

"Oh, maybe if the evening goes well you'll get to see my file in its entirety." Dereath was standing close to him again, and his strange scent reached Volle's nostrils. His nose reached just to Volle's collarbone, and it was pressed there now, snuffling in his fur.

"We'll see," Volle said, turning away. "Can you really get to all the files?"

"He keeps some locked up, but I can get to most of them. I can't see the one on the King, if that's what you want to know. You wouldn't want to read that. He's boring anyway. Devoted to his wife, no secret vices." The rat giggled.

"Could you get me information about anyone I was about to meet with? Like the Exchequer?"

Dereath pressed up again, half-lidding his eyes in what he probably thought was a sultry look, but which made Volle think he was about to fall asleep. Nonetheless, the want in his eyes was unmistakable. "I might. It would depend on how grateful you were for it. Not the Exchequer, though. He's one of the locked ones. Pity, too. I bet he'd be interesting reading. Why you interested in him?"

Volle explained as briefly as possible his situation. Dereath's eyes glittered. "Ah, that Ullik. You can always check the books, you know. He'd have every entry in there labeled and dated. Every Lord is supposed to be able to see the account of his holdings, just not of any others."

"I might as well wait until I have my own proof now, in case he'd falsify a book or something."

"Oh, he wouldn't do that. He's—"

Welcis interrupted them. "Excuse me sir. Miss Llana Drosian." Behind him, a timid-looking coyote stepped into the room, wearing a blue lace-trimmed dress. She stood and looked at Volle, then at Dereath, then back at Volle.

"Good evening, Miss Drosian, and thank you for attending." Volle took her paw and bowed, touching his nose to it.

She giggled softly and curtsied. "My pleasure, sir."

They talked awkwardly for a few minutes, during which Volle learned that Llana was an assistant to the head of staff for the palace. When Lord Vanadi arrived, he greeted them all with a warm smile, and shook paws all around.

The dinner was as superb as all the others had been, the conversation somewhat less so. Volle found himself encouraging Lord Vanadi to talk, because Llana was too shy to do more than giggle, and Dereath kept talking directly to him. Not only did Volle generally want to discourage that, it excluded the others from the conversation. So his recollection of the dinner later was largely of Lord Vanadi saying things like:

"If you read the Books of Panbestia—and I mean all of them, not just the one of your House—you begin to see a pattern that really puts a new light on the actions we take every single day. Really, the other people we interact with are all parts of the same glorious whole, and when I really started to appreciate that was when I read the Books, with a group of youngsters of other species. We all grow up in our separate worlds, and that's a necessary stage, but if we're to mature into the holy beings that Gaia intends us to, we must at some point achieve an awareness of the other branches of the tree of life from which we came."

To which Volle usually nodded and smiled and ate another bite of food, ignoring Dereath's attempts to catch his eye.

Mercifully, the dinner came to an end, though Volle could have sworn it took twice as long as it had the previous night. Lord Vanadi said his goodbyes with the smile of the oblivious, and Llana followed him out. Volle waited for Dereath to follow them, but the rat shut the door, remaining inside.

"Good heavens, I thought they'd never go," he said. Volle could smell the wine on his breath and noted that he'd had several refills over the course of the dinner. "Hasn't that fox ever heard that too much of a good thing spoils it? Church is fine, once a week, but I certainly don't want it at the dinner table."

Though Volle agreed with him in principle, he didn't feel like discussing it. "You know, I do have to get up early for the tribunal tomorrow…"

"Oh, don't be a pill, Volle." Dereath seemed to savor the sound of his name. "Tribunal's not 'til the afternoon. You have plenty of time to go for a run with Lord Ikling and make it to the tribunal in time. I'm feeling a bit chilly. Where's the fireplace?"

He went back into the sitting room before Volle could stop him. Volle went after him, but he'd already made it into the bedroom. Volle found him in there, regarding the cold fireplace sadly. "I guess you've got thicker fur," he said, wrapping his arms around himself, though Volle thought the room was very comfortable. "There must be some way I can get warm in here."

Volle ignored the sly look and walked in, leaving the door open. "Listen, I really am tired."

"It's okay. We can lie down if you want." Dereath sat on the bed and lay back, letting his vest fall open. "Oh, don't look at me like that. You were interested enough in me earlier, when I was telling you things." His voice had a sad overtone to it.

"I appreciated the information, but really, it's been a long day."

Dereath shook his head. "You shouldn't lie to me, Volle. I know things. I know that you just went out and walked around town today."

Suddenly, Volle was seized with the fear that Dereath had seen him talking to Seir. "Oh? Where did I go, then?"

Dereath shrugged. "Out. No big deal. Get to know the town, it's a nice town." He smiled. "Or I could save you time. I can tell you all about it—where the good restaurants are, where the good plays are, even where you can get some good ass cheaper than at a brothel."

Volle sensed where that last comment was leading, and didn't take the bait. "I'd appreciate that, but maybe we should talk about it some other time."

"Oh, you're right. We shouldn't be talking now." He put a lazy emphasis on *talking*.

Volle rubbed the bridge of his muzzle. "Why are you still here?"

"I like you, Volle. And I thought you liked me. Isn't that why you invited me to dinner here?"

"No…I mean, yes, but…"

"Don't you like me?" He was staring straight at Volle.

"Look, that's not the issue. It's late, and…"

Dereath shook his head and got up. He walked over to Volle, who couldn't think of anything to do, even when the rat grabbed his shoulders and pressed his muzzle up to the fox's. The kiss was hard and rough, and not at all like the gentle sharing he'd had the previous night with Arrin. There was quite a bit of wine on Dereath's breath, but it didn't seem to be impairing his arousal, which was pressed squarely into Volle's leg. His thin paw rubbed Volle's sheath through his pants, then tried to slide down inside them.

The rubbing against his fur, the sour breath, and the clumsy groping were more than Volle could take. "No…NO!" He pushed Dereath away roughly and stood there panting, aware his tail was bristling. "What is wrong with you?"

Dereath didn't seem to have heard him. He had an odd smile on his muzzle. "Oh, you like it rough? That's okay, I do too." His pink tail was lashing behind him, and Volle could now smell his excitement even over the wine.

There was a cough, and Welcis stood at the door. "Sir? I was about to retire for the night." He glanced at Dereath and then back at Volle.

The rat spoke before Volle could. "Fine. Goodnight, Welcis."

"Sir?"

Volle looked at Dereath with what he hoped was a stern glare. He felt disgusted, but also felt sorry for the rat. Not sorry enough to let things progress any further, but at least he didn't want to be too cruel. "Yes, Welcis, I was going to retire as well. Mister Talison was just wishing me a good night. Would you be so kind as to see him out?"

Dereath glared at him with hurt and anger mingled. Welcis reached out to take his arm, but he shook off the skunk and stalked through the door. Volle heard him slam the parlor door behind himself on his way out.

He sagged against the wall. "Thank you, Welcis."

The skunk bowed. "It is a pleasure to be of service, sir. Good night." He retreated, closing the door, and Volle staggered to the bed and sank down on it without even bothering to remove his clothes. He wished he'd handled Dereath better, but he couldn't see how. Let him grope and kiss all he wanted? He would've just wanted more, and they'd have ended up naked on the bed, and just thinking of that made Volle's fur prickle again. The rat would have been a good ally, true, but certainly there were others Volle could befriend who wouldn't ask so high a price.

And maybe things would be okay with Dereath once he sobered up. Maybe he'd come and apologize for being so forward.

Volle sighed. "Right," he said aloud. "And maybe he'll just hand me a file with all the details of the secret plot I'm supposed to uncover." His lack of progress nagged at him, but in the interests of being an effective spy, he felt he had to devote some energy to fitting in to palace life, and that meant throwing dinner parties and serving on the tribunal, not sneaking around Lord Fardew's office.

He sighed, wishing Seir had stayed longer, and fell asleep without even undressing.

In the morning, once he'd recounted the events of the previous evening to Helfer, the weasel was more amused than sympathetic. "Dereath drunk and in your bedroom? Good Mustela, Volle, if you want to get into self-flagellation, use something less painful, like pulling your claws out. At least the little prick left when you told him to."

Volle rolled his eyes and nodded, keeping pace. "I'm a bit worried about making an enemy of him, given all the information he has access to."

"Oh, don't worry about him. He'll sulk for a while and get over it, then he'll be on to the next object of his desire."

"He still worries about you."

Helfer shrugged. "Nothing I can do about that. Anyway, let's talk about more pleasant things. Did you like the books?"

Volle grinned. "I found them very…inspiring."

"I thought you might. You can borrow more if you want."

"I think I'd rather head back to the Jackal's Staff."

Helfer flashed him a smile. "I don't think they have a fox working there."

"Doesn't matter, really. I kind of wanted to give that cougar a roll."

"Jonas? He's pretty cute, yeah. If you're going to be with him I might try Richy, since you gave him such high marks. That is, if there aren't any cute rabbits around. I keep telling Tally to hire one, but she says they're not in demand." He snorted. "Three wolves on staff and not a single rabbit."

Volle grinned. "Pity the world doesn't cater to your particular fetish, eh, pal? So when do you want to go?"

"Tonight's okay with me. You have money?"

Volle's ears fell. "I forgot about that. Let's wait a couple days. I should hear by then."

"All right. It's a bit soon for me to go again anyway. Not that I have to go with you, but it's more fun, eh?"

Volle nodded and patted Helfer on the shoulder. "I appreciate the company. And I guess it'll do me good to wait."

Helfer grinned widely. "I don't know about *that*."

After the run and a quick bath, Volle spent fifteen minutes searching for the tribunal room. He had been listening for the sound of arguments and discussion, but in the end, when he found the room, it was silent. The three Lords who made it up were seated behind the bench: a bear seemingly asleep with his head on his arms, a wolf leaning back staring at the ceiling, and an elderly raccoon who waved Volle over as he spotted him.

"Lord Vinton?" Volle nodded. "I'm Lord Creane. You'll be taking my place. This is Lord Oncit," he gestured to the wolf, "and the snorer there is Lord Boursin."

The wolf extended a lazy paw without otherwise moving. Volle thought he recognized him as one of the Lords who'd been at the table when he'd attended the luncheon, talking about 'Old Blood'n'Guts.' He shook the paw, and then shook Lord Creane's.

They sat all afternoon without hearing a single case. Lord Creane got some files of previous cases and went over them with Volle, who had the annoying feeling that he was back in the Academy studying. One would think, he reflected after about five indistinguishable cases had gone through his paws, that these matters and questions would at least be somewhat interesting. Sadly, people seemed inclined to complain and argue about the pettiest things, and his job apparently was to pretend he cared long enough to help make a decision.

"I've done this for twenty years," Lord Creane told him, "and I've finally had enough."

"Twenty years!" Volle shook his head. "I was bored after twenty minutes!"

"M'boy, you do occasionally get interesting ones in here, though most of the really juicy ones go to the King. You just have to wait out the interesting ones. Meanwhile, bring a book or a conversation. We ran out of things to talk about months ago."

Volle looked at Boursin, who had shifted to another position but was still snoring, and Oncit, who was now apparently counting the hairs on his paw. "I wouldn't count that your fault," he whispered.

Creane chuckled. "They're good folk, just quiet." He himself seemed delighted to have someone new to talk to, and much as Volle wanted to ask Lord Oncit about 'Old Blood'n'Guts,' he couldn't break away from Lord Creane's amiable chatter.

The afternoon finally ended, and Volle was able to escape back to his chambers. Welcis met him with a glass of wine, which he sipped gratefully.

"I believe I would like to eat alone tonight, Welcis," he sighed.

"As his lordship wishes. The tailor delivered the first of your lordship's clothes today, if you would care to see them."

"Oh, yes!" Volle sprang to his feet and followed Welcis into the sitting room. There he saw two pairs of smart yellow pants, one a pure yellow and the other more orangish. The tailor had also left three skirts, all emblazoned with the Vinton crest, and three shirts, two white and one a soft brown.

"Nice. I can still wear my doublet over these." He fingered the material admiringly.

"Yes, sir. The tailor wished me to tell you that the formal garments will be ready in two days, for your lordship's dinner with Lord Tistunish."

"Good F--Canis, I'd almost forgotten about that." He wondered if the vixen they'd found for him would be at all interesting.

"Yes, sir. In addition, the King has announced a banquet for junior nobles two weeks from tomorrow night."

"Do you think I have to dress formally for the dinner with Lord Tistunish?"

"I would recommend it, sir."

"Oh, all right." He grinned. "Maybe I will go eat dinner after all. I'd like to show off my new clothes."

"Indeed, sir."

Welcis helped him dress, and brushed his fur, and thus attired, he set off for the dining room.

He was disappointed to find neither Helfer nor Tish there. Lord Vanadi found him rather quickly, and though Volle was apprehensive at first, without the distraction of Dereath, he managed to have quite an interesting conversation about the differences between the Reformed Panbestian Church ("Well-meaning but trying too hard to please everyone," sniffed Lord Vanadi) and the Orthodox Church. He was aware, for example, that the Reformed Church did not lump the species into Houses, as the Orthodox did, but he wasn't aware that the Orthodox Church had not only a Gaiavox, but a Cantor for each House.

The dining hall was large and crowded, and so it wasn't until Volle had gotten up to leave that he noticed Ullik and his wife in another corner, laughing merrily with an ursine couple. He tried to leave quickly, but Lord Vanadi insisted on accompanying him and finishing their conversation, and he was sure Ullik had seen him by the time he left.

No harm done, though, he thought as he bid the grey fox good night and walked across the main hall towards his chambers. I just need to avoid him for another couple days...

The hall was deserted; everyone was at dinner, either in the dining room or in their chambers. He stopped when he heard footsteps and looked around, but there was nobody there. A bit more nervous, though he couldn't have said why, he hurried past the Lion Stair and toward the Wolf. Rounding the corner of the staircase, the sight of his corridor, with his rooms just a few yards away, helped him relax.

Silly, he thought. Who would be stalking you in the palace? But when he stepped into the corridor, a draft brought him the scent of dry dust and old ink, with a subtly unpleasant undertone, and he knew who was stalking him even before the weight slammed him into the wall and the voice hissed in his ear.

"Been avoiding me, little lord? Trying to shirk your duty?"

Muzzle pressed against the wall, Volle found it hard to talk, especially with Ullik's weight crushing his lungs. "Couple...days..." he coughed.

"Days," the squirrel snarled, and let him go. "You need to wait for your governor's word? You don't trust me? I think we should go to my office and make another deposit right now. Or maybe..." his eyes traveled thoughtfully along the corridor, "your rooms are closer." His paw gripped Volle's muzzle, forcing him to look the squirrel in the eyes. "We can get rid of your servant."

Volle wrested his muzzle free, repressing a snarl. "No, let's go to your office." Ullik's eyes brightened, then flashed suspiciously at Volle's agreeability. "Then you can show me the Vinton books."

Ullik folded his arms. "I think we should use your chambers."

His attitude now radiated muted anger, but also wariness. Volle was now sure he was right: Ullik had somehow heard about his dispatching a messenger to the governor and wanted to get in one last session before the official receipts returned and Volle could confirm his lie. He silently thanked Dereath for telling him about the books; the rat had probably saved him from another disgusting muzzleful.

"Once I see the books, we can come back down here," Volle said, crossing his arms over his chest to mimic Ullik's position.

The squirrel looked him up and down and then shrugged, with a crooked smile. "No need for that, Lord Vinton. I'll send down a report in the morning. It was fun while it lasted." He leered and then started to walk away.

"Hey!" Volle's claws were bared and he wanted nothing more than to rip long gashes in the squirrel's fancy clothes, if not his disgusting hide. He restrained himself, but Ullik, turning, could see his frustration.

"Yes?" The squirrel smirked at him, and Volle knew there was nothing he could do.

Volle stared at him for the space of half a dozen heartbeats, and then forced himself to relax. "If twenty years accumulated eight hundred gold pieces, and you'd forgiven me one year, shouldn't that be added to my account now?"

Ullik stared at him, and then burst into laughter. "You're a Lord after my own heart, Vinton. Forty gold for a little tongue action! My boy, you'd be the most expensive in Tephos—and I should know." He gave Volle a leering wink, and walked away, still laughing.

Volle sighed, entering his chambers. He had felt at the dinner like he was finally starting to fit in, to relax, and then the encounter with Ullik had tightened up his insides again. He dismissed Welcis for the night, stripped off his new clothes and hung them carefully in the wardrobe, then curled up in bed with "The Ringing of the Belle."

Kris's slender legs could not hold him upright before that sight; like a flower wilting before the sun, he dropped to his knees gently. His muzzle hung open as his cornflower-blue eyes traveled over the creamy white fur that highlighted each firm muscle, from the sculpted chest down to…down to…the enormous white ridge between his legs, above which the raccoon's staff waited, firm and ready, for whatever attention the petite wolf cared to bestow upon it…

Volle felt the warmth in his own staff, picturing the scene in his mind, and as his fingers traveled lightly along it, he let his mind wander to fantasies of Prince Gennic again. He was as muscular as the raccoon, and Volle could be the petite fox who was holding the prince's staff in his muzzle…and then being laid gently on his back as the prince's desire pressed into him, filling him with warmth and passion. *The raccoon's paw moved as smoothly as silk around Kris's arousal, each touch of pads against skin like a soft kiss, each one building upon the last, sending sensations through the young wolf's body that he had never before known.* Volle knew the sensations well, and knew exactly when to set the book aside, when his body would shiver and convulse and the familiar warmth between his legs would blossom outward to the rest of his body as his paw worked harder and his belly was *splashed with the warm fruits of his passion.*

He panted, and smiled, leaning back and setting the book aside before falling into a contented slumber.

He had to clean up early the next day, Gaiaday, to attend the Church services that the entire palace was expected at. They were held in the enormous cathedral, and people lined up outside to watch the lords go in.

The service was similar to what he was used to, except that the lords were seated by House, so he was separated from Helfer and ended up next to Lord Alister and two down from Lord Vanadi, who waved at him. Alister's tail kept distracting Volle by twitching throughout the service, brushing his leg as it did, so that what he remembered of it went something like: "O Gaia above, bless ye all the Children of Canis and keep them…" *twitch* "…and keep them safe and prosperous. O Gaia above, bless ye all the…" *twitch.* And so forth.

He found the differences interesting, but initially hard to follow, so he just stayed quiet when he couldn't figure out what to say, moving his muzzle and trusting his silence to be lost in the group noise. And he had to admit that the six-part hymn sung at the end of the service was more beautiful than anything he'd heard in a church in Ferrenis. The hymn was called "Dicit a vocibus omnis," but the people around him called it the "Our Mother," and told him when he asked that it closed every service

When he'd entered the church, he'd considered it part of his cover as a spy. He was Reformed and would stay Reformed. But talking to Vanadi and listening to the service, he began to see that many of the differences were largely cosmetic. He recognized half of the prayers and most of the hymns (save the last one). At first, he'd thought that keeping the Houses separate was too divisive, but at the end of the service the Cantor paired the Houses up, and each noble had to greet some of their counterparts in the other house. They were then called to stand wherever they were, and the six-part hymn that concluded the service was sung at that time.

"Go in the light of your spirits on the path of Gaia, and blessings run with you always," the Cantor concluded.

"May your path be smooth and true," the congregation responded, and then there was a general shaking of paws and patting of shoulders as they filed out of the cathedral.

As they were leaving, he found Helfer, and they arranged to change and take their run immediately. Volle beat him to the main gate by only a couple minutes, and as they started out, he told Helfer about his encounter with Ullik. "Good for you!" the weasel said. "So you have money now, eh? Up for a trip to the Jackal's Staff tonight?"

The fantasies of Prince Gennic superimposed on the memory of the cougar Jonas floated in Volle's mind. "You bet. You know, those books are good, but they're no substitute for the real thing."

"I know." Helfer chuckled as they climbed the wall. "But for a while they were all I had. My folks wouldn't let me go out alone until I was sixteen."

"Sixteen? When did you start reading those?"

The weasel grinned. "Um. I think I got my first one when I was nine."

Volle barked a laugh. "I don't think I was even interested in sex until I was twelve." And he hadn't done anything until fifteen, when he'd registered at the Academy and been surrounded by good-looking young males his age, away from his mother's watchful eye. There had been furtive orgasms under sheets after lights-out, sneaking through darkened hallways to make the midnight bed-check, various scent-maskers passed down by the older boys, to cover the scent of semen. And on weekends, there were plenty of older males waiting to offer mead or money to the adolescent cubs who filled the bars.

"Weasels mature faster than foxes. It's a known fact."

"Ha. Unfortunately, they also stop sooner." Volle reached down to pat Helfer's foot-and-a-half shorter head.

Helfer flashed him a look. "You think so? I could outrun you if I weren't holding back to let you keep up."

"Go for it," Volle said, and they both took off at top speed, heading back to the main gate. Helfer really was fast, and it was all Volle could do to keep up with him. He passed him briefly, but then Helfer sailed back into the lead and beat Volle back to the main gate by four or five seconds.

"There," he grinned, panting hard. "You foxes are supposed to be so fast."

"That's not always a good thing…" Volle said, collapsing next to him on the stairs and panting as well. It wasn't that good a joke, but it started them giggling, and their recent exertion made it hard to stop. A lord and lady bear, walking out, gave them a curious glance, and Renaldo, after helping the lord and lady into a carriage, looked at them disapprovingly, but they didn't care.

After they'd laughed themselves out and lain basking in the sun for a bit, the wind started to pick up, and they walked back inside the palace. Near the Wolf Stair, Helfer patted Volle on the shoulder. "Say, why don't you come to dinner tonight? I'll give you the official tour of my chambers."

"Sure." Volle smiled. "And we can head out after."

"Sounds good. See you around seven."

Volle waved as Helfer jogged across the main hall, then turned around the staircase and found himself face to face with Dereath. "You two are certainly getting very cosy," he said. His arms were folded across his black vest, and his expression carried anger, jealousy, hurt, and longing. His scent was more sour than Volle remembered it.

Volle shrugged. "We're friends," he said noncommittally.

Dereath just looked at him. "Well?"

"Well? Well what?"

Dereath sighed. "Are you going to apologize for the other night?"

"Apologize?" Volle stared at him. He honestly had no idea what could possibly be going through the rat's mind.

"Yes, apologize! You invited me to dinner, you invited me into your bedroom, you practically begged me to kiss you, and then you push me away and kick me out with barely a good night!" He gesticulated violently with his paws. "And then I wait a whole day for you to send an apology, and nothing. Nothing!"

Volle just stared, stunned. "Keep it down, will you?" he finally managed to say.

"What, am I embarrassing you?" Dereath practically shouted. He lowered his voice to say, "I thought you were nice, you know, not like that Ikling. But he's turned you against me, hasn't he?"

"Look!" Volle exploded. "Helfer has nothing to do with this. And I didn't invite you into my bedroom, you forced your way in there, and then tried to force yourself on me, and that's why I kicked you out. You were drunk."

"Oh, that's very convenient. I suppose you'll say that's why I don't remember it that way at all." Dereath glared at him icily.

"Either that or it's because you're completely insane." Volle tried to push past him to get to his corridor, but the rat blocked his way.

"Insane, am I? Wouldn't that be convenient for you? Saves you having to be considerate of anyone with your shameless flirting. Oh, don't think I don't know about you. Going out to the brothel, hitting on that fox in Alister's office, probably going to screw Ikling tonight. And I know about Ullik, too."

Volle stared at him. How could he know? Dereath's eyes widened and his expression became triumphant. "Ah-ha! I thought so. That old lech would take a blow job from anything on two legs—or four, if he could get it to hold still—and I thought he would've pressured you since you were new and all. And now I know." He clapped his paws and practically danced with glee. "Ah, I feel much better, Volle. This makes up for a lot. Thank you." Smiling sweetly and nastily at the same time, he slipped past Volle and up the stairs.

Volle sagged against the wall. He didn't know who Dereath would tell, and likely Dereath would time it to be the worst possible person at the worst possible time. But it wasn't all that bad a piece of information. Apparently Ullik had done the same before, and he'd been new and afraid. All in all, he thought things could be worse.

But he was definitely starting to hate that rat.

Chapter 8

He told Helfer about it over dinner, and the weasel nearly choked on a piece of cucumber. "Ullik? Oh, poor thing. I'm surprised you can still eat."

Volle sighed. "It was probably the worst thing I ever had to do. I mean, not harmful, just horrible."

"Yeah, I bet. Ugh." Helfer patted his paw sympathetically. "I can see why you wouldn't want that spread around, but really, most everyone knows what Ullik is like, including his wife. If it gets out, people might snicker for a bit, but most of them will be sympathetic. Believe me, Ullik will come off worse than you will."

"I don't know about that, if that's what everyone thinks he's like anyway."

Helfer shrugged. "I wouldn't worry about it. It was your first day. All the young lords have done stupid things. I got drunk at my first banquet and threw up on a footmarten."

Volle giggled. "Did you really?"

"I think so." Helfer grinned. "I sort of remember being at the table, and then everything went all spinny, and I grabbed at a uniform. The next thing I remember is the horrible smell and people pulling me off the poor thing. Then I think I passed out."

"I don't throw up when I drink," Volle mused. "Don't know why."

Helfer leaned across the table. "So...I really don't want you to have to relive it any more, but I have to ask. Is it as small as they say?"

Volle blinked at him. "Is what small?"

"You know. Ullik."

Volle grinned and held his thumb and forefinger an inch apart. Helfer howled with laughter. "There you go! If that story gets out, and people ask what it was like, you can just say 'stick your thumb in your muzzle and that's about the size of it.'"

They laughed over that for a while, and when he had calmed down a bit, Volle smiled. "Thanks, Helfer."

"Aw, what are friends for? And speaking of friends, my good friends call me Hef."

Volle grinned. "My good friends just call me Volle. Sorry."

"So how do you tell them apart from just your friends?"

"Well, the good ones make me laugh." He winked.

While Caresh cleaned up dinner, Helfer showed Volle his 'laying room.' "I got tired of cleaning the bedsheets," he explained, "so I set up this room to conduct my more, ahem, messy activities in." He plopped down on a couch and patted the seat next to him.

Volle grinned. "Not sure I should, in here."

"Piffle. I already told you, I don't ride mounts from the palace stables."

Volle sat down. The couch was certainly more comfortable than anything in his chambers, and he resolved to speak to Welcis about that. "So why did your bedsheets keep getting messy? Too much P. Zinsky?"

"That, plus I do have the occasional visitor." Helfer grinned, and kept going before Volle could ask any more. "Those chests have lots of fun stuff in them. You can go through them and borrow whatever you like. I keep the really private stuff elsewhere."

Volle eyed the small chests. "Maybe another time. I don't really have anyone to use them with now."

"Oh, there are things you can enjoy yourself," Helfer said. "Plus, you'll get that fox into bed eventually."

"Mm. Maybe." Volle thought about Arrin. He should invite him to dinner again. He added that to the list of things to discuss with Welcis.

"Anyway." Helfer pointed at the doors. "Private bath there, which you saw. And, by the way, you're welcome to use it if you need it. Wardrobe in that one. I've accumulated a lot of clothes." He grinned. "Bedroom behind the curtain there. My parents didn't like doors. I wanted one for my room when I lived there, but when I moved out here I decided I liked the curtains, so I left them."

"It's a nice effect." Volle smiled and looked around. "Feels very open."

They talked for a little while longer, and just when Volle was thinking that his meal felt pretty well digested, Helfer stood and stretched. "Ready to go?"

Volle grinned. "You read my mind." He stood, tail wagging, and followed Helfer out the door.

The street was less crowded than on their last visit. It was a bit earlier, at that crepuscular time between day and night; the nocturnals were just stirring and the last of the diurnals were winding down their day. Volle thought again about home as they walked. All the things that made Divalia different from Caril stood out in sharp relief to him: the grey of the palace walls, the absence of certain odors (the river had a very different smell), the presence of others (he'd identified one of the unfamiliar smells as the odor of one of the wood types that was used in the buildings here), and just the whole feel of things was somehow different.

When they walked into the Jackal's Staff and Tally greeted them each with a warm hug, the feelings diminished somewhat. Enclosed in this now-familiar environment, he could pretend that anything was outside. In here were lust and perfume and bright colors and soft music. It was its own little world, existing apart from the rest of his life. Fleetingly, he felt irritation that Seir would have to invade it.

Tally had dyed his ears blue this evening. They twitched as he put an arm around Volle. "Richy's available if you want him."

"Actually, I was wondering if Jonas is available."

"Jonas." Tally tapped his muzzle. "He should be in about fifteen minutes. What about you, darling?"

Helfer grinned. "I'll spend an hour with Richy."

"Don't tire him out now. He's got a whole night to work."

Helfer raised a paw. "I promise." His grin belied his promise, though.

Tally patted him on the back of the head. "I'll send Richy out, and Jonas when he's done. Have a drink, darling."

This last was to Volle, who nodded and poured himself some water. The raccoons were playing again, and though they weren't experts, the music was pleasant enough. It wasn't any tune Volle recognized, but then, he mostly just knew bar songs.

Richy emerged from the back a moment later and walked slinkily up to them in a tight green loincloth. His fur was just as clean and soft as it had been the other night, and once again the sight of the loincloth and the edges of white fur below it brought Volle's sheath to life. Now that he knew what lay under the loincloth, he was more aroused still, because the bit of white fur he could see showed lines that he could trace up along the sheath, and that brought back memories of the wolf sitting in his lap, arms and legs wrapped around him, tight rear warm around his hardness.

His muzzle was just as adorable, too, with soft grey ears and bright green eyes. He smiled at Volle. "So you're abandoning me?" He put on a mock pout.

"No, no," Volle grinned. "I just talked so much about you that my friend insisted on seeing for himself how lovely you are."

"Flatterer." But his ears went back and a smile curved further up his slender muzzle. Volle wished he could change his mind, go and take the wolf in his arms at that moment, but Helfer was already stepping forward and offering his paw courteously.

Richy took it, and led him to the back. Volle's sheath throbbed harder at the sight of the wolf's rear swaying back and forth and the tail swinging over it. He knew Richy knew he was watching him, and just as he ushered Helfer into the back, he turned and blew Volle a light kiss.

Volle sighed and drank his water. And next week he wouldn't even get to see Richy, because he'd be meeting Seir. He looked unenthusiastically ahead at the next two weeks. Mister P. Zinsky was going to get several reads, he thought.

He barely noticed the fifteen minutes going by. His mind floated along aimlessly from one memory to another, carried along by the music of the raccoons. The worries about Dereath and Ullik, the wondering about the dinner with Tish, the anxiety over a possible plot—all this faded away, and when Tally came over, he greeted him with a warm relaxed smile.

"Jonas is ready, darling. Room three."

"Right." He stood, but Tally was still standing there waiting, and it took him a moment to realize what for. "Oh. Sorry. How much?"

"Five, dear." It was the only time Volle had ever heard him speak quietly, and though he was still smiling, his eyes were all business.

Volle counted out five silver pieces from his purse and slipped them discreetly into Tally's paw. The white fingers closed around it and Tally purred and gave him a kiss on the cheek. "Enjoy, dear." And then he swept away to another customer, paws outstretched. Volle had no idea where he'd put the money.

He let himself in the back and found room three. It was very similar to the room he'd been in with Richy the last time, except that the bed was oriented differently. Stretched out on it was Jonas, naked, one paw draped over his long pink erection. He smiled as Volle came in.

"Close the door." His voice was a musical baritone, and Volle could hear the purr behind it. His yellow eyes traveled up and down Volle's form, while Volle waited. He wasn't sure why he was waiting, nor what for, but the echo of royalty in the panther commanded his respect. He looked at the lithe form stretched out on the bed, and his eyes were drawn to the long pink erection, more slender than Richy's, but with the characteristic feline ridges near the tip, almost like barbs on an arrow.

"Let's see you." The cougar moved one paw lazily toward Volle, up and down, while with the other, he stroked himself slowly.

Obediently, Volle lifted his shirt off, then undid his trousers and stepped out of them. He was breathing a bit more quickly and was not surprised to feel his arousal growing. Because of the royal family, cougars always held a sense of majesty for him, and the interest in him was very exciting. Jonas's scent was strongly feline, and though it wasn't quite the same as the royal family's, it was at least the same species, and in this situation Volle could easily pretend. The pretending, of course, made him much more submissive, but he enjoyed that as well—letting himself go at the whim of the beautiful creature on the bed.

"Rrr. Very nice." Volle's erection grew harder at this, and his tail wagged slowly. "Come here."

He followed the cougar's crooked finger to the bed, and onto it, scrambling up on his paws and knees. The scent was more powerful here, and if he glanced to the side, he could see the muscles rippling under the short tawny fur. A large, velvety paw stroked down his back, along his rear, up his thigh and hip to his chest, and then down to curl around his rock-hard member. "Oh, you like this, do you?"

He panted agreement. The paw stroked slowly. Volle's arms trembled on the bed. He saw movement, and turned his head slightly so he could see the cat reaching for a pawful of lubricant. With a low moan, he closed his eyes and lowered his head.

"That's a good fox," the cat purred, and Volle could almost hear the Prince's voice saying that. In his mind, Jonas became the prince, and it was Gennic's paw that rubbed gently under his tail, first with the back of the knuckle, just teasing the fur, and then with a soft pad slick with lubricant. The pressure on his tail hole reminded Volle how long it had been since he'd been mounted, and produced another moan from him. His tail arched high in anticipation.

He heard a low chuckle from the cat and a gentle nibble at his tail. "Patience, patience." The paw stroking him slowed its strokes so that they became light caresses, feeling and exploring every inch of him in detail. The paw cupped his hanging sac while the other continued to play under his tail, rubbing and probing, relaxing him.

Volle sighed, moaning again, and spread his legs a bit more. After long and gentle caresses, he felt the weight behind him shift on the bed, and the panther switched paws, bringing the slick one to his member. "Ready?" Volle nodded his head once, and felt a warm pressure under his tail. He lifted his head and moaned, pressing back into it, and the entry was tight and smooth as the cougar slid into him. On the thrust in, Volle barely felt the ridges on the cougar's length, but when Jonas pulled out, they plucked at his muscles, sending electric sparks of pleasure through him.

He shivered, gasping, and clenched his muzzle tight. It felt so good, and the cougar's muscular body atop him pushed him further into his fantasy. The prince's paw stroked him, the prince's maleness pressed all the way into him, the prince's hips pressed tight against his rear, and it was the prince's purr he heard with backswept ears and felt through his back. He felt as though he might burst from the dizzying sensations, but somehow he managed to hold himself back, to keep himself on the edge of orgasm.

Until the cougar's warm breath hissed in his ear, the paw stroking ever more insistently, and Volle felt the surge of pleasure explode through him. "Oh…oh…highness!" he cried, his whole body straining as it finally gave in to the sensations. He felt himself clench around the member inside him, heard the cougar's hiss of pleasure, and felt the spasms in his groin send warm splashes all over the stroking paw and the bed.

It lasted forever, and was over far too soon.

He lay on his side, panting. The prince was gone, and Jonas was cleaning him up. He looked with half-lidded eyes at the cougar's lithe form, and noticed his erection, still firm and full, and now clean of lubricant. He sniffed the air, and though his musk was thick in the air, he didn't smell any sign that the cougar had finished. Remembering that Richy also hadn't finished, he didn't say anything. He did, however, lean forward and lick gently at it when it came into view.

The cougar favored him with a smile, and kissed his muzzle. "What did you call me?" his baritone rumbled softly.

Volle's eyes widened slightly as he played back in his head the words he'd said. Oh, Fox, had he really said 'Highness'? "I…said 'Jonas.'"

The cougar shook his head. "That's not what I heard."

Volle gave a weak smile. "Well, I'm sure I said that. There was a lot going on. What did it sound like?"

"It sounded like…" Jonas considered, looking thoughtfully at Volle, and then smiled. "It's none of my business what your fantasies are. There, you're all clean."

Volle smiled and wagged his tail slowly, sitting up. "Mm. Thank you, Jonas."

"Thank you, sir."

Volle would have liked a bit of a cuddle, but the cougar was more aloof than Richy had been, and he couldn't work up the nerve. His fantasy of Prince Gennic was still fresh in his mind. "How did you know what to do?"

Jonas smiled and rubbed his chest with a paw. "When someone comes in and just stares, and waits for me to tell them what to do, it's not too hard to figure out. I was right, wasn't I?"

"Oh, yes." Volle panted for effect, and Jonas chuckled softly. "I'm glad."

Volle was enjoying the chest rubbing, and he returned it, rubbing his claws over Jonas's stomach and enjoying the resultant purr. After several relaxing minutes, Jonas was still showing no more interest in cuddling, and Volle's arm was getting tired. He knew he could ask for a cuddle, but that didn't seem as right with Jonas as it might with Richy; then again, Richy would have offered. So Volle just got up and stretched, enjoying what he imagined was the cougar's admiring gaze, and then slowly got dressed.

He turned to Jonas and smiled when he was done. "Thank you again, Jonas. Good night."

The cougar was lying back on the bed again. "Good night, sir. Please do come again." He had a small smile on his muzzle, and his overall impression was one of superior aloofness. Volle reflected that it suited him very well, and turned and left.

Once again, he had to wait for Helfer. He waved to Tally, and gave him another silver when he came over. Tally smiled, pocketed it in the same mysterious way, and, as the place was nearly empty, sat down beside him. "Liked Jonas, too?"

"Oh, yes." Volle sighed, and smiled. "Cougars just do something to me." He grinned, and Tally batted him softly on the nose.

"Oh, you cutey. Jones is a sweetie, but not to everyone's taste, and he and Richy are pretty different. You're a worldly fox of many tastes, dear."

"I suppose so," Volle chuckled. "Mostly I like wolves and big cats." Tally looked shrewdly at him. "Not foxes?"

"Oh, well, foxes too. I thought that went without saying."

The white cougar shook his head. "Not everyone likes their own species. Take your friend. Never been with a weasel, as far as I know."

"Really?" Volle rubbed his muzzle thoughtfully.

"Really, dear." Tally placed a paw over his on the table, and whispered confidentially, "I just wanted to let you know that we're all set up for next week. You and your friends won't be disturbed. And I don't want to know what you're doing in there!" He giggled. "All right, I admit it, I do. But what I wanted to ask is, will that be all, or will you want Richy to join you?"

"Not joining us," Volle said, "but maybe for after."

Tally's eyes widened. "So maybe foxes have more stamina than I'd thought." He held a paw to his muzzle and smiled. "You'll have him, too. Just pay when you come in, then, dear. Oh! Customers." Tally stood, and kissed his ear. "Good night, darling. See you soon." He swept off to greet the new arrivals.

Volle grinned, and listened to the raccoon combo. Sex usually relaxed him, and it was probably mostly that which gave him a comfortable, happy feeling. His homesickness had evaporated, and that was probably because he felt at home here. Tally's friendly, open manner made him feel like one of the family, and even Helfer's friendship and Welcis's precise dedication hadn't given him that feeling at the palace. He sighed and closed his eyes.

"There's an extra charge for sleeping." Helfer slipped into the chair beside him, a wide grin on his muzzle.

Volle grinned and sat up. "Want a drink, or are you ready to go?"

"Oh, let's go." Helfer left a silver piece on the table, calling Tally's attention to them before he followed Volle into the street.

Once outside, Helfer took a deep breath and stretched. "He's a nice bottom, that wolf. Warm and tight and small enough that I can hold him." His paws drew a vaguely wolf-shaped outline in the air. "I can see what you liked in him."

"Enough to compare with a rabbit?" Volle grinned.

"Well, no." Helfer chuckled. "Ears are too small, and he was panting pretty hard by the time I was done."

"Panting? What do you *do* to them?"

The weasel giggled softly. "It's not really the sort of thing one describes. Much more fun to show."

Volle smirked. "I thought you didn't ride from the palace stables."

"Well? Doesn't mean you can't watch."

They shared a laugh, and teased each other all the way back to the palace. There, they parted with pats on the back and "see you in the morning." Volle found when he got back to his chambers that Welcis was asleep, so he crawled into bed and followed suit.

In the morning, he mentioned the loveseat and the dinner with Arrin to Welcis, who promised to take care of both. The tailor had dropped off a formal suit, which reminded Volle that he had dinner with Tish, his wife, and some vixen the following evening, which reminded him that he had yet even to meet any of the three lords Tish had wanted him to ingratiate himself with. His memory had been trained well enough that he could remember all three names, but Tish hadn't told him who they were or what they looked like. And while he might've been able to ask Dereath a few days ago, that was out of the question now. So he would have to ask Tish when he saw him for dinner.

He ran with Helfer and then went to the lunch anyway, but the only lord there he recognized was Oncit, the wolf from the tribunal. He sat near him and tried to engage him in conversation, but with little success. Half-hoping to run into Seir again, he spent the afternoon wandering around the town, but apart from the fried pastry vendor, saw nobody he recognized. He returned for dinner, taking it in the common area, and this time he heard one of the names Tish had given him: "Ikinna."

He turned and saw a chubby weasel responding to the name. The weasel was slightly taller than Helfer, but also wider; he obviously didn't take a daily run. He had Helfer's energy, though, and showed it in his flamboyant gestures and incessantly tapping foot and wagging tail. He was sitting with four other lords who were all four or five years older than Volle was, and they were drinking plenty of mead. One was a wolf, one a badger, and the other two were bears.

Volle swiveled one ear to try to catch his conversation without being obvious about it. He only caught snatches here and there, but it appeared the group was talking about the Ermine Dancers, with Ikinna boasting that his wife could outdance any of them. Volle was rather amused that they were still talking about the dancers a week later, but then again, they were all much more excited by them than he'd been. He thought about going over and introducing himself, but the group reminded him of some of his groups of friends in the Academy. Nobody was more annoying or more quickly and firmly excluded from the group than the hanger-on who tried to push his way in. Better to find Ikinna and meet him one on one.

He was about to stop listening when he heard Ikinna say "Ryshko, you're an idiot." He turned again and saw that they were all laughing, but he couldn't tell which one was Ryshko. He finished his dinner, making absent conversation with the other lords at his table, and didn't realize until he was back in his chambers that he hadn't caught their names.

The next day, he asked Helfer about Ikinna, but Helfer didn't know him all that well. "His family and mine are from different areas," he said, "and he's five years older than I am, so we never played much growing up. I never did have any other weasel friends." He shrugged and smiled. "Didn't much miss it."

"Who were your friends?"

"I don't think you've met any of them," Helfer said. "Lord Black is one, he's a raccoon. We used to be best friends until he got interested in girls. And Lord Tallio's son, until he went off to the Winfield School. Other than that, I was always kind of a loner. What about you?"

Volle shrugged. "They're all far away now. Joey, another fox, was my best friend growing up. He got the plague and died. And probably my best friend lately was Reese. He's a hare."

"Ooh. Gay?"

Volle laughed. "Sadly, no. But maybe you'll get to meet him sometime anyway."

Helfer just licked his lips and kept running.

Preparing for the dinner that night was more of an ordeal than Volle had thought it would be. First, Welcis insisted he take a bath, a water bath, and then he had to brush out every inch of his fur, even the parts that Volle would have preferred to take care of himself. The skunk handled it very professionally, so Volle was thankfully able to keep from showing his usual reaction to being touched there. After the brushing, Welcis brought out a scented powder, more expensive than the common powder used in the baths, and brushed Volle lightly with it. It smelled of lavender, but the scent was so light that even Volle's sensitive nose had trouble detecting it further than a few inches away. The powder absorbed some of the moisture from his fur and neutralized most of the strong smell it gave off. It was considered impolite to conceal your scent, but foxes, mustelids, and other strong-smelling animals often muted theirs at formal occasions, out of consideration for others.

When he was dried and scented, Welcis helped him with his new formal clothes. Volle was glad of the help, because there were a few things he would definitely have put on incorrectly: the cravat, for one, which Welcis tied so deftly that Volle couldn't see how he'd done it, and the cloth belt for another, which apparently had to be tied particularly to one side and to the back, not the front. And then there was the lace collar, and the feathered cap ("which you must take off when you arrive," Welcis told him, and didn't reply when Volle asked "then why even put it on?"), and finally, Welcis deemed him ready.

He looked at himself in the mirror rather longer than necessary. The clothes not only looked very nice, but were also warm. Hopefully Tish wouldn't have a fire going. He steeled himself to meet his prospective wife, and followed Welcis to Tish's chambers.

Tish greeted him at the door with a formal grasp of his paw and touching of muzzles, then smiled and patted him on the back. "Come on in, boy! Everyone's here." Volle remembered to take off his hat as he entered the room.

Tish's chambers were laid out much like his. There was no foyer, as Helfer had, but the parlor was larger than either Helfer's or Volle's. Because it was on the third floor, the windows were also larger and both were open to let the cool fall air in.

It was the furnishings that really set the room apart. Tish and his wife had decorated with two elegant tapestries, both depicting heroic wolves in battle. Tish's desk was twice as large as Volle's and was in immaculate condition, as far as Volle could see under the papers that threatened to engulf it. Behind it, two large windows looked onto the rear gardens. Two plushly upholstered chairs and a loveseat faced the large fireplace, and behind them, against the wall, two simpler chairs were set around a small wooden table. The door to the sitting room was also ornate, of dark polished wood that Volle thought might be ebony. It was unadorned except for the golden handle.

The two ladies were standing between the loveseat and the door, the larger wolf in front of the vixen. "You remember my wife, Tika." Tika came forward and curtsied, and Volle kissed her paw.

"Of course." He smiled, and she returned the smile.

"And this is Ilyana," she said, stepping aside.

She was attractive, Volle had to admit. He stepped forward and took her paw as she bowed, brushing his muzzle across it. Her scent was muted, probably with a powder like the one he'd used, but he could tell it was rich and warm. It reminded him in vitality of the smell of the inns he'd stayed at on the plains, though he supposed she wouldn't appreciate that comparison. Lightly laid over it was a flowery scent he didn't quite recognize.

Her light purple dress went well with her reddish fur. She too had a lace collar, though hers was more elaborate than his and cut lower. The swell of her chest tapered to a narrow waist, defined by a dark purple cloth belt that rested on her wider hips. Her long tail was quite fluffy, and the white tip at the end was clean and bright.

She smiled and brought her paw to her muzzle, breathing in the scent he'd left on it. "Ilyana, this is Lord Vinton," Tika said belatedly.

"A pleasure to meet you," he said, straightening.

"The pleasure is mine." She had a high voice, but it was warm and soft.

Tish smiled. "Shall we sit down for a first round of wine?" He ushered his wife and the foxes into their sitting room.

The sitting room, also large, was divided in half by an archway. The half they entered initially was set up as a traditional sitting room, with two loveseats, four chairs, and four small tables. At the back of the room was a handsome cabinet that smelled of liquor.

To their right, through the archway, a six-person table had been set with silver place settings, two candlesticks, and linen napkins. A formally dressed raccoon stood at attention to one side, where a tray of platters rested. He pulled the chairs out for the ladies and arranged their napkins, and then poured a glass of wine for everyone.

"Thank you, Alcis," Tish said, and raised his goblet. "To our friends. Your very good health."

"And yours," Volle replied as he took a drink. The wine was excellent, full and smooth, with a rich taste that lingered on his tongue even after he swallowed. He caught Ilyana looking at him, and she smiled as she lowered her own goblet.

"So, Ilyana, why don't you tell Volle about your upbringing?" Tika prompted.

The vixen's ears swiveled demurely downward. "I was raised in lower Divalia by my parents, who are former nobility. I'm the youngest of five children, and I was schooled by a private tutor. My brothers and sister all have cubs already." She flicked her ears and smiled. "I've been studying with Madame Duschene for the last year, but I could leave whenever I need to. She says I'm ready to enter society."

"Madame Duschene is a friend of mine," Tika interjected. "She says Ilyana is head and shoulders above anyone else in her finishing school. She's planning to have a cotillion just as soon as her family can raise the money. Oh, I'm sorry, dear."

Ilyana waved a paw courteously, but her ears had folded back at the mention of money. They came back up quickly, so quickly that if Volle hadn't been watching her, he wouldn't have seen the motion. "And what about you, Lord Vinton?"

Volle was getting tired of reciting his childhood history, but he did it nonetheless. If he hadn't known it before, he certainly did now, and the biggest challenge was refraining from embellishing the story. It had to remain consistent, not only in case people he told it to talked between themselves, but also so that he wouldn't have to keep track of what details he'd told to whom.

Ilyana looked genuinely thrilled at the story. "Imagine!" she said. "A farmboy who discovers he's nobility! Oh, it's like a fairy tale."

"I suppose so," Volle said. "I really hadn't thought of it that way. It's not like I'm king or anything."

Tish and his wife chuckled, and Ilyana lowered her eyes with a smile. "It's still wonderful. You must be so thrilled."

"It's certainly been a wonderful experience so far," Volle said sincerely as Alcis served the appetizers.

Ilyana seemed to take the comment personally, and smiled more widely. She ate delicately, as did Tika, while Tish was less graceful. Volle wasn't sure whether to emulate the more graceful ladies or the other male, and in the end he struck a middle ground, taking small bites but using his paws as Tish was doing.

Tika took over the conversation during the meal, talking about the palace gossip, which mostly consisted of who was sleeping with whom. Tish met most of the tidbits with a chuckle, or a short comment like "didn't know old Villutian still had that much energy."

Volle merely listened, fascinated that this much fooling around went on, even in a palace of this size with fifty or sixty nobles and their families under its roof. The nobility's focus on procreation was evident in Tika's stories; most of them were inter-species relationships that were considered 'dalliances' and weren't serious. Volle gathered that they might even take place with the blessing, or at least knowledge, of the other spouse in some cases.

Adultery with a member of the same species, however, was much more serious, and the one example Tika had was revealed last, over dessert, and in hushed tones. "Lady Barclaw told me that he saw Lady Oncit coming out of Lord Deverin's quarters, and he said that her fur bushed up when she saw him, and she went very quickly in the other direction." Volle was confused momentarily by the pronouns until he remembered that 'Lady' Barclaw was the male mate of Lord Barclaw.

Tish grunted, losing his good humor. "Deverin better watch himself. Oncit's only got one cub. He could mess up the family line."

"I know, that's what I told Farris when he told me, and he said that *he* heard that Lord Oncit hasn't exactly been trying lately, if you know what I mean."

Volle glanced at Ilyana, but he couldn't tell whether she was really listening. Her ears were down and she appeared to be concentrating on her plate, smiling very slightly. Perhaps it wasn't proper for her to listen to or comment on this sort of thing. "Lord Oncit's on the tribunal with me," he said.

"Oh?" Tish looked up at him. "Talk to him much?"

Volle shook his head. "Lord Creane kept me busy. I tried to talk to Lord Oncit at lunch, but he didn't seem very talkative."

"He isn't, but he's a good wolf. Wonder if something's bothering him." Tish tapped the table thoughtfully.

"Well, anyway," Tika said, "are we all finished?" Seeing the nods, she rose first, signaling Ilyana to rise with her, and Tish and Volle followed them through the archway into the sitting room. The females went into the parlor, but Tish waved Volle to a seat while he went to the cabinet in the back. He returned with two small glasses of a light amber-colored liquid.

"Finest port in Tistunish," he said, handing a glass to Volle.

Volle eyed the liquid dubiously. He hadn't had port since his first year in the Academy, but he remembered the sweet taste that he'd quickly tired of. He sniffed its strong sweet scent and coughed.

"Don't stick your nose in it, boy! Just sip it." Tish sat down and sipped at his own. "So what did you think of Ilyana?"

Volle shrugged. "She seems okay. I didn't talk to her much."

"You'll get to talk more when you take her home."

"What?"

"It's late. It's the gentlemanly thing to do. You don't expect her to ride home alone, do you?"

"Never really thought of it." Volle took a sip of his port and swallowed. It burned his tongue and nostrils, but only slightly, and the sweetness complimented the flavor rather than overwhelming it. Perhaps he should have invested in better port at the Academy.

"Well, that's why Tika and I set this up." He chuckled. "You're still bound to be a bit rough around the edges, but Ilyana's no farm girl, you know. She's a genteel vixen of good breeding, and she's accustomed to courtesy and decorum. Speaking of which, if you do take a fancy to her, it would be nice to offer to sponsor her cotillion."

Volle looked narrowly at the wolf. "How much would that cost?"

"Oh, don't worry about the cost, boy. A few dozen gold, and Tika and I will chip in, of course. But it would be a nice gesture and it would ensure that you get her undivided attention all night."

"Can I bring a date?" Volle asked wryly.

Tish laughed. "This is all business, my dear fox. Appearances. If you like her, we'll do another dinner again in a couple weeks, and then you can start seeing her on your own. Oh, come now," he said, seeing Volle's expression. "She's pretty, and she likes you."

"How can you tell?"

"She kept looking at you all night, and if you'd looked at her, you would have noticed it too." He sighed and chuckled. "Can't see how you can ignore a pretty chest—er, muzzle—like that."

Volle laughed. "Depends what you're looking for, I suppose." He suddenly wondered if the ladies could hear them in the other room. He swiveled an ear, but couldn't hear anything, and upon turning, he discovered that the door had been closed.

Tish followed his look. "They're chatting on their own and leaving us to do the same. We're supposed to be talking about politics and they're supposed to be talking about us."

"Speaking of which, I saw Lord Ikinna in the dining hall, but didn't talk to him. Ryshko was with him, but I couldn't tell which he is."

"Wolf. And Whassel's a beaver. He's easy to pick out; there are only two of them, and he's the one with gold-plated teeth. Keeps to himself a lot of the time, though, so I doubt you'll see him in the dining halls."

Volle nodded. "Can I ask you something?" Tish nodded. "You said something about the later kings using Bucher's gold. What did you mean?"

The wolf settled back in his chair and took a sip of port. "Let me see if I can explain it better. From what I told you about Bucher, and what you know, you might regard him as evil. And you might regard Halloran as good. Barris I think you don't know enough about yet. Nor do many of us." He brushed his whiskers with a finger. "At any rate. The gold that Bucher collected was not collected by beating peasants or raising taxes or killing rich nobles and appropriating their holdings. It was collected as the natural result of a time when the kingdom was larger and more prosperous than ever before. As time passes, more and more people remember that prosperity as a golden age—never mind that it was built on the blood of our neighbors and our children.

"Similarly, there is nothing good or graceful about his prison. It was adorned with reliefs of his victories, but I believe I told you that those are gone. It is a horrible place of pain and despair, and why do you think it is still standing?" Volle shook his head. "It is still standing because no matter how good the king, there are still people he wants to lock up, criminals or traitors or dissidents, and Bucher's prison is a convenient place for people to be locked up.

"His shadow is fading, but it still stretches over the land. Some remember him as an evil tyrant; some remember him as a near-holy leader. Admittedly there are fewer of the latter. But he was neither. He was only a fox, a creature of Gaia as surely as the rest of us, and so are all the kings. And I believe that the good that came of his reign—the gold and prosperity—is intertwined with the bad—the prison—and the succeeding kings realized this. Perhaps not consciously, but they knew that everything he left would be of use, and it comes to the same thing.

"Now, I am not trying to defend the things Bucher did, because some of them were truly horrible, and a violation of the contract between a king and his people. Was Halloran a better king than Bucher? By most standards, yes. But he also had good advisors. About Barris, I am not so sure. And my point, I think, was this: that in every king there exists the potential to be good or bad, peaceful or warlike. He is influenced not only by the temperament his ancestors bestowed upon him, but also by the advisors around him and also to a degree by the wishes of the people."

"So what can we do?" Volle asked. "I mean, I'm not one of his advisors."

"We can suggest and advise. I am close to Alacris, the king's closest advisor, and I can give him some ideas, but not all my ideas are popular. I would like to see us at peace. Some would like to see us at war. The king, predictably for a bear, is riding the middle course, unwilling to commit to a war, but also afraid to back down completely to peace. But lately, lately…" He sighed. "If I didn't know there was a group devoted to bringing us back to war, I would have guessed it. And some of the things Alacris has told me he's heard from the king indicate that they are as active as we are, if not more. But we don't know who all of them are, nor who their conduit to the king is."

"There can't be that many with close access to the king," Volle said.

Tish shrugged and counted on his paw. "Barclaw, Villutian, Quirn, and Wallen among the landholders, Fardew, Alister, and Prewitt among the landless. It would help us to know whom, but there's another matter. They've been quiet lately, at least given what Alacris tells me, and Lord Dewanne is worried about that. He thinks that they may have given up on convincing the king to go to war and are trying to bring it about themselves. But as he's back from vacation now, I'll let him talk to you about that."

"Dewanne." Volle tried to remember where he'd heard the name.

"He's the other fox in the peerage. And he's the one who found you, by the way."

The door creaked open then, and Tika poked her muzzle through. "Are you boys done? Ilyana needs to be home before ten, and it's a half hour ride back."

Tish waved to her. "Yes, just wrapping up."

"How did he find me?" Volle said as they got up.

Tish looked at him with some surprise. "He's the one who hired Derrik. Dewanne wanted to restore a fox noble to the peerage, so he sent a couple mercenaries out to Vinton and Merinland and a couple other places the last Lord Vinton had been, to see if he could find any children the Lord might have left behind. And Derrik found you in Merinland."

"Oh, right. Derrik. Um, he just mentioned he'd been hired, but didn't say by whom. I thought it was you since you wrote the letter."

"No, no. Dewanne is just attaining mid-ranking in the peerage. He needed a letter from someone higher up so there wouldn't be lots of questions. Derrik told us about your loyalties and I wrote the letter based on that." The wolf's eyes met his, bushy eyebrows lowered. "And don't think I haven't been double-checking his work."

Volle's ears flicked. "I hope I passed."

Tish clapped him on the back. "I'm reserving judgment on that, but I certainly approve of your character, m'boy."

"Thanks." Volle's tail was wagging slowly as they entered the parlor.

Ilyana stood next to Tika by the door, talking in low tones. They looked up and smiled, Tika broadly, Ilyana demurely. They didn't say anything, and neither did Volle until Tish elbowed him, hard.

"Ow. Oh. Ilyana, might I have the pleasure of escorting you home?"

"That would be lovely, Lord Vinton, thank you." Her smile grew a little wider.

"Alcis has gone to fetch a carriage from the palace stables," Tika said. "It should be waiting at the main gate."

"Thank you very much for the meal," Ilyana said, curtsying.

"Yes, thank you both." Volle shook Tish's paw, and the wolf smiled at him.

"Remember, my boy…duty." He grinned. "I'll see you soon."

Volle nodded and embraced Tika as well, then walked Ilyana down the stairs to the main gate. She didn't speak the whole way, and so he didn't either, but when they reached the main gate and saw a fancy carriage waiting there, with Alcis holding the door open, Volle said, "That's a nice carriage. I didn't know we could do that."

Ilyana smiled. "Do what?"

"Oh, take a carriage from the palace. I've just walked everywhere."

"Lords shouldn't have to walk." She stepped delicately up into the carriage, holding his paw as she did. "But it shows independence and resourcefulness."

He paused in the midst of getting into the carriage. "Oh, Alcis, I, uh...where are we going?" he asked Ilyana.

"I have the address, sir," Alcis said before Ilyana could respond.

"Oh, good. Thank you." He seated himself across from her, and Alcis closed the door of the carriage. A moment later, he slapped the side of the carriage, and they were off.

Ilyana produced her certificate and handed it to Volle. He rummaged for his and found it just as they arrived at the front gate, where the guard opened the door. Volle handed the certificates out, and the guard looked them over, then handed Volle's back. "Hope you enjoyed your visit, ma'am," he said, bowing to Ilyana as he closed the door.

"I did," she murmured, and smiled at Volle. The carriage drove out of the gates and clattered onto the street.

Volle had to raise his voice to match the street noise. "I'm glad," he said. "I'm sorry if I wasn't a good host, or guest. I don't really know how to behave at these things." He half-lowered his ears and smiled apologetically.

She grinned back. "It's okay. You're cute." Her fingers had been resting on her lace collar, and now she tugged at it. "I'm sorry, but I really must get this off. It's been itching all night. Do you mind?"

"Er...no."

A moment later, the collar was sitting on the seat beside her, and the dress was slightly less modest. Ilyana brushed the fur with her fingertips and sighed. "Much better. I do deplore some of the constraints of fashion."

"Oh, uh, me too." Volle tugged awkwardly at his lace collar, but couldn't figure out how to get it off. It wasn't that itchy, but he felt as though he shouldn't be more formal than she was.

"Here, let me help you." She leaned forward and deftly unfastened his collar. Her fingers were slender and quick, and her scent was a little richer. He could smell some excitement on her, and realized two things at the same time: first, that she was lingering over the collar so he could smell her, and second, that she could undoubtedly smell the lack of excitement in him. His ears flattened as she sat back.

"What's the matter?" Her soft smile suggested that she knew already.

"Oh. Just...I never had a beautiful vixen undress me in a carriage before." He smiled, hoping humor would help.

Her ears flicked down and back up. "Why, thank you, Lord Vinton. Yes, I know, Tika told me about your preferences."

Volle blinked. "She did?"

"Yes, and don't worry. I wouldn't be very demanding. Just, you know, one or two times. Whatever it takes to have a cub or two." Volle gaped. "I'm not looking for romance. To be honest, I think I'd much rather be secure."

"Secure?"

She was relaxing more now, tail spread comfortably across her lap. "Yes, secure. The mother of a future noble, wife of a noble. I don't know about living in Vinton, but I'd be happy with my own apartments at the palace. Really, it's not that uncommon an arrangement."

He shook his head. "I know, but…it just seems strange to be planning it in advance."

"Why? Isn't it better for both of us to know what we're getting into?"

He chuckled, still discomfited. "You know, you're a lot different than you were at dinner."

"I believe in being honest first, and then courteous. Tika said you'd be pleased by that, and that I didn't want close ties."

He couldn't keep the grin off his muzzle when she said 'ties,' and she did have the grace to lower her ears and smile back. "I do appreciate it," he said. "I'm just a little startled by it."

"I wouldn't have thought you'd have time to get used to all the protocol and court customs."

He shrugged. "I was told you were decorous and that I had to be polite."

She laughed softly. "I am when I have to be. In this case, I thought it would be better just to clear the air. We'll still have to do the traditional 'courtship' for a little while, but I don't see much other reason to wait. If you find me acceptable."

Volle left the last question unanswered. "How long?"

She smiled, and counted on her fingers. "It's another month and a half to my season, about, so it would be good to be official by then. If I have my cotillion in a month, that would work well. We could dance there and then it would be all proper. A vixen in season shouldn't be with anyone who doesn't intend to marry her. Well, she shouldn't be anytime, but especially not when she's in season."

Volle knew about vixens being in season, but hadn't had to worry about it much in the past. He viewed it as a delicate subject, and the mention made him slightly uncomfortable. "Oh. I can help you pay for the cotillion. I mean, sponsor it."

"Oh, would you? That would be so delightful." She brightened, and he reflected that she was really pretty.

"Can I ask something? I mean, since we're being personal and all." She nodded, the smile fading slightly. "How is it you're not engaged yet? I mean, you're beautiful, really, and I'm surprised you haven't found a fox yet."

The smile returned, but her eyes had a trace of sadness. "Thank you, again, Lord Vinton. But I'm the fifth child, and my family wasn't rich to begin with. I only have one brother and three sisters, and my parents have no more dowry."

"Dowry?" Volle remembered Seir mentioning something about that, but couldn't recall what it was.

"The bridal gift from the family to the groom. Oh, I suppose as a farmer you never worried much about that."

Volle shook his head. "When a couple wants to get married, both families sponsor the wedding and help the couple get started."

"But isn't the male the main worker in the family? That's why he receives the gift, for taking the responsibility of the female."

"No, the females work alongside the males when they aren't tending children." It was that way all over Ferrenis, but he didn't want to start an argument about different customs.

"Amongst the noble families the dowry is important. If a lady does not have a dowry, she must either marry below herself or find a noble who does not need the dowry—a landholder. Florina, who was born a year before I was, married a woodworker, and we help them where we can, but they live in poverty. The cub runs around naked, and Florina is reduced to wearing the simplest of garments. I swore I would not let my cubs be brought up like that. Only," she sighed, "that meant I needed to find a rich, noble fox to marry. And those aren't exactly common." She smiled at him. "I'm surprised you haven't been besieged by scores of vixens wanting to be Lady Vinton."

"It's only been a week," Volle said. "Give it time."

He liked her laugh; it was light and joyful. "I do hope you'll give them even less consideration than you normally would."

He grinned. "I wouldn't dream of dating one that hadn't been approved by Tika. She'd chew my ear off."

"I think she would, at that. If it were left on when she'd done talking."

"She certainly had a lot of news to share."

"Mm. Life at the palace seems very sordid. I'm quite looking forward to it. I mean, that is…I'd like to be a part of it." She lowered her ears at her boldness, glancing at him.

This time, he felt he had to make an answer. He wasn't quite willing to commit, but he honestly couldn't see anything wrong with her. "We'll see how it goes," he said. "But I feel good about your chances so far."

"Thank you, Lord Vinton."

"Please, call me Volle. If it's proper."

"Technically, I shouldn't until we've seen each other two more times. But I believe I can make an exception." She smiled. "Ah, here we are."

The carriage stopped outside a large brick building, and a moment later the driver opened the door. Ilyana looked at Volle expectantly, so he got out and helped her down.

"Thank you for the evening, Lord Vinton." She curtsied to him.

He took her paw and brushed his muzzle to it gently. "My pleasure, Ilyana. Good night."

He waited until she was safely inside the house, and then climbed back in the carriage to head back to the palace. Her scent was still in the carriage, and he thought that this arrangement might not be bad after all. Tika had found a vixen who just wanted to have noble cubs, not a noble attentive husband. Surely he could manage one or two nights with a vixen. He'd never really wanted to have cubs, but that would be okay, because she'd raise them, and then there would be cubs to carry on his line when...

But he wasn't noble.

He'd been so immersed in the part that it was easy to forget that he couldn't have cubs with this vixen. It was likely that one day, he would be discovered, and then his title would be forfeit. That was fine for him; it had never been his to begin with. But what would happen to Ilyana and their future cubs if he were found out? Their lives could be ruined. They could be thrown out onto the street. He couldn't let that happen.

He couldn't reject her immediately, either; Tika would just find another vixen, and another. He supposed that in time he could run through all the ones she knew, but he preferred to put that off as long as possible. She wouldn't stop until she'd found him a mate, he was quite sure of that. So, he concluded, he would have to play along for a while with Ilyana, maybe even pay for the cotillion, and then find a reason to break off the engagement. It bothered him, but the only alternative was to tell her the truth, and he couldn't see any way to do that.

He told Helfer about the date the next day, of course, and to his surprise the weasel was encouraging. "Sounds like a good situation. She sounds pretty and honest. Rare combination. You should go for it."

Volle grinned. "What about you? Going to carry on the Ikling name?"

"Eventually. There are a couple ladies back home that Burren keeps trying to get me to marry. I told them that the first one to have a cub will be my wife, so the race is on."

"But you said you only go home once a year."

"That's partly why."

"So you actually sleep with them?"

"They sleep somewhere else, but I do the deed, yes."

"Do they interest you at all? I mean, for me, there's nothing." Helfer shook his head. "So how do you manage?"

The weasel grinned. "I get drunk and then I mount 'em from behind."

"Does that work?"

"I guess so. No cubs yet, so hard to tell. I come, if that's what you're asking."

Volle grinned and shrugged. "Not really. Just curious."

"It's not that bad, really. Couple bottles of mead, and maybe stick something in your nose to mask the scent—they can get pretty strong in bed—and you won't be able to tell the difference between her butt and what's his name's, Arrin's."

"Haven't seen his yet. I'll see him for dinner tonight, though. I got some flowers for him."

"Oh, yeah, the romantic one. Careful, they always want attachments."

"I'm not sure that's not what I want."

"Better you than me, foxy boy."

Volle grinned. "Someday maybe you'll want to settle down too."

Helfer just snorted.

Chapter 9

When he returned to his chambers after a bath, Volle found a
sealed message from Anton waiting for him. It included receipts for all
the taxes Vinton had paid for the last twenty years, scrupulously up to
date. It also included a note from Ullik dated twenty years before stat-
ing that the Vinton income would be held in the palace treasury until a
new lord came forward to claim the title. The figure Ullik had written
for the yearly income was one hundred and six gold. Volle multiplied
that by twenty in his head and found that he had to sit down.

While he was still trying to absorb the size of that credit, he noticed
another note from Anton. It bore two more items for him to present
to the king, which reminded him that he hadn't presented the other
items yet. And today was Ursiday; the king would be hearing this afternoon—meaning now.

Tish had told him at the banquet that he needed to be dressed at
least semi-formally to petition the king. With Welcis's help, he put together a nice-looking outfit in red with yellow trim and set off for the
audience hall.

The king was hearing the petition of a bobcat noble whose name
Volle didn't catch, but there were no other nobles waiting. His stomach
reminded him that they were probably all at lunch.

After some fifteen minutes of discussion, the bobcat bowed and
left, and Volle walked up to the king.

"Lord Vinton." His voice was a low bass rumble, befitting his stat-
ure and size. Though he was stocky, he was not as overweight as some
of his nobles, and Volle thought he could see the lines of some muscle
in the king's arms and legs. He wore a deep purple robe and wore a
simple gold circlet on his head. Below the thick eye ridge, his eyes were
dark, alert, and intelligent.

"King Barris." He knelt and touched his muzzle to the king's paw,
as etiquette demanded.

"Delighted to see you in the palace. How may we be of service to
you?"

"Your Majesty, there are several requests the people of Vinton have
made for royal assistance with their lands. We have paid our taxes du-
tifully these twenty years and although they are a proud and capable
people, some things remain beyond their power."

"Show us the list." Volle handed the king the two lists he had; they
disappeared into the bear's enormous paw. He spent a few minutes
reading and considering each item.

"Hmm. Except for the dispute with the mead merchants, these are
all easily remedied. I will remand the dispute to your care. See Lord

Black about them; they come from his province. If the two of you cannot work out an agreement, return to me."

"Your Majesty is too kind," Volle murmured.

"We thank you for your estimation, Lord Vinton." He sounded amused. "Welcome, again, to Divalia, and may you continue to serve your people for many years, and your cubs after you."

Cubs again, Volle thought. "May your Majesty reign for ever," he said ritually, bowed, and departed.

Arrin greeted him for dinner that night with a worried expression. "I need to ask you about something. You know that rat in Lord Fardew's office?"

Volle sighed. He'd almost let Dereath slip his mind. "Yes. Why?"

"Well, he said the oddest thing to me the other day. He asked me if I tasted Lord Ullik when I kissed you. I asked him what that meant and he laughed and said I should ask you."

"Come on in and sit down." Welcis poured them both glasses of wine, and Volle waited until the skunk had left the room before answering. "It was my first day here, and Ullik scared me by telling me I didn't have any money and he would kick me out of the palace if I didn't do something." He shrugged. "It was unpleasant, but I didn't want to get kicked out. I didn't really know any better."

"Oh, you poor thing." Arrin patted his knee. "Was it really that bad?"

"Oh, he smells awful." Volle made a face. "But at least it was over quick."

Arrin giggled, and then, with an inquiring look at Volle, held his paws apart about six inches. Volle grinned and pushed them four inches closer together, and Arrin put his paws to his muzzle, stifling more giggles. "Oh, dear."

"Let's eat," Volle grinned. "If you still have an appetite after that story."

"I think I can manage." Arrin took his paw and walked with him into the sitting room.

During dinner, Arrin asked him what he'd been doing, and he mentioned the dinner with Tish almost without thinking about it. Then, under Arrin's questions, he had to tell him about Ilyana. He was afraid the fox would be jealous, but to his surprise, Arrin smiled and nodded enthusiastically. "You should definitely marry her. She sounds perfect."

"You wouldn't mind? I mean, wouldn't that interfere with the romance and all?"

"Not really. I know you have to get married and have cubs before you can think about mating for your own pleasure." He grinned, less shyly than usual.

Volle didn't return the grin immediately. "What if I didn't get married?"

"What do you mean? You have to."

"What if it doesn't work out? What if I don't think she'd be a good mother, or something?"

Arrin laid his fork down. "Volle, you can't avoid marriage just because you don't want to…you know…with a vixen. It's not that bad."

"It's not that," Volle retorted.

"Then what?"

"I just don't know." He really didn't. He couldn't think of what to say that would convince Arrin.

Fortunately, Arrin thought he knew what the problem was. "Aww, if you don't think you're ready for cubs…is that it? Trust me, she'd do most of the work."

Volle ran with that. "Yeah, but it's bringing another life into the world."

"You're going to have to do it sooner or later."

He didn't respond to that, and hoped Arrin would think he was just thinking it over. The other fox obliged him by changing the subject.

By the time they were relaxing after dinner, the subject was forgotten. Welcis hadn't procured a loveseat yet, so he and Arrin reprised their kiss by the door, taking longer about it this time. He moved his paws down Arrin's sides, noting a bit of plumpness, and rested them on the fox's hips. After some hesitation, Arrin's paws mimicked the movement of his. They kissed like that for a good long time, tongues curling around each other and exploring the two muzzles, noses flared to the scent of the other, whiskers twitching and brushing.

Hesitantly, Volle let his paw slide down to Arrin's rear, and though the other fox didn't object, he also didn't move his own paws. Volle's fingertips brushed his tail, first atop, then underneath, and it was then that Arrin drew back gently. Volle could smell his arousal and feel it against him, but the other fox just smiled and said, "I should go. But oh…maybe next time I'll stay longer." He licked Volle's nose, and Volle licked back, smiling.

"Good night, Volle."

"Good night—oh, wait!" Volle smacked his head.

"What's the matter?"

"Stay here." Volle ran back into the bedroom and came out with a bouquet of yellow roses. He handed them to Arrin. "I got these for you, and then when you came in asking about Ullik, I forgot all about them. I'm so sorry."

"For me?" Arrin took the flowers and held them wonderingly. He brushed his nose across them and smiled. "That's the sweetest thing." He gave Volle another warm kiss, tail wagging rapidly. "I don't know if I have anywhere to keep them. Oh, I'll keep them on my table." He smiled. "This is really wonderful. Thank you so much."

"You're welcome." Volle couldn't help his smile; the fox's joy was infectious. He found himself hoping he could make Arrin's tail wag like that many more times. One fox at a time, he thought as the door closed, and headed for his bedroom and the book on the side table, aiming to make at least his own tail wag.

After the requisite teasing by Helfer the next day ("flowers? roses?"), he walked around the town again. When he passed a little odds and ends shop that had a small brass trumpet in it, he thought of Arrin and bought it for five copper pieces.

That afternoon, Tish summoned him to a meeting room where he met Lord Dewanne and Lord Ryngs, a raccoon. Both were on the portly side, though Ryngs had a stockier build and wore the weight better. Dewanne was a middle-aged fox who had a notch out of one ear and a perpetually bored expression. He kept his ears and tail well under control, but Volle could see small twitches that betrayed his alertness and interest in what was going on around him. Ryngs, a slightly younger raccoon, was less serious than the other two and kept interjecting jokes into the conversation.

"There are a couple more who think the same way we do, but we are the main ones," Tish said. "A couple years ago, we realized that we all more than anything wanted this country to be at peace."

"We are aware of the benefits of war, but also of the risks. The last time war was undertaken it was disastrous." Dewanne spoke slowly, in a deep voice that held Volle's attention. "We don't wish a repeat of Bucher."

"I told him about our history," Tish said. "He agrees that peace is the best road to prosperity, and has agreed to help us."

"Of course, the road to prosperity is paved with bad intentions," Ryngs put in.

"Be that as it may," Tish acknowledged the comment with a grin, "it is our goal. We don't meet often, but we felt we should introduce ourselves."

"I am pleased to meet you," Volle said. "I can't help but wonder, though, why do some want to risk war again? I would think they would have learned their lessons."

"Some never do," Dewanne said. "Some are mostly interested in their own short-term gain, seeing only the spoils of war."

"And not the spoilage of war," Ryngs put in.

"Quite." Tish smiled at the raccoon. "Ikinna is one of the obvious choices as he is not only directly descended from one of Bucher's advisors, but also the lord of one of the provinces that adjoins the Reysfields, and believes that some of that land should also be his. The other two we suspect may be going along because they agree with him, or because of their friendship, or out of respect for their ancestors."

"Some of us have been well-served by our ancestors," Ryngs said slyly, glancing at Tish.

"Hush," Dewanne said before Tish could reply. "Our disadvantage here, Vinton, is that we have formed in reaction to their group. Therefore we are always a step behind. We can talk to the king in vague terms of peace, but it is a weak argument compared with their plans, their goals, and their imagined rewards. What are we to say? 'Your Majesty, if you simply stay the course, everything will stay the same and that is good.'? It is like trying to walk without your tail to balance you; without a pro-war argument to push against, the statement topples. That's why we need someone to join their ranks and report back to us what they're telling the king, and what, if any, their other plans are." He leaned forward. "Can you do that, Vinton? Can you be a spy?"

Volle looked around at the three of them, trying not to smile. "Yes. I think so."

He found himself falling easily into the routine of the palace. Every day, he ran with Helfer, ate his lunches and dinners in the common room, except when he dined with Helfer or Arrin, and attended his tribunal on the appropriate day. Helfer finally took him to the Lonely Cock, twice in one week, and the second time disappeared with a rabbit, leaving Volle to make his way back alone.

Arrin loved the trumpet and spent a couple hours in the conservatory with him, helping him fumble around with the piano and the pipes there, and Volle was amazed that by the end of the time, he was able to play a simple tune he remembered from his childhood. There were only three notes in it, but still, he was proud of his progress.

He only saw Dereath once that week. The rat passed him in the corridor on his way to lunch, and gave him a haughty glare. He glared back, still annoyed that the rat had told Arrin about his encounter with the Exchequer. Fortuantely, nobody else came up to him and asked him to explain it, and it wasn't too long before he'd relegated it to the back of his mind.

He was to meet Ilyana again, but had to put it off a day because the day Tika proposed was the day of his rendez-vous with Seir and Reese. She looked askance at him when he said he'd promised to go out with Helfer that night, but rescheduled it for the following night without comment.

"Going for someone new tonight or back to the wolf or cat?" Helfer asked as he walked down the street.

"Wolf, I think." Volle grinned. "How about you?"

"I have a good feeling about tonight. I'm going to hold out for a rabbit. There are a couple that sometimes show up looking for me, you know."

"I don't doubt it. That one in the pub the other night seemed to know you pretty well."

Helfer chuckled. "He does."

"Say, where did you go with him, anyway? The bartender told me you weren't in any of the rooms."

The weasel winked. "I have a few places. Sometime I'll show you some of them."

They walked into the Jackal's Staff, which was busier than usual. They still found a table, and Helfer was delighted to spot not one, but two rabbits in the bar. When Tally finally made his way over to them, Helfer already had a note written out and was tapping his paws impatiently.

"Oh, just a minute, darling," Tally said as he thrust the note at him. He turned to Volle. "Richy's waiting for you in room seven." He gave a broad wink.

"Thanks," Volle grinned, and got up.

"What's that about?" Helfer asked. "Got him tied up or something?"

Volle patted the weasel on the head. "I have some secrets too." He ruffled the fur, which he knew Helfer hated, and while the weasel was smoothing it down, he handed Tally five silver pieces and let himself in the back.

He slipped quickly into room seven, shut the door behind him, and looked around. Seir was in a chair, Sherr the porcupine was on the floor well away from everyone else, and Reese and Tella the weasel were sitting at opposite ends of the bed.

Volle made as if to take off his shirt. "So who's first?"

"Ha ha." Reese looked especially out of sorts.

"What, no hug for your old friend?"

"What's the idea of sending me all the way back down to Vinton for a piece of paper? Ben could've done it."

"What's the idea of telling me they were all strict Orthodox here?"

Sherr and Tella sniggered, and even Seir smiled. Reese just grinned. "That was a good one, eh? I couldn't have done it without Seir."

"All right, all right." Seir chuckled. "Derrik caught a coach to the border two days ago, but he left you this note." She handed it to Volle. "You're supposed to burn it after you read it."

Volle unfolded it. It read, "Volle—if you should ever need to get out of the palace in a hurry, there are two spots. Between the two rear gardens there is a wall. You can climb up atop that and run across to the rear wall, where there are handholds to get over it. Jump over the other side into the river. That way is the easiest but is also the most exposed; use it only in emergencies. The other way is through the passage behind the Lion staircase on the first floor. Go into the baths, and in the privy second from the left, there's a loose flagstone in the floor. You should be able to lift it. Underneath is a tunnel—don't worry, it doesn't go to the sewers—that leads into the basement of Andronico's Butcher Shop. Andronico stores sausages down there, so you can hide without being smelled for a while. Good luck. Hope you never need these. –Derrik."

He nodded. "Have you all read it?"

"We're not supposed to," Seir said. "We know that in an emergency we should stay posted along the river, and Andronico's meat shop, but we don't know where in the palace the passages lead."

"Okay." Volle crumpled the piece of paper and put it in his purse.

"So," Sherr said. "You haven't left any messages for us. What have you found out?"

Volle related the gist of his meetings with Lord Tistunish, and the history he'd learned. Seir nodded. "We know about Bucher. You were deliberately not told a lot of history so you could play the part of the innocent better. Bucher left his mark, but is already being forgotten out in the hinterlands—sometimes deliberately." She brushed her whiskers with a paw. "He was unusually aggressive for a fox."

"Yeah, usually they like to make love, not war." Reese smirked. "I mean, really, Volle, could you have picked a grosser place to frequent? The smells here must be making it hard to concentrate. Good thing some of us don't like males, eh, Tella?"

The weasel ignored him frostily and went on picking her claws. Sherr spoke up. "But what else have you found out? You were supposed to be uncovering this plot."

"Tish doesn't even think there is a plot."

"Marina thought there was. Haven't you even checked Lord Ikinna's chambers?"

"Well, you wanted me to be a long-term asset," Volle snapped heatedly. "I can't very well go sneaking around in people's chambers if I'm going to be a respected Lord for years on end. What else do you want me to do, go around the palace asking the nobles, 'Excuse me, but are you planning some sort of secret violent plot'?"

"You could do a sight more than you're doing," Sherr replied. "What kind of fish have they been serving? What spices do they use? These things tell us what countries they're trading with and who they have good relations with. What is the current slang? How people speak tells us who they're in contact with. What proclamations has the king issued?"

"None that I know of." Volle pounced on the one he could answer quickly. "As for the meals..." He rattled off what he could remember. "All the food is really good. Oh, Fox. You have no idea."

Reese looked sour. "Yeah, well, we're eating pub food, so shut up about it."

"But Sherr asked," Volle said innocently.

"Enough, you two." Seir smiled and walked over to Volle, and gave him a hug. "You're doing great. Just try to keep in mind the things Sherr mentioned and jot notes. Leave them in one of the drop sites around town when you can."

"I will." Volle hugged her back.

"Anything else to report?"

"Well... I met Lord Tistunish, as I said, and his wife is trying to set me up with a vixen." Reese snickered, and Volle grinned. "Apparently the lords have to have cubs to keep their lineage intact."

"It's the same in Ferrenis," Sherr rumbled.

"He's being facetious, Sherr," Reese said. "Ignore him."

Volle shrugged. "So now there's all this pressure to have cubs. I'm trying to put it off as long as I can."

Sherr grunted. "Might be good. It'd cement your standing."

"But it'd ruin the vixen and her family if I'm ever found out."

"So don't get found out."

Volle shut up. It was easy for the porcupine to be so cavalier about the situation, remote from it all. Having met Ilyana, he was not willing to risk her life against his spy skills, no matter what Sherr said.

"Anything else?" Seir asked.

Volle mulled over the events of the past week. "Nothing worth mentioning."

"All right. You guys go on out. I want to talk to Volle privately for a minute."

They filed out, and Reese gave Volle a pat on the shoulder and a smile as he left. Seir kept the door partly open, listening in the corridor, and then said, "Listen, Volle, I really admire your scruples in this matter of the cubs. I'll leave it up to your discretion to decide what to do. Sherr doesn't really have any idea of what it would do to a vixen to have her standing and her family wrenched away from her, and if we can avoid being cruel, we will. But at some point you are going to have to have cubs if you're going to be a Lord there, and there's no getting around it."

He sighed. "I know. I want to wait until I'm better established. I mean, I've only been there a week. Maybe in a year I could figure out how to set aside some money for her, or something."

She nodded. "I know. Don't make excuses and put it off longer than necessary."

"I won't."

"All right." She patted his back. "Hang in there. It gets easier."

"Oh, I'm getting used to it already."

She smiled. "Attaboy. I'll see you in two weeks." And then she slipped out the door, closing it behind her.

Volle lay back on the bed and sighed, resting his head on the pillow. Life at the palace was hectic enough without him worrying about all the other little things he was supposed to be doing. And he was bothered by Sherr's implication that he hadn't done anything. Hadn't he spent two weeks trying to convince everyone he was a Lord, and pretty much succeeded? But he hadn't really done any spying, that was true. At most he'd identified some people who might possibly know something about the plot, if there was one, but he hadn't approached them.

He was lost in thought, so he didn't see the door open and shut silently. A paw touched his side, making him jump.

"Sorry." Richy giggled. "I just wanted to know if this is a private party or if anyone can join."

Volle grinned and motioned for him to sit down. The wolf was wearing his loincloth and a nice herbal scent. He sat with one leg on the bed and one on the floor, and petted Volle's head between the ears. "You paid for me, so I thought you might as well get the benefits since all your friends left." He mock-frowned. "They left so quickly, and you with your clothes on!"

"You know, they weren't very attentive to my needs."

"Aww, well, that's what I'm for." Richy smiled and kissed the top of Volle's muzzle. "So what are your needs, my fox?"

Volle slid a paw gently up and down Richy's leg, and thought. "I think," he said slowly, his paw sliding under the loincloth to curl around the wolf's warm sheath and sac, "that I would like to feel this inside me." He felt the sheath expand under his paw, and kept rubbing it, enjoying the feeling.

"Very good, sir." Richy smiled. "And what shall I do with this?" He rested his paw over the growing bulge in Volle's trousers.

"Surprise me." Volle grinned. His ears flicked and he looked up at the wolf. "Can you finish in me tonight?"

Richy patted his sheath gently. "Oh, I don't know if I can. It's still too early. I need to be careful. I have a long night ahead of me."

Volle nodded. "All right." An idea struck him, and his ears perked up. "Say…do you think you could tell me how you, um, enter someone but don't finish? There's a vixen who wants me to get her pregnant, and I thought maybe I could just pretend to be trying…"

Richy laughed. "You nobles have such interesting lives. Sure, I can tell you. Here, look." He slipped his loincloth off, revealing his erection. He spanned a length about two inches down from the tip. "I'm most sensitive here. So when I'm going in and out, I try to make sure not to catch this section or rub it against anything. And I try to think of something else, but not so much that I lose it altogether. It takes some practice."

Volle grinned. "How about you demonstrate?"

The wolf nuzzled him, smiling, and helped lift his shirt off, then gently removed his trousers. By this time, Volle's erection was hard and full, and Richy spent a little time brushing it gently with the fur on his paws. He leaned over and nuzzled it, then slowly drew his tongue along it, bringing a shiver to Volle's legs.

"That's a nice surprise," Volle murmured. He spread his legs and let Richy's tongue work, closing his eyes as his sheath jumped slightly at every pass of the warm tongue. The wolf moved around on the bed, crouching between Volle's legs, and his tongue curled down around the fox's sac, lifting it and damping down the soft white fur. Volle clasped his paws behind his head when his paw fell away from the wolf's sheath, and made soft murrs of pleasure.

Richy's nose brushed below Volle's sac, slightly chilly, and Volle squirmed. Richy grinned. "Mm, nice and clean." He applied his tongue there, slowly licking down to the opening under the fox's tail, pressing against and then inside it, over and over, while Volle panted with delight. The wolf's slick tongue traced lines of pleasure along his rear, and the tip pressing into him sent a tingling down to his toes that made them curl.

After a blissful few minutes of this, Richy paused to lick his own erection. He smiled up at Volle as he straightened. "Is this okay, or do you want the stuff?"

"I'll tell you if it's not," Volle panted, looking at the long pink length between the wolf's legs. "Go ahead."

Richy smiled, and brought his hips up to Volle's rear. Volle felt the warmth of the wolf against him, and then the pressure under his tail again. Where Jonas had thrust into him, Richy took his time, working the tip gently in and then slowly feeding his whole length into Volle's tail hole.

Volle moaned happily. Richy was wider than Jonas, but he was looser than he'd been the previous week, and the wolf's shaft slid nicely into him with only a little stretching. The stretching felt good, and made it feel like Richy's length was pushing his own further out of his sheath. He was painfully hard and automatically reached down to grasp himself, but Richy's paw gently moved his aside.

He'd barely opened his eyes to look when he felt the wolf's muzzle envelop his length in warmth. Richy looked up at him with a grin, and slowly started moving in and out, holding Volle in his muzzle and indicating his hips with his eyes.

Volle could feel the motion, and sensed how Richy stopped just short of the tip. He grinned and nodded, tongue lolling out of his muzzle. Every thrust made him shiver, and Richy seemed happy just licking the drops of fluid that leaked from the end of his shaft. He kept this up for several more minutes, until Volle felt his body was on fire with arousal. His moans became higher in pitch, and Richy responded by beginning to lick a bit more firmly. Volle thrust up into his muzzle, working his hips in time with the wolf's, and closed his eyes as the sensations built and built in him.

Richy finally started to move his muzzle up and down Volle's shaft, holding the fox's thick knot in one paw, and that was enough to finish him. Volle's body tensed and he felt his fur prickle all over, and then came the release, and Richy was lapping eagerly at him, swallowing everything that splashed on his tongue and coaxing still more out. Volle heard himself moaning, low and guttural, and felt his fingers clawing at the sheets, but seemed to be disconnected from it somehow.

And finally, it was over, and he lay back, panting. Richy slipped slowly out of him, making his body twitch, and then eased his muzzle off of Volle's erection. He grinned and lay beside Volle. "Nice surprise?"

"Very…nice…" Volle panted. "You should do this professionally."

Richy giggled and kissed him, and Volle could smell himself on the wolf's tongue. He licked back and slid an arm around the wolf, holding him close. Richy returned the embrace, resting his head on Volle's chest.

Volle ruffled his fingers through the wolf's fur, enjoying the softness and the scents, the herbal aroma mixed with the scents of passion. He nuzzled Richy's ears and smiled, enjoying the warm closeness and the silence. So much of his life, in the palace and the Academy, was about keeping up appearances with words and clothes, or hiding sex behind layers of etiquette and propriety. He understood the need for it, but also appreciated the chance to step back from it and just be a fox, in a bed with a wolf, neither of them worried about status or what would happen in the morning or anything other than the other's pleasure.

Part of his training as a spy had been the subversion of his identity, the assumption of traits that others expected of him. He was used to the idea, knew how to keep himself separate from the persona he played, while at the same time putting enough of himself into it that it was easy to maintain. Over the long term, especially, it was necessary to minimize the role-playing, because that could easily burn out even the most well-trained spy. It was exhausting work, and here in the brothel he could forget about it as he had never been able to before, not since he'd entered the Academy.

He hadn't been in the habit of frequenting the brothels in Caril, no matter what the others thought; he couldn't afford it and couldn't see why he should when with a little effort, he could get anything he wanted in the pubs. Those encounters had carried with them some concerns, as liberating as they'd felt. Here—as long as he was paying, of course—he didn't have to worry. Richy would be here whenever he wanted him.

On four nights out of the week, anyway. Where was he the other nights? Didn't matter. He'd be here, and Volle could escape once a week, to a place where he didn't have to be a Lord, didn't have to be a spy, didn't have to be anything but a fox.

Book 2: Xiller

Chapter 10

His life over the next two weeks continued the routine he was building up. He spent time with Arrin in the conservatory and at dinner, and on his new loveseat, they progressed to deeper kisses and gentle explorations under clothes. He'd been embarrassed when Arrin asked to see his bedroom and the latest P. Zinsky book he'd borrowed ("The Slippery Slope," whose cover showed an otter lying on his back, tail hole exposed) was sitting right out there in the open. Arrin had just laughed and said, "I like "A Brush With Love" best, don't you?" and then it was okay.

Ilyanna visited for another dinner with Tish and Tika, and they spent the entire dinner discussing her cotillion. Volle hadn't known quite what the event would entail, but he had gathered that it would be a dance of some sort, and that it marked an entry into society for Ilyanna. By the end of the evening, he was dazed from the discussion of invitations, manners, catering, flowers, music, venues, and dance steps. Tish took him aside and gave him some words of advice: "You only need to know three things: how to eat, how to dance, and how to hand over far too much money. And Tika and I are taking care of that last part." Volle had protested that he had plenty of money, but Tish had overruled him. "We're getting you into this, the least we can do is pay for it."

Which was fine with him. He had pondered many different ways of getting out of the engagement, as he'd found himself increasingly unwilling to reject Ilyana. She was too nice, and the only flaw he could find in her was that she was too honest, but rejecting her on those grounds would mean a parade of dissembling vixens, a thought that made him shudder. His best option, he thought, was to get her to reject him somehow, and though he hadn't quite worked out how to do that yet, he felt certain he could behave badly enough if the situation warranted. The meeting with her parents was arranged, which would be his first opportunity—if they didn't like him, the courtship was off. He began to practice rude comments in his spare time.

The Secretary sent word that some of the requests the governor of Vinton had made were in the process of being addressed—meaning, he was told, that in a couple weeks someone would be hired to begin the process of putting together a team to make the changes, but at least the process was moving. At least the king had sent some of the weapons they'd requested. He sat down with Lord Black and hammered out an agreement, and ended up inviting the raccoon to the pub with Helfer, where the two of them made a start towards rekindling their friendship. Everyone had a good time, even though Black kept getting propositioned, which annoyed him and Helfer both; the former because he didn't want to be bothered, and the latter because he did.

He and Helfer ran every day, had dinner several times, had clothes made at Helfer's tailor, and visited the pub together. And once a week they went down to the Jackal's Staff, and Volle lost himself in the arms of the young, sexy wolf. After the slip with Jonas, he'd decided it was better not to see him again, and anyway, Richy was delightful enough that he didn't miss the cougar.

At the second meeting with his team, when he still had nothing concrete to report, Sherr browbeat him into letting Tella into the palace via the secret entrance, over Volle's objections that it could compromise him, the passage, and the whole team. They arranged a time the previous Gaiaday; Volle was to let her in immediately before the church services, when the palace would be empty, and she was to finish and get back out before services ended. Sherr also insisted that he start using more anti-Ferrenis rhetoric when he talked to other lords, and this Volle found reasonable, and agreed to.

Apart from his nervous twitches during Tella's mission, Volle thought everything was going well. Tella hadn't found anything new for him to investigate, so he didn't feel like he was missing anything. His mission and life were progressing smoothly, and everyone seemed to think he was doing a good job, even if he hadn't uncovered anything yet. He had begun to think that the palace held no more surprises for him.

As a trained spy, he should have known better.

The Ursiday after that meeting, while he and Helfer were preparing for their run, he saw Dereath lurking in the main hall. The rat vanished quickly into a corridor, but Volle was sure it had been Dereath. He hadn't seen the rat in two weeks and had hoped the rat had forgotten him. Helfer and Lord Black had joked about him at the pub, but Volle hadn't joined in. He was not inclined to discount a potential enemy nor the damage one could do.

Now, he felt uneasy again as they jogged down the main steps, but he didn't want to let on to Helfer, who was chattering about an upcoming banquet. He nodded and made short replies, trying to put Dereath out of his mind. It didn't help that the last of the flowers had died the previous week. Several of the trees and bushes in the garden were glowing a fiery red or a bright yellow, and the muted blues and violets of several shrubs were more visible now that the flowers were gone. But overall the garden looked darker and more sinister, and the gardeners had not removed all the dead flowers. They seemed out of place in the lively garden. Volle tried to avoid looking at them.

Helfer looked at him oddly as they were making their way through the section of the palace that separated the front gardens from the first rear garden. "Are you okay? You've been in another world since we started."

"I'm fine. Just…" He hesitated to mention Dereath, because Helfer didn't take the rat seriously. "Just thinking about the cotillion."

"Oh, that. Don't get so wound up about it. You'll do fine. Besides, everybody will be looking at her, not at you."

"I'll be dancing with her all night," Volle pointed out, "so they'll be looking at me as well."

The rear garden's familiar emptiness seemed more ominous to Volle today. It was chillier than the front garden, as the path ran through the shadow of the palace. He felt his fur prickle, and lifted his nose to the wind, but the only scent he could catch was Helfer's strong musteline smell. The bushes rustled slightly in the shifting breezes, making his ears swivel back and forth. He glanced at the palace windows to his right, and thought he saw a shadow move across one of them, but when he looked again, it was gone.

His sense of unease grew, but he was still reluctant to mention anything to Helfer; the weasel would laugh at him for jumping at shadows. So he kept running, ears alert, scanning the garden while Helfer talked about the ladies his governor was lining up for him at home.

They rounded a corner, and Volle's whiskers twitched a half-second before a large shape leapt out from behind a large bush, not two yards in front of them. They froze, startled, and the shape closed the space in a heartbeat. A large paw lashed out at Helfer, who spun and ran.

Volle's fur was bristled out and he had just enough time to register the shape as a large cougar before it was on him, knocking him down and landing heavily on top of him. Dizzy, breathless, he felt its paws pin his arms and its weight slam his hips to the dirt path. He had snapped his muzzle downward to protect his throat, and now he could hear its low growl and feel the hot breath on his whiskers. He struggled, but the feline only shifted his weight, pinning Volle more firmly as his muzzle sought purchase in Volle's throat.

Volle squeezed his eyes shut and whimpered, trying to remember his unarmed combat training. Most of it, unfortunately, was devoted to avoiding precisely the position he now found himself in. He tried squirming out from under the heavier body, but the legs spread out to either side of his and pinned him in. The teeth were searching at his throat, but so far he was able to keep them away. The one thing he remembered was that as a canid, his long muzzle was vulnerable in this situation: an enemy could get his jaws around it and bite down, which would essentially end the fight. So he kept his muzzle moving quickly, alert for the first attempt to bite it.

"Get away from him!"

The cougar was so heavy that he was having trouble breathing, even as he squirmed. And he couldn't help noticing that the cougar was very male, and very excited. What made it worse is that Volle himself was getting aroused, though he certainly wasn't thinking about sex. But the cougar's scent was strong and feline, and his body was strong and taut, and his breath was hot and musky and passing right over Volle's nose.

Gradually, he realized that the cougar wasn't trying very hard to bite him. In fact, the growls sounded like chuckles. Warily, he stopped moving his muzzle and opened his eyes. The cougar placed his muzzle gently around Volle's throat, just enough for Volle to feel his teeth, and then looked up, hazel green eyes bright.

"Scared ya, huh?"

Volle wheezed out, "Who *are* you?"

"Get away from him!"

It was Helfer's voice, and when Volle turned his head he saw the weasel in an aggressive stance, waving a large stick of wood he'd picked up somewhere. "I said get off! *Now!*"

The cougar shifted his weight, and before Volle could cry out a warning, had launched himself at Helfer. A moment later the stick of wood was lying on the path and Helfer was holding one paw in the other, dazed. The cougar growled softly at him. "I'm off. Now what?"

"It's okay, Hef," Volle called, sitting up slowly. "He's just trying to scare us."

The feline face looked back at him with a grin that had some savagery to it. "I was only trying to scare *you*," he said, and turned back to Helfer.

The weasel took a step back, looking much less sure of himself now that he had no stick and Volle wasn't in danger. But Volle could see the twitching of the cougar's tail; it wasn't lashing in a hunting mode, it was twitching with excitement and amusement. The cougar himself, now that Volle could get a good look at him, was taller than he was, and kept his fur trimmed shorter than Jonas did. Volle could see the tight thigh muscles below the line of the supple leather armor he was wearing; they rippled beneath the fur, flexing as he shifted his weight back and forth, staying alert. His chest was armored, with flaps running across his shoulders but not around them, giving him more flexibility at the expense of some protection, and the way he was keeping his arms moving and ready suggested he knew how to use them.

This evaluation was done in a second; Volle twisted, reached up, and grabbed the lashing tail, kicking out wildly at the cougar's legs. He clipped the edge of one of the leather knee braces the cougar wore. It wasn't enough to knock him down, but it did throw him off balance, and Helfer took advantage of the moment to charge at the cougar's midsection. That did knock him backwards, onto Volle's legs, and for a moment they thrashed around, a frenetic tangle of fox, cat, and weasel.

Volle was struggling to get his legs free, keeping hold of the cougar's tail, while the cougar was trying to contain the squirming weasel. The idea of calling for help in the deserted gardens hadn't occurred to Volle at all, and apparently it only occurred to Helfer when the cougar's huge arm clamped across his chest, pinning him to the chest of the prone cat.

"Help!" he shouted. "Help!"

The cougar's other arm was grabbing at Volle's legs. It paused for a moment, the cougar's weight shifted, and he growled, "Stop."

Helfer stopped.

Volle didn't know what had happened, but he was almost free. He pushed a bit harder, holding onto the tail with one paw and batting away the cougar's with his other, and then the paw slid up his leg, under his skirt, and closed on his sheath and sac. "You too," the cougar growled.

Volle gulped, and stopped immediately. The paw was soft, no claws extended, but the threat was there. It was huge, too, easily enfolding his privates, and was not squeezing nearly as hard as he was sure it could.

"First rule of fighting is to protect your valuables," the cougar growled softly.

"We didn't come out here to fight," Helfer said, panting.

"You should still protect yourselves better." The paw was starting to move on Volle, and his sheath was responding no matter how much he willed it not to. Looking up, he could see Helfer's skirt lifted and movement under it.

"Hey," Helfer started struggling again weakly. "We're out here in the open...you can't..."

"Oh, but I am," the cat purred. "Nothing quite as relaxing after a nice tussle, wouldn't you say? Besides, there's nobody else out here. And you don't seem to mind."

"I..." Helfer twisted his neck around to look at Volle, and their eyes met.

Volle gave a small shrug, eyes wide. "I don't understand either, Hef, but I'm sure not moving while he's got his paw...oh, there..." He panted as the large, soft paw slid along his fully erect member.

Helfer's eyes slid down and Volle realized the weasel could see up his skirt, but he didn't care. He let go of the cougar's tail and lay back, submitting to the caresses, which were now moving more quickly. The paw slid back and forth along his length, and through his own pants he could hear Helfer making small chirps of pleasure. The stroking continued until Volle was panting and his claws were pressed into the dirt of the path.

"Nice to see you both so cooperative," the cougar murmured. "I wonder which will be faster. My, you're a squirmy little thing." This was to Helfer, who was having some difficulty keeping still on the cat's chest. "Do you want me to stop?"

Volle thought he wasn't quite so far gone that he couldn't have said yes to that, but Helfer moaned, "No…" A few moments later, he was curling up around the cat's paw and moaning loudly into his own paws, trying to muffle his cries. Even from his prone position, Volle could see the lithe body's twists and turns as he came, and then lay back panting. The strong scent of weasel floated to him on the air, and he thought, that's just what I'd expect him to smell like after sex.

"Mmm. You win." The cat paused in stroking Volle to feel his knot, which was quite swollen. "But I think your friend isn't far behind. Just lie still. You can watch if you want." Volle squirmed, whimpering slightly, as the stroking resumed, and he saw Helfer's head flop over towards him, the half-lidded eyes watching him lazily.

And now, if the cougar had asked him if he wanted to stop, Volle would have moaned "No" as well. He dug furrows in the dirt with his claws, staring at the sky as he felt himself shiver and tense, and then felt the familiar rush of climax. His body shuddered, and his semen spurted out onto the cougar's paw and his skirt, warmth flowing into his belly fur as the musk filled his nose. He let out a long, low moan, not as concerned with Helfer about keeping it quiet, and then lay back, panting.

The cougar rolled Helfer onto Volle and got to his knees, looking at his paws. Both were rather sticky, and he sniffed them before sticking them into the nearest bush and rubbing them on the leaves. After a few moments, he was apparently satisfied, and knelt with his paws on his thighs watching Volle and Helfer.

"Now, will you tell us what that was about?" Helfer had recovered a little more quickly than Volle and sat up. The front of his skirt was stained dark from his orgasm, but for the moment he was more concerned with the cougar, staring up at the big cat defiantly.

"I was supposed to scare you two." The cougar shrugged his broad shoulders. "Dunno why. The rat said it'd be funny to see you two wet yourselves and come running into the castle, but you didn't at first." He licked his lips. "So I thought of a more fun way to do it."

"Rat…" Volle propped himself up on his elbows and looked at Helfer. "Dereath."

"Yeah, that's his name. He said you guys play jokes like this on each other all the time."

Helfer rolled his eyes. "Not really. He hired you just to frighten us?"

The cougar's smile faded a bit as he looked from Helfer to Volle and back. "Nah. I'm here on other business. But I'm staying with him— for a bit."

"You know him?" Volle was still leaning back, but his ears were perked.

"Nah. He's just who they put me with."

"Who's 'they'?" Helfer asked.

The cougar shook his head. "I think my work here is done." He got to his feet, looking down at them as he brushed the dirt from his haunches. He was still smiling, but the smile looked almost apologetic now. "Maybe I'll stick around to see you two come back into the castle."

Helfer spread his arms. "What more could you want to see?"

The cougar shrugged, and jogged back toward the front garden, tail lashing behind him.

Helfer sighed and looked at Volle. "This is definitely the strangest morning run I've ever been on. You really must've gotten that rat stirred up."

Volle shook his head. "I don't know. I thought he'd forgotten about that, or at least let it go. I saw him in the main hall just before we left. What do you bet he was watching out one of those windows?"

"I don't think he meant for that cougar to show us such a good time." Helfer grinned. "He's probably more irritated now."

Volle's adrenaline had subsided, and with it the immediate terror of the attack. He was still worried, but it was a more theoretical worry than the visceral fear he'd felt earlier. "I don't know if that's a good thing, Hef. We could've been hurt. What'll he do next time?"

The tension of the initial fight had obviously vanished for Helfer, too. "Oh, he wasn't going to hurt us. And I think he's too good to let us hurt him."

Volle shrugged. "Maybe." He looked down at his stained skirt. "So now what do we do?"

"Well, we can either wait here until it dries, take the clothes off and run naked, or just finish up as we are." The weasel grinned. "I'll run naked if you will."

"Isn't there some rule against that?"

"I think there's a rule against shooting your load in the gardens, too, but we've broken that one already."

Volle grinned. "How about we just turn the skirts back to front and let our tails cover the stains? It still smells, but at least it won't show."

Helfer scowled. "Easy for you to say, with that carpet you're dragging behind you." He twisted to look at his small, black-tipped tail. "You think it'll cover?"

"Yeah, I think so. Try it and let's see."

Helfer stood up and loosened the drawstrings of his skirt, then slid it around his hips. "Aw, come on," Volle teased. "Take it off. You got to see mine."

The weasel just stuck his tongue out at Volle and tied the strings under his tail. He wriggled his hips. "Feels funny, but I think it'll stay. Does it show?"

"Nope. Not unless someone looks under your tail, and I think you can get back to your room without that happening." Volle grinned. "Unless we run into a big scary rabbit soldier maybe."

Helfer put his paws on his hips and glared down at the fox. "You know, I could take that skirt completely off for you."

Volle's grin widened. "Yeah, I saw the way you took care of that cougar."

"Oh, like you did better. At least I got away. I only came back for you."

"Yeah." Volle got up, his smile gone. He reached out to Helfer. "Thanks, Hef. That was really brave. You risked a lot for me."

Helfer stepped into the hug briefly, then stepped back. His dark eyes glinted in the sun as he looked into Volle's. "Well, you know…" He scuffed the ground, ears flicking self-consciously. "I, uh, couldn't just leave you here to have all the fun. Come on, let's jog. Just finish the one circuit and then in. I think we've had enough exercise for one morning."

"Definitely." Volle fell into step beside his friend, and chuckled. "What?"

"Oh, just that…it was kind of fun having him on top of me. Except for the part where I thought he was going to rip my throat out."

Helfer grinned. "It was fun being on top of him too. That arm… ooh."

"Tell me about it." The cougar's hazel eyes lingered in Volle's memory. They were clear and honest, playful and humor-filled, and he remembered the strong embrace of the muscular body as the eyes had met his. He remembered the cougar's groin pressing against him, his excitement palpable even through the sturdy leather of his armor, and he found himself wondering whether he'd see the cougar again.

Those thoughts led him to Dereath. What was the rat doing with a soldier in his quarters, and who had ordered him there? "Is it common to have soldiers in the palace?"

Helfer shrugged. "From time to time. Depends on what's going on, I guess. I usually don't know what's going on. But I've seen soldiers around before."

"I wonder what he's doing here."

Helfer wagged a finger at him. "Don't get mixed up in politics, I'm telling you."

Volle grinned. "It's just weird, is all. The first soldier I see attacks me."

"No wonder, showing off your butt like that. All soldiers are gay, didn't you know?"

Volle laughed. "No."

"Think about it. Cramped together in close quarters, separated into male and female units…"

"Sounds like a great life."

"Except for the lousy food, the curfews, the orders, the constant exercise, and the going off to be killed."

"Right. Except for that."

They passed through the large archway and back into the main garden. Except for the rapidly stiffening stain on his skirt, and the musky odor he could still smell, Volle could almost have believed that the whole episode had been just a daydream. The morning sun was brighter here and birds chirped gaily in the trees. He shook his head and followed Helfer back into the palace. Renaldo was standing on duty at the door, and as they passed, he bowed slightly to them. Volle saw his nose wrinkle as they passed, and he hurried on with a quick wave.

"Want to change at my place? It's closer," Volle said as they approached the Wolf stair.

"No thanks. I'll take my chances. Want to come use my private bath?"

Volle considered it, then shook his head. "I'm right here." He gestured to the corridor, then lifted his nose. He caught the cougar's scent a moment before the shadow appeared behind Helfer. "Hef," he said warningly, and the weasel heard his tone and saw his look, and was at his side in a second. Together, they watched the cougar approach.

He stopped at the base of the stair, looking at the two of them. He still looked cheerful, though his ears were laid back. "Hey, just wanted to say I'm sorry. I shouldn't have frightened you. And then I just got kinda carried away. Friends?"

Volle felt the tension melt away from them, and heard Helfer chuckle. "I don't mind the carried away part, but next time, buy me a drink first or something, okay?" He slipped past the cougar and up the stair. "I gotta go get changed. Volle, see you tonight?"

"Oh yeah. See you then, Hef." The weasel darted up the stairs and disappeared.

"I should go, too." Volle started to turn towards the corridor.

"Wait." The cougar was shifting on his paws. "Look, there's something else I wanted to ask."

Volle turned back and caught the warm hazel eyes in his. There wasn't much guile in the cougar, if any, and what he was about to ask was plain in the arch of his eyebrows, the uncertain flick of his ears, and the way he was kneading his paws. Volle grinned even before he heard the question. "Go ahead."

"Well, I told you I was staying with that rat. But I didn't like him all that much, and he's pretty upset with me. I guess he saw what I did after the scaring part." He scratched the back of his head. "So all in all, it looks like I need another place to stay. It'd just be for a few days," he added hurriedly. "You know anyone who has an extra room?"

Volle looked at the tall, powerful body, the cougar's scent in his nose, and heard himself say, "I've got an extra half a bed."

The cougar grinned, and Volle's ears flicked back. "Oh, Fox, I can't believe I just said that." He returned the grin abashedly.

"That's okay," the cougar said, tail waving more animatedly now. "I was sort of hoping you might."

Volle glanced to the left as a raccoon and weasel wandered into view in the main hall. "Maybe we should go look at it now. More private there, and I still need to clean up anyway."

"I've got a few things in the rat's chambers. I'll just grab them and meet you back here. Which door are you?"

Volle walked him along the corridor to his chambers. "This one."

"Okay. See you in a couple minutes." The cougar wrapped his arms around Volle and squeezed him. "Thanks. I really appreciate this."

"Oof. Sure. Hey," he called as the cougar padded quickly away, "I'm going to take a water bath, so if you get back and I'm not here, just make yourself at home, and I'll be back soon." The cougar gave a wave of understanding and disappeared.

Volle opened the door and saw Welcis tidying the parlor. "Ah, Welcis..."

"Sir?" The skunk turned to face him.

"We'll be having a guest here, for a few nights, I guess. A big cougar. He'll stay in the bedroom with me. I think."

"Yes, sir."

"I'm going to take my bath. If he comes by while I'm gone, er, show him to the bed. Bedroom, I mean."

"Yes, sir. Might I remind his lordship of his dinner plans tomorrow night?"

"Oh. Arrin." Volle chewed his lip.

"Will I be setting a table for three, sir?"

"Let me think about that."

"Very good, sir."

He walked over to the bath, still thinking about Arrin and what he would say. The large hot water bath that lay beyond the main archway was occupied, so he headed to one of the two smaller private baths behind it. He didn't mind bathing with others—had done it all his life—but he preferred to be alone at the moment. Besides, he wasn't sure the stain on his shorts had dried, and a stain that appeared to be on the back was even more embarrassing than one on the front.

The water was clean, if not very hot. He grabbed some soapstone and started scrubbing his fur. As he cleaned the area around his sheath, he thought about the cougar's warm paw, his confident touch, and easy manner. What harm would it do to have him stay for a few nights? It would save him some money at the Jackal's Staff, anyway. Arrin already knew about his trips there and tolerated him, and this wasn't that different, really. It wasn't like he had some attachment to the cougar. He didn't even know his name.

All the same, he probably should cancel his dinner with Arrin. There'd be no way to juggle them successfully, and if Arrin wouldn't sleep with *him*, there was absolutely no chance he'd end up in a three-way with the cougar...

Volle jerked his paw back from his sheath, where his erection was growing quickly. He looked down at himself and grinned. This could be a very interesting week. He wondered if he had enough stamina for it.

When he returned to his chambers, towel wrapped around his midsection, Welcis greeted him. "Your lordship's guest is in the bedroom, sir."

"Thank you, Welcis." He slipped through the two doors, holding the towel, and found the cougar examining the bricked-up doorway.

"That used to lead to a bathroom. Before I lived here."

The cougar turned and smiled. "I was wondering. How long have you lived here?"

"About a month now." Volle closed the door behind him. "My name is Volle, by the way. Volle of Vinton."

"I guessed you were a Lord." The cougar shook the proffered paw and grinned. "I'm Xiller."

"Ziller?"

"Close enough. It's an 'X,' so you actually pronounce it 'ch-ziller'." He aspirated the 'ch' sound so that it sounded almost like a purr. "Non-felines have trouble with it though, so 'Ziller' works too. I'm used to both."

"Ziller. K-ziller." Volle tried a couple times and couldn't the aspirated sound to work. "Oh, well. It's nice to meet you."

"Same here. So, did you mean it about sharing the bed?"

Volle flicked his ears. "Well…"

"If you don't, it's okay, but I'd be okay with it. I mean, I wasn't going to do the scaring thing, but when he pointed you two out to me, I thought you were pretty cute. And I guessed you probably liked males, 'cause he said you and the weasel were sleeping together. So I thought, what the heck? Maybe I could meet a couple other people. And honestly, if I slept another night with that rat I think I might tear his throat out."

Volle watched his claws flex as he said that, curved lethal daggers springing from those soft paws, and shivered. "I'm not sure that would be a huge loss."

"Maybe not, but I think it's bad form to kill your host."

"I sure hope so!"

Xiller grinned. "You don't have anything to worry about, unless you suddenly become about five times pushier."

"Tell me about it. How did you end up with him anyway?" Volle leaned against the bed.

The cougar shrugged. "I showed up day before yesterday, stayed in an inn that night, then they moved me in here once I got my paperwork. I shouldn't have said anything about being gay, but he started talking about it and …I dunno, I'm not that clever. Just said whatever came to mind."

"Well, you're welcome to sleep here, in the bed or on the loveseat, or wherever. I promise I won't touch you unless you ask."

The cougar gave him a searching look, then walked slowly over to him and placed both his paws on the towel. His muzzle lowered until it brushed the top of Volle's and his feline scent filled Volle's nostrils. Hazel eyes met amber, and feline lips pulled back in a slow smile. The towel fell away from Volle's hips as if of its own accord. The cat purred. "What if I touch you first?"

Volle slid his paws around the supple midsection, between the leather shorts and the hard leather chest plate. He brushed his nose against the collarbone, inhaling the scent of leather, cat, exertion, and desire. The paws on his hips pulled him close, pressing his body to the hard leather and hard muscles, and when he felt a warm breath and the brush of a tongue in his ear, his knees buckled and he felt exactly like a character in a P. Zinsky book.

Xiller chuckled, softly and deeply, and supported him. "You can touch me whenever you want," he whispered into Volle's ear.

Volle exhaled slowly into the tawny fur. "You're nice to touch," he murmured, and then mentally kicked himself. Could he have been less original? But Xiller didn't seem to mind.

"You too." He pushed his fingers through Volle's thick fur. "Not many foxes where I come from. No gay ones."

"Pity." He drew his claws through the exposed fur on Xiller's back, and rubbed the base of his tail.

"Mmm. I didn't know what I was missing."

Volle laughed, and gave the top of the cougar's broad chest a lick. He tried to step back, and the big paws parted slightly to allow him to. Their eyes met again, both muzzles smiling, and Volle said, "Mmm. I should really get dressed so we can go to lunch."

"What's the hurry?" One paw slid smoothly around to cover Volle's sheath and erection, which was quite full again.

"Ooh. But I'm hungry."

The paw kneaded slowly. "I can give you something to eat."

Volle grinned, pressing slightly into the paw. "With a cream sauce?"

"Oh, I think so." The paw rubbed more firmly up and down, and Volle let his tongue hang out.

"Okay, okay. If you insist…"

Xiller chuckled. "Hey, you got done once today already. I just got worked up."

Volle managed to get the armor unbuckled from the cougar's hips. It dropped to the floor with a thud, revealing a pair of linen undershorts that were stained with sweat and musk. They did little to hide the large bulge of the cougar's arousal, which jutted up through the thin cloth. Volle grinned and slid the shorts carefully down, remaining on his knees, at eye level with the sheath and protruding member.

He looked up and saw the cougar's warm hazel eyes and soft smile. Gently, he reached up with a black paw and brushed his fingertips down the long pink member, the soft white sheath, and the compact white-furred sac that hung below it. One of Xiller's paws came to rest between his ears, pushing the soft fur back and forth, as the cougar purred in reaction.

Volle reached up again; even kneeling up, he had to pull the long shaft down slightly to angle it for his muzzle. His paw closed around it, feeling the thickness—unusual for a cougar—and the warm softness of the skin. The tip was already dripping with the cougar's excitement, but Volle took his time licking it clean, with little darts and licks of his tongue. Xiller squirmed and moaned, and the lashing of his tail quickened.

When the tip was clean and glistening with nothing but Volle's saliva, the fox took pity on the moaning cougar and gave the long shaft several long, slow licks. The paw atop his head relaxed somewhat and the moans became deeper, then louder as he held the cougar's erection still and slipped his muzzle over the tip. It was the first time he'd felt a cougar's penis with his tongue, and feeling the ridges around the tip that he knew from previous matings was an interesting sensation. He explored them with his tongue for a bit, and judging from the sounds he made, Xiller didn't mind his interest.

The whole length was too long to fit entirely in his muzzle, but he could stroke up and down with his paw as he moved his muzzle up and down. With his other paw, he held one of Xiller's thighs, which was so large he couldn't get his paw even halfway around it. He felt the muscles shift and twitch as the cougar's arousal grew, and the paw on his head clenched tighter, pushing his head up and down with the rhythm he'd started.

Volle didn't know if Xiller was naturally quick to come, as many felines were, or if he'd just gotten himself very worked up this morning, but he felt the contractions in the cougar's legs and shaft and only had a moment to prepare himself before his muzzle was pressed down hard on the cougar's spasming length and salty fluid coated the back of his tongue. He swallowed and licked for more, using his paw to brace his muzzle so that he didn't get the whole shaft pushed back into his throat. Xiller was moaning and pressing hard on his head now, convulsively, and the cougar's legs were spread far apart for balance.

Volle kept stroking and licking until he felt the cougar's body sag and relax. "Oh, oh, fox," he was panting, "I needed that. Wow."

Volle slid his muzzle off the dripping shaft and licked his lips. "Mm. I enjoyed it."

"Oh, me too." He dropped to his knees and pulled Volle into a tight embrace, nuzzling him hard.

"Oof. Careful with the squeezing there."

"Sorry." Xiller grinned and gave Volle's nose a lick.

"So, want to grab some lunch in the dining room? I could make all the women and gay nobles jealous."

Xiller laughed. "Sorry. I'm not supposed to be in busy public places. And I have briefings all afternoon and dinner after that. But I'll be back this evening."

Volle flicked his ears. "Okay, I'll be here. What exactly are you doing here?"

The cougar's smile wavered a bit. "I can't really tell you. I'm doing secret work and I'm not supposed to talk about it."

"All right, all right." Volle smiled. "Get your armor on and go ahead."

Xiller kissed him and stood up, stretching so Volle could get a good look at him, and Volle took advantage. The cougar's tawny fur came down his back and around his hips, covering his legs below a 'V' of white fur on either inner thigh. The white rose up around the area Volle had just become familiar with, over his tight stomach, and disappeared below the protective chest plate. He wore leather pads on his knees and elbows as well, and a pad around his foot that protected the top of it, leaving the bottom free for better mobility.

The rear was just as nice, Volle saw when he turned. Xiller's black-tipped tawny tail waved back and forth, more expressive than Volle's was. Below it, his nicely shaped rump tightened up when he bent over to retrieve his shorts. Volle whistled appreciatively, and Xiller turned to glance at him with a grin as he stepped into his shorts. He made a show of wiggling his rump, tail held high, as he pulled his shorts up.

Volle went to his wardrobe to get some clothes of his own. His selection was the largest it had ever been, thanks to a visit to Helfer's tailor as well as the palace tailor dropping off more clothes every now and then. He selected a silk shirt and trousers that were among his more expensive clothes, just because he felt like dressing up.

"That looks really nice." He turned to see Xiller watching him, armor back in place.

"Thanks." It seemed at that moment as though he'd known the cougar for ages, and they were just starting another day in their life. The next moment, the sensation passed and he remembered that he'd known Xiller for an hour or two at most.

"So…I can just come back here, right?"

"Sure." Volle smiled. "Welcis sleeps in the sitting room. If I'm not here I'll be out with Helfer, but I'll be back before too late." He was already thinking that he might limit his pub visit to one drink or skip it altogether.

"Okay." The cougar stood indecisively for a second, then padded quickly over to Volle and licked his nose. "Bye."

And as quickly as that, he was gone.

Chapter 11

After a short rest, Volle brushed himself off and walked down to the dining hall for lunch. The group of lords that usually took lunch in the hall was more familiar to him now, and he sat down and talked comfortably with some of them about palace politics and the upcoming events. If they noticed his slightly dazed manner and occasional inability to follow the conversation, they didn't remark upon it.

He'd scheduled a meeting with the Secretary the previous week to discuss sitting in on some of the councils, but it was only with Welcis' help that he remembered it. He found his way to the Secretary's office easily and sat in the anteroom for a while, thinking about Xiller. It wasn't until one of the assistants cleared his throat that Volle realized he'd been sitting for about half an hour.

"I'm sorry, but the Secretary is very busy today. He should be back any minute."

Volle nodded. "It's okay. I'll wait." It was odd, though. He'd met with some of the ministers and functionaries half a dozen times or so, and even the hyper-busy Alister had never kept him waiting more than ten minutes.

He was more than willing to lose himself in thoughts of the cougar, but the thought of Alister reminded him of Arrin. He chewed his lip thoughtfully, wondering whether it wouldn't be best just to avoid the fox for this time. After all, Xiller would be gone in a few days, and it wasn't going to be anything long-term. Arrin might be worried about him if he knew, but Xiller himself was apparently trying to keep a low profile, so the chances of anyone finding out he was staying with Volle were pretty small.

Dereath would know, though. And he wasn't above telling Arrin, Volle knew that already. If he'd been angry at Xiller for how his childish attempt to get at Volle and Helfer had turned out, Volle could only imagine how he felt towards the two of them now. So he had to expect that Arrin would find out somehow. He sighed. Maybe he should just send Xiller to stay somewhere else. Helfer's wardrobe would probably do. That would be the safest solution, to keep things right with Arrin.

Except…except Arrin had never made his knees feel weak.

Xiller's energy and simple joy in life (yes, and his libido, which seemed a match for his powerful muscles) were refreshing and delightful, and a stark contrast to Arrin and Ilyana's seemingly endless courtship rules and protocol lessons and etiquette guidelines. Volle was extremely reluctant to give that up. He felt that after dealing with the other two, he deserved a bit of liberty, some fresh air, and a little freedom. After all, he hadn't made any commitments to anyone yet.

And there was also the fact that he couldn't seem to stop thinking about the cougar. Even the impressions of him from the attack in the garden had been leached of the fear they'd initially contained, and now all Volle could think of when he brought the incident to mind was the warm press of muscles against him, the paw creeping up his leg and grasping him gently, the tail like something alive and independent, tugging at his paw.

Maybe he'd talk to Helfer tonight and see if he had any advice, then just wait and see how the situations played out.

"Lord Vinton?"

He looked up from his reverie to see the golden fur of the Secretary. "Oh. Mr. Secretary."

"Please, I told you, it's Prewitt. I can't stand those titles." He smiled and extended a paw. "So sorry for the delay. Come into the office?"

Volle nodded and shook his large paw, then followed him into his office. Prewitt sat down behind his desk and waved Volle to his seat. "Now, you wanted to talk about sitting in on some councils. You've been here about a month?" He shuffled a few papers as he talked, sliding a couple out of sight very discreetly, but Volle noticed.

"Yes. I'm starting to pick up on what's going on, and I'd like to get more involved. I think I could follow the Taxation council well enough, and I'd like to sit in on Defense."

"Hm." Prewitt scratched his muzzle. "I'd have thought Agriculture would be more natural, given your background. I think you're in a unique position to offer some insights into the farming community, since you grew up on a farm. Not many nobles have that pedigree." He laughed. "In fact, I can't think of one."

Volle joined his laugh. "I'd be happy to help there. I was interested in Defense, though."

"Why is that?" The bear was still smiling, but his eyes were more serious as he examined Volle.

"My father died fighting the Ferrenians, and they as good as killed my mother, too. I've picked up a bit of the history of Tephos, and I know they took the Reysfields from us. I want to help make sure they don't take any more."

He'd used variations on that speech enough that he could put his heart into it. Prewitt leaned back and nodded. "Very interesting. Yes, I think we could arrange for something. I'll have to talk to Lord Fardew, of course; it's his council. You don't have a lot of experience, but experience can be acquired. Enthusiasm is more rare and precious. Yes, I think that will work out fine."

"Thank you, Prewitt." Volle wouldn't allow himself a smile of relief.

"It's interesting you should mention that. I learned just now that you have a guest in your chambers. I was debating whether to ask your guest to move to a more discreet location. But I think it will be fine. I do want to ask you not to discuss your guest with anyone at the palace."

"How did you hear about that?" Volle's eyes had widened, and his ears had perked straight up.

"Dereath, of course. Very clever rat, but if he's not careful, he's going to cripple himself with his emotional problems. That's just between you and me. He couldn't find Fardew, so he came and told me." Prewitt laughed. "I told him that there wasn't much I'd be able to do about it. I think he wanted me to bodily remove your guest back to his chambers. I told him that Fardew was in charge of that, and that Fardew wasn't going to be too happy that Dereath had exposed…well, that you and Lord Ikling had seen him."

"What's he doing here?"

The bear shrugged his large shoulders. "Search me. Fardew has him in, but he just filed the paperwork with me because it's his department. Anyone in there could have sent for him."

"Could Dereath?"

Prewitt laughed. "Not likely. Dereath's just an assistant. I'm sure he volunteered to host when he met the guest."

Volle chuckled. "Probably. Knowing him."

"Do be careful of him, though, Lord Vinton."

"Please, call me Volle."

"Volle, then. Be careful. He is clever, as I said, though as you noticed today, somewhat immature and prone to impulsive acts. He could easily do some harm."

Volle nodded. "I'm trying, but I think we got off on the wrong foot, and I don't really know how to mend that."

"I'm not saying you have to mend fences. Just watch your step. Hopefully he'll forget and get caught up in some other new thing that gets in his fur."

"I hope so. I don't think he was very happy that his…guest moved out."

Prewitt shrugged his massive shoulders. "Brought it on himself, no doubt. I don't know what happened," he held up a paw, "and I don't want to. Just be discreet, like I said."

"Okay. He doesn't seem to have much inclination to go outside anyway." Volle's ears flicked as he realized that that could refer not only to Xiller's being discreet, but also to him being happily occupied in Volle's chambers.

Prewitt either didn't get the second meaning, or didn't care. "Good. He's supposed to be discreet; I just didn't know about you. Nice to know we can count on you."

"You can." Volle felt good about building his reputation as someone trustworthy. And he was apparently involved in an intelligence operation, if only peripherally, so that could only help his standing. Maybe in the future he'd be let in on more secrets.

"Is that all? I do have some things to get back to."

"Yes, I think so. I appreciate the time, Prewitt."

"My pleasure, Volle." They shook paws, and Volle left the office.

He wandered slowly through the palace, having a few hours to kill before dinner with Helfer and nothing in particular to do. In the wing by the Goat stair, he found an open door to a large room that proved to be a library.

For a while, he perused the books, and skimmed one on the history of Tephos. By and large, it gibed with what he'd been taught, though he was amused at the depiction of the Ferrenians as the villains in all the confrontations. Two nobles came in while he was reading and set up a game of chess, which he soon put down the book to watch, as they didn't seem to mind his attention. He'd played it occasionally in the academy, but wasn't sure whether as a farmer's cub, he would be expected to know how, so he didn't comment on their play, which he judged mediocre. He would have to get Tish to 'teach' him so he could legitimately play later on.

When his stomach started rumbling, they were deeply engrossed in their third game. He excused himself and returned to his chambers to see if Welcis had any messages for him.

"Nothing today, sir. May I inquire whether his lordship has come to a decision on the disposition of tomorrow's dinner?"

"Not yet. I need to think about it a bit more."

"Very good, sir." Welcis's tone seemed a bit stiffer than usual. "Will his lordship's guest be requiring any special amenities?"

"No, thank you."

"Then, with his lordship's permission, I would like to retire for the night."

"Yes, certainly." Volle waved a paw. "I'll be back after dinner, but I'll be okay."

"Thank you, sir."

Volle stood for a moment watching the skunk. It was clear that he didn't approve of Xiller staying in the bedroom, but Volle wasn't sure whether to ask him directly about it or just let it go. He decided that he had enough to worry about without getting into a discussion about it. If it persisted, he would ask Welcis about it later.

Helfer was in good spirits when Caresh let him into the weasel's parlor. "Hey, Volle! Come and have a seat. My good man Burren just sent up a case of mead, and I'm keeping it here, not in the palace cellars. It's smoother than last year's even. You must try it."

Volle grinned, sat, and obligingly took the cup that Caresh handed to him. He lapped it tentatively, then took a sip. "Nice. Apricot?"

Helfer nodded and sighed. "My favorite." He took another drink and looked at the cup tenderly. "I may not get out to the pub tonight."

"Yeah. Me neither."

Helfer's ears snapped up. "Really? I was kidding."

"Well, see, I've got sort of a guest…"

"You sly fox. How'd you sneak him in?"

Volle blinked. *Sneak him in?* Could Helfer know about the secret passages? And then he remembered the weasel's sudden disappearance. He hadn't known about the other passages then, and now it seemed very likely that Helfer knew about one, maybe even had one in the room.

"I didn't," he said casually, watching the weasel. "I'd need some sort of secret passageway for that, wouldn't I?"

Helfer just stared at him for a moment, then sat back. "No," he said, taking another drink of mead. "You could bring him in in a carriage or something."

"And is that how you do it?"

Helfer got a quirky smile on his muzzle, and tapped a claw on his cup. "All right, look. I'm going to share a secret with you. Even my parents didn't know about it. I think. Caresh knows, but nobody else but me does. Come on."

Volle followed him into the laying room and then into the wardrobe, where the weasel shut the door and dropped a bar across it. "It's here in the back. Close your eyes, would you please?"

Volle saw him set down his cup on a chest, then closed his eyes. He heard a click and a soft creak, and then smelled mildew and felt a cool breeze across his whiskers. Helfer said, "You can open 'em."

The back corner of Helfer's wardrobe had swung out to reveal a passageway. It was dark and dank, and from what Volle could tell, it dropped down immediately. Helfer was watching him nervously. "You can't tell anyone about this, okay?"

Volle nodded. "Sure. How did you find it?"

"Messing around as a kid. I don't think it was anything but a storage room before my parents put me in here. I never told them about it. I did sneak out a bunch, though." He grinned sheepishly, but with pride as well. "They wouldn't ever take me out to the town, so I had to explore by myself."

"Wouldn't buy you any Zinsky books, either, would they?"

Helfer grinned. "By luck, there's a book merchant three doors down from where this comes out." He swung the door closed. "So I still use this to go out sometimes, when I don't feel like being bothered with guards and papers. And when I might want to bring people back." He leaned against the door. "So how did you get your guest in? Is there another passage?"

Volle shook his head, feeling slightly guilty that he wasn't returning Helfer's confidence. "No, he was already in the palace. It's, well… it's the cougar."

"The one that attacked us?"

"Yeah." Volle flicked his ears. "He came back to my rooms… he'd been staying with Dereath and wanted out, and so I offered him my bed. I mean, my rooms. Well, it ended up being my bed, too." He grinned.

Helfer's expression was half a grin. "Are you sure it's safe? And what about Arrin?"

"Yeah. I wanted to talk to you about that. Can we go back outside?"

They walked back into the parlor, where Caresh had set the table for dinner. He set appetizers in front of them, and though Volle was hungry, he just picked at his while Helfer ate.

"He's so sexy, Hef." He sighed. "He made my knees weak. Wrapped me up in his arms, and he's so strong. And he thought I was cute. He said he wouldn't have jumped at us if not for me."

The weasel looked a bit jealous, but smiled. "He was pretty strong all right. Had me caught right up 'til I decided I didn't want to get free."

Volle grinned back, tail wagging. "He was pretty persuasive, wasn't he?"

"Yeah." Helfer adjusted his pants casually with a paw.

"Anyway, I'm worried about what Arrin will think. On the one paw, we're not really not seeing other people yet and what I do should be my own business. And I really like him. On the other, I know he doesn't mind me going to the Jackal's Staff, but it might be different having someone here. So what do you think? What should I do? Keeping in mind I really like him."

Helfer finished his mead and called Caresh over to refill it. "Well, are you going to give up Arrin for this cougar?"

Volle shook his head. "He's only going to be around for a bit. Which means I want to spend as much time with him as I can."

"You've only known him a day. Not even!"

"I know, but…didn't you ever just have a crush on someone? You know I have a thing for big cats, and he's forward and sexy, and he's sweet too."

"So just send him up here when Arrin visits. I'll make him feel welcome."

Volle grinned. "I don't know if he'd agree to that, but I could ask. It's not a bad idea, except that Dereath probably knows he's with me and he wouldn't lose a chance to tell Arrin."

"He could stay with me for a couple nights. Then when Arrin checks, he'll figure Dereath was just lying."

"Canis's teeth, Hef, are you that desperate? Don't you think you'll be able to hook up tonight?"

The weasel grinned at him. "I'll take a sure thing over a gamble any day. And he was pretty."

"Yeah." Volle saw the cougar's eyes again, and the rippling of his muscular frame, and fell silent.

Helfer watched him for a bit, sipping his mead, and finally waved a paw in front of his eyes. "Hey, Volle. Wow, you have it for him bad."

Volle looked at him sheepishly. "He's gorgeous. And he likes me."

"I guess so. Look, why don't you just tell Arrin you have to host him, that he was staying with Dereath and didn't like it, and don't tell him you're sharing a bed. It's none of his business anyway."

Volle nodded slowly. "That makes sense."

"Sure it does. So stop worrying and eat. They've made something with berries tonight, it's fabulous."

It was. As Volle devoured it, he thought about the other question he'd wanted to ask Helfer. "It's usually safe in the gardens, isn't it?"

"Now it is. But even before, nobody was really in danger. There are always some commoners who want to do away with the nobles, but more likely anyone you meet would just want to rob you. The only ones who'd want to kill you are other nobles." He grinned.

"Or Dereath."

"Nah, he just wants to tie you up and rape you."

"I think I'd prefer it if he killed me."

Helfer snickered. "Don't tempt him." He grinned at Volle's look. "Oh, don't worry, he'll forget about you soon enough."

"I hope so. Sure doesn't seem like he is. How did you get rid of him?"

"You came along." Helfer laughed at Volle's stricken expression and flattened ears. "I'm just kidding. I don't know that I did, actually. He seems to be upset that you and I are friends."

"He thinks we're more than that."

"Oh, right. That would explain a lot of it too. He's jealous of us being together when we both rejected him."

"Great."

"And now you've taken his big cougar toy away from him."

"Mmm." He pictured the cougar again, and fell silent. They moved on to dessert, and Volle kept seeing the lithe, muscular form waiting for him. He bolted down the cake almost without tasting it, and Helfer laughed at him.

"If you want to get away so much, you should've just said so."

Volle flicked his ears. "Sorry. It's just…"

Helfer waved a paw and grinned. "I know, I know. Is he even back yet? What does he do during the day?"

"Don't know. He won't tell me. Secret work or something, and he was being taken to dinner."

"Not by Dereath, I hope."

Volle shook his head. "I got the impression that Dereath was just his host and wasn't involved otherwise."

"By who, then?" Helfer's eyes sparkled. "He's a mysterious stranger! How exciting. It *is* just like a Zinsky book."

"Yeah, but I'm still curious. What is he here for?"

Helfer waved a paw. "Don't get involved, whatever it is. If you haven't noticed, the only thing the nobles here love more than finding out secrets about each other is keeping secrets from each other. He's probably being hired by Quirn to go steal something from Wallen or something."

"Maybe. But Prewitt knew about him," Volle said, remembering.

"So he has papers. Prewitt knows about everyone who gets papers."

"Why would he be staying with Dereath, though? Doesn't he work for Minister Fardew?"

"That might not have anything to do with it. I wouldn't be surprised if Dereath asked for him once he got wind of him."

"Right, that's what Prewitt said." Volle grinned and shrugged. "I shouldn't worry too much. He's waiting for me downstairs, or will be soon."

"Have another cup of mead and then get on down," Helfer said. "And I'll be off to the pub. Caresh!"

Volle's stomach was still warm from the mead when he took his leave of Helfer some time later. He felt pleasantly lightheaded as he skipped down the stairs, though he would have attributed it as much to the cougar he was going to meet as to the apricot mead.

Flickering candles along the staircases and the hallways lit his steps. Evening had fallen quickly, and the skylights were reflecting the inner light rather than letting in the outer. Volle knew the way so well that he could have walked it with his eyes closed, but to his light-sensitive eyes, the candles were as bright as day.

None were lit in his chamber, though. The light from the windows was more than enough for him to navigate by. He lifted his nose to the air and caught Xiller's scent, fresh. Smiling, he padded quickly to his bedroom door and opened it.

A head lifted slowly from his bed. Eyes gleamed, collecting the meager light from the windows and reflecting it to him.

"You're here," he said softly, tail hitting the doorframe as it wagged. He closed the door behind him.

"I couldn't wait to get back," came the whispered reply.

"Me neither." He unbuttoned his shirt and let it fall to the floor. The eyes watched him as he shed his trousers and tunic and stepped forward, naked.

"So come to bed," the cougar said softly, and Volle came.

He closed his eyes as the warm arms enfolded him. The smell of cougar was rich in his nose, reminding him of all his fantasies and yet somehow more real than all of them. Xiller was no prince, but Volle didn't need a prince with him there. The echo of royalty in his scent was enough to make Volle's fingers tremble as they brushed the short fur, feeling the soft and rough texture against his pads.

Although they'd never spent a night together, their paws seemed to know exactly where to roam. "Your fur is so soft," Xiller murmured as he let his claws out just enough to drag trails down Volle's back, making the fox shiver delightedly.

"You smell wonderful," Volle said back muffledly, his nose buried in Xiller's chest.

"You taste divine." He felt the long soft tongue lick between his ears, and then along his ears, and down his muzzle. He opened his muzzle slightly, and then words became unnecessary as well as impossible.

When he woke the following morning, the cougar's body was wrapped around his, strong tawny arms across his chest, serpentine tail draped across his hips. His tail was trapped between the cougar's muscular legs, except for the tip. He inhaled deeply; the scent of their lovemaking was still noticeable over their own scents. What he focused on in that half-awake blissful moment was the texture of Xiller's scent.

Scents were perceived as a whole, but up close, they were made up of many different aromas, all combining to make a recognizable whole. Like the walls of the palace, grey and uniform from a distance, but made of many different shades and sizes of stone up close, a scent was a combination of the fur itself, the body oils, anything the person habitually wore or carried, and the places he frequented. Lying close in Xiller's embrace, Volle passed a few dreamy moments sorting out the layers of his scent, breathing in and out slowly. He couldn't remember the last time he'd woken up this happy.

A knock at the door disturbed his reverie. Welcis's black and white muzzle poked in discreetly, and he coughed.

Volle flicked his ears to let him know he was awake, and Welcis said softly, "Lord Ikling will be expecting his lordship in just a few minutes."

Volle looked up and nodded, and Welcis shut the door softly. Xiller shifted against him, and his paw tightened across Volle's chest. "Mm. How long is a few minutes?" he murmured as the paw slid lower down the fox's body.

Volle squirmed and grinned. "Maybe ten."

"Hm. Maybe fifteen?" The paw had found its target and rested there, while the other slid between them to push his tail gently out of the way.

"Ohh…maybe…"

"Good." The single word quickened his blood and curled his toes with anticipation. Warm breath caressed his ears, sending shivers down his ribs even before the soft paw with just a hint of claws caressed him elsewhere. He pressed back into the warm cougar, holding the long, tense tail in his paws, stroking it with his own claws, which seemed dull and crude compared to the keenness of the razor-tipped ones being held just above his skin. He knew there was no real danger, but the sense of it added to his overall intoxication as he lost himself in the cougar's embrace again.

Some twenty minutes later, he jogged down the main hall towards an impatient weasel, whose foot was tapping the stone floor. "What took you? Oh, don't answer that, I can see it in your grin. Phew, and I can smell it, too. Come on, let's go."

Volle followed the weasel out. "I hoped the fresh air would get rid of some of the scents. Didn't really have time to clean up much." Helfer just snorted. "How'd your night go?"

"Ah, nobody was interested. Plus my head is killing me."

"How much of that mead did you have?"

"Two bottles before you came over. Two with you." He paused. "Two when I got home."

"And how much at the pub?"

"I drank ale at the pub. Their mead tastes rancid."

Volle chuckled. "If you don't want to do the whole run, that's fine."

"Nah, I can make it as long as I don't look at the sun. Or anything it's shining on."

He was more cheerful when they got to the shady back garden. Volle, in turn, fell silent as they approached the bush where Xiller had been hiding the day before. Had it really only been one day? He couldn't help but feel that he'd known the cougar for weeks or months.

Steady on, he told himself. He's leaving in a few days and you don't know when he'll be back. Don't throw your life into turmoil just because he happens to be stunning. And fabulous in bed. And somehow infatuated with you.

Helfer was waving a paw at him. "Hello? I asked what you're doing today."

"Oh, sorry. Tribunal. Then dinner with…well, alone, I guess."

"And then another wild night? How many more 'til he goes?"

Volle shook his head. "Don't know. Less than a week."

"Enjoy him while you can, my friend."

"I am." Volle grinned. "Thanks."

"Maybe I'll just head to the Jackal's Staff myself tonight. See who's there. My trip home is coming up in a month or so, so I'll miss a couple of our dates then."

"Oh? How long are you gone for?"

"Usually it's two weeks. Takes a few days to get there, a week to go through all the stuff with Burren, visit my mother and sisters and all their kids, and then a few days to get back here."

Volle calculated ahead. "I think you might just miss Ilyana's cotillion. Lucky you."

Helfer grinned. "Don't get married without me."

"Don't worry about that."

"She seems driven enough that she might just have the wedding on the floor there."

"You know, it's going to be painful enough without me thinking about that all the time. Do you know that it's even more complicated than a banquet at the palace? Not only do I have to remember all the place settings and how to use them and when to drink the wine and how to make a toast and who dances with whom and who sits with whom and who I'm allowed to dance with and for how long and to what kind of music, but I also have to be part of the official presenting. Her father brings her out and presents her and asks if there is anyone present who will escort her and I have to do this whole question and answer thing with him."

Helfer clucked sympathetically. "And then you have to remember all the wedding stuff on top of that." He ducked Volle's swipe at him. "Hey, I'm just saying, if you see a Canid Cantor there, better ask him what you need to say."

"I know what to say: help!"

By the time they reached the main entrance again, Helfer felt a little better, so they did a second tour. Panting, Volle bid the weasel good bye and headed for the baths, where he rolled in the powder for a while, rubbing his fur thoroughly. When he returned to his parlor, wrapped in a towel, he was a bit surprised to find Arrin waiting for him.

The fox was sitting in one of his chairs, resting his muzzle on one paw as he stared blankly at one of the tapestries Renaldo had had brought up the previous week. His ears were down and his tail rested limply on the floor. Volle had stopped with the door half-open, his tail against the doorframe, and Arrin looked up at him with a pained expression. He stepped in and closed the door as Arrin got up. He was holding a piece of paper, which he held out to Volle.

"I was going to ask if this is true, but it is, isn't it? I can smell him."

"Listen, he's just staying here because he wanted to get away from Dereath…" Volle's protest died away as Arrin thrust the paper at him. He took it and read it.

It was a notice from the Steward. A warning, more properly, that "improper conduct in public areas" was not permitted by royal decree, and that "complaints had been lodged" regarding Volle's conduct in the garden the previous morning with Lord Ikling and "an unknown cougar." Nothing was going to happen to him, but the tone made it clear that future incidents might be treated more harshly.

"Oh," he said. "That."

"You know," Arrin said in a low tone, "what you do is your business."

"Dereath filed this complaint, didn't he?"

"I mean, we never promised to be true to each other. And I know you go out to that brothel."

"Arrin? Was it Dereath?"

"But I thought—what?"

Volle had grabbed his shoulder. "Was it Dereath who filed the complaint?"

"Yeah. Him and Lady Oncit. But he's the one who identified you. She just said she saw…it."

Volle threw the paper down to the table. "He set it all up. He hired the cougar to attack us, and the cougar just got, um, carried away."

"Can you prove that?" Arrin's ears had lifted slightly.

"Yes. No." He remembered that he wasn't supposed to tell anyone about the cougar. "Look, it doesn't matter. Do you believe me or him?"

"Well, you, of course, but…"

"He set it all up and then when it didn't go like he'd planned, he tried to screw with us some other way. Damn him."

"Why is he here?"

"What? Who?"

"The cougar. It is the same one, isn't it?"

Volle chewed his lip. "Yeah, it is. I told you, he was staying with Dereath, and Dereath got upset with him over that. He doesn't know anyone else at the palace, so he asked if he could stay. I said yes."

"Is he staying in your bed?" Arrin met Volle's eyes and then turned away. "I'm sorry. I guess that's really none of my business. But I believed you when you said you and Lord Ikling weren't lovers, and now after this…"

"We're not. We were out running together, the cougar jumped out and attacked us. Helfer ran away but came back, I knocked him down, we ended up in a pile together, and then he, um, grabbed us both." Arrin's eyes flicked back to him, then away again. "Honestly, Arrin, that's what happened. Hef and I are good friends, nothing more."

The fox sighed, his tail twitching, and then he looked up. "All right. So how long is he staying?"

"I'm not sure. Less than a week."

"And is he coming back again?"

Volle opened his muzzle to say 'no,' and then thought better of it. "I don't know." He shrugged. "I don't know if he'll want to stay here if he does." Although technically true, he had a pretty good idea that Xiller would be back in a heartbeat, given the chance. He tried to assuage some of the guilt that rose up at that remark. "I think he's just here on a single assignment. I don't know how long it'll last."

Arrin was quiet for a while. His paws were clasped together in front of him, and he kept working his fingers through each other and back. Finally he said, in a small voice, "Do you want to keep seeing me?"

Volle stepped forward and wrapped his paws around the other fox's. Arrin looked up, and Volle smiled. "Of course I do. I'm just enjoying being single before I have to get married and pick a mate. I like you a lot, and I have a lot of fun with you." He touched his nose to Arrin's gently.

Arrin smiled. "All right. I guess we should postpone our dinner tonight?"

"If we could. Next week, same night? Maybe we can make an evening of it and go to the conservatory again."

"Okay." Arrin licked him and smiled. His ears had come back up. "I'll see you then."

Volle squeezed his paws. "Count on it."

Arrin headed for the door, and tapped the paper on his way out. "Oh, Volle. Do please try to keep your activities private from now on?" It was said lightly, but there were still traces of hurt in his eyes.

"I promise." Volle lifted a paw as Arrin left. When the door was closed, he sighed and sank into an armchair.

"Glass of wine, sir?" Welcis approached him from behind. He hadn't heard him come in from the parlor.

"No thanks. I've got to dress for the tribunal. Oh, Welcis, dinner one week from tonight with Arrin."

"Yes, sir." Welcis held the door open for Volle, who looked at him suspiciously.

"You heard the whole thing, didn't you?"

Welcis followed him into the bedroom. "It is invaluable in the management of his lordship's affairs that I gather what information I can." He searched through the wardrobe and laid out an outfit as Volle dropped the towel. The room still smelled of cougar, but the cat and his armor were gone.

"What else have you gathered?" Volle asked as the skunk took a brush and applied it to his fur.

"None of the servants know very much about his lordship's guest. Several saw his lordship's, ahem, indiscretion in the garden. Between that and his friendship with Lord Ikling, I fear his lordship is acquiring something of a reputation."

Volle gave a resigned sigh. "What else?"

"His lordship's interest in Madame Rodion is well regarded. It shows a dedication to his line that is admirable, especially given how quickly he is pursuing it."

"Well, I have Tish to thank for that. Or Tika."

Welcis pulled the brush through an unruly tangle. "There was some speculation initially about his lordship's authenticity, but I am pleased to say that his lordship's interest in furthering his line and his interest in the tribunal have laid such rumors to rest."

"Speaking of which, I'm going to be late for that. I just heard the clock sound."

"His lordship has enough time to be brushed and dressed." Welcis continued the brushing imperturbably, and as usual, he was right. Once Volle had dressed and walked quickly to the tribunal room, he found that he wasn't the last to arrive. Lord Oncit walked in five minutes later and slouched down in his seat.

They actually had several cases to hear; with the fall came harvest and markets and disputes over ownership and gold. Volle had been approved by Lord Creane to take his place, and the older lord would now sit as a spectator for the next month.

He found the cases interesting, but the demeanor of the other judges indicated that the interest wouldn't last. Oncit in particular was especially taciturn; not that he was ever talkative, but on this day he seemed angry about something. When he was outvoted on the first case by Volle and Boursin, he scowled, laid his ears back, and muttered, "Guess my opinion doesn't matter at all." Volle thought that was rather extreme, as they had listened to his opinion, but obviously something else was bothering him.

The wolf kept glancing at Volle, though he did it while he thought Volle wasn't looking. Volle caught him at it once, and after that, he listened for the rustle of the wolf's neck turning. Oncit had shown only cursory interest in him for the past few weeks, and he wondered what had changed. Surely he couldn't know about Xiller too? That seemed too much a coincidence to be possible.

Finally, he asked Creane during a break if there were anything different about him. The raccoon inspected him, then shrugged. "Nothing I can see or smell, but my eyes and nose aren't what they used to be. Why, you using a new scent or something?"

"Lord Oncit keeps looking at me. I'm not sure why."

"Yeah, I noticed that. Maybe he's annoyed at you for taking Boursin's side in that first case."

"I don't think so. It's more like he noticed me for the first time."

Creane shrugged. "Maybe he fancies you. I've heard he doesn't pay much attention to his wife these days." At Volle's look, he grinned. "I pay attention to *my* wife, and she talks to the other wives."

Volle grinned back and shook his head. "It doesn't feel like that."

"Well, then, who knows? He's always been a moody one. Look, the next case is coming in."

They finished in time for dinner, and as they were heading out, Volle felt a paw on his shoulder. He turned to see Lord Oncit.

"Lord Vinton. I wonder, if you're not busy, if you'd join me for dinner in my chambers?"

Volle breathed in, but got no scent of arousal or desire. Puzzled, he flicked his ears. "I'm not otherwise occupied, but may I ask, er, why?"

The wolf managed a smile of sorts. "I thought that since we've been serving on the tribunal, we should get to know each other a little better."

Volle nodded. "All right. Let me go change, and I'll be right up."

Oncit gave him directions to his chambers, and they parted. Volle pondered the odd invitation until he returned to his chambers, where he told Welcis about it.

"What do you know about Lord Oncit?"

"He is a lord in good standing, sir, a resident of the palace for twelve years. I have heard from the servants that he and his wife are no longer on the best of terms. It is likely that he has another…interest somewhere, but nobody knows who or where."

Volle nodded. "I've heard that from several places. About his wife, I mean. I didn't know he had a mistress."

"Begging your pardon, sir, but that is merely speculation on the part of the staff. My own thought would be that if the servants have not seen her, then either he is going to great lengths to hide her or she does not exist."

"Why would he hide her?"

"It is not my place to speculate. Please, sir, lift your head. There." Volle adjusted the shirt slightly as it settled over his shoulders. "Anything else about him?"

"I will investigate, sir."

"Thank you, Welcis."

Lord Oncit's chambers proved to be more spacious than Volle's. He saw what he assumed was Lady Oncit's touch in the decorating; much of the large parlor had frills and lace on it, and the curtains over the windows were a cream-colored sateen that Volle liked, but couldn't fit with the dour wolf he knew. Lord Oncit greeted him with a curt "Thanks for coming," and waved him to a table.

The wine and appetizers were already laid out. Volle looked around for a servant, but none appeared. Oncit saw him looking around and said, "I dismissed Chauncy for the evening."

"Is your wife joining us?" Volle was beginning to be a little worried.

"No, she's out." He waved a paw vaguely and sat down. "Wine?"

Volle nodded. The wolf filled both glasses, then raised his without ceremony and took a long drink. Volle sniffed the wine and then sipped it. It was good, though not remarkable. He looked up at Oncit, expecting him to say something, but the wolf just started eating the appetizers. Volle didn't know what to say, so he followed suit.

After a period of silence, he said, "I thought that third case was interesting. You know, the one where the weasel cub stole a knife and threw it?"

Oncit grunted, and nodded.

"I'm Volle, by the way. Please don't use 'Lord Vinton,' it sounds so formal."

Now the wolf looked up. "Maron," he said. "Maron of Oncit."

"Pleasure." Volle took another bite, but the wolf didn't.

"So, you grew up in Ferrenis." Volle nodded. "Liked it?"

"I've fonder memories." Volle trotted out his story of how the Ferrenians took his farm and killed his mother.

"Of course, of course. And your father…"

"Died fighting them." He put on a morose look. "I just hope I can avenge him somehow."

"Yes." And now Oncit looked a bit disturbed. He flicked his ears and set down his fork. "How serious are you about that?"

Volle met his gaze. "Pretty serious, I guess."

"It's easy to talk like that, safe here in the palace. Would you go out and fight on the front line?"

Volle frowned. "Are we at war?"

"I mean hypothetically."

"I…suppose I would. I mean, it wouldn't be fair to ask someone else to fight if I weren't willing to as well, would it?"

"Quite." The wolf seemed pleased with his response. "We're not at war, but we might be someday."

"Why? I mean, I presume not everyone has my reasons."

"Oh, the Reysfields, for one. Richest cropland in the river valley and they took it from us. Oncit borders the Reysfields, you know, which means we're on the frontier now. Unstable situation. Sure, they don't maintain any military presence there, but it's still theirs. My grandfather remembered when Oncit was larger and included some of the Reysfields."

"I see."

"Plus there's the matter of pride. That land, plus the land to the south, well, it's always been Tephossian. Except for the last fifty years or so. Someday, we will get it back."

"How?"

The question provoked an odd reaction from the wolf. His ears flattened and he looked down, his energy gone. "Yes," he muttered. "How, that is the question."

Volle didn't know quite what to say to that. Maron went to the sideboard and fetched the dinner, which he served very gracefully, to Volle's surprise. It was a small Cornish hen with bread stuffing and small tomatoes around the side, and while he was eating it, the wolf began talking again.

"So what do you do in your spare time?"

"Oh, walk about town some. Visit a pub or two. In the palace, I just noticed some people playing a game in the library that looked interesting."

"Yes, chess. I play myself, with Lord Ikinna. He's much better than I am, I'm afraid. I'd be glad to help you learn if you like."

"Maybe when tribunal slows down again."

Maron nodded. "Should have one or two more busy weeks, then winter will set in."

"I'd like that, then."

"I'll bring a set." For the first time at the dinner, the wolf smiled.

"What about you? What do you do for fun?" Volle regretted saying that immediately, as the wolf looked like he hadn't had fun in a very long time.

"Oh…" His eyes took on a faraway look. "I read. Play games."

"How long have you been here?"

"Dozen years or so. Sometimes it seems longer."

"What do you like best about it?"

That made the wolf pause. He stared at his plate and said, "I used to think I could make a difference. I wanted to do something for my people. That's what I liked."

"We made a difference for some people today."

"For a couple. In a year, nobody will even remember that they came to the palace, much less what the decision was or who handed it down."

"But it is important now."

Maron sighed. "You're right, of course. Sometimes you just get carried along in the course of things and you find that where you are isn't where you set out to be. And you look back and can't quite see how it happened, but it's too late to change it, really."

Volle smiled. "I don't think it's ever too late."

The wolf paused again, and gave him a long look. "Well. Hopefully you're right."

Dessert was a bowl of berries with fresh cream, and Volle stayed for only one glass of sweet wine, as visions of Xiller were starting to dance through his head. He shook paws with Maron and took his leave, thinking as he walked back to his chambers that he was surprised at how much he'd enjoyed the dinner. The wolf had turned out to be an interesting dinner companion in a number of ways, not least of which was that Volle had the distinct impression that he was being tested or sounded out.

The scent of the cat drove those thoughts from his mind as he closed his parlor door behind him. He stopped and breathed in, trying to sort the layers out as he had that morning, but the scent was too faint. Smiling, he eased the sitting room door open, padded in, and then eased the bedroom door open.

He could see the shape of the cougar, sprawled across the covers, but there was no eye-shine to greet him. Standing there in the shadowed doorway, he slipped his clothes off slowly, padded towards the bed where the cougar's scent was strong, and stopped abruptly.

Two gleaming orbs had appeared as the cougar opened his eyes, and a line of white slowly appeared as he grinned a feral grin. He stalked to the edge of the bed, and Volle felt his heart race. Instinctively, he took a step back, then another, as the cougar leaned forward.

He pounced at Volle, who twisted away and ran for the bedroom door, the cougar just a step behind. He had to dodge around the table in the sitting room, but the cougar matched him step for step. In the parlor, he hesitated between the door and the window, and just as he turned for the window, the large, muscled body tackled him from behind and bore him to the ground.

They hit the floor, but not hard, and Volle realized the cougar had cushioned the fall with one arm while holding him with the other. Teeth grazed his ear, and Xiller's soft voice hissed with amusement. "The little fox was running from me, but I seem to have caught him."

Volle squirmed a bit and gave a little whimper. The paw holding his chest let him feel the prick of its claws, and he stopped moving. His heart was pounding and his nerves felt as taut as a harpstring, though he knew the danger wasn't real. Blood pounded in his head and loins, his arousal pressed almost painfully hard against the cold stone floor as it grew. He could feel the cougar's arousal under his tail, which seemed by contrast almost unbearably warm.

A warm tongue pushed up the fur on his neck, and then powerful jaws circled it. He felt the pressure of teeth on his neck as they scraped through his fur, and a brief stinging pain that was lost in the flood of sensations. The jaws retreated, and the tongue licked up to his ear. "And what shall I do with him now I've caught him?" the cat's voice whispered.

"Whatever you want," Volle whispered back.

"Yes," came the chuckled reply as the cougar's other paw moved down Volle's side and slid under his hips. They moved together, desire uniting them under the starlight until even the stone of the floor was no longer cold.

Later, Xiller watched with amusement as Volle returned from the bedroom with a towel to clean the floor. "Doesn't your servant do that?"

"I don't know if I want him knowing about this. The servants all talk to each other."

Xiller traced a claw over Volle's bare rump. "You think we didn't wake him up?"

Volle sniffed at the floor and wrinkled his nose. "I don't know how lightly he sleeps. I didn't hear him moving when I went through, though." He took another swipe with the towel.

Xiller chuckled, a deep, throaty chuckle. "I thought our chase might have woken him. You were bad to run like that. It got my predatory instincts all up."

Volle leaned over and licked the cougar's nose. "Maybe that's what I wanted. I admit I didn't expect you to be that fast. It ended well, though."

"Mmm. Sure did. I hope I didn't hurt you."

"A couple scratches. I've had worse."

Xiller purred and nodded, resting on his side. "You're a tougher fox than you look."

Volle looked at the eyes shining in the darkness, half indignant, half amused. "How tough do I look?"

"That's not what I meant. I mean, all the foxes I know are light, slender, and mostly biters. You've got good muscle tone and you know how to use it."

"Thanks. Must be all that farm living."

"You were raised on a farm?"

"Yeah."

"Hm. I don't smell it on you."

"I haven't been on the farm for a long time. Nearly a year."

"Oh."

Volle sniffed the floor again, and this time detected only a faint odor of sex below the stronger scent of the towel. He sighed. "I think that's the best I'll do."

"Let's get to bed, then." He stood, extending a paw, and pulled Volle into a tight hug before walking with him to the bedroom.

Curled up together in bed, Volle murmured sleepily, "How much longer can you stay?"

The cougar nuzzled his ears. "Two more nights. I leave Ursiday morning."

Volle sighed deeply. The cougar's arms tightened around him. "I know. I'll be back, though."

"When?"

"I don't know. As long as it takes."

"A month? A year?"

"It shouldn't be a year. But I really don't know. I'm not supposed to come back here, but I'll find a way."

"Okay." Volle yawned. "I'll be here." The thought of Arrin lurked on the fringe of his consciousness, but it seemed so remote as to be beneath his notice. He was warmed by the cougar's body and his promise to return, and when he slept, his sleep was deep and peaceful.

Chapter 12

Welcis woke them both in the morning, setting out an outfit for Volle to attend services that morning and then retiring, without saying a word. Xiller grinned from the bed as Volle got dressed. "Think he heard us last night?"

"Maybe." Volle pulled on his shirt and shook his fur into place. "I think he just generally doesn't approve of you being here."

Xiller shrugged. "As long as you do."

Volle wagged his tail. "Most certainly. Aren't you coming to services?"

The cougar's ears slid back and he mumbled, "No. They told me not to. Too public." He fidgeted. "I haven't missed a Gaiaday service in years, and I so wanted to see the cathedral. Felis forgive me."

"She will," Volle said. "Maybe you can worship this evening, when the cathedral's empty."

"Without a Cantor?"

"I'm sure there are some around. I'll talk to one and make sure."

Xiller smiled, and his ears came back up, and Volle thought he would promise just about anything to see that expression on his muzzle, that light in his eyes. "Will you?"

Volle nodded, and the cougar sprang out of bed and wrapped his arms around him. "Thank you, fox. That would mean a lot to me."

"Then of course I'll do it." Volle ruffled the cougar's bare back with his claws.

Xiller was kissing him soundly on the muzzle when Welcis walked back in. The skunk coughed delicately. "Sir, the palace is assembling for services." He seemed to be avoiding looking at Xiller's naked form, as difficult a task as that was.

Volle licked the cougar's nose and smiled. "I'll see you tonight and we'll go over."

The cougar's tail swished back and forth, mimicking Volle's wagging, as the fox accompanied Welcis out to the sitting room. Even though Welcis continued to avoid looking at the naked cougar, Xiller seemed completely at ease, making no attempt to cover himself.

Outside, the palace was assembled in a gaudy show of finery. Everyone was wearing their colors or crests and their best clothes. They had loosely assembled into the six Houses prior to going across the street, and when the foot-fox signaled that the street had been cleared and secured, they all walked across together.

Volle sang more confidently with the services now. Even though Fox wasn't mentioned by name here, he held Fox in his heart and knew that his prayers to Canis were heard by Fox as well. He joined in the song at the end confidently, and ended the service suffused with a feeling of protection and well-being.

The Canids and Herbivores had been placed together at the end, so Volle had to look around to find the Felid Cantor, a slender bobcat. It wasn't until the cathedral was mostly empty that he spotted him talking to another bobcat, a noble Volle didn't recognize. He walked over and waited patiently until the noble was finished and left.

"Yes, my brother's cub?" The bobcat turned peaceful eyes on him.

"Father's brother," Volle said respectfully, "I wonder if I might ask you a favor."

"If it is within my power to grant, I will be delighted to help. But why not ask Cantor Juvicius?" He indicated the coyote who was the Canid Cantor, walking back towards the back of the cathedral.

"A friend of mine was unable to attend services this morning, and must leave the city in two days. He very much wanted to have a service in the cathedral before leaving."

"He is a son of Felis?" Volle nodded, and the bobcat stroked his muzzle thoughtfully. "We normally spend the evening in private observance. I do hold a small service on Feliday, but that's five days away."

"It is very important to him."

The priest smiled. "Importances are all relative, my brother's cub. Does the importance to one outweigh the importance to another?

"It is important to me as well. That makes two." Volle smiled tentatively, and the priest returned his smile.

"For someone so devoted to Felis and not even of her flock, I can spare half an hour from my observances to lead a small service tonight. At what time will your friend be ready?"

"Nine?"

"That will be fine. Come in through the side entrance, there, and wait for me here. I will lead you to one of our private chapels."

"Thank you, brother's father. I won't forget this. Should the Church need something in the future…"

"We have all that we need inside us, but there are always those unfortunates whose needs cannot be met by Gaia alone. A donation to one of our orphanages is never unwelcome."

Volle nodded. "I will remember that. Thank you again."

"Good day, brother's cub. Go with Gaia."

"And you as well."

He walked out of the cathedral with a happy arch to his tail. The secured area along the street was still lined with a few locals, but most of the ones that had turned out to watch the nobles go to church had gone home or to their own services.

Helfer was waiting for him. "Seeking some extra spiritual guidance in your dilemma?"

"Dilemma?"

"About Arrin."

Volle patted the weasel on the back. "No, that seems to have worked out. Oh, did you get a warning from the Steward?"

"Yeah. May that rat catch the plague. Writing us up for something that was his fault in the first place."

"No way to prove that, though."

"Can't you bring the cougar to the Steward? I'm sure they're curious who he is."

"He's not supposed to be exposed to any more people than necessary." Helfer snickered. "You know what I mean."

"It's not likely to be a big deal, anyway. It's not like I plan to go screwing in public again."

"Don't include me in your plans if you do."

"With as long as you took? Perish the thought!"

Volle grinned. "Yeah, I actually gave him time to get interested before *I* sprayed all over his paw."

"Hey, I could've come twice in the time it took you. Would've, too, if he hadn't stopped. He must not know about weasels."

"Or else he knows all about them."

They bantered, grinning, all the way back to the palace and all the way through their run, and as they stood panting in the main hallway, Helfer said, "Look, why don't you bring him up for dinner tonight? It would be nice to meet him a bit more formally, since you think so much of him."

Volle considered. "He's usually busy for dinner, but I can come up and tell Welcis to send him up when he returns. We'll have to leave around quarter to nine, though. He wants to see the cathedral and I told him I'd take him."

"Won't leave us much time."

"Sorry. I don't have much time to see him either."

"I know, I know." Helfer grinned and waved. "See you tonight, then."

"I'll be there." Volle waved and watched the weasel jog up the stairs, then headed down the corridor for a bath.

He took a walk through the town in the afternoon. Most shops were closed for Gaiaday, but a few eateries were open. He visited the fried pastry shop, as had become his habit; they knew him there now. Munching his pastry, he slipped into the alley three doors down, made sure he wasn't being observed, and then slipped a note into a space behind a loose stone in the wall. It was one of their rotated drop sites, which he made sure to visit at least once every few days. Today's note mentioned the odd behavior of Lord Oncit and his discussion of a Ferrenian war, as well as a loosely worded suspicion that something was going on at the palace that Dereath was involved in.

He'd agonized over whether to mention Xiller, and in the end had decided to wait and see what else he could learn before doing so. He was afraid that he would be given instructions to do something that would damage their fledgling relationship, or to stop seeing the cougar altogether. In a couple days, he knew now, Xiller would be gone and he could write a report detailing what he'd managed to learn. The decision was not made without a great amount of guilt; he knew that really he should have reported Xiller as soon as he showed up, and only his personal issues kept him from doing so. But, he reasoned, what could they tell him to do? Capture the cougar? Lure him to a place where he could be questioned? Neither of those seemed very plausible to Volle, and he was trying to get information as best he could. Better to ask forgiveness than permission, he thought as he sauntered out of the alley, licking crumbs from his muzzle.

The air had a definite chill to it, but he only noticed it at the tips of his ears and in the breeze past his nose. He thought about winter and what the snow would be like in Divalia. In Caril it was beautiful on the tops of houses, but often melted to slush in the streets and pooled in holes that became invisible. Many a soaked paw trod the cold stone floors of the Academy in the winter months.

For now, though, the snow was weeks away, and the chill in the air refreshed and invigorated him. He wandered off his normal route, and found himself in a dark, cramped street. At the end of it, a group of large badgers turned to look at him. He knew that look from the streets of Caril, though he'd never been on the receiving end of it there. For the first time in his walks in the town, he felt nervous, and he turned back to the more open street.

He'd been warned about his walks in the town. Near the palace, there were guards posted, and a noble was never more than a shout away from help, though still vulnerable to cutpurses. The better businesses were located there, to attract the nobles' money, and so generally there was little danger. Further away, though, rescue was not so close, and not only his money but his person might be in peril. He'd always trusted to his instincts and his speed to get back to safety in time, and now he paused downwind of the alley entrance and slipped into a doorway, keeping his nose to the wind.

For ten minutes, he waited, while people walked by and smells floated through the air, but he didn't smell the badgers. Probably they wouldn't chase him beyond their street, but he waited a couple more minutes to be sure. When they didn't appear, he edged cautiously out and padded quickly towards the palace.

"They wouldn't have done anything besides take your money," Helfer assured him over dinner. "Might have been a little more rough than a cutpurse, but they wouldn't have killed you. Like I said, you have more to worry about here at the palace."

Volle took a sip from his second glass of apricot mead, and nodded. "I'm not used to that." He meant that he wasn't used to being a target. In Caril, he and the other students had walked around in plain clothes through some of the worst sections of town and had barely even been jeered at.

Helfer took it another way. "City's a lot more dangerous than the farm, you know."

"I know, I know. But hey, at least here you can't end up with a leg sheared off by a plow."

"Did that happen to someone you know?"

"Yeah." It had happened to Reese's older brother's friend, who really did work on a farm, but Volle co-opted the story. "They had to take the leg off. Now he can only drive the plowing team. He can't help much with the harvest."

"That's too bad."

Volle shrugged in what he hoped was an appropriately nonchalant way. He'd been horrified when he'd heard of the accident. Granted, he'd lost a childhood friend to disease, but mutilation was something he'd never thought about before Reese mentioned it. Now he repeated what Reese had said when he'd told the story. "It happens. Goes with life on the farm."

Helfer nodded. "Glad I don't have to work on a farm." Which amused Volle, as it was very nearly exactly what he'd said to Reese.

"Anyway, they didn't follow me, so I didn't have to find out."

"I don't know what you see out in the city anyway," Helfer said around a mouthful of rice and vegetables. The kitchen had prepared a rare vegetarian dinner, but after some initial grumbling from Helfer, they'd found it quite good.

"Just curious about it," Volle said. He had always known the streets of Caril and enjoyed walking around the streets here to see how different and similar they were, but again, Helfer interpreted his remark differently.

"Very different from the farms, eh?"

"Quite."

"You should be okay. I used to wander out too, though I don't think I ever went as far as you did."

That suited Volle. The fewer nobles wandering the city, the less chance he'd be seen dropping a note or receiving one. He was worried about Dereath following him, but he'd remained attentive and had yet to see the rat outside the palace.

They were just licking the last traces of lemon tart from the dessert plates when they heard a knock at the door. Caresh answered it, and ushered in the large cougar a moment later. His eyes brightened when he saw Volle, and he barely let the fox stand up before sweeping him into a hug.

"Hi." Volle licked him and hugged back, tail wagging. "You remember Helfer?"

Xiller grinned. "Quite well." He extended a paw.

Helfer stood and chuckled. "What do you want me to put in that?"

Xiller laughed. "Just a paw, this time. I am sorry for getting carried away."

"I'm just sorry you stopped." Helfer smiled as he shook the large paw.

"I did have a fox to take care of." The cougar grinned down at Volle.

"So you did. And I hear you're doing a good job of it."

"I'm trying."

Helfer sat down, and Volle did the same. "Have a seat, won't you? Cup of mead? It's from my personal stock."

"Certainly, thank you." Xiller wedged his large frame into one of Helfer's chairs and took the cup Caresh handed him, holding it steady while the fox poured mead into it. He took a sip, and then another. "This is delicious."

Helfer smiled and nodded. "I know. Thank you. So what brings you to the palace?"

The cougar's eyes slid to Volle, then down. "Oh, I'm not supposed to talk about it."

"Secret mission, eh? Exciting." Helfer grinned at Volle. "More than just molesting a couple nobles?"

Xiller chuckled, unabashed. "That was just a side benefit."

"May all your missions be as beneficial, then." Helfer raised his cup, and the others joined him. "Seriously, good luck. I hope you get back soon. I haven't seen the fox this happy ever before."

Volle flicked his ears and looked down when Xiller looked at him. "He's made me happy, too," the cougar said softly. "I feel like I have a friend here."

Helfer patted the large tawny paw that rested on the table. "I hope you feel like you have two. Though not necessarily in the same way."

"Thanks." Xiller downed the rest of his mead, and set the cup on the table. "Where are you from, Lord Ikling?"

"Vellenland. Hence the mead." Helfer lifted his cup again. "Best in all the land. And yourself?"

"I don't think I should talk about myself much."

"Ah, well, there goes my plan of learning more about you. I think it is about time for you two to leave anyway, right, Volle?"

"Quarter til? Yes, we should be going. Thank you, Hef. I'll see you in the morning." He embraced the weasel as they stood, and Xiller shook his paw. Caresh showed them out.

Walking through the palace, Volle's tail was wagging almost of its own accord. Even though it had been a short time, and they hadn't talked about much, he was glad Helfer'd had a chance to meet Xiller. The two of them had seemed to get along pretty well, and that made him feel good enough to wag his tail.

Xiller noticed. "You and he are pretty good friends, eh?"

"Yeah. He really made me feel welcome here. We get along really well."

"I'm glad I got to meet him more formally." Xiller chuckled a deep chuckle.

Volle grinned. "I'm glad you got along."

"He seems pretty nice. I wish I had more of a chance to get to know him."

"Hopefully you will."

They crossed the garden in silence and presented their papers to the guard on duty. He eyed Xiller, but didn't say anything as he let them pass. The nocturnal traffic had started, making the streets busy, but the space around the cathedral was quiet and still. They took a moment to walk around it so Xiller could admire the graceful spires, the arch of the doorways and windows, and the many reliefs that crowded the outside. The cathedral predated the palace, and it showed: the palace's outer walls were starkly functional, and the inner, though painted nicely and decorated around the windows, were not nearly as elaborate as the baroque lines and numerous detailed animal heads that decorated the large edifice.

Volle remembered his first impression of the cathedral as austere and forbidding, when he'd thought it was the symbol of the repressive Orthodox church. After going to services, he had softened his views somewhat, for although the building was still grey stone, with many impressive sculptures, candles illuminated many colorful frescoes inside the walls, and the services were generally welcoming and uplifting. He had never looked this closely at it in the moonlight, and he found that the loss of color made the building less friendly, but more impressive. Lit by the stark silver light, the faces of the animals seemed more mysterious, as though they might really be the ancestors or even the gods, caught in a frozen moment. Their expressions were benevolent, for the most part: peaceful, contemplative, and smiling, but here and there a terrified or furious visage stood out among the others.

The church by day, the church by night, the church during services: all these were aspects of the cathedral, just as each of the reliefs was. Each single relief had its own characteristics, its own message to convey, and provoked a particular sensation in the viewer. Each was different from each other and from the whole, Volle thought, and yet they came together fluidly to express that yes, all these individuals were indeed part of the world. The silver light and deep black shadows seemed to him to underscore the importance of remaining on Gaia's path, and yet the overall lines of the church reached upward without straining, extending the inclusion to Gaia's World and promising that they would be lifted from this earth, in time.

Xiller was as entranced as he was, but rather than standing still, he paced back and forth, examining the reliefs in silence. His tail, usually so active, was held almost perfectly still behind him. Volle shifted his attention from the cathedral to the cougar, watching his rapt examination of the stonework and feeling the wonder he was feeling. He imagined how the cathedral must look to someone who had really been raised in a small farm town, and felt echoes of Xiller's delight and amazement.

The cougar's eyes were wide when he turned back to Volle. He padded to the fox's side and whispered, "It's amazing."

Volle nodded, smiling. "They did things differently back then. Much bigger."

Xiller shook his head. "We have an old church in our town, but it's crumbling and covered with moss and stuff. We don't even go there anymore. For services, anyway. The kids still play in it. This is just…this is so much different."

"Yeah." The cathedral in Caril was prettier and more open, but Volle saw this cathedral as more solid and reassuring. It stands apart from the people, he thought, welcoming them in but remaining above them, where the Caril cathedral strove to be a part of them. He got the sensation that should the people abandon it, the cathedral in Caril would fall quickly into decay; this cathedral, similarly abandoned, would endure.

"We're supposed to go in the side," he said softly to Xiller, indicating a walkway around the corner of the cathedral. The cougar followed him down the unevenly lit path, pausing every now and then to admire another detail of the stonework on the sides of the cathedral. When they reached the door, Volle opened it slowly and peered inside.

The church was dark, lit only by a few stations of candles around the periphery. Both Volle and Xiller could see perfectly well by that small light, and stood just inside, looking around as the door closed behind them. The space inside the cathedral seemed somehow larger than it looked on the outside, perhaps because the ceiling was dim with shadows. Wooden pews filled the floor in six groups, and the six stations where the Cantors stood looked very different, wreathed in shadows as they were. A few furred shapes occupied some of the pews, and the murmured sound of praying was an undertone in the cathedral.

As they looked around, the bells in the tower above them tolled nine slowly. Xiller's ears folded back briefly; the sound was much louder in here than it was outside. Slowly, he brought them back up again, looking up with an awed expression. Volle kept his down the whole time; the loud sound made his ears ring otherwise.

The last stroke had barely faded when a quiet voice said near them, "Welcome, my cub, and my brother's cub."

They turned to find the Felid Cantor standing to one side, smiling, his ears lowered as well. He carried a book under one arm and was dressed in the same priestly robes he'd worn that morning.

"Hello, my father's brother," Volle said. "Thank you again for disturbing your schedule."

"Thank you," Xiller echoed, a little awestruck.

"My children, I merely do the work of Felis and Gaia. Come this way."

They followed him down the side of the cathedral towards the front. The decorations were all Felid here, but Volle noted that all were tapestries and statues that could easily be moved; indeed, some showed signs of movement. The frescoes were less specific, being mostly scenes of the Creation and Birth of the six Houses. He guessed that with the succession to the throne of a certain House, that House was placed at the front of the cathedral, or at least the part closest to the street, as the Ursid decorations dominated the entrance and surrounding area.

The Cantor led them behind a curtain, and Volle was surprised to find a small chapel there, complete with two short pews and a Cantor station, smaller than the large ones in the main building, but unmistakable. The bobcat drew the curtain back and then closed a door behind it. He stepped up into the station and arranged his book, while Volle and Xiller took their place on the pews.

He looked down at them. "My cubs, welcome home. Let us pray."

The service was similar to the morning's, except that the songs seemed much more personal to Volle. He joined in at the Cantor's urging, and the three of them sang two hymns: one that was particularly Felid, called "With Clawless Paws," and of course, the "Our Mother," though they only sang two of the parts to it. Volle's baritone melded nicely with Xiller's bass and the Cantor's pleasant tenor, and when they ended, the Cantor said, "Go into the world, and the world goes with you."

"Gaia's blessing on you," they replied, and stood, shaking paws to end the service.

"Thank you again, Cantor," Xiller said with a huge smile, shaking the priest's paw.

"Bless you, my cub," the priest replied. "I am glad to help you praise Gaia and Felis."

Volle had brought a small purse with five gold pieces in it, and pressed it into the priest's paw. "Here, father's brother," he said. "Please take this to the orphanage with my compliments."

"Bless you, my brother's cub," the bobcat said, sliding the purse into a pocket of his robe. "Go with Gaia, both of you." He smiled and opened the door, and slipped out through the curtain.

Xiller clasped both of Volle's paws in his, and kissed the fox firmly on the muzzle. "And thank you, for arranging this. None of the others thought it would be important for me to attend a service, even though I told them I wanted to."

"It was important to you, so it was important to me." Volle kissed him back and smiled, his tail already wagging. "Let's head back home."

Xiller's tail curled around his and then slid off. "Yes, let's."

They walked arm in arm back to the palace, strolling slowly through the night. Back in Volle's chambers, they made their way to the bedroom and undressed each other in the soft moonlight. They nuzzled each other, and their muzzles sought each other out.

At the touch of the cougar's tongue, Volle felt weak again. He sagged in Xiller's arms, and the cougar supported him, carrying him over to the bed and laying him down on his back. He smiled at the cougar as the long legs straddled his form, admiring the lithe grace with which the muscular body moved, and the large sheath that rested on his stomach as the cat straddled him. He brushed a paw gently along it, and up the waiting erection.

Xiller's rear rubbed over Volle's matching hardness. "Up for something a little different tonight?"

Volle pushed upwards. "Can't you tell?" He smiled, tail wagging against the bed.

"I sure can." The cougar licked his lips, then leaned over to lick Volle's.

Volle kissed him back, and reached paws up to Xiller's sides to pull the cougar down against him. His heart was beating fast again, and he could feel every beat in his ears, his chest, and his maleness. He could feel the heat and heart of the cougar too, as their bodies pressed close. His arms clasped the strong body tightly to him, and his paws ruffled the short fur down the crease of the cougar's spine and rump. Their heartbeats sounded loud in his ears and then merged and became indistinguishable. Volle felt so much a part of him then that the later joining, as wonderful as it was when it happened, seemed almost a formality.

Chapter 13

He woke before Xiller again, and discovered that he had squirmed out of the cougar's embrace at some point during the night. The morning's light was coming in at an angle through the window, so the curves of the cougar's body appeared as a rough silhouette against the bright wall. He reached out and drew a finger across the tawny fur.

Xiller's eyelids fluttered and then opened. He looked at the fox and smiled. "Morning."

"Hi."

A large paw draped itself over Volle's hip. "Sleep okay?"

"Great. You?"

"Mm."

"You have another full day?" The cougar nodded slowly. "I guess I'll see you tonight, then."

"I'll be here."

Volle brushed the short fur down Xiller's side, enjoying the cat's purr. "You don't have to tell me what you're doing, but I'm just curious how you got picked for it."

"I volunteered." The cat smiled. "My dad used to read me the stories about Makale, and I loved them. You know, the great cougar hero who served with King Kohai? Do foxes tell the same stories?"

Volle smiled. "I was brought up on stories of Granzer, the great wolf who rallied his regiment to hold back the Crivens at Vista Pass. There aren't many heroic foxes in the legends. But I've heard of Makale and Kohai, of course."

"My family sent me to the army when I was twelve. I had the body and skill for it even that young. And what I wanted more than anything was to be in the service of the King, taking on his enemies with my sword, earning glory in his name. I bothered the commander every month once I'd been appointed an officer, and finally last month he told me he had a mission for me."

Volle touched his chest. "How old are you?"

"Seventeen." He puffed his chest out. "I'm the second youngest officer ever in Villutian."

"That's where you're from?" Xiller's expression fell. Volle laughed softly and kissed him. "It's all right. I won't tell. So you must be excited about this mission."

"Kind of. It's not exactly what I'd pictured. More sneaking than anything else. But they said I'd be in line to do more heroic things later if I did well at this."

Volle smiled. He was reminded of Maron's words from two days before, and hoped Xiller wasn't in for the same bitter disillusionment. "I'm sure you'll be a great hero."

"You think so? I hope so."

"Just be true to yourself. You've certainly done a good job catching a fox."

Xiller grinned and brushed his paw across Volle's chest. "Oh, that's not heroic. That's—what's this?" He rubbed at something on Volle's chest.

The place he was rubbing was a bit sore. "I don't know."

Xiller leaned closer and sniffed at his paw, then Volle's chest. "I think it's blood. I must have pushed my claws out deeper than I meant to, the other night." He looked up contritely, ears down. "I didn't even notice, yesterday. Sorry."

Volle smiled. "I didn't notice either. It's okay. You used your other weapon quite well."

"I certainly didn't meet a lot of resistance."

Volle shook his head. "I was awed by its mighty power."

Xiller laughed and pulled him into a warm embrace. He returned it happily, tail pushing against the sheets as he wagged it.

Over his morning run, he realized he'd forgotten to tell Helfer about his dinner with Lord Oncit. Once he had, Helfer shrugged. "Who knows? I've never met him, personally. Doesn't sound like he wants to sleep with you, though that would've been my first guess since he sent his servant and wife away."

"That's what I thought too, but it definitely wasn't that."

"Who knows? Maybe he's just lonely and wants someone to play chess with."

"Could be."

"It's nice to have friends around here."

"Glad I met you," Volle said sincerely, and Helfer chuckled.

"Yeah, me too. Glad I sought you out, I should say. I haven't really had anyone to pal around with in a while."

They ran on in silence for a while, until Helfer said, "I guess you're not going to the Jackal's Staff tonight, then?"

"No, it's his last night. He leaves tomorrow morning."

"Too bad. I'll say hi to Richy for you."

Volle grinned. "I'll see him next week."

"I'll tell him that."

They chatted for the rest of the run lightheartedly, and Volle took a quick bath before dressing and going to lunch. He didn't see Lord Oncit there, and realized that he couldn't remember the last time he'd seen the wolf at lunch, though he had been at services the previous day. Ikinna and Ryshko weren't there either. He ate with a couple other nobles he knew slightly, talked about the weather and when the first snow would fall, and then set off to spend an afternoon walking around the town.

His wanderings took him to the park, where he saw a statue of a fierce lion warrior. He'd seen it many times before, but never really looked at it, and today, it reminded him of Xiller. He smiled, wondering who had carved it and why. The muscles were well done, and the armor was similar to Xiller's. Only the flowing mane was different; no doubt that was why the statue was here in a park rather than in the palace gardens or in a noble's chambers. The maned lions all lived across the arid southwestern deserts, according to the stories, and there was a history of enmity between them and Tephos. This was probably a trophy brought back by some long-forgotten army, judging by its age.

The expression and the active pose spoke to why it was still on display, however. The lion's jaws were open in a defiant roar, and there was a hole in the curve of his paw that had probably once held a sword. His other arm bore a shield, but it was swept out to the side rather than held in against the body. The heroism in the pose more than anything else was what made Volle think of Xiller.

He sat down near the statue and rested his muzzle in his paws. The cougar was leaving tomorrow, and Volle was going to have to let him go. He wasn't looking forward to it, but he knew he could do it. The fabric of his life had become a complicated one, and he couldn't let a single encounter disturb it. He had too many duties to too many people, and he couldn't afford to be impulsive—as impulsive as he had been the last few days, he reminded himself guiltily.

For a moment, he contemplated throwing it all away to accompany Xiller on his mission. The romance and simplicity of it appealed to him, for though he recognized the complexity of his life, he didn't necessarily enjoy it all the time. Pretending to be someone else could be fun, but without a break it became arduous, especially when he had to pose as several different people at different times and remember which was which. He'd been trained for it and was good at it, but he was good at knife fighting, too; that didn't mean he sought it out. He was important but not critical to anyone. Seir and Tish and Helfer and Arrin and Ilyana would all get along without him if he ran away.

He let himself wander into romantic fantasies wherein he and Xiller would be an unbeatable espionage team, hiring themselves out to the highest bidder, undertaking dangerous missions by day and romantic escapades by night. The fantasies brought a smile to his muzzle even as he realized how impossible they were. No, when the morning came, he would have to bid the cougar good-bye and face the upcoming months not knowing when he would see him again, if ever. He would have to hold the memory of their time together to his heart, in case it never came around again.

There would be Arrin, and there would be Ilyana, but they and even Richy would pale next to the memories of these few days. It was strange, he thought, that only a week ago, leaving services, he'd been thinking how his life here was going better than he'd imagined it might, and now he was lamenting the sacrifices he had to make for it. He smiled at himself and lay back with his eyes closed, enjoying the sunlight that warmed his fur despite the chill air.

When the sun had sunk low in the sky, he wandered down to a row of short houses and walked around the back, where each house had a small yard that was shared by all the inhabitants. The thick wooden fence behind the third house hid him from sight, allowing him to bend down and lift a loose cobblestone. Underneath it was a small folded piece of paper on which Sherr had written in his neat slanted handwriting, "Investigate Oncit further."

Volle read the note while walking down the rest of the alley. If anyone had been watching, they might think he had only paused to adjust his trouser leg, or pick a stone out of his toes. When he'd read the terse instructions, he chewed the note into a pulpy mass and spit it into the gutter. The ink left a sour taste in his muzzle, so he stopped by the nearest pub and ordered a cup of wine, which he lapped slowly as the shadows grew over the city.

He was hungry by the time he headed back to the palace, so he headed straight for the common dining area and took a plate of spicy duck to a table. A few minutes later, Lord Black, who was in a jovial mood, joined him. He explained to Volle that he'd expected to lose some income this year as a result of an infestation of locusts in his land's fields (the proliferation of insects was why his lands were called 'Black,' but the locusts were a rare plague on top of everything else), but as it turned out, his resourceful farmers had harvested the locusts and cooked them with the help of some of the elders in the town. They now had plenty of food for the winter, and had enough to sell to neighboring lands besides. The rodents especially considered the locusts quite delicious. He was having some trouble with the herbivores, because plants were scarce, but he thought they could easily trade a few bushels of preserved locusts for enough vegetables to get through the winter.

Volle had eaten locusts as a child, he vaguely recalled, but all he could remember about them was that they were "crunchy." He was glad to accept the raccoon's invitation to come over and try a jar, when the farmers sent some up. He promised to drag Helfer along, too, and they discussed strategies for getting the finicky weasel to try one. Eventually the strategies became more and more outlandish, and Volle was still chuckling when he bid Black goodnight and wandered back to his chambers.

The smell of cougar was old in the parlor and also in the bedroom. Welcis was asleep and Xiller was nowhere to be found. Volle sighed, undressed, and crawled into bed to wait. Every moment that passed brought some small worry that Xiller had already left without saying good-bye. He wouldn't want to, of course, but maybe he'd been forced to.

Volle had just about resigned himself to never seeing the cougar again when he heard movement in the parlor. He hadn't heard the door open, but he heard it close. His bedroom door inched open slightly, and a figure stepped through.

It was Xiller's height, and moved like a cat. Volle sat up, about to say 'where have you been,' and then froze. Jaguar's spots were clearly visible on the naked body.

The jaguar moved towards him, and he was a second from crying out when the scent caught up to him and he recognized Xiller. "What happened to you?" he whispered.

He pirouetted for Volle, his spotted tail flowing gracefully around him like a ribbon. He was spotted all over, and the spots were expertly done. "It's my disguise," he whispered back. "Like it?"

Volle reached out to brush the fur around a spot. "You look like a jaguar," he said. His fingers didn't smear the spot when he touched it. "But your fur won't match."

"The fur's yellow. You just can't see it. It took them all day." Xiller wiggled his rear and then turned, grinning.

"I can see one place they didn't do," Volle said, reaching out with a smile.

Xiller purred at the touch and then leapt onto the bed, landing astride Volle. His eyes looked down into the fox's. "I wasn't supposed to be here. They wanted me to stay in the pub and not be seen. But I couldn't leave without saying good-bye."

"I'm glad." Volle lifted his muzzle and they kissed, slowly and tenderly.

When they broke apart, Xiller settled beside him with a smile. "You knew what I was. I'd never seen a jaguar. I guess you grew up in the south?"

Volle had seen the occasional jaguar in Caril. He found them exotic but also very aloof and stuck-up. "I saw one in town once," he said vaguely. "On his way north to the city."

"There's so many creatures here I'd never seen in our little town. White foxes, golden bears…I haven't seen a jaguar, though. I wish I had. I'd know how to act then."

"Act like you're better than everyone else," Volle grinned. "That should about do it." He brushed a spot again. "Won't this come off if you bathe?"

Xiller shook his head. "It bonds to the fur somehow."

"Even in a water bath?"

The cougar nodded. "There's a special cream that removes it. They gave me a bit of it, but it's outside with my other things."

"Really." Volle stroked the cougar's chest. This was news that Sherr would find interesting. The Tephossians had the fur pigment. Most likely they'd stolen it from the Ferrenians. He grinned widely as he thought of one way he could make sure. Conveniently enough, it didn't require him to change any of his plans for the evening.

He rolled over and pressed his chest and hips against Xiller, draping an arm over his chest. He licked the cougar's short spotted muzzle and smiled. "Let's say good-bye properly."

Xiller kissed him once, then again with more passion. His eyes reflected starlight. "I thought you'd never ask."

When they lay together afterwards, panting slightly, Volle drew his finger through a sticky area of Xiller's fur and across one of his spots. The spot smeared, and Volle's fingerpad left a dark smudge across the cougar's hips. He smiled, and Xiller followed his eyes.

"Yeah, I'll need a water bath for sure. You were pretty messy—oh no!" He saw the spot and sat up, brushing at it with his own paw. The black marking smeared a bit more. "Oh, I've ruined it already. I can't go back. I'm not even supposed to be here."

Volle grasped his paw, brought it to his muzzle, and kissed it. "Shh. Don't worry about it. Look, it'll be hidden under your armor anyway."

"I guess so." The cougar scratched at the spot. "They said it wasn't supposed to come off."

Volle grinned at him. "Well, now you know to be careful when pawing yourself off."

"Mmm. Good point. I guess it was a lucky chance, you smearing it there."

Discretion warred with openness, and finally Volle confessed, "I've seen this sort of thing before. I was curious as to whether it was the same one."

Xiller stared at him. "You did that on purpose?"

"Not entirely! I mean, you had a lot to do with it too."

"Oh, did I?"

"Yeah. I mean, you had this here, and this here, and what's a fox to do?"

"I don't quite get what you mean. Maybe you'd better show me."

"Well...if that would help you understand."

A long, loving, wonderful time later, Xiller looked up at the fox's panting muzzle and said, "I'm aiming you at my chest this time," and Volle laughed as he leaned over, surrendering to the physical and emotional joy coursing through him, his tail curled around Xiller's.

And then they lay together, the fox on top, the cougar holding him in strong arms, and Volle murmured, "Now that's what I call a goodbye." Those were the last words he remembered uttering before the light of morning filtered through his eyelids.

Xiller woke as Volle shifted, tugging at their stuck fur. The cougar yawned and smiled up at him. "Morning."

"Morning, you."

They kissed, and then Volle buried his nose in Xiller's fur. "I want to remember your scent," he murmured. "When do you have to leave?"

"I shouldn't even have stayed this long." He licked Volle apologetically, rolling the fox to one side, and winced as their sticky fur protested the separation.

Volle sighed and nodded. He brushed a paw over the cougar's fur. "I'll miss you."

Xiller gathered up his bushy tail and buried his muzzle in it. "I'll miss you too," he said muffledly, and then inhaled deeply. "I won't forget your scent."

Don't cry, Volle told himself. He resisted the pressure in his throat and just nuzzled the cougar gently. "Hurry back," he whispered.

"I'll try." Xiller nuzzled him back, sounding near tears himself. "I don't know when I'll be able to."

"I'll be here." It sounded bitterer than he meant it.

Xiller's eyes brightened. "Wait a minute." He got up and ran out, and returned a moment later with his arms full of his leather armor. He set it down and rummaged through it.

"Here," he said finally, holding up a small purse. "I want to leave this with you."

"What?"

"This is the payment I'm getting." He handed the purse to Volle. It was small, and felt like it contained a few more than ten coins. Hopefully gold, if the number was that few. "I want to leave it with you."

"Oh…"

"I have enough of my own money for expenses. I'll come back for that." He smiled. "I promise."

"All right." Volle slid the purse under his pillow. "I'll keep it here."

He watched Xiller put his armor on quickly. "I'll wash at the pub," the cougar said, and then bent to pick up the fox. He held him to his chest and bent his muzzle for one last kiss. Volle responded eagerly, closing his eyes as he felt the cougar's warm tongue against his. He held tight to the cougar, and the cougar held him close, and they both knew when it was time to end the kiss. They looked into each other's eyes as Xiller lowered Volle back to the bed.

He smiled at him one last time. "Good bye, Volle."

"Bye, Xiller. Good luck."

"Thanks." He let his gaze travel down Volle's body, and then returned to his muzzle. He smiled, turned, and walked out the door.

"I'll come back for that. I promise."

Chapter 14

Volle lay in bed as the cougar's aroma faded. Half an hour later, Welcis knocked and discreetly looked in. "Sir, Lord Ikling will be awaiting you."

"I'm not running today," Volle said. "I'll see him tomorrow."

"Very good, sir. May I remind his lordship of his dinner appointment with the parents of Madame Rodion tomorrow evening?"

Volle sighed. "Consider me reminded, Welcis."

"Yes, sir." The skunk withdrew his muzzle and closed the door.

He had, in fact, forgotten that he was dining with Ilyana and her parents the following night. It was one of the steps leading up to the cotillion. Though Ilyana had assured him that her parents would love him and would agree to the courtship, he technically had to get their approval before wooing her. She had assured him that the process would go well, but he was still feeling some apprehension, which was ridiculous because he didn't really care if the meeting went well or not. He had no intention of getting engaged to Ilyana anyway.

Tika would be angry with him, he thought, but at this point he didn't really care about that. It would be easy to be rude tomorrow night. He just had to pine openly for his departed gay cougar lover, ignoring Ilyana entirely, and presumably her parents would be shocked at his rudeness and forbid her to marry him. And if that failed, he could get drunk.

He was still lost in his miserable reverie when another knock came at the door. "What?" he called irritably. The door opened, and Helfer walked in.

He glanced at the naked fox and shook his head. "Put a skirt on and let's go." He walked right to the wardrobe and rummaged through it.

Volle didn't bother trying to cover himself. "I don't feel like it."

Helfer tossed a skirt onto him, neatly covering most of his sheath. "That's exactly why you need to go. I know your cougar left, but he's going to be gone for a while. You need to get out and get back to your life now. Go ask Arrin out to dinner or something."

Volle sighed. "You're not going to leave until I come with you, are you?" Helfer crossed his arms and grinned smugly at him. "Fine."

He slid the skirt on, stood, and stretched. Helfer waved a paw. "Phew. I can smell him on you." He grinned. "Reminds me of last night." When Volle followed him out silently, he said, "Come on, don't you want to hear about last night?"

Volle really only wanted to go back and bury his nose in the pillows. But Helfer was looking at him with such a wide grin, and such a sparkle in his eye, that the fox finally said, "All right, all right. What happened last night?"

"I said hi to Richy for you when he came out, but I didn't really feel like a wolf, so I asked Tally for Pike. He's one of the raccoons there. And just as I was about to go back, this gorgeous rabbit walks in—all white fur, about your height, and he'd dyed these stripes into his fur. Well, I'd already ordered Pike, and he was waiting, so I couldn't really leave him there."

Volle took his cue from the silence and asked, "So what did you do?"

They were heading down the outside stairs into the garden, and Helfer's narrative grew more jerky as he ran. "I ran up, and asked if he wanted to join me. I said I'd pay for Pike's time."

"You didn't!"

"Sure did."

"I guess he accepted."

"Sure. Wouldn't you, for a freebie? Before you were a noble, anyway."

"Probably." He thought back to his Academy days. "Definitely."

"So we go back and it's not awkward at all. Pike—you've got to try him sometime, he's like *this* long—he's all ready, and we get undressed, and the rabbit watches me mount him, then he wants Pike in him, so we do a sandwich with the raccoon in the middle. Then one with me in the rabbit and Pike in me. Then there was a lot of licking."

Volle laughed. "How many times did you come?"

"Um. Counting the licking? Four."

"In an hour? That's got to be a record."

They were just entering the archway under the palace, and Helfer's smile flashed through the shadows as he looked back. "Nope."

Volle grinned. "You weasels."

"And rabbits. The rabbit came about four times too. Poor Pike even came by the end of it."

"Really? I'm impressed. I haven't gotten Richy to finish yet."

"We were pretty insistent." Helfer grinned. "He has good control, but there's only so much he can do. I left him an extra few gold pieces to make up for any business he might lose."

Volle smiled, but fell silent as they approached the bush where they'd met Xiller only four days earlier. Helfer hung back to jog at his side until they'd passed it, and then patted his shoulder gently. "You know, a cougar tree takes about six months to fruit again."

Caught between sadness and surprise, Volle just stared at Helfer and then started laughing. He lunged for the weasel, who skipped out of the way and then started running full bore. Volle chased him and managed to catch one paw as Helfer scrambled over the wall, but the weasel kicked free and jumped down the other side.

He stayed just ahead of Volle until the fox panted, "Enough," and slowed down.

Helfer grinned. "Feeling better?"

"Yeah." Volle smiled. "Thanks. I'll be okay. Just sad."

"Sad is all right, but don't let it mess up your life or my running. Got it?"

Volle nodded, grinning back. "Sorry."

"Let's finish up and then you can clean up and be presentable. What are you doing today?"

"I think I have some councils to sit in on. I'll have to check with Prewitt."

Helfer rolled his eyes. "I'm telling you, Volle. Stay away from that stuff."

Volle grinned. "Can't be helped." And fortunately, Helfer left it at that.

Volle was considerably cleaner and in better spirits when he visited Prewitt's office after his bath and lunch. The bear received him promptly and sat him down.

"Good afternoon, Volle."

"Afternoon, Prewitt. I just came by to check on the councils."

"Ah, yes." Prewitt shuffled through papers on his desk. "We have the Agricultural council meeting just before dinner today for an hour. I'll notify Lord Barclaw that you'll be observing."

Volle nodded, suddenly distracted by the shine of Prewitt's golden fur in the sunlight. Xiller had mentioned a golden bear and a white fox. He hadn't seen any white foxes at the palace, but he'd seen one golden bear, and only one.

Prewitt caught his stare and returned it curiously. "I gather from the paperwork that your visitor left this morning. Was he a courteous guest?"

Volle smiled. "All I could have asked for."

"Good. I'm glad to hear it. Did you ever find out what he was visiting for?" The question was asked casually, but Volle thought he could hear the tension behind it.

He shook his head. "No. He was very closed-mouthed." About that, at least, he said silently to himself.

"Ah, well. Some mystery gives spice to life, eh?" He smiled, but the smile was as much one of relief as of humor. Volle's fur prickled with the certainty that Prewitt knew something about Xiller, and had at least talked to him directly.

He had enough time for a leisurely walk to one of his drop sites before the council meeting. He scratched out a quick note about the fur pigment and folded it up, stuffing it into his purse before walking out.

A light drizzle dampened his fur as he walked through the city. He stayed close to the buildings, trying to stay dry, and made his way down the side streets until he got to the drop site, a rock under a bench hidden by some bushes in the park. Normally he would have sat down for a while, but the rain was getting into his clothes and the fur of his tail, so he hurried back to the palace and dried off before attending the council.

The council was led by the Minister of Agriculture, Lord Barclaw. He remained very low-key, and the council followed his lead, discussing the issue of the crop expectations from the southern provinces. Volle had introduced himself, and found himself caught embarrassingly unprepared when asked about the projections for Vinton. He told them that the governor was probably not used to having to send projections to the capital, and that he would send for them immediately.

Barclaw was very genial, and apologized afterwards for putting him on the spot. "I figured you were attending because you had figures to share," the large bear said. "Otherwise I wouldn't have asked you."

Volle smiled. "I had no idea. I'll send a message down."

"All right." Barclaw shook his paw. "Thanks for attending. I look forward to seeing more of you there."

"Thank you. Oh, you know what? I have no idea how to send a message to my governor. Do we have messengers here in the palace?"

"Sure. Let me take you down there myself."

"Oh, thank you." Volle followed him down the corridor and stairs to the main corridor. "I have actually corresponded with my governor, but it was right after I arrived."

"About the business with Ullik?"

Volle's ears flattened. "Er, yes."

Barclaw chuckled. "Ullik and I are friends, after a fashion. He likes to talk about his exploits, real and imagined. He was quite tickled by your request for forty gold. Couldn't stop laughing while he was talking about it."

"You're friends?"

"After a fashion, I said. He's a useful friend to have, so I listen to his stories and laugh at his jokes, and he does me favors from time to time. Without asking the same sort of price he asked of you."

Volle lowered his head, and the bear patted him on the back. "Oh, come now. You're not the first, nor will you be the last. He's the King's little embarrassment, but he does have a head for figures and he knows plenty of little secrets around the palace, so he sticks around. And you're on his good side now, or at least not on his bad side."

"Still feel humiliated," Volle muttered.

"Look," Barclaw said, lowering his voice as he pushed open a small door Volle hadn't been through before. He was surprised to find that it gave onto the rear garden. The air was still cold and the light drizzle hadn't abated, but Barclaw seemed not to be bothered by it, and Volle followed him somewhat reluctantly. "Think about it another way. He exposed himself to you. No, I don't mean just in that way. You know something he wants. That gives you a certain amount of leverage, should you ever need anything from him."

"I hope I'm not reduced to doing *that* again."

"Don't dismiss it so lightly. I know it's probably not pleasant, but think how much worse it would be for someone who was straight." He grinned at Volle, and the fox felt his mood lighten. "And you've done it once, so the worst part is over."

"Still, I hope it doesn't come to that."

"Divalia is a complex and sometimes dangerous place, Vinton. We're often required to do things we find unsavory for our own good or our people's good."

"Don't I know it." Volle thought of what he was doing for Tish's group, for the people of Vinton, and for the Duke back in Ferrenis.

"If sucking off Ullik is the worst thing you do here, you will have had a fantastically successful career. Here, the messenger station is just there." They were walking along a path, thankfully far from the place Volle would forever associate with Xiller, and the stables had just come into view.

"Could you please not talk about it like that?"

"The messenger station? I know, I know, I'm just kidding. Sure, if it bothers you. But trust me, one day you'll look back and wish you could solve your problems with one blow job. Okay, there's quill and paper here, and there's always a messenger on duty. Hello, Tarka."

A sleek otter had risen as they approached, and now he bowed. "Good eve, Lord Barclaw."

"Young Lord Vinton here has a message to send to his governor. What's the fellow's name?"

"Anton. He's a raccoon."

The bear turned to Tarka. "You know where Vinton is?"

"Yes, sir."

"All right. Vinton, write out your message, and Tarka here will deliver it. Have a good evening."

"Thank you very much for the help and advice," Volle said as he took a quill and dipped it in ink.

Barclaw started to walk down the path, and then turned. "Do you have plans for dinner tonight?"

"No."

"Why don't you join Farris and I? We'd be happy to have company. We usually eat in our chambers."

"I'd be glad to," Volle said, pausing in his writing. "Where are your chambers?"

"If you won't be long, I'll just wait. It's a nice night."

Volle smiled, very aware of his damp tail. He scribbled the note quickly, asking Anton to send back harvest predictions as soon as possible, and then confided it to Tarka.

"Waiting for a response, sir?"

"Yes, please."

"Very well." He bowed. "I will be back in about a week."

"Thank you, Tarka." He followed Barclaw back to the palace and couldn't resist the urge to shake himself once he got inside, though he did wait until the bear was a short ways ahead.

He was still damp, though not uncomfortably so, when they arrived at Barclaw's chambers, on the third floor by the Bear stair. Volle stepped inside and thought for a moment that he'd stepped into a different palace.

It was obviously only the foyer, but it was nearly as large as Volle's parlor. The door to the servant's quarters was solid oak, carved with some detailed flourishes, and the walls of the foyer were paneled in a similar oak. The oak door to the parlor, which stood ajar, bore a beautifully painted crest depicting a bear, a sheaf of wheat, and a fleur-de-lis. The crest was raised as well as painted, and Barclaw let Volle pause to examine the detail, obviously pleased by the attention.

"This door was sent to us by a master craftsman from Tyrus, the largest city in Barclaw. It was a gift, so we invited him up to the palace to see it hung. He's an aging beaver, and he was so delighted by his trip up here that he made us a set of matching chairs last year."

He pushed the door open a little further, and Volle saw a huge, beautiful parlor. The windows were wider even than Helfer's, and had blue velvet drapes held back with matching ropes. A cool breeze floated into the room from one of the windows; the other two were closed. Beneath each of the closed windows sat a large mahogany desk, one more piled with papers than the other, but both clearly examples of fine craftwork. The oak paneling from the foyer extended into the parlor, covering every wall save for the small area around the fireplace, which was lined with polished obsidian. Portraits adorned the walls: Lord Barclaw by himself, with another male bear, with a female bear and two cubs, and one of the female bear alone.

The other male bear sat in one of the chairs Barclaw had mentioned. They were wide, sturdy wood chairs, built to accommodate the heavy frame of a bear, but no less beautiful for that. Volle could see the crest on the back of the unoccupied one, as well as the flowery detail down the arms. The legs were bowed outward slightly, and ended in claws gripping wooden spheres.

The floor was hardwood, but covered with two lovely carpets. Volle stepped forward onto one as the seated bear got up to greet him, and sighed at how comfortable they felt on his paws.

"Farris, Lord Vinton is joining us for dinner tonight. He's just joined the Agricultural Committee as an observer."

"Welcome." Farris's voice was as deep as Barclaw's, maybe a little deeper. He resembled his mate, if about half a foot taller. He took Volle's paw in his and squeezed it gently.

"Thank you. Nice to meet you."

"I noticed you at the banquet the other night. So Dewanne isn't the only red fox any more."

"I guess not." Volle smiled.

"Have you met him?"

"Once or twice." He kept his voice neutral, wondering if Farris knew about Tish's group or not. "He's pretty nice."

"Just because they're both foxes doesn't mean they spend all their time together," Barclaw rumbled, amused.

"I know that, Ray. Lord Vinton spends most of his time with Lord Ikling, isn't that right?"

"Hef's a good friend," Volle confirmed.

"Well, we'll just leave it at that." Farris arched his eyebrow at Barclaw, and then waved Volle into the next room. "Come on in and sit down. I'll grab another chair."

The dining room was not quite as luxuriously decorated as the parlor, but was still far nicer than any other room Volle had seen in the palace. Oak paneling again, two windows in the far side with blue-green curtains, and a side table with a small sculpture formed the backdrop for the large table in the center. It was covered with a white cloth and set with two settings of china and silver, and even the wine goblets atop it were silver. A doe and a marmot were busy placing a third setting between the other two. They finished just as Farris brought another chair over from a row of four sitting against the wall.

"Thank you, ladies," he said, holding the chair out. "Lord Vinton?"

"Thank you." Volle sat down and let Farris push him in. The bears sat on either side of him, smiled at each other, and said a short prayer to Ursa. Volle lowered his head respectfully, though he didn't join in. And then the dinner was served.

Farris talked nearly as much as Tika had, Volle found. He heard many of the same stories he'd heard from Tika, with minor changes, and wondered if those same stories were retold for years and years. He certainly felt sorry for Lord Oncit if that were the case. Farris spent a good deal of time speculating on his problems and the indiscretions of his wife.

"I'm on a tribunal with him," Volle said, seizing an opportunity when Farris was chewing on a large piece of potato.

"Oh?" Barclaw spoke up for the first time. "Does he say much?"

"Not really. I did have dinner with him the other night."

Farris swallowed, and asked, "Did he come on to you?"

Volle grinned. "Everyone asks that. No, he didn't."

"Was his wife there?" Farris asked knowingly.

"No, nor the servant. But he just wanted to talk."

"Interesting," Barclaw rumbled.

"Quite." Farris tapped a fork against his plate. "What did he want to talk about?"

"Farris," Barclaw chided gently. "If Oncit didn't want to share it with his wife and servant, I'm certain he would not have wanted to share it with you."

"He wouldn't, but perhaps Vinton here would, eh?" He turned to Volle with a winning smile.

Volle returned the smile. "It really was just small talk and politics. He said his wife had another engagement."

"I bet she did." Farris looked meaningfully at Barclaw, and sat back in his chair, his mind already racing ahead. "You know, Lord Deverin postponed his troop inspection last month. That normally takes him out of the palace for a week."

Barclaw smiled. "I'm sure Lord Vinton has other things to talk about, Farris."

"Not really," Volle said with a smile, which Farris took as the cue to keep on going. Volle watched Barclaw while his mate chattered on. The smaller bear ate slowly and deliberately, and watched his mate with genuine affection. Volle concentrated on his food as well, taking his time since the bears ate slower than he did. Amazingly, Farris seemed to be able to eat at the same pace as his mate without slowing his patter much.

Volle enjoyed the dinner. He found himself relaxing and letting his memories of Xiller recede. He thought of him often, especially when Farris told a particularly salacious story or when he remembered that he didn't have to hurry through dinner. He missed the cougar, but tried hard to channel that emotion into looking forward to his return.

The three of them sat for a bit after dinner, sipping a sweet liquor that tasted expensive and talking about Volle's past. The inevitable questions of his childhood had come up, and he answered them in good spirits. When he'd finished one glass of the liquor, he put it aside and bid his hosts good night.

"Thank you for joining us. We must do it again sometime," Farris said, shaking his paw.

"I'd love to. You have a beautiful place here. It looks too good for the rest of the palace."

Barclaw, taking his paw in turn, grinned. "Farris did all the decorating himself. He has a eye for it."

"Really? It's wonderful."

"Thank you." For the first time that night, Farris appeared to be speechless. It lasted only a minute. As Volle was on his way out, the large bear patted his shoulder. "If you ever want a few nice things for your place, we've got plenty that we could loan you."

"Thanks," Volle smiled. "I'm sort of used to it the way it is and I'd be afraid of ruining something nice."

"At least come and see what we have sometime."

"All right. Good night, Farris. It was a pleasure to meet you. Good night, Lord Barclaw."

"Good night, Lord Vinton. See you in Council in two weeks."

He was a little bit tipsy from the liquor, which was deceptively strong, but made it back to his chambers without incident. When he collapsed in his bed, he sniffed the pillow for Xiller's scent. Nothing. Welcis had cleaned the linens.

He sighed and called up the scent from memory, imagined his arms around the big cougar, and fell asleep.

The next day, he awoke in somewhat better spirits. After a run with Helfer in which he heard more details than he needed to about the upcoming batch of ales from Vellenland, he returned to his chambers to be informed by Welcis that Arrin had requested his company for dinner the following night, and in the conservatory in the afternoon if he was free.

He told Welcis that he would be delighted to join Arrin. The thought of seeing the fox again was a pleasant one now that Xiller was gone. He was about to go for a walk in the town and check his drop sites when there was a knock at his door. Welcis answered it, and a moment later ushered Tish into the room.

"Hello, Volle." He extended his paw. "All ready to meet Ilyana's parents tonight?"

Volle shook his paw and nodded. "I think so."

"Good, good. I'm sure you'll have no trouble. They're nice foxes. Tika just wanted me to check in on you, make sure you weren't nervous, that sort of thing."

"No, no, I'm fine." He was nervous, a little, at the thought of how deliberately rude he was going to have to be, but he'd manage.

"Good." Tish sat down in one of the chairs and stroked his muzzle thoughtfully. "The others want to get together again too."

Volle nodded. "I had a couple things to talk to them about too. Could you excuse us, Welcis?" The skunk bowed and retreated to the sitting room, closing the door behind him.

"What's been happening?"

Volle told him briefly about his talks with Lord Oncit. "Is he part of the group with Lord Ikinna, do you know?"

"We don't really even know that Ikinna's in the group. It makes sense for him to be, but we don't have any proof at all. Oncit…he could very well be. He's always been quiet, and even after ten years I don't know much about him."

"I'll keep talking to him."

Tish nodded. "Keep me posted. Anything else?"

Volle hesitated. He wanted to ask about Prewitt, but that would entail talking about Xiller, and he wasn't quite prepared to tell that whole story. Especially with Xiller being disguised as a jaguar—he was likely headed for the southern countries for whatever his mission was, and that was probably not related to the Ferrenians. "I heard a rumor that Prewitt might be involved in some espionage against the southern territories," he said finally.

Tish waved a paw. "The southern operations don't interest me much, though the fact that Prewitt is involved does. The southerners are hard to figure out and Fardew's always got some scheme or another to enhance our trading position with them. But Prewitt...wonder what his interest could be. What else did you hear?"

Volle shook his head. "Nothing definite. I don't even know what the operation is. But he dropped a couple hints that made me think he knows something about it."

"Like what?"

"Dereath was hosting this visitor, and Prewitt knew all about him. He claimed it was just because he'd had to do the papers to process him, but he seemed more interested."

"Makes sense for Dereath to be hosting someone. He works for Fardew, after all. How did you find out about the visitor?"

Volle sighed. He couldn't think of a reasonable way to keep evading the issue, so he told Tish about Xiller, omitting the sexual parts. The grin on the wolf's muzzle indicated that he'd probably filled in those parts for himself, but he kept quiet about it. "So that's the cougar scent in here. I wondered but wasn't going to ask. None of my business, you know. How did they paint him up like a jaguar?"

"It was some sort of fur pigment," Volle said. "I'd never seen it before."

He stumbled over the lie, but Tish didn't seem to notice. "Fascinating," he said. "I think you're right, though. It sounds like a southern operation. I wouldn't worry about it too much. I'm sure you'll see him again before long."

Volle returned the wolf's grin with a sheepish one. "Hope so."

Tish got up and stretched. "All right. You've got a dinner to attend, so I should let you get to that. No doubt Welcis is fretting to get you all dressed up. Oh, come now, it's only for one night," he said as Volle stuck his tongue out.

"I know, but still. I hate lace."

"So do we all, m'boy. Give it another ten years to go out of style."

"Thanks."

"Enjoy your dinner," the wolf said. "I'll see myself out." And he did.

Welcis did indeed have an armful of clothes when Volle opened the door to the sitting room. He indicated the bedroom. "If his lordship would allow me to assist him in his preparations?"

"Sure." Volle gave the skunk a long look, but was met with unruffled equanimity. He was certain Welcis had listened to some of what was going on, but he didn't know how much. He didn't think the skunk would do anything that wasn't in his interests.

Unless it involved lace, of course. After brushing him thoroughly, Welcis fixed the lace collar firmly around his neck, going over the first formal shirt he'd gotten from the palace tailor. "But I like those better," Volle said, indicating the newer shirts Helfer's tailor had made for him.

"I share your affection, sir, but I must point out that the older generation is unlikely to."

"Oh, very well." Volle submitted to the dressing without another word, staring at his window while the skunk straightened his pleats and smoothed down the wrinkles, and finally pronounced him ready to go to his dinner.

He took a carriage, but sat back the entire journey, immersed in his thoughts. It would be easy enough to pull off the performance tonight, but then he would never see Ilyana again. He found that he felt mildly sorry for that, and for the behavior he was going to assume, and he wondered idly if she would see that it was all an act. To take his mind from that, he focused on Xiller, and what the big cougar would say and do if he were there now. He'd tell me not to worry, he thought with a grin, and then he'd put his paw down my pants.

He barely realized the carriage had stopped, and only got up when the driver rapped gently on the door. Adjusting his pants somewhat self-consciously, he stepped down and was greeted by a diminutive grey wolf, who led him up to the door.

Despite the servant, he could see the financial straits of her family the moment he stepped in the door. The paint on the wall was chipped and peeling, and the floor was dirty and in obvious need of washing. Not only that, but the house was divided into several parts, and it looked as though two other families lived there. The wolf ushered him to a staircase that led him up two flights to a door in similar disrepair, which the wolf opened. "Lord Vinton," he announced.

Volle stepped forward into a sitting room that, while it did not quite match the Barclaw's, was still very nicely maintained. The floor was clean and it was clear that the family had made an effort to keep the room brightly lit and tidy. He eyed the decorations with the prejudice of the palace, but decided they were quite nice, given the circumstances.

The family that rose to greet him could be described the same way. Instantly he felt overdressed and mortified, certain that his formal attire was rubbing his wealth in their muzzles. Their clothes were older than his, and as they rose he could see a well-concealed patch in the father's trousers. His gaze flicked across the father's eyes to the mother's, and rested there. He saw her ears flick back, then forward, saw the narrowing of her eyes, and knew that she could see what he'd seen, and resented his pity.

Could he use that? No, he couldn't flaunt his wealth any more than he already was. In the first place, he just wanted to be rude, not arrogant, and in the second, they wanted their daughter to be well off, so showing off wealth wouldn't endanger the courtship.

"Thank you so much for coming by, Lord Vinton. I'm Ilyana's father, Marcel." Marcel was about fiftyish, with graying fur along the sides of his muzzle and ears, but his paw gripped Volle's with the firmness of a fox twenty years younger. His clothes were rather bright, Volle thought: sunburst yellow and a bright blue that almost hurt his eyes to look at.

"Please, call me Volle."

"And this is my wife, Katiana." Volle lifted her paw to his muzzle and brushed it gently, inhaling her scent. She smelled like Ilyana, but worn down and faded. And yet...as he raised his head to look into her amber eyes again, he could see that there was a strong core that had survived. He released her paw and she bowed her head.

"A pleasure to meet you, sir."

"Please," he said again. "Volle."

Ilyana stepped forward and embraced him, touching her muzzle to either side of his. Her eyes sparkled as they drew apart. "Good evening, Volle. Thanks for coming."

He smiled. "Thank you for the invitation, Ilyana."

"Papa, I'll let you two talk over drinks." She guided Volle toward the liquor cabinet and stepped outside with her mother. "We'll see you at dinner in about ten minutes."

Marcel smiled fondly after her. "She's my favorite," he said. "I'd never tell the others that, but she's bright and charming..." He laughed. "And what am I telling you this for? You already know that. Can I offer you some wine?"

"Sure. Yes, thank you," Volle said, remembering his etiquette a moment too late. "Yes, your daughter is very charming."

"She'll make a good mother." Marcel handed him a goblet of wine. Pewter, Volle noted as he lapped briefly from it. The wine was good but not remarkable, and he couldn't help comparing it to the wine he'd had the previous night, as unfair as that was.

"I'm sure she will." He couldn't quite figure out how to start being rude.

"And I understand you're not really in the market for a wife."

Volle blinked. "She told you that?"

"Sure." Marcel sipped his wine. "She tells us everything. Got a boyfriend?"

"Sort of. I mean, not at the moment." He took a drink of wine to cover his confusion.

"Oh. Had a fight?"

"No, I mean, he's gone. But he'll be back," he added hurriedly, and gave an exaggerated sigh. "I miss him."

Marcel patted his shoulder. "I know just how you feel. When my boyfriend broke up with me, I was depressed for a month. Katiana tried to comfort me, but she doesn't really have the right equipment, you know?"

He was grinning. Volle stared blankly at him, and he put down his wine goblet and held his paws about eight inches apart. "Germain was like this, you know? Mmm. I still miss him sometimes." He sighed and picked up his goblet, taking another drink.

"You...you're..."

"Did you think you were the only one?" Marcel grinned at him and put a paw on his arm. "Volle, I just wanted to make you feel comfortable about marrying my daughter. I had a very full life with Katiana and it didn't stop me from visiting Germain. Or the Tattered Sheet, after Germain took up with that slut from Whitemarch."

"Tattered Sheet?" Volle said, trying to regain his footing in the conversation. *He* was supposed to be the one pining over his departed lover.

"It's a lovely establishment just down the street. They have boys and girls and the prices aren't too bad. Do you go to the Jackal's Staff?"

"Um. Sometimes."

"Lucky. They're supposed to be the best. At the Sheet, it's about a three in four chance of getting a good boy. Other nights you get someone who thinks that just laying there is the extent of his job. Are the boys at the Jackal good?"

Volle found himself nodding. "I've only been with two there, but they were both great."

"I bet. Well, I think dinner's ready. Shall we go in?"

Volle recovered quickly from the shock of exchanging brothel recommendations with Ilyana's father, but he couldn't quite bring off the effect that he wanted at dinner. They waited politely for him to talk, and when he belched, they pretended they hadn't heard. It hurt his throat, so he gave that up quickly. He tried talking about Ilyana as though she weren't there, but she grabbed his paw and joined the conversation, and he couldn't ignore her after that.

The whole thing was complicated by the fact that he really did like her, more than Arrin even, and if she'd been male he would've been happy to spend time with her and court her. But the fact that he liked her made him even more reluctant to risk ruining her life.

In desperation, he turned to her mother, who had been quietly following the discussions, and tried to praise the dinner in unflattering terms, like "This is a nice little stew. It reminds me of a wonderful dish we had at the palace the other night." He meant to imply that the food at the palace was much better, but he apparently wasn't very good at being subtly insulting, because she actually smiled and thanked him. He assumed that she'd made the food herself, and decided to continue along that line.

The problem was that main dish was rather good, he thought as he ate the honey-dressed chicken. The beans served on the side were the only thing about it that he didn't really like, so he left them carelessly untouched.

"Do you not like beans, Lord Vinton?" Katiana asked partway through the course.

"Oh, I do. Just not these." He indicated them with a dismissive wave of his paw. Surely she couldn't help but be offended at the outright rudeness.

"You know, I did think there was something a little off about them." She took another taste. "Yes. I will definitely have a word with the cook. What a refined palate you have!"

Volle glumly took another bite of chicken.

Ilyana walked him to the front door after dinner. She held his paw and smiled. "I knew they'd like you. What was wrong with your stomach?"

"Stomach?"

"The, um…noises."

"Oh. Just something I ate at lunch, I guess."

"Is that why you didn't like the beans?"

"I guess." He sighed, and she squeezed his paw.

"Don't worry about it. I'm sure everything will be okay anyway. I'll explain to them that you weren't feeling all that well."

"I was worried I offended your mother by being overdressed."

"Oh, no. I told them what a smart dresser you are." She smiled and took the lace off of his collar. "There. You don't need that now."

He smiled crookedly. "I guess I didn't mess things up too badly, then."

Ilyana laughed. "I don't think you could have messed them up even if you'd tried."

Well, that was some consolation, though he was sure she didn't know how true her words were. "I'll see you next week, I guess."

"Yes, Tika's got more planning for me to do. It's only three weeks away." Her tail was wagging quickly, and her eyes glinted brightly.

Volle smiled. "It's going to be lovely," he said, and kissed her on the nose.

He was going to have to go through with it, he realized. He didn't have it in him to ruin her cotillion. At least he could let her have that, and let her down afterwards. She'd said her season didn't start for another couple weeks, so he had plenty of time. He sighed. It was all so complicated. He felt as though Xiller's presence had given him a vacation from all that, taken him away from courtships and spies and pretense, and no sooner had the cougar gone than here he was plunged back into it all.

She flicked her ears back and smiled shyly. "I know, I'm like a little cub with this. But it's a year overdue for me. All this time we were waiting to find the right fox, and…well, I was waiting. I'm glad I did, though. I think you'll be a good father." Hastily, she added, "If you want me, that is."

Volle smiled. He was touched, but not quite enough to tell her he wanted her, when he knew that was a lie. But he had been impressed with how close her family was, how much her parents cared for her, and how much she still cared for them. "I think you'll be a good mother," he said softly, and she seemed contented with that.

After a short silence, he asked, "So what happens now? Do I have to ask your father for permission to court you?"

"Didn't you?"

"Er. No."

"I thought that's what you and Papa were going to talk about when we left you alone."

He shrugged apologetically. "I didn't know. He didn't ask."

"He was probably waiting for you to bring it up. What did you talk about?"

"Er...just small talk, you know." He didn't quite feel that he could tell her what they'd really talked about.

"Oh. Male stuff."

Volle almost giggled aloud, repressed it, and kept his ears up. "Yes, that's right."

She smiled. "I'm glad the two of you got along. You should go out together sometime. I'm sure he'd like that."

Volle couldn't stop the giggles this time, so he coughed to cover them. Ilyana patted his back. "Are you okay?"

"Fine," he wheezed. His first image had been of him taking her father on a date; the second had been of him taking her father to a brothel. He drove them from his head with some difficulty.

"Do you want a drink or something? I can run back upstairs."

"No, no, I'm fine." He glanced at the house and changed the subject. "Who else lives here?"

"Oh, my uncle lives on the second floor with his wife. They don't have any children. And my grandparents used to live on the first floor until a few years ago. Now we have renters there."

Volle nodded. "It must have been crowded when you were growing up."

She smiled. "We liked it. Some of us stayed with our aunt and uncle, and my oldest brother moved in with my grandparents when he was old enough." He could hear a wistful note in her voice.

"You miss your brother and sisters."

She nodded. "I still see them sometimes, but they all have families now. Mama and Papa are wonderful, but I think sometimes they worry about me, and I know I'm costing them money."

"I never had much of a family."

Ilyana took his paw. "There's another incentive for you to pick me." She was trying to be coquettish, and it almost worked.

Volle kissed her paw and smiled gently. "As if I didn't have enough."

At that, she smiled widely and flicked her ears, and her tail wagged more quickly. "Oh, you flatterer. Go on home, Volle. I'll see you next week. And thank you."

He bowed. "Thank you, Ilyana. Good night, and thank your parents for me."

She stood in the doorway while he walked to the carriage. The driver had been waiting; having seen him at the doorway, he'd prepared the horse and was ready to go. Volle stepped into the carriage and looked back at Ilyana as the driver closed the door. She waved, and then stepped back inside.

He sat back on his seat and sighed. Who could have told him that romance would be his biggest problem as a spy?

When he joined Helfer the next morning, the weasel was practically hopping up and down. "Have I got news!" he said, setting off without asking whether Volle was ready.

Volle sprinted to catch up with him. "What?"

Helfer grinned. "Seen Dereath around lately?"

"No. But I sometimes go days without seeing him." He hadn't been around the whole time Xiller was with him, though, Volle recalled, and that seemed a bit odd now that he thought about it.

"You'll go a few more. I heard from Caresh that he made quite a scene over Xiller leaving him, and Fardew told him that it would be better if he weren't around the palace for the next few weeks. Practically fired him, but sadly didn't go quite that far."

"Really?" Volle grinned. He'd become used to thinking that Dereath would get away with whatever he tried or did. "Where'd he go?"

"Nobody knows. But Caresh says the chambermaid who overheard him said he didn't stop cursing from the time he packed a bag to the time he rode out of the palace gates. For all we know, he still might be."

Volle chuckled. "And the rest of us can finally stop."

Helfer laughed. "Well, he'll be back, but hopefully he'll have cooled down a bit. I wonder why Fardew was so mad."

"You remember Xiller was supposed to keep a low profile? I heard from Prewitt that Dereath was complaining to everyone that I stole him. Not exactly keeping his existence secret."

"Ah, that would do it. Fardew likes his secrets. Now I'm surprised he didn't fire him. Maybe he knows something about Fardew."

"Maybe he threatened to come back if he were fired."

Helfer grinned. "Maybe Fardew just doesn't want to lose his best cock-sucker."

Volle laughed. "Come on. This is Dereath we're talking about, right?"

"How do you know he's not really amazing in bed?"

"Wouldn't be worth it."

"No, you're right."

They jogged on a bit further. "Wonder where he went," Volle mused.

"Don't really care," Helfer said cheerfully. "He's out of our fur for another couple weeks, and hopefully he'll be a bit calmer when he gets back."

"Or else be worked up about something else."

"Makes no difference to me."

This time, when they passed the bush in the rear garden, Volle felt only a small pang, and smiled at the happy memories. Had that all really happened? He came so quickly and was gone so quickly, it felt like a dream now.

A good dream, anyway, and that was better than nothing.

Lord Oncit was back in the dining room over lunch, sitting near Ikinna but at a separate table. Volle sat down near him, but Oncit was so absorbed in his thoughts that it wasn't until a servant brought Volle his food that he noticed the fox. "Oh. Hello, Volle."

"Hello, Maron. Got a lot on your mind?" Volle started eating, keeping his ears politely turned toward the wolf.

"I suppose." He was eating slowly, and certainly looked preoccupied.

"I was thinking about what you said, about taking back what is rightfully ours." He kept his voice low, and though they were alone at the table, looked around somewhat anxiously. "Is it likely that we'll go to war?"

The wolf chewed, and thought this over. "Not at the current time."

Volle sighed. "If only there were something I could do. I just feel like I'm doing nothing here."

"I know what you mean," Oncit muttered.

"How do you deal with it?"

"Hm?"

"You want to get the fields back. Are you just waiting until something happens to bring them back?" He was talking almost in a whisper, but Oncit shushed him.

"I trust to Canis to bring me back what is mine," he said, and turned back to his meal.

Volle thought that was all, but as the wolf finished and stood to leave, he patted Volle on the shoulder and said, "Don't worry. All things come in time." He was gone before Volle had a chance to ask him what he meant.

"I wish people would just say what they mean instead of talking cryptically," he muttered. He spent the rest of the lunch listening to Ikinna's loud dissertations on his family's lands.

Arrin was in good spirits when he got to the conservatory, and gave him a short kiss. "Hi, Volle. I've been practicing. Listen." He picked up the trumpet and ran through the royal ceremonial march, which was similar to most of the other royal marches but contained a couple extra notes that Arrin had always found difficult.

"That's terrific! I haven't been practicing, I'm afraid." Volle picked up the pipes and blew experimentally into them. He played a quick scale, faltering over only one note.

"That's not bad." Arrin smiled. He picked up another set of pipes. "Want to play these today?"

"I think so."

They played together, Arrin coaching him as they did. He enjoyed playing, and was getting better at it. He'd never studied music in the Academy, but the pipes were pretty easy to pick up and Arrin was teaching him simple tunes that he knew from his cubhood.

When they stopped, they sat back together. Volle put his arm around Arrin's shoulders out of habit. The other fox sighed and leaned into the embrace. "So," he said, "how are things going with Ilyana?"

"Good. I met her parents last night. They were nice. I think they'll approve the courtship."

"That's good." Arrin rested a paw on his knee.

"How's your mother?"

"Oh, her leg's bothering her, as always. The herbist was by last week and made her some tea, and she's walking easier now."

"Glad to hear that." He nuzzled Arrin's ear.

"It wasn't serious. It never is."

"I know, but it still worries you sometimes."

"Yeah." He sighed. "She keeps saying she probably won't be around much longer, but she seems pretty healthy."

"I'm sure she'll be around for a while."

Arrin nodded. Volle rubbed his shoulder gently and tried not to think about Xiller. What did he really know about the cougar? Did they share any interests? Would he be as good a companion out of bed as in it? To his distress, he found that he didn't care. He buried his nose in Arrin's fur, inhaling the soft musky scent, and tried to relax against the fox. The scent was safe, familiar, and comforting, but it wasn't exciting. It didn't set his fur a-tingle as the cougar's had.

Maybe that's not good for me, he thought. Isn't being a spy excitement enough?

The truth was that it hadn't been very exciting yet. Xiller was the most excitement he'd seen at the palace, and now that he was gone, everything was falling back into the same normal routine he'd had for over a month. He knew how the rest of the evening would go. He and Arrin would go to dinner, talk about their lives over eating, repair to the loveseat, and spend the rest of the evening curled up together. He would get his paw up the fox's shirt, ruffle his chest fur, slide down to his abdomen, and remain there. Arrin might be daring enough to mimic the action with his paw, or he might feel more restrained and restrict himself to stroking Volle's tail. Either way, the evening would end chastely with a kiss, and Volle would end up alone in his bed with his paw for company.

Was that so bad? Arrin held the promise of future security, a bed-mate who would always be there and not have to run off on secret missions. But is that what he wanted, when he couldn't promise that in return? He didn't know what he wanted, for sure. It would be nice to have a companion at the palace, but he couldn't honestly say it was something he longed for, the way he longed to have the cougar's arms around him one more time.

Arrin nuzzled him. "What are you thinking about?"

"Dinner," he said, and strove to turn that lie into truth.

Over the next few days, Volle kept the memory of the cougar close by reaching under his pillow at night and finding the purse there. He often slept with his paw closed around it, and that made him feel that wherever he was, Xiller was thinking of him.

Apart from that, his life at the palace slowly returned to normal. The tribunal was busy again, so he didn't get a chance to talk to Lord Oncit there, nor did his efforts to talk to him at lunch lead to anything more. He checked twice for notes from his team, but found nothing all week, so it was with some nervousness that he showed up at the Jackal's Staff with Helfer the following Gaiaday. Had they not gotten his note? Had they misinterpreted it? Or had they just been busy acting on it?

"Richy's waiting for you in back, dear." Tally was done in green to-day, a mint green dress and green stripes around his muzzle, as though he were a jungle cat of some sort. His tail had one green stripe running from base to tip.

"You look like a sweet today, Tally," Volle said as he walked by and handed the cougar the five gold. "Fitting, I guess."

Tally laughed and patted his shoulder. "Aren't you the adorable one!"

Volle wagged his tail and walked to the back. The Jackal's Staff felt comfortable to him, more so than anywhere but his own rooms, and partially that was because there were no expectations of him here. He almost resented Seir's intrusion on that world, but in fact he preferred it to be here than anywhere else, because he felt so comfortable.

They were seated around the room as usual, and Sherr barely waited for the door to close before barking, "What's this about the fur pigment?"

"I saw a cougar painted to look like a jaguar. Yellow paint, black spots, and all."

"How do you know it was the same pigment we use?"

Volle flicked his ears. "Ah, well, it did smear when..." They were all staring at him. He sighed. "When I used the paint, I noticed that it smeared when certain, um, fluids got spilled on it."

"What fluids?" Sherr asked.

"You have to ask?" Reese snorted. "You obviously don't know Volle."

"Oh? Oh."

Volle's ears went back. "Anyway, the black spots smeared in the same way."

A chuckle went around the room. Seir said, "How did you meet this cougar?"

"He was in the palace. This rat was hosting him for some secret mission and asked him to jump me and Lord Ikling, because he doesn't like us. Not 'jump' the way you're thinking, Reese. After we'd met, he confessed that he didn't like the rat very much, and so he stayed with me for a few days until he left."

"And of course you spilled some fluids on him by accident."

Volle couldn't quite bring himself to banter with Reese in front of the others. Luckily Sherr spoke up. "What mission?"

"I couldn't find out exactly," Volle said, "but they do run espionage down south, so I guessed that's why he was painted as a jaguar. They're not exactly common here."

"Makes sense."

"You couldn't get any better information from sleeping with him?" Reese teased.

"Well, he didn't get any information from sleeping with me," Volle retorted.

"Touché."

"We sent word immediately that there may be a spy in our alchemical laboratories," Seir said. "We wanted to wait until we heard the whole story from you before issuing further instructions. So you have no idea who it was who did the painting, here?"

"I have a clue, at least. I think the Secretary, Prewitt, was involved. Xiller—the cougar—talked about meeting a golden bear, and Prewitt is the only one I know of. And he seemed to know about and be interested in Xiller even though he was supposed to be keeping a low profile."

"Can you get closer to this Prewitt?" Sherr asked.

Volle shrugged. "I can try, but he's very busy and our meetings are always brief. I've been trying to get more information on Oncit, too, but he's been too quiet lately."

"Do you think he might have been involved in the cougar?"

"I've no idea."

"This is certainly interesting, and helpful. At least it will help us root out spies in our country. Good work, Volle."

Volle's ears came back up at the rare praise from Sherr. Reese added, with perhaps a touch of jealousy, "Good to see your libido might actually help you with your work."

Heartened, Volle smiled. "It's nice to mix work with pleasure. I'll report more when the cougar comes back."

"Oh, you're expecting him back? This wasn't just a two-night stand?" Seir arched her eyebrows.

Volle flicked his ears. He couldn't keep himself from answering, even though he knew it wasn't the right thing to say. "I think he'll come back. He promised."

The silence stretched out for a minute, until Seir walked over and placed a paw on his knee. "You know, Volle, that emotional commitments are something you can't afford to make unless you know you can break them."

"I know." He sighed. "I can handle it."

"All right. See that you do. What about that rat you mentioned? Could he make more trouble for you?"

"Not for a little while. He's been sent away from the palace. Apparently the Minister of Intelligence wasn't too happy with him using their soldier for a juvenile revenge prank."

"All right. Try not to make too many enemies, okay?"

"Just the one." Volle shrugged. "I couldn't really help it."

Seir nodded, and looked at Sherr and Tella. "Anything else for him?" They shook their heads, and stood. "Good use of the drop sites. Keep using them and we'll do the same."

The others filed out, Reese stopping to press his paw to Volle's. Seir said, "I'll be right out," and closed the door behind them. She went to the bed and sat next to Volle.

"Listen," she said. "We didn't think commitments would be a problem for you, given your...history. It worries me a little bit, because you're a good fox. Maybe too good to be a good spy as well. I just want to be sure you know that you need to keep a part of yourself outside."

"I know," he said, "but that doesn't mean I'll be able to do it. But I know the risks. I've thought about it a lot, but sometimes you don't have a choice in what you feel."

Seir grinned. "Spoken like a youngster. Well, if you ever really need to talk to someone about your double life and your entanglements and all that—I know it's hard not being able to talk to anyone—just leave a note in the drop box with my name on it and I'll meet you in the park the following afternoon if I can. Deal?"

"I thought we weren't supposed to be seen together."

"We're not. But once in a great while, as long as we're careful, we can risk it. And I don't want you doing anything stupid like telling your cougar boyfriend about your secret life just because you're frustrated that you can't talk to anyone. All right?"

"All right." He smiled and hugged her. "Thanks, Seir."

"You can thank me best by never taking me up on it." She nuzzled him, then hopped down from the bed. "Now I'll let you get on with your evening. See you in two weeks."

He lay back on the bed as the door closed behind the mouse, closed his eyes, and sighed. After a moment, he heard the door open and close, and a familiar scent reached his nostrils. "Hi, Richy," he said without opening his eyes.

He felt the motion and heard the soft chuckle. A moment later, the wolf settled beside him. A gentle paw tugged at his shirt fastenings. "I haven't seen you in two weeks. I thought you'd forgotten me."

"How could I?" Eyes still closed, he lifted his arms to permit the wolf to lift off his shirt.

"You want me to blow out the candle?"

He realized Richy was wondering why his eyes were closed. He opened them, looked up at the wolf's clear green eyes, and smiled. "Sure."

"Just a minute." He folded Volle's shirt and laid it on the table near the bed, then cupped the flame in his paw and puffed softly on it. The room grew darker, but Volle's vision adjusted quickly. He could see as well without the candle as with it, but the colors were more muted and the room seemed more peaceful and serene.

Richy had already removed his loincloth, he saw. The wolf's silvery pelt was bright as he knelt on the bed, and his sheath hung invitingly between his thighs. Volle lifted a black paw and cupped it, stroking gently with his fingers as Richy worked with the fastenings of his pants. He was rewarded with the slow emergence of the wolf's member, dark against the light belly fur. Volle smiled and brushed a velvety finger up and down the length as it appeared, making the wolf raise his head and smile.

"Patience, foxy," he said with a smile as he slid a paw into Volle's pants and found his sheath as well. Volle lifted his hips to allow the pants to slide the rest of the way off, revealing his erection under Richy's white paw. The wolf drew his pad up the length and smiled. "And what is sir's preference tonight?"

By way of answer, Volle reached back under Richy's sheath and drew a single claw down his tail hole. "I think I'll have a wolf," he said softly. "On his back."

"Yes, sir." Richy grinned and laid down on the bed as Volle scooted to one side. He raised his knees and lifted his rump slightly. "Will this do?"

"It'll do wonderfully." Volle leaned over and drew his tongue along the wolf's length, tasting the soft musk and filling his head with the wolf's delicate scent. "I think I would like a muzzleful tonight as well."

The wolf's gently protesting paw fell back. He murmured, "I guess that would be okay."

Volle lifted his muzzle and smiled. "I hope it's more than just okay. The cream's in the chest?" Richy nodded assent, and Volle lifted the lid of the chest and peered inside.

He found the cream immediately, but paused to look at the rest of the contents. He held up a silk rope and chuckled. "You use this often?"

Richy turned his head and smiled. "More than you'd think. You want to use it?"

Volle shook his head. "Not my thing. What about this?" He held up a polished wooden dildo with a knot at the end. "Good heavens, it's nearly as thick as my arm."

"That's a popular one."

Volle eyed it, and considered trying it just to see if it would fit. It was slightly larger than even Xiller had been, but not so much larger that he thought it would hurt. But he was trying to let his memories of the cougar settle and rest, and so he put it back in the chest. He grinned at the wolf. "Some other time."

He closed the chest and returned to the bed, kneeling in front of the prone wolf to give him a good view of his erection as he rubbed the slick cream up and down it. He took another pawful and rubbed it gently on Richy's pink opening, pressing a knuckle into it to push some of the cream inside too.

"I'm fine," Richy said softly, his tail thumping the bed.

Volle set the cream down and guided himself gently into the wolf, his tail wagging as well. He sighed at the warm tightness surrounding him as he pushed his length further into the panting wolf. He slid easily in, looked up at Richy and received an encouraging smile, and bent over to take the wolf's erection into his muzzle.

He held it without moving as he began to thrust in and out, feeling the motions through the wolf's hips with his paws. Then, slowly, he lowered and raised his muzzle, tongue caressing the long stiff length as he did so. Richy moaned appreciatively and pushed his hips up into Volle's muzzle as Volle was pushing his own hips forward into the wolf, his shaft sinking in all the way over his growing knot and then back out. Richy clenched his muscles expertly around the fox's tip, making him shiver and moan himself around the hard length in his muzzle.

He could feel the swelling of his knot, both as a pressure at his groin and in the resistance with each thrust into the wolf. He moved his paw, still slick with cream, to the base of the thick shaft, feeling the knot there grow along with his. He wrapped his paw around it and stroked in time with his muzzle's movements, tasting Richy's musk with every lap of his tongue.

Time seemed to slow for him, or maybe he was keeping his thrusts deliberately slow in an attempt to keep the moment going. Richy's knot was full and he was ready to come; Volle had been teasing him with tongue pressure on his sensitive tip until the knot in his paw was nice and hard. Volle himself was close, to the point that he was waiting to push his knot into the wolf. The back and forth was exciting but also relaxing, in a blissfully hazy sort of way, and maybe it was five thrusts later or twenty-five that he pressed his hips all the way in, his knot resisting and then sliding in all at once, sealing him to the wolf.

He squeezed Richy's knot at the same time, licking quickly, and the wolf cried out, tensing on the bed as he came onto Volle's tongue. Volle shuddered himself, lapping at the musky fluid as it spurted onto his tongue, his hips moving with a life of their own until his body matched Richy's shudders and he emptied himself into the wolf, moaning loudly around the dripping length in his muzzle.

They stayed locked like that for several heartbeats, and then Volle let Richy's length slide out of his muzzle. He panted and smiled at the wolf, who gave him a bright smile in return. "That was great," he said.

Volle nodded. "Me too." He arranged his knees until he was sitting a bit more comfortably, and then rested his paws on Richy's taut stomach. He rubbed the fur gently, and Richy's tail, which had been wagging, wagged harder.

"How many clients do you usually get a night?"

"I really shouldn't talk about that. I don't think."

"I'm just wondering how much business I might have made you miss." Volle licked his lips and smiled.

"Oh, that." Richy giggled softly. "It's okay. I have enough time before the next one, and I'll just tell Tally to send in someone who doesn't want me to be on top. I don't get a lot of bottoms anyway."

Volle leaned over and licked a few white drops off of the wolf's pink member. "You always seemed reluctant to finish, though."

"Well…" Richy reached up and touched his muzzle. "It does keep me more enthusiastic if I haven't come that night. But for special clients I can make an exception."

Volle smiled and nuzzled Richy's paw. His mind wandered as his paws roamed through the soft white fur, and he said, "What happens if you fall in love with a client?"

Richy stiffened, and his eyes became instantly wary. Volle saw this, and hastily amended, "Not me. I'm just curious."

The wolf relaxed somewhat. "It's all business," he said softly. "We're not allowed to meet clients outside the building."

"Have you ever wanted to?"

The wolf shook his head slowly. "I don't mean that I don't enjoy my time with you, Volle. But you understand. You don't really know me. And I don't really know you."

"I think you know me better than I know you. You just react to me. You're pretending to be someone else, someone I want to be with. So you have to know me, at least a little bit."

Richy shrugged, with a smile. "You know the business." He covered Volle's paw with his. "But I do enjoy being with you."

Volle grinned. "You don't have to worry about losing my business. I'm just wondering. Trust me, I've been very happy with your service." He wriggled his hips, tugging at their tie.

Richy grinned. "There have been some clients who I wanted to see again here." He traced a fingertip over Volle's paw. "I usually tell them so."

"Don't you tell everybody that?"

"No. Really, I don't. Sometimes I just wipe up and smile until they leave."

"Do you ever play with any of the other workers?"

Richy's eyes slid to one side. "I shouldn't be talking about the others."

"About yourself, then. Have you ever been in love with someone who wasn't a client?"

He continued to run his dark paws through the wolf's white stomach fur, waiting for an answer. He felt Richy draw in a breath and let it out slowly, and felt the vibrations as he said, "Once." He didn't look at Volle as he said it.

"What happened?"

"He died."

"I'm sorry." He rested a paw on Richy's stomach. "How?"

Richy moved his hips, and Volle slid out of him easily. "Let's get you cleaned up," he said softly, sitting up and grabbing a towel from the side of the bed. He bent over and wrapped the towel around Volle's member, rubbing gently. As he did, Volle leaned over and nuzzled his ears.

He glanced up and smiled at Volle's contrite expression. "It's okay. It was three years ago. He had his leg stepped on by a horse. It got infected..." He sighed. "Nothing I could do."

"I'm sorry," Volle said again.

Richy finished, and licked his nose. "Not your fault. Nothing you can do either."

Volle started to put on his clothes. "I hope you can find someone to be yourself with. I think that's pretty important for everyone."

Richy gave him a questioning look, but didn't say anything. He rubbed the towel along his own glistening member, smiling when he saw Volle watching him. "I'm all right. I may not have chosen this life, but I'm not unhappy."

"All right. Would you mind if we talk a little more next time? If not, I won't bother."

Richy shook his head. "As long as it's just about me. Or you," he added, "if you want."

"Of course." Volle did up his shirt and smoothed it out, and leaned over to touch his nose to the wolf's. "Thank you, Richy. As always, it was delightful."

The wolf smiled back, his tail thumping the bed. "Thank you, Volle. See you in a week?"

"Yes, I won't miss it this time."

"Good. Your weasel friend wears me out." He winked. "At least, you can tell him that."

Volle laughed. "I will. Until then, wolf." He walked back out to the front, where he gave Tally a tip for Richy that was equal to his regular fee for the night, making the green-dyed cougar mock-swoon.

After his morning run with Helfer ("Well, of course I wear him out!"), Volle tried unsuccessfully to get Oncit to talk over lunch again, and then met clandestinely with Tish, Dewanne, and Ryngs.

"Volle thinks that Oncit might have something to do with them," Tish told the others after the greetings.

Dewanne stroked his whiskers. "Oncit, eh? Certainly possible. He's on the border. We hadn't thought of him before because he doesn't seem to be interested in much of anything. Why do you think he's involved?"

"He invited me to dinner, with no servants and without his wife, apparently only to talk to me about whether I wanted to invade Ferrenis."

"He said that?"

"Not in those words," Volle conceded. "But he asked if I would fight on the front lines if the country went to war, if I would do anything to get the Reysfields back."

"Did you tell him they weren't yours to begin with?" Ryngs interjected.

"What did you say?" Tish asked, ignoring the raccoon.

"I said I would. If the country went to war. Then I asked if there were any indication we'd be going to war, and he changed the subject."

"But he hasn't talked to you since?" Dewanne said.

Volle shook his head. "Not at all. I mean, pleasant chit-chat, but whenever I bring up Ferrenis, he clams up."

"I wouldn't have thought he'd even be capable of pleasant chit-chat," Ryngs said. "With his wife running around behind his back and all."

"She what?" Dewanne turned to look at the raccoon, who seemed pleased to find an audience.

"You must be the last person in the palace to hear. Lady Oncit and Lord Deverin?"

"I never hear anything," Dewanne muttered. "With Lady Dewanne being indisposed and all."

"Ah yes, how is dear Delia?" Tish said, cutting off Ryngs, who was about to make another remark.

"She's very well, thank you. The two weeks at Salinas Springs did her a world of good."

"What's wrong with her?" Volle asked.

"What isn't?" Ryngs got his remark in this time.

Dewanne shot a glance at him before continuing. "Lady Dewanne has a very delicate constitution," he said. "She suffers from an imbalance of humours…"

"And a lack of humor," Ryngs muttered so low that only Volle heard him.

"…and she is congestive and has trouble breathing sometimes."

"She's not consumptive?" Volle asked cautiously.

"Thank Canis, no. But she is very delicate and stays in bed most of the day. She thinks she has a weak heart." He smiled fondly as he said it.

"It astonishes me, Dewanne," said Ryngs, "that you laugh only at that self-diagnosis and treat the others seriously."

"Her condition is real," Dewanne said stiffly, "even if her speculation as to the cause of it is rather naive."

Ryngs sighed and turned away, giving up so quickly that Volle was sure they'd had the same argument many times.

Dewanne turned pointedly to Volle. "I hear you're courting a young vixen yourself."

Volle flicked his ears and nodded. "Tika introduced us."

"How is that going?"

"Is she 'delicate'?" Ryngs put in, earning a glare from Dewanne and Tish both.

"Drop it, Ryngs," Tish said softly.

"All right, all right. Just looking out for a friend."

They were silent for a moment, so Volle answered Dewanne's question. "It's going very well. She's a lovely, bright vixen, and her family is very nice. She's having her cotillion in a few weeks, and I'll formally announce my courtship then. Or she will," he said with a glance at Tish. "I confess I haven't quite figured it out yet."

"You will dance the first and last dance, and that will serve as the announcement," Tish said with some amusement. "Don't worry. We'll go over it all several more times before it comes up."

Volle's ears flattened involuntarily, drawing chuckles from around the table. "No, really, I'm glad," he protested.

"And Tika and I will be there too. You'll do fine."

"You're helping with the planning, I hope," Dewanne said to Tish, who nodded. He turned to Volle. "Good. Tish knows everybody. I wouldn't plan a trip to the pub without consulting him."

"You don't drink, anyway," Ryngs pointed out.

"When Lady Dewanne is not present, I have partaken of the occasional glass of wine."

"You should get stinking drunk sometime. Do you good."

"It doesn't seem to have done you much good," Dewanne retorted. "Didn't you end up in the moat last time you got drunk?"

"Only because you pushed me there." Ryngs grinned at the fox, who clapped him on the shoulder. "Hey, how am I supposed to get revenge if you won't get drunk?"

"Children," Tish rumbled with a smile. "Perhaps we could do the socializing later."

"That's what I'm trying to set up!" Ryngs said. "Volle will come with us, won't you?"

"Sure." Volle grinned.

"All right, all right. I can't think of any way to get at Oncit without alerting him, so Volle, just stay available and talk to him. Maybe something will happen to make him talk." Volle nodded. "Dewanne, are you taking the wife on another vacation again soon? Maybe see what's near Oncit this time. I think there are some hot springs in or near his borders."

"What about me?" Ryngs said.

"What have you been doing?"

"Nothing. But I always hope you'll give me something." He grinned. "Okay, I've just been nosing around Fardew and the Defense council."

"Did you hear about Dereath?" Volle interjected.

"That he got sent away? Yeah. Good riddance. He's far too anxious to make a name for himself and he asked me a lot of questions a couple months back about my loyalties. Since then I just try to stay out of his way."

"Good luck," Volle said fervently.

"Easier with him gone."

"What was he sent away for?" Dewanne asked.

"Fardew had some operation going on that he wanted kept low-profile, and Dereath blabbed to a couple people about it."

"What operation?"

Ryngs shook his head. "Don't know. But Fardew wasn't happy. He kept showing his fangs all through the day."

Tish looked at Volle, who laid his ears back a little. The wolf nodded very slightly and remained silent. Volle didn't especially want to discuss the whole experience again, and if Tish thought it wasn't important enough to tell them, then he preferred to hold off.

Chapter 15

The cotillion dominated most of his conversations for the following few weeks. Ilyana came to the palace a few days later, the same day Tarka returned with a scroll from Anton that Volle could present to the Agricultural Council.

To his surprise, Ilyana wanted to come see his chambers. "Why?"

"You say you have other clothes. I just want to see them. We're going out to get me fitted for my gown, and if you don't have anything suitable, you can come along and get fitted too."

"Oh, that would be ...great."

"You'll love it." She winked. "The tailor is a cute little bunny boy."

"I'll alert Helfer," he said, trying to think whether he'd left any Zin-sky books out on his table. He didn't think so, but he still hesitated after telling Welcis that Madame wanted to examine his wardrobe.

The skunk picked up on the hint. "I was just cleaning the bed-room," he said smoothly. "If Madame can wait five minutes? Or I could bring the formal outfits out."

"No, I can wait," Ilyana said, wandering over to the windows of the parlor and looking at Volle's desk, which had become as messy as any Lord's in the palace.

He followed her there and indicated the scroll from Anton. "I just got word from Vinton that they're expecting a good harvest this year."

"That's good." She smiled, and turned to the window, looking out over the gardens. "This is a nice view."

He stepped up beside her and put his arm around her waist. "I like it. It's nice to sit here in the evenings and watch the light fade over the flowers—and trees, this time of year. Most of the flowers are gone. It's interesting to watch the scene with all those colors blending into each other, and then as the sun goes down the colors fade and turn grey. But they're not gone." He paused. "Just sleeping."

She nuzzled him. "That's poetic. I like that. The flowers are sleep-ing, or the colors?"

"Either. Both." He chuckled. "See that bare patch there?"

"The one between the red bushes?"

"Yes. The flowers that were there before were yellow. The whole garden looks different now, even though just that one bed was changed. Know what I mean?"

"I think so."

"Nighttime is like that. It's the same, but it's different. You can see different patterns when you take the colors away."

"I just see that those red ones shouldn't be next to the violet shrubs. That's too much red."

He smiled. "You have good color sense."

Welcis coughed behind them. "His lordship's bedroom is ready."

As they turned, Volle extended a paw. "After you, Ilyana."

She smiled and glided after the skunk. He watched her tail swaying in front of him, imagined Arrin's, and was excited for a moment. But her scent was undeniably feminine, and he just couldn't sustain the illusion. He sighed inwardly. With luck it would never get that far.

"I warn you, it's not as luxurious as you might expect." She had already stopped at the entrance.

"Good heavens, Volle, don't you even have a carpet in here?"

He shook his head. "Never really needed one. There's a fire, and I spend most of my time in the bed anyway."

"But just for appearances!"

He smiled. "Maybe you can help me pick out a nice one."

She brightened, ears perking up, and walked over to the wardrobe, which stood open.

Volle turned to Welcis and spoke in a near whisper. "Thank you, Welcis."

The skunk whispered back. "You're welcome, sir. I moved any potentially embarrassing items to my own cot in the sitting room."

"Thank you, again." He patted the skunk on the back.

"Simply doing my job, sir."

Ilyana had taken down the formal outfit Helfer's tailor had made, which Volle liked quite a bit. "This might do. Is there another set of pants to go with it?"

"No, just those."

She eyed them critically. "They're not bad, but would you be upset if I asked you to get another pair? The cut is a bit too new and the color is a little darker than it should be."

He started to reply that he liked the color and the cut, and then remembered that it was her big day. "That would be fine."

"Thank you." She replaced the clothes, came over, and kissed him on the muzzle, and her eyes were sparkling. "Let's go back up and get Tish and Tika."

They took a carriage to the tailor, though it was a distance Volle could easily have walked. The wolves sat together on the front seat of the carriage while Volle and Ilyana sat in the back facing them.

"Where did you find this tailor?" Volle asked Ilyana.

"Tika found him for me." Ilyana smiled. "Last year, when I needed a new dress."

"Tish found him, actually," Tika put in, and her husband smiled.

"Friend of a friend," he said.

Volle chuckled. "Is there anyone in Divalia who doesn't meet that description?"

"Very few," Tika said with a smile. She nuzzled Tish and he put an arm around her as the carriage bounced down the road. Ilyana leaned closer to Volle, who was looking at Tish and thinking hard about something. It took a couple nudges before he got the hint and put his arm around her. Tish returned his gaze with equanimity, almost inviting him to ask a question, but Volle remained quiet.

"What sort of color are you looking for, Ilyana?" Tika asked.

"A blue, I think. Something light."

Tika nodded. "That should look nice. So a darker blue for Volle?"

"Yes. With purple trim, I think."

"On both? I'm not sure it's proper to have outfits that are that closely coordinated."

"I could have green," Volle put in, but the two of them ignored him.

"It'll be okay. Mine will have more of a lavender color, and his will be royal purple. It won't be quite the same. And the proportions will be different."

Tish grinned at Volle and shrugged his shoulders, and Volle grinned back, settling against the seat as the two ladies discussed the color patterns and fabric and myriads of other details.

At the tailor, Tish took Volle aside while Tika and Ilyana were getting their measurements taken. "Just let her take charge of everything," he said. "It's her day. The wedding will be like that too, except you'll get even less to say."

"Wedding?" Volle coughed. "What if I—what if there isn't a wedding?"

Tish flicked his ears. "What do you mean? You don't like her? You should have said something before now."

"No, I do like her. But what if…what if I screw up at the cotillion or something and she doesn't want to marry me?"

Tish clapped him on the back. "Is that what you're worried about, m'boy? I wouldn't. I think you'd have to set fire to the place and poison her parents before *she* would call off the engagement." His eyes searched Volle's. "As long as you're not thinking about it."

"No," Volle said, but Tish pressed on regardless.

"You know, Volle, if you're worried about giving her the kind of affection you think she expects, don't. She knows what she's getting in for."

"I know."

"She was Tika's first choice over all the others. If you reject her, I won't be able to stop Tika from moving down her list, and likely the second one won't be as good a match."

"I know."

"I know it's strange for you, having only known her a while and having this marriage thrust upon you. You've never had a chance just to get to know her. But that's the way things are done. My father arranged my marriage to Tika when I was sixteen. Luckily, it turned out well. You have even less to worry about—just get an heir and send her off to Vinton to live, then go about your life here. It's an obligation; maybe it will be easier if you think of it that way."

"All right. I'll try." He resolved not to leak any more of his doubts to Tish, at least.

"Volle." Ilyana poked her muzzle out of the door and beckoned him. "Your turn."

Tish laughed and patted Volle as he walked toward the door. "Enjoy, m'boy."

"Tika says you're next," Ilyana said to him saucily, and disappeared. Volle turned in time to see the wolf's crestfallen expression, and his folded-back ears, though from the twinkle in the dark eyes he was sure at least some of it was an act.

He laughed. "I'll stall them as long as I can."

"You're a good fox," Tish said with exaggerated relief, and sprawled back onto the chair.

The tailor was a very cute young bunny, as Ilyana had promised, and he was wearing a short shirt and short pants that showed off his stomach and hips to good effect. Volle supposed that he had made the clothes himself and was just modeling his wares, but he was also selling himself, and that accounted for the giggling he and Tish had heard even out in the waiting room.

"Isn't he cute, Volle?" Ilyana said, and the tailor's resigned expression and spread ears told Volle that he'd been putting up with a lot of this sort of teasing.

"He is, yes. I should tell Hef about him."

The tailor shot him a quick glance as he dropped to measure Volle's waist. Volle didn't know how to interpret it, but he thought maybe he should stop teasing.

Ilyana and Tika commented on his measurements as the tailor called them out, especially the hip. "How does he stay so trim?" Ilyana wondered, with a teasing look at Volle.

"He runs with Lord Ikling every day," Tika said. "I don't know what other exercise he gets."

They giggled again, and this time, the glance that the tailor gave him was sympathetic. Volle smiled and shrugged slightly, and the tailor smiled back.

He and Ilyana went out to the waiting room when it was Tish's turn, and she kissed his muzzle. "Thanks for going along with this. It means a lot to me."

"I know," he said softly, nuzzling her back.

"My father said for you to come by anytime to make your request." She lowered her eyes shyly at that last word.

"All right. How soon will these clothes be ready?"

"One week. They're paying him extra to rush. I hope they turn out okay."

He stroked her fur and nodded. "I'm sure they'll be lovely."

They were. The tailor delivered them himself and waited while they tried them on. He made some small alterations to Ilyana's dress on the spot, but the other three all fit perfectly. Volle saw Tish give the tailor a gold piece on the way out the door.

"They're just as lovely as I'd pictured!" Ilyana was enraptured, running her paws through the fabric. "I'll never be able to pay you back for these."

Tika smiled. "Consider them an engagement present. An early one." She smiled at Volle, who flashed a quick smile back. "Your intended looks good too."

"We're not official for another two weeks," Ilyana reminded her, but she was beaming and her tail wagging.

"You're nearly there," Tika insisted.

Volle had visited her father two days before and formally asked to court her. Her father had happily given his permission, and had been delighted at Volle's gift of a free night at the Jackal's Staff, which he'd set up with Tally the previous day. He'd invited Volle to join him, but Volle had declined, feeling slightly awkward about it all. To make sure he didn't run into her father, he'd put off his weekly visit to Richy until the next night the wolf was available.

He and Ilyana dined with Tish and Tika that night before Volle's appointment, talking mostly about the arrangements for the cotillion. Tish got Volle alone for a few moments after dinner.

"Any progress with Oncit?"

Volle shook his head. "I'm just trying to get him to chat at this point. I think Ikinna isn't part of any group, though."

"Oh? Why's that?"

"He talks too much. He talks about everything and he loves being the center of attention. If he had a secret, you can bet everyone would know he had a secret, even if they didn't know what it was."

"Hmm. I'll trust your judgment. What about Rhyshko?"

"Not sure, but I tend to think the same. He hangs around with Ikinna all the time. I can't imagine one of them being in on a secret without telling the other."

"All right. I'll consider that."

Tika opened the door. "Volle, Ilyana's ready to leave."

He escorted her home, and met Helfer on his return to the palace. The weasel had postponed his weekly visit to the Jackal's Staff to match Volle's, for which the fox was glad. He liked the weasel's company; even if they took their pleasures separately, they still talked on the way there and back, and often shared a drink afterwards.

"I hardly see you anymore," Helfer complained as they left the palace. The air was chilly enough that Volle kept flicking his ears to keep them warm. It wouldn't be long until the snows came, he thought.

"You see me every day for the run."

"I know. You just postponed our visit to the Jackal's Staff and didn't have dinner with me, so I thought I'd give you a hard time."

Volle rolled his eyes. "I'm already marrying someone else. I don't need a hard time from you."

"But you do need it from Richy, eh?"

Volle laughed. "That's different. I pay him and he goes away afterwards." He shook his head. "I can't believe I missed that setup."

"See? That's what I mean. Sooner you get this cotillion out of the way, the better. I only wish I could be there to see it."

"I wish you could, too. How are things back in Vellenland?"

"Burren has the usual contingent of weasel ladies lined up for me to service, and papers to sign. On the whole, I'd rather sign the papers, but I don't get a choice until there are at least three little Iklings running around."

"Three?"

"At least a year old, too."

"Oh. Sounds like a lot of work."

"It wouldn't be if they would actually be in season. It's easy to fake with weasels. They have multiple seasons, so the scent doesn't really change at all. So of course any lady who wants to have a noble kid *says* she's in season, and we can't tell whether she is or not."

"Glad foxes aren't like that." He could remember the strange smell when his mother was in season, and how she'd sent him to stay with friends for a week whenever it started, once he turned ten. And his friend explaining to him, both of them wide-eyed at eight years old, that the smell was a little troll that came around selling babies, and if he found a tod and a vixen together he would make them take one and put it in the vixen's tummy for six months.

"Lucky. Likely you'll be done in one night." Helfer grinned. "Let me know if you need some mead."

"I will." They arrived at the house, and found it rather busy. Three female bobcats were sitting around a table, the first time Volle could remember seeing more than one female in the club. They had to wait for an empty table, but only a few minutes, and Tally was bustling busily all over and didn't see them at first. The scent of lust was even stronger than usual, and Volle found himself fidgeting and trying to ignore the tingling and slow swelling in his groin.

"This is why I usually go on Gaiaday," Helfer said, settling in with a mug of watery wine. He didn't seem as affected by the smell as Volle was, nor did he notice Volle's reaction.

"Hope there's not too long a wait."

The weasel shook his head and sipped. "There won't be. Most of these are hooking up with each other. Except them." He nodded toward the bobcats. "But they look like they're here for some group thing."

Volle grinned. "I don't know whether to be impressed that you can tell that, or curious." But as he looked at the bobcats, he saw that they were all immersed in each other, not looking around at the other tables as most of the patrons were doing.

Helfer just snickered. Tally came over to them then, hurrying.

"Darlings! On our busiest night of the week! You should stick to your regular night."

"This was sort of impromptu," Volle said. "I didn't want to meet my guest."

"Oh! He had a lovely hour with Celann, and even tipped. He's certainly a gentlefox. Friend of yours?"

"Future father-in-law," Helfer put in, grinning.

"Oh my! I'd love to hear more, but…" He gestured around at the room. "Volle, you want Richy, right? He'll be free in about fifteen minutes. Hef, there's a lovely bunny who usually comes in around this time, if you want to wait for him."

"Sure." Helfer paid for a room, and Volle paid for Richy. The silver disappeared, Tally blew them both a kiss, and hurried away to another table.

"I should never have told you about Ilyana's father." Volle grinned. "Didn't know you'd tell the first person that asked."

Helfer looked hurt. "I haven't told anyone else!" The hurt expression slid into a grin. "Besides, it's too funny."

"It is that," Volle admitted, lapping at his wine with a grin. "I'm just glad he appreciated the gift. I wasn't sure it would be appropriate."

"I guess his wife knows?"

"I'm not sure about that. I would think she'd have to, but maybe it's just one of those once-in-a-while things that he does and she doesn't ask questions about."

"Maybe. So how are your preparations going?"

"Ilyana's really excited. I guess I'm a little excited for her, but…" Volle sighed. "I'll be relieved when it's all over."

"Won't we all," Helfer chuckled, taking another sip of wine and then craning his neck at what seemed to Volle to be a painful angle to get a look at the rabbit who'd just walked in. "Wow. That one is a looker."

"I'm surprised you're letting him sit down." Volle grinned as Helfer scribbled a note and waved Tally down. "What do you write on those, anyway?"

"Oh, just my species and some of the things I like to do. Thanks." Tally patted his head as he took the note. "Saves time, you know."

Volle grinned. "There never seems to be much question in your case. Ever had someone turn you down?"

Helfer, watching the rabbit, shook his head. "No, but I usually pick the rabbits. I know what to say to them. See?"

The rabbit was looking over and nodding. Helfer stood up and grinned to Volle. "See you after."

Volle chuckled and nodded. "Have fun." He watched Helfer make his way over to the rabbit's table. The two of them disappeared into the back within a minute.

"Don't know how he manages it. He sure is charming." He took another drink of wine, and then felt a gentle touch on his shoulder. A piece of paper fluttered down to the table.

"Two tables back and to your left, dear," Tally murmured. "In case you don't want to wait for Richy."

Volle unfolded the note. In a neat, curliqued handwriting, someone had written, "You look like a cute fox. I'm a tender buck and I'd love to have you on top of me."

He craned his neck back and saw a handsome stag watching him alone from a table. He was young, with only three points to his antlers, but he was dressed handsomely in a green linen outfit (which reminded Volle of Reese's 'hunter' outfit). He smiled when he saw Volle turn, and mimed getting up, with a questioning raise of his eyebrows.

Volle considered it, but he'd been intrigued by his talk with Richy and felt that he owed the wolf an appointment, even though he knew the wolf didn't really care if he missed a week or not. He shook his head and pointed at the back, and the stag, though he looked disappointed, smiled gracefully and started scanning the room for someone else. He'd started writing another note before Volle turned around.

He spent the next fifteen minutes listening to the raccoon combo playing, and thinking about Tish, Xiller, Ilyana, her father, and Arrin, before Tally came over with a smile on his purple-whiskered muzzle. "Richy's ready, dear. Go on back. Room seven."

"Thanks." He smiled, got up, and walked to the back.

When he opened the door to room seven, the young wolf was lying on his back, nude, one knee crossed over the other. His tail thumped the bed when he saw Volle.

Volle closed the door and smiled. "Hi, Richy."

"You're two days late." But he said it with a warm smile. He lowered the crossed leg to expose his sheath and pink erection, lying flat on his stomach fur. "I've been waiting and waiting."

"I'm sorry." Volle grinned. "Let me make it up to you." He knelt at the side of the bed and leaned his muzzle over, lifting the wolf's length with a paw and running his tongue over it. Richy rubbed behind his ears as he did it again, curling his tongue around the sensitive tip and then letting it go. He took his time, tracing the long hardness with his tongue over and over while he felt his own erection grow to match it. Finally he slid it into his muzzle, closing his lips around the swelling knot and pressing the hardness against the roof of his muzzle with his tongue. He slid his muzzle back and forth, paying particular attention to the tip, until he heard the wolf moan and felt his body shudder.

Slowly, he lifted his muzzle free, giving the glistening tip one last lick before he let it fall back to the warm, white-furred stomach. "If you want to finish me, you can," Richy said quietly. "Some customers pay just for that."

"I bet they do." Volle teased his fur gently.

"Why don't you take those clothes off and join me?"

"I will." He wagged his tail slowly back and forth, and ran his paws up Richy's stomach and chest, feeling the muscles and ribs below the fur. "I like feeling you."

Richy settled back against the pillow. "You can do that too. Careful!"

But Volle's paw had already reached up to the shoulder and felt an ugly lump, hidden under the fur. "Sorry," he said as the wolf winced. "What's that?"

"Bite," Richy said shortly. "From a client last week. It still hurts."

"Sorry. Was it a cat?"

"I really shouldn't talk about..." Richy sighed. "He was a squirrel."

Volle winced. "Ouch. Sharp teeth." The wolf nodded. "Any other areas I should stay away from?"

Richy grinned and placed the fox's black paw back on his long pink shaft. "If you stay here, you'll be fine."

Volle rubbed the length appreciatively and then stood up, slipping out of his pants and shirt quickly. He took a moment to draw his paw up his erection, which was already fully out of his sheath, and then reached for the cream in the chest.

"I can do that," Richy said, but Volle stopped him with a paw.

"Just lie there and look beautiful," he said, scooping some cream onto his fingers. He rubbed it under his tail, then wiped his fingers on a towel. Smiling, he slid onto the bed on his paws and knees, and applied his tongue to the wolf's erection again, licking until it was glistening, teasing the tip with his lips until Richy's control was wavering and he was moaning.

Then he swung his leg over the wolf, kneeling astride him. He reached down, lifted the wolf's shaft from his stomach and positioned it under his tail. Wiggling his hips, he lowered himself quickly onto it, gasping as the slick length penetrated him. He felt the bulge of the wolf's knot slide into him and out again with difficulty, the pressure forcing drops of fluid from his tip. He tightened his rear and slid almost all the way off, pressing around the wolf's tip as he slid back and took him all the way in. It had been over two weeks since he'd been mounted; since Xiller, actually, and the memory came back to him as he raised and lowered his hips, though the knot made the experience very different.

No less pleasurable, though, and the length of time it had been since his last visit manifested with a vengeance in the surge of blood that went through him as he felt the hard length inside him. He moved up and down, just savoring the feel of it, and noticed that he was already leaking some fluid from his tip. "I've missed this," he murmured, starting to pant as he slid up and down, tail twitching.

"I can...tell." Richy panted, and brought a paw up to brush the fluid from Volle's tip. He licked his finger and grinned, then curled his paw around the fox's erection, stroking back and forth as it dangled over his chest. Panting, Volle moved his hips faster, trying to squeeze the wolf's knot with every stroke. From the rate it was growing, and the sensations that were building up in him, he thought this would be a very quick session.

Perhaps sensing that too, Richy tried to slow down once, but as his knot grew, every time it slid into Volle it was squeezed more, making him moan softly. After a few more of these strokes, his paw started moving faster. Volle moaned himself, his paws resting on the wolf's chest as he levered himself up and down, and then he pressed back and met resistance. He pressed harder, and Richy pushed his hips up, and with a slick sound, his knot slid through Volle's tail hole and locked him to the fox. Volle kept tugging with his hips, unable to stop himself as the flood of delightful sensations took over his muscles; Richy pumped harder along his erection, writhing and panting and finally howling softly as his body tensed under Volle, hips shivering back and forth.

Volle smiled, very close himself, and waited as Richy's paw paused. It started again as soon as the wolf began to relax, smiling up into the fox's muzzle. With the warm fullness inside him and the soft paw stroking him, it wasn't long before Volle moaned loudly, shivering and clutching at Richy's chest as he came. His seed spurted onto the wolf's chest and paw with every convulsive spasm, and he dimly registered that the orgasm seemed to go on and on, until he thought he must have soaked the wolf's fur all the way through.

The smell was certainly strong in the air, he noted, and then realized that it was because he was panting, head hanging down not four inches from the small pool of white fluid in Richy's fur. He looked up into the wolf's bright eyes, and licked his nose.

"Wow, the extra two days make a difference, don't they?" Richy's eyes sparkled teasingly.

"I guess so." Volle smiled, tail wagging. He didn't tell Richy that he hadn't been pleasuring himself for the past few days either, not because he wanted to save up, but because he found himself occupied with Ilyana's planning or related matters, and exhausted when he got to bed.

"You came pretty quickly. And lots." He licked his dripping paw with a smile.

Volle wiggled his hips. "You came too."

"You made sure of that. I shouldn't have told you my weak spots." The wolf grinned and brushed the back of his paw along Volle's shaft gently. "Oh, I thought of something else for you, for if you don't want to come. Just paw yourself off right before."

"I thought of that, but she'd be able to smell it. Unless I completely washed off, and I wouldn't have time for that really."

Richy grinned. "You can use what we use. It masks the smell very well."

"Oh, really?"

"Sure, just remind me before you leave. I'll give you a bit."

"Thanks. I won't need it for a few weeks yet. A month, actually, I think." He tried to remember when she'd said her season would be. Two weeks after the cotillion, so a month was about right.

"Wedding night?"

Volle grinned. "Something like that. The big social event is in a couple weeks and she comes into season after that."

Richy teased his shaft with a finger. "You'll still come see me, right?"

"Of course I will." Volle squirmed, squeezing the wolf's shaft, and giggled. "She doesn't have one of these."

"She'll have yours."

"But then I won't."

Richy laughed. "True enough. Well, you've got mine when you need it."

"Mm, I know." Volle wriggled again, feeling the knot, which hadn't gone down much. He smiled down at the wolf. "How long have you been doing this?"

"About two and a half years now. Ever since Jonn died. I needed some way to support myself."

"What about your family?"

Richy shrugged. "They didn't like Jonn. Thought he was taking advantage of me. I think they were happy when he died so they could laugh at me."

"That doesn't sound very nice." Volle stroked the wolf's chest.

"That's my family," Richy replied.

They were quiet for a moment while Volle stroked his fur, trying to avoid the sticky patches. "What was Jonn like?"

"He was an older cat. He trained horses. I took riding lessons with him, and other lessons, without the horses, in the stables..." He sighed and stroked Volle's paw, smiling. "It's okay. It's been a long time, and I'm all right. I'll do this for a while and then buy my own stable."

"How long?"

Richy shrugged slightly. "A few more years before I'm not quite young and pretty enough for everyone. If I'm lucky. A couple of the boys here got beaten up by customers and quit. One died of—something else." He looked suddenly wary. "I shouldn't be talking about this. Any of this, really." He smiled and nuzzled Volle's paw.

"It's all right." Volle guessed he'd been about to mention a disease, which he knew was common in the brothels, but of course they wouldn't want to talk to the customers about that.

"Really, you come here for escape and I shouldn't be talking about myself like this." He squirmed a bit, his knot looser.

Volle sighed as he felt the wolf's member slide slowly out of him. "I do get a nice escape here. I'm not—a noble, a courting fox, or any of that here. I'm just Volle, and you're just Richy, a sweet young wolf." But as he said it he realized how false that was; Richy was putting on a persona for his benefit, and no matter how much he opened up, this wasn't what he was like.

Richy didn't respond to the comment as he cleaned them up with the towel. When he'd finished, he rummaged in the chest and then handed Volle a small packet of herbs. "Mix some water into this and rub it around your groin. It masks the come smell."

Volle put it in his purse as he pulled his pants on. "Okay. Thanks again."

Richy smiled. "Good luck."

Volle slipped into his shirt, adjusted it, and gave the wolf a hug. "I hope you find someone you can just be yourself with," he said softly. "I think that's very important."

"Thank you," Richy nuzzled him.

"I'll see you in five days. Promise."

Richy traced his sheath with a paw, leaning back against the bed. "I'll be here."

Volle grinned and walked back out to the main room, where of course Helfer wasn't. The crowd had thinned a bit, so he sat down at a table and lapped a mug of wine. As he usually did after visiting Richy, his problems seemed to recede. The cotillion was far away, he was making progress in investigating the palace, and he would see Xiller again, maybe not this year, but hopefully next. The raccoons were in fine form, he thought, the crowd looked happy, and he felt content, relaxed, and at peace.

Book 3: Lord Vinton

Chapter 16

The morning of the cotillion, Volle looked out of his bedroom window and saw tiny white flakes drifting to the ground. "Is snow lucky or unlucky?" he wondered, standing at the window and looking outside, letting the cold air drift past his muzzle.

"Beg pardon, sir?" Welcis had entered the bedroom quietly and now stood at the wardrobe.

"Oh. Good morning, Welcis. I was just wondering if the first snowfall on the day of Ilyana's cotillion was a good omen or a bad one. What do you think?"

"I believe, sir, that snow is commonly associated with the coming of winter, a cold, dry time that most consider the least pleasant of the seasons."

Volle couldn't tell whether he was being serious or not. "So you would opt for bad omen?"

Welcis's muzzle twitched in a way that suggested the possibility of a smile. "I would not be so bold as to predict anything but success for Madame's event. In my experience, sir, Gaia sends her seasons regardless of the activities of her children."

"So you're saying I shouldn't worry about it."

"In a nutshell, yes, sir."

"Thank you, Welcis. Still, it is the first snow." He watched some more flakes fall, reached out and caught one, and brought it back to his muzzle.

"Yes, sir. I believe that winter is also considered among the more romantic of seasons. Many people remain inside during the cold nights, and romance is often the result."

"An excellent point." Volle smiled. "Now, you are aware of the preparations for today?"

"Yes, sir. Lady Tistunish described the necessary procedures at length." He started to lay out the formal clothes the tailor had produced for the cotillion. "I do have one piece of information, sir. His lordship may remember that some time ago he had asked me to procure information regarding Lord Oncit."

"Oh, yes. Turn up anything?"

"My inquiries have been discreet, and until last night had produced no results. Lord Oncit is a very quiet, private lord. However, last night I happened to encounter his servant again, and he told me that some two or three weeks ago, he overheard Lord Oncit mention your name."

"What did he say?" Volle had turned from the snow and was watching Welcis eagerly now.

"He only heard him say 'I tell you, he's not suitable!' or something of the like. His voice was raised, which is why he had overheard that."

"Who was he talking to?"

"He would not tell me at first, sir, but I gathered from some of the other things he said that it was Secretary Prewitt."

Prewitt? "What did he want to know if I was suitable for?"

"Precisely, sir. I could not gather that, I fear."

"Well, thank you for what you did get, Welcis. I'm lucky to have you."

The skunk did smile then, and nodded. "If his lordship will come over to the bed, we can begin with a brushing. His lordship did take a water bath today after his run?"

Volle nodded. "I'm mostly dry." He sighed. "I hate running alone. I can't wait 'til Helfer gets back."

"Lord Ikling left two days ago?"

"That's right. We had dinner and he said he'd be gone early the next morning. It's dull without him around. I wish he could be around tonight." Volle sat back as Welcis worked the brush through his fur.

"How long is his trip?"

"Two weeks, I think he said. One week of travel, another week to attend to his affairs there."

"Two weeks will go by quickly, sir, especially with Madame's company."

"I suppose so." Volle sighed. Helfer would have caught his sly double entendre about 'affairs.' He closed his eyes. The brushing usually felt good, but today it seemed rough and irritating. Probably due to his worries about the cotillion.

"What time are Tish and Tika coming by?"

"I believe Lady Tistunish has decided to help Madame prepare for this evening. Lord Tistunish will be here for lunch in approximately one hour."

Volle's stomach rumbled at the mention of lunch. He wanted to eat, but at the same time he felt shaky and wondered if he really had an appetite. He'd been unable to prevent himself from getting nervous about the cotillion; no matter how many times he told himself that he was prepared and that it didn't matter anyway, he had horrible visions of himself doing something totally inappropriate, people laughing, and Ilyana's crestfallen expression as her cotillion was ruined.

"They should've taught us this at the Academy," he thought to himself. "What good is it if I can recite all the kings of Ferrenis in order, if I can't make it through a simple cotillion?"

Welcis was arranging the clothes and helping him with them. First the pants, which had fasteners in the front and back, then the undershirt, which was plain linen, then the overshirt, which was dark blue sateen with violet ruffles on the sleeves and a violet collar. The buttons down the front were a lighter purple, so they stood out against the blue. All in all, Volle liked the outfit well enough, but it took the better part of half an hour to put on. He was glad that Ilyana had chosen to leave off the lace trim, no matter how fashionable it was.

He busied himself while waiting for Tish's arrival by finishing a note to Anton delineating some requests the Agricultural Council was making. He found that lately, he wasn't able to finish any of the few administrative tasks he had, what with keeping Seir informed of his progress (or lack thereof), spending lunches with the taciturn Oncit, and trying to calm an increasingly frenetic Ilyana.

Perhaps, he mused as he sealed the letter, he was picking up nervousness from her. It was certainly likely enough, as she was communicating it with scent, not just body language. Even Tika seemed more jumpy lately, though that could've just been her natural worrying about the event as well. Only Tish seemed completely calm about the whole thing.

Just as he thought that, he heard Tish's knock at the door. Welcis admitted him to the parlor, and he stood before Volle in his own new outfit.

They looked at each other for a moment, and then Volle said. "You do look good in that."

"It was expensive enough," the black wolf grumbled, but his ears perked happily at the compliment. "You do yours more than justice as well."

"Thank you. Have a seat?" Tish took one of the chairs, and Volle handed the letter to Welcis. "We can get lunch. Can you take this to the stables and have it sent to Vinton?"

"Certainly, sir. Lunch is on the sideboard." Welcis bowed and picked up his cloak, then left the room.

"Glass of wine, Tish?"

"Thank you, I believe I will. How are you feeling, m'boy?"

"Oh, nervous." Volle poured two goblets of wine and brought them over to the small table, seating himself across from the large wolf. "I just hope it all goes well, for Ilyana's sake."

"I'm sure it will. We've coached you properly and I'm sure you'll do fine." Tish lapped at his wine and nodded appreciatively. "This isn't from the palace cellars."

"No, Helfer gave that to me. He doesn't like wine and says Vellen-land doesn't do very good wines, but I rather like it."

"I do too. Perhaps I'll trouble him for a bottle. When he returns, of course."

Volle nodded. He swirled his wine and looked into the goblet, missing Helfer again. He felt much more weighed down with duty and work when the weasel wasn't around.

"Want to run through the ritual again?"

"Not really." He smiled at Tish. "Maybe after we eat."

"All right. Lead on."

They shared a simple lunch from the kitchen: a salad and some cold chicken, garlic-roasted. Afterwards, Tish settled back with his second goblet of wine and smiled at Volle. "Who will escort my daughter from her home into the world?"

"I will." He grinned. "That was an easy one."

"And who are you?"

"Lord Volle of Vinton, a fox of noble breeding and good character, true to Canis and Gaia and King Barris."

"And who will vouch for this fox?"

Volle snickered. "You're doing them out of order, and anyway, that's yours!"

"So it is. 'I, Lord Marcher of Tistunish, true to Canis and Gaia and King Barris, vouch for Lord Volle of Vinton.'"

"My parentage is: Lord Wiri of Vinton, whose father was Lord Taurin of Vinton, whose father was Lord Fyrin of Vinton, whose father was Lord Beri of Vinton, whose father was Lord Geri of Vinton, who was granted his title by King Telas IV, son of Gaia."

"Very good. 'Will you protect her from ill, and show her beauty, guide her from the wrong path and accompany her on the right?'"

"I will." Volle's tail swished the floor. "Wish I didn't have to do this in front of all those people. It feels like a wedding."

"It's best to have the courtship begin at an event if possible. Often a cotillion is just for the young lady to meet the eligible bachelors in her society, but if there is one who plans to court her, he announces it there. This ritual just makes it fit into the cotillion better."

"I know. Well, I think if I can get the parentage question, I can get any of them. When should we leave?"

"In a bit." Tish smiled. "Don't get too worked up about tonight. In the grand scheme of things, it isn't that important. Your courtship will happen regardless of what you do, but the formal words will make it easier. They're important to Ilyana and her family, but not so important that they'd jeopardize this union. So relax and have a good time."

"I'll try." He sighed. "I just don't think I'm the best choice."

"Tika and I do, and so does Ilyana, so you're outvoted."

"As if that had anything to do with it."

Tish grinned and levered himself up from the chair. "You're right, of course."

"Nice to know it." Volle got up as well, and smiled. "But you've never steered me wrong yet."

"Nor will I." For a moment, he looked beyond Volle, and then his eyes snapped back to the fox. "Now, speaking of steering, shall we be off?"

Volle bowed, extending a paw towards the door. "Age before beauty."

Tish grinned and clapped him on the shoulder. "I almost regret we picked out such a pretty vixen for you, you disrespectful fox!"

"Too late now." Volle followed him out.

It took them about half an hour to get to the house that was hosting the cotillion. It belonged to a relative of a friend of Tish's, or a friend of a relative. It was a beautiful old house that Tish told him had been a retreat from the palace for a lord in the past, but now was the permanent residence of the family of one of that lord's illegitimate children, to whom he'd bequeathed the house, since he couldn't leave him his title.

Volle had seen similar mansions in Caril, but not in Divalia; then again, he hadn't been far from the palace, which was surrounded by shops eager for noble patrons and housing for commoners who owned and worked in the shops and the palace. In this area, he saw several large mansions, and the one the carriage stopped in front of was neither the largest nor the smallest.

Greenery and hedges surrounded the house, though nothing as fancy as the gardens of the palace. Everything was white with the first snowfall, and the flakes swirled around Volle and Tish as they stepped down from the carriage. The front sported several white columns and a shallow flight of steps leading up to the gold-and-blue-painted door. In a little while, a servant would be waiting at the door to greet the guests, but for now, there was nobody, and Tish opened the door himself.

Volle looked at the snow before walking inside. "First snow," he said half to himself, rubbing it between his fingers.

"It's a bit early," Tish said. "Looks like it might be a hard winter."

They walked into the mansion, into a small hallway that led to a larger one. Both hallways had candle sconces and mirrors, but only a couple paintings, both of a noble-looking stag. Volle didn't see any legends near the paintings, but he supposed they were portraits of the original lord who'd owned the mansion. They looked rather old.

The whole place looked old to him, and slightly dingy. The floor was dirty, though it had been recently swept. He and Tish were leaving wet footprints as they walked along, although Volle suspected they were getting as much dirt on their paws as they were leaving on the floor. The palace was always quite clean, and he was surprised to find himself missing that, especially as the Academy floors had been anything but.

"Here's the room," Tish said. "What do you think?"

It was gorgeous. The floor was polished and shining in the light that filtered in through the many windows along the far wall. Each of the white marble squares was joined at the corner by a small red diamond to the other four squares. A black border ran around the edge of the room, separated from the white squares by a line of gold. At one side of the room, two marmots and a raccoon were working on a wooden platform, while a fox and a bobcat distributed place settings around a number of small tables. Opposite the platform, a larger table was being set by a mouse and a goat, who were talking in low tones as they worked.

The six windows reached from about two feet above the floor to four feet below the ceiling. Each one was made up of dozens of small, diamond-shaped panes, and was surrounded by a decorative golden relief, surmounted by the insignia of one of the Houses of Gaia.

"The windows were done by Farrish—you know him?" Volle shook his head. "He did the staircase sculptures in the palace—well, all but the Wolf one—and a lot of religious icons for the nobility. Wonderful work."

"The Wolf stair used to be the Fox stair, didn't it?"

Tish nodded. "You figured that out, did you? Good thinking. Yes, they destroyed the fox heads, more's the pity. The wolf ones are nice, but there's nobody alive today who can sculpt like Farrish could."

Volle indicated the large table with his muzzle. "That's where we're sitting?"

"Yes. Others should be arriving soon. I see the musicians are here."

Volle looked at the wooden platform again, where the marmots were unpacking instruments and setting up chairs and music stands. The raccoon was still inspecting the platform.

He walked with Tish over to the large table once the mouse and goat had finished setting it. Their names were marked on the place settings, next to each other, for which Volle felt profoundly grateful. Ilyana was seated to his left, and Tika to Tish's right.

He and Tish talked quietly while the musicians finished setting up, and then listened while they warmed up. The two marmots had violins, and the raccoon played cello. They played a couple snatches of airs that Volle didn't recognize, and then launched into one that he did, a classic piece that was making the rounds of the palace.

As if on cue, the guests began to trickle in. Volle didn't know most of them, because few were from the palace. Mostly they were upper class canids, although there were a few mustelids and ursids thrown in. "We only invited the bears because ursids make for a classy occasion now that it's their turn," Tish confided to Volle as the bear couple entered. "To be honest, I called in a favor on them. They don't really know Ilyana's family at all."

"Why aren't there more lords here?"

"I thought Tika told you that. Ilyana's not in that circle yet, and you're not courting her yet, so she has to be introduced to the appropriate level of society first. When you get married, the palace nobles will be there."

Married. Volle chewed over that for a couple minutes and then decided to let it go. A few of the guests were venturing out onto the dance floor—until Ilyana arrived, it was fair game, but after that, she had to have the first dance. For the next half hour, the room filled steadily until some seventy people were sitting at tables, talking, dancing, and wandering around the room. At the large table, Volle found himself seated across from two elderly foxes whom he guessed to be Ilyana's aunt and uncle even before they introduced themselves. He made polite small talk until Tish nudged him and pointed him to a shy young vixen who was looking his way.

"Go on, dance with her." He grinned. "It would give her a thrill, and besides, you're only single for another half hour or so."

"Will you dance with me afterwards if it would give me a thrill?" Volle muttered with a grin as he got up.

"I'm not single," Tish replied with a wink, and pushed him towards the vixen.

Her name was Mariana, and she was a graceful dancer, but after saying, "I'm Mariana" in a near whisper, she didn't speak the whole time they were dancing. Volle was concentrating on remembering the steps he'd been taught, and so didn't initiate any conversation. Mariana seemed uncertain about how closely to hold on to him; her paw rested on his hip, then wavered uncertainly and moved up, only to slide slowly back down. He held her across her back, and held her other paw in his own.

By the end of the dance, Volle was happy that he'd remembered the steps and thought he'd acquitted himself well. They stepped back from each other, and Mariana looked up with a bright smile. "Thank you, Lord Vinton," she said in a soft whisper.

"Thank you, Mariana." He bowed to her and tried to make his way back to Tish, but another vixen stepped in front of him, and so he asked her to dance as well.

Two more vixens and a lithe young bobcat later, he was still trying to make his way over to Tish when he felt a tap beneath his shoulder blade, and a familiar voice cooed, "Oh, could I have the next dance, great Lord Vinton?"

He turned and saw Helfer grinning at him. For a moment he just stood stunned, then he laughed and swept the weasel up into a big hug, tail wagging. "Hef! What in Gaia's name are you doing here?"

"You think I'd miss this?" The weasel hugged back and then smoothed out the wrinkles in Volle's clothes. "I postponed my trip for a bit. Lousy weather for it anyway." He winked.

"Weather's not going to get any better," Volle said. He couldn't stop grinning. "But I'm glad you're here."

"Yeah? So how about that dance?"

Volle laughed and grabbed the weasel's paws, twirling him around the floor a few times. Helfer kept time pretty well, though Volle was taking larger steps than the short-legged weasel.

"Where did you learn to dance?" Volle asked.

"Oh, here and there." Helfer grinned. "Tish gave me a refresher when I told him I'd be coming."

Volle glanced over at the broadly grinning black wolf. "He knew?"

"He talked me into it. We decided to surprise you. He thought it might relax you to have a friend here."

"I'm glad he did." The song ended, and Volle squeezed Helfer's paws as they slowed to a stop. "Thanks. I'm glad you're here."

"I am too." Helfer patted him on the back. "Now get back to your table. I think your intended is about to come in."

Volle watched Helfer move to a small table off to the side, where he was talking to a hare who looked familiar. Was that Reese? Volle stopped to take a closer look, but everyone was clearing off the floor as Tish stood up, and Volle hurried to get back to his side.

Tish smiled as he scrambled into place, then addressed the crowd. "Sons and daughters of Gaia, it is my pleasure to welcome you all to this happy event. We are here to witness the entrée into society of a dear friend of mine, a young vixen whose family is among the most highly regarded in Divalia. I know that all of you here will provide an appropriate welcome for her as she makes the exciting transition from her home to the greater home of our society. Sons and daughters, ladies and lords, I present to you for the first time: Madame Ilyana Rodion."

He turned toward the door, and Volle did too. The whole room stood and followed suit. After a moment, Ilyana stepped elegantly through the doorway, showing off her light blue and lavender gown to excellent effect. It was blue across the shoulders and down the front and back, with a slightly darker blue bodice. The lavender sleeves were ruffled down the side, and the skirt of the dress was blue with lavender stripes down either side.

She walked proudly, head held high, ears up, tail arched. Behind her, her mother and father walked, looking just as proud, and Tika flanked them. All four stopped when they reached the open area in the center, and the crowd applauded appreciatively. Ilyana curtsied deeply to all sides of the room, and then walked gracefully to the large table, where she stood next to Volle. Her mother stood beside her, her father behind them, and Tika took her place beside Tish.

Tish motioned the crowd to their seats with both paws, but he, Volle, Ilyana, and her father remained standing. "We are doubly fortunate tonight in being present to witness not only the introduction of Madame Ilyana Rodion to society, but also her courtship by a recently arrived noble. He has agreed to take responsibility for Madame Rodion, and her father has acquiesced to the courtship. Sons and daughters, lords and ladies, Lord Volle of Vinton."

Volle felt his ears flush at the polite applause. He bowed to each side of the room. Tish continued. "The lady's father, Marcel Rodion, will officially question Lord Vinton."

Marcel stepped forward. "Who will escort my daughter from her home into the world?"

Volle faced the older fox. "I will."

"And who are you?"

"Lord Volle of Vinton, a fox of noble breeding and good character, true to Canis and Gaia and King Barris."

"What is your lineage?"

"My parentage is: Lord Wiri of Vinton, whose father was Lord Taurin of Vinton, whose father was Lord Fyrin of Vinton, whose father was Lord Beri of Vinton, whose father was Lord Geri of Vinton, who was granted his title by King Telas IV, son of Gaia."

"Do you know me?"

"You are Marcel Rodion, son of Razum and Avdotia, husband to Katiana."

"Do you know my daughter?"

"I know Ilyana Rodion and hold her in the highest regard."

"Will you protect her from ill, and show her beauty, guide her from the wrong path and accompany her on the right?"

"I will."

"And who will vouch for this fox?"

Tish said, "I, Lord Marcher of Tistunish, true to Canis and Gaia and King Barris, vouch for Lord Volle of Vinton."

Marcel continued. "As this fox has presented himself and been vouched for, I see no reason why he may not escort my daughter." He turned to them and smiled. "Goodbye, Ilyana, from our home, and hello and welcome, to our society."

He leaned forward and kissed her, and she kissed him back, then stepped aside. He shook paws with Volle, smiling at him, and then stepped aside so Volle could take Ilyana's paws. Her eyes sparkled even in the muted afternoon light as he touched his nose to hers and kissed her.

She smelled like lavender as well as wearing the color, he noticed, and of course Welcis had applied the lavender scent to him that morning, so their scents and clothes matched. He wondered vaguely if that were proper, given the fuss over the clothes matching or not, but decided he wouldn't worry about it. The hard part was done, and now he just had to dance, eat, and make it home.

"I'm so happy," she whispered to him as they walked to the center to dance the first dance alone. "The snow is so beautiful, it's just like

The music started, and he led her in slow, elegant circles around the floor.

a fairytale. I couldn't have asked for a better setting, or a handsomer prince."

Genuinely touched, Volle kissed her again. The music started, and he led her in slow, elegant circles around the floor. "It's all the clothes, you know," he said with a smile. "Really, I'm not that handsome."

"You're handsome inside," she said softly. "And outside too, no matter what you say."

"Thank you." He smiled and nuzzled her ears. "But I know that nobody in the crowd right now is looking at *me* dance."

She laughed. "That vixen over there is."

"Nope," he said without turning around. "She's looking at you jealously and thinking that she'll never look that good even if she had this same dress."

"You're so sweet," she murmured.

He nuzzled her ears again. "I think your father wants to dance with you for the next song." He'd spotted Marcel waiting eagerly at the edge of the floor, though the thought crossed his mind that he didn't know for sure which one of them the older fox was waiting eagerly for.

"All right," she said as the song faded away. The company clapped politely, and some other couples came out onto the floor with them.

Volle handed Ilyana to Marcel, and he seemed happy enough, so perhaps he really was waiting for her. "See you again in a bit," he said as the two of them spun away. He intended to head back to the table, but found his way blocked by Tika, who grabbed his paw and shoulder.

"You didn't really think you'd get away without giving me a dance, did you?"

"Shouldn't you be dancing with your husband?"

"Oh, he says he'll dance with me later, but his foot is bothering him right now."

"Right," Volle said, grinning. "I'll have to remember that one."

Tika chuckled, letting him lead her through the dance even though she was taller, heavier, and more skilled than he was. And after Tika, Ilyana came back for another dance, and then Helfer swept her off and Volle found himself with her mother. After that, he begged for a rest and wandered off the dance floor, intercepting Helfer and walking back to the table with him.

"Who was that hare I saw you with earlier?"

"Him? Oh, I think he said his name was Reese. Nothing doing, though—he's straight. Pity, too, with a rump like that." He scanned the room vaguely. "There he is, over there with the vixen you were dancing with earlier."

Volle followed Helfer's muzzle. "I was dancing with all of them earlier, I think. My paws are about to fall off." He patted Helfer on the shoulder. "Excuse me a moment. I think I remember him from somewhere. Just want to make sure."

"Sure," Helfer called after him.

Volle made his way across the room and tapped Reese on the shoulder. "Excuse us, Mariana, for a moment?"

The vixen nodded and slipped away quietly. Reese frowned. "Why'd you have to do that? I was getting somewhere with her."

"What are you doing here?"

"Seir said I could come. Thought I might enjoy it. You know, music, dancing, good food. At least, I assume there will be. Won't there?"

Volle sighed. "Yes. Though most of the people here are carnivores, so I don't know if they'll have any herbivore food. She asked you to keep an eye on me, didn't she?"

Reese shrugged. "Yeah, so? Doesn't look like you needed anyone watching out for you. Don't worry about it." He looked hurt. "Don't I even get a 'thanks' for coming all the way out here?"

"Thanks." Volle grinned. "Just don't talk to anyone."

"Too late for that, buddy. Think I have a chance with Mariana?"

"Not really. Maybe you should try the servants."

"Hey, if I wanted to date trash, I'd have asked you out long ago."

Volle shook his head, chuckling. "Good luck with Mariana. You here alone?"

"Yep. Tella drove me and is going to pick me up. She didn't want to come in." He smoothed down his green velvet doublet, which he was wearing over a nice-looking white linen shirt. "I think she just didn't have the clothes for it."

"If I don't get to see her, say hi for me."

"Will do. Congratulations, by the way. I always knew you'd go straight in the end."

"Depends whose end you're talking about." Volle smiled and strode off to sit with Tish, now that the black wolf was done dancing with Tika.

"Enjoying yourself?" the wolf asked as Volle sat down.

"I am, yes, thank you," Volle said. "And thank you for all you did to arrange this. Ilyana's very happy."

"Who's that hare you were talking to? Friend of yours?"

Volle shook his head. "I was just trying to warn him off Helfer. But I was wondering if he even knows Ilyana. He didn't go up and congratulate her."

Tish shrugged. "Could be a friend of a friend. Tika did want to make sure we had enough people here to make it impressive. I'm sure word got around."

"Well, that's probably it, then." Volle scratched his muzzle and watched Ilyana dancing with a coyote he didn't know.

"Food will be served in a little while." Tish patted his stomach. "I'm starving."

"Me too." Volle stopped watching the coyote and leaned back. "I wasn't sure I was going to be able to eat, but it wasn't that bad."

"You did well," Tish said. "I know you have reservations, but trust me. This will all work out for the best."

"I think you just might be right."

The food, when it came, was delicious, easily up to the standards of the palace. Volle suspected that Tika had procured the services of some of the palace cooks, but she wouldn't say, just smiled at the compliments. Ilyana and her parents devoured the Cornish hen appetizers, which were the one thing Volle didn't feel measured up to the palaces; they seemed too salty to him. Ilyana's family ate more daintily when the main course of roast leg of lamb arrived, surrounded by beans, the whole thing covered in a red wine sauce. Volle found the lamb slightly more to his tastes, but he supposed the Cornish hens at the palace had spoiled him.

Tish and Tika ate with their usual enthusiasm, as did Helfer, but Volle spotted Reese picking unhappily at the lamb and eating only the beans out of his plate. Serve him right, coming to a carnivore's event.

Ilyana couldn't stop her tail from wagging throughout the dinner. She kept saying things to Volle like "Isn't the music wonderful?" and "See Tarina there? She's been staring at my dress all night. She's so jealous." and "This food is amazing." He smiled at each of the comments and agreed with her, and at the end of the meal, she kissed his cheek and said, "Thank you so much."

He nuzzled back and smiled. "You deserve it," he said. "I'm happy to be here with you."

Her muzzle moved closer to his ear, and she whispered, "After a few dances, I want to show you something upstairs."

His ear flicked, and he looked at her with some surprise, but she just smiled and turned to her parents. She can't have meant what he thought she meant. He could tell she wasn't in season, for one thing. She must have some fond memories of the house that she wanted to share, or maybe there was something interesting in another room that she wanted to show him. He shook his head and found Tish looking at him with a smile.

"What?"

"You look confused." He patted Volle's shoulder. "What's the matter?"

Volle shook his head. "Nothing." He smiled. "How long do we have to stick around now?"

"Well, you should do one more dance after dinner, when everyone's had a chance to digest their food. After that, you can leave if you want, but I would hope you'd stay for Ilyana's sake for a bit longer."

"Oh, I will. She wants to show me the house, I think."

"It's an interesting one," Tish said. "This is the nicest room, of course, but there are some antiques around that are worth a look. I didn't know she was interested in that sort of thing."

"I didn't either, but an interest in the arts is a nice sign." People were starting to get up following the meal, and Volle spotted Helfer looking at him. "I think I'm going to go talk to Helfer for a bit. Please excuse me?"

Tish waved him on, so he got up, said "I'll be right back," to Ilyana, and walked over to where Helfer and two young female wolves were sitting and talking.

The wolves giggled as he came up. They smelled like sisters, at least as much as he could distinguish their scents in the crowd. "What about his, ladies?"

"Oh, nicest one yet!"

"Definitely!" The two wolves giggled.

"Dare I ask?" Volle sat down at the table.

"We need to go." The two wolves rose at almost the same moment. "But it was so nice to meet you, Lord Ikling."

Helfer grinned and waved a paw lazily. "Thank you for the company, ladies. Good luck with your fiancés."

"Thanks for the advice!" the other wolf said as they wandered away.

"What was that all about?"

"Oh, they were having some man trouble, so I gave them some advice." He chuckled. "They agreed that you have the nicest tail at the cotillion."

"Tail, eh?" Volle grinned. "Well, I appreciate it. I wanted to thank you again for coming. Is it going to be a tougher ride now the snow's fallen?"

"No. Just colder. Less risk of bandits."

"Oh." Volle remembered what Tish had told him about Helfer's father being killed by bandits, and didn't know what else to say. "If you need anything for the trip, let me know."

"You could give me my books back. About time you got your own anyway."

"Done." Volle chuckled. "It was pretty boring running without you these last couple days. Did you just hide in your room?"

Helfer nodded. "Took meals there and all. Tish helped. I think he wanted to give you a nice surprise, and I did too. I know this is a stressful thing you're doing, but really, it won't be that bad."

"I know." Volle sighed. "I just feel like a fraud, you know? Going through all this like we're going to be in love forever. I like her a lot, but I don't feel anything, you know? No excitement, nothing."

"Well," Helfer said logically, "that would be because you're gay. Volle, she knows that and it's fine."

"No matter how many times people tell me that, it doesn't make me feel any better. I still feel like she's going to expect more from me."

Helfer patted his paw. "They always will. But you're not leading her on. Just remember that."

"All right." He grinned and scanned the crowd. "Any luck here?"

"I can't tell," Helfer complained. "The only ones who want to talk to me are the females. Which is fine, you know, but I'd rather talk to someone I can go home with."

"Not many rabbits here."

"No. Maybe I'll just go visit the Lonely Cock tonight."

"You can go now if you want. I don't know how much longer I'll be here."

"Oh? Going to get a little courting action in?"

Volle snorted, but then it occurred to him that Helfer might be right. "I hope not. It's Ilyana's day, and she wants to show me the house, so I'll go along with whatever she wants. I think it's too early for that, anyway. She's not in season yet."

"You never know with these vixens." Helfer chuckled and got up, and Volle got up with him. "I think I will go, if you're sure it's okay. But I'll be around tomorrow to run with you. Should be fun in the snow."

"Great. See you then. Thanks again, Hef."

"Anytime." They embraced, and the weasel left, blowing kisses to the wolf sisters as he passed them.

A few other people were drifting out, and Reese intercepted Volle on his way back to the table. "Tella's back," he said. "Or will be soon. I'll see you at the meeting in a couple days, okay?"

"Okay. Say hi to everyone for me."

"Will do." Reese shook his paw and slipped out the door as well.

Volle made it back to the large table, but no sooner had he sat down than Ilyana was tugging him up, back to the dance floor. The music had started again, and a few couples were already dancing. Volle went along with her, reminding himself that it was her day, and put his arm around her, leading her into the waltz that the trio was now playing. He stumbled once, but caught himself and hoped nobody had noticed.

They remained out on the floor for the next number, going back to the more common dance steps, for which Volle was grateful. He finished a couple more dances, and then Ilyana tugged him back to the table to pay their respects to Tish and Tika.

"I want to show Lord Vinton the upstairs." Ilyana smiled, her tail still wagging. Volle didn't think he'd seen it stop the whole evening. "Thank you both for coming, and for everything you've done. I hope someday I can find a way to repay you."

"Just live a healthy, prosperous life," Tish said.

"And have healthy cubs," Tika added with a smile. "We're happy to be part of this, dears. Go on now, have a good time."

Ilyana grasped Volle's paw and curtsied. "Thank you!" Volle bowed quickly as she tugged him out the door.

"I'm surprised you're so anxious to leave your party." He followed her along the hallway to the stairs.

"Oh, I've talked to everyone there now, and it's more or less over already."

"You're right about that." Volle looked over his shoulder and saw more people leaving. "I think people are worried about the snow."

"I thought they would be." She let go of him to mount the stairs, but kept checking to see that he was following.

"I'm coming, I'm coming." He grinned and sprang up after her.

"Here, it's down the hall here, I think. This door." She pushed open a door, letting Volle into the room before slipping in after him and closing the door.

The room, he saw, was about the size of his bedroom in the palace, or maybe he was reminded of his bedroom because this room was dominated by a large four-poster bed. No portraits hung on the walls, and although the windows were diamond-paned like the ones below, these were grimy and cracked. The room was chilly, and it didn't look like there was a fireplace to heat it.

"What did you want to show me?" He rubbed his paws together.

She walked over to him and clasped her paws around his. "Chilly?"

"Just the pads. Not too bad." He looked around the room.

"Maybe I can warm you up a bit." He had his back to the bed, and as she stepped forward and pressed a paw against his pants, he stepped backwards and ended up sitting on the bed, crushing his tail.

"Wait, what...?" But she was pressed up against him already, her muzzle seeking out his. "I thought ...you're not in seasonmmmf."

She held the kiss and then broke it, her paws questing inside his pants. "I know," she said softly. "But I wanted to get some practice in. You don't mind, do you?"

Her expression made him hesitate. "Mmmf. I..." But she was already on top of him, pushing him back until he was lying on the bed, her paws undoing some of the fastenings at his pants. He made a feeble attempt to stop her, but he didn't think she even noticed.

Her paws found his sheath and circled it, rubbing a little roughly. "There." She smiled at him. "That's not so bad, is it? Not so different?"

Except that he wasn't aroused at all. Oh, his body was responding to the touch, but the scent, the feel, and the mental part that was so important to him was completely absent. He considered asking her to stop again, but then thought that maybe he needed some practice too. If he came, this time, it wouldn't result in cubs.

Gently, he reached up and caressed her chest. She lifted her muzzle and panted softly, and he saw that her other paw was busy under her dress. "You don't have to do that," she said softly. "I'll do the work."

"I want you to enjoy it." His paws felt the rounded shape of her chest. He had never been with a vixen, or any female, before. He did know what to expect, from Reese's stories (and others), and as he brushed her nipples through her clothes, he felt her shiver.

"I'm enjoying that," she panted. Her paw had brought him mostly out of his sheath, and now she smiled down and straddled him, spreading out her dress to cover him.

"Have you...done this before?" He couldn't think of a delicate way to ask the question, and so just blurted it out.

Her ears flicked, and her smile faded for a moment before returning. "I know what I'm doing," she said softly. "That's all I'll admit to." She lowered herself slowly and guided him up into her.

He felt warmth around his member, not as tight as the tail holes he was used to, but slick even without any creams. He moved easily into her, and she gasped as he slid all the way up. "Oh!"

His paws moved down to her hips and held her there, letting her lever herself up and down on his shaft. She moved slowly at first, lifting her whole body up and down. Volle found that just lying there, letting her move on him, he didn't get very aroused at all. Enough to stay hard, apparently, because she started pumping faster, now moving just her hips up and down. His knot swelled a bit as she rubbed up and down his length, but not nearly as quickly as it did when he was with a male. Her scent was getting stronger, and even if he closed his eyes and pretended she was Richy, his nose told him differently.

If he focused just on the sensations, he found, he got aroused a bit, and could see himself getting excited enough to finish. He deliberately opened his eyes to look at her and inhale her scent, and thought about her rather than what was going on under her dress.

She was rather cute, panting and looking from him to the snow outside the windows and back again. He could see the twitching of her tail behind her dress, and smiled as he saw her enjoyment. His paws guided her hips, keeping pace, and every so often he gave a little push up with his hips, because she squeaked when he did that and seemed to enjoy it.

The experience was similar to his previous experiences, but the differences were interesting. Ilyana's movements, even when fast, were much more leisurely. Most males (including Volle himself) would have been close to finished by now, but she seemed to still have a ways to go.

"Are you...okay?" she panted down to him.

He grinned up and nodded. "Just fine."

"Going to...oh..." He figured she was going to ask if he was going to come, but she hit a sensitive spot or something partway through the sentence and never finished it.

For a few more minutes she rode up and down. His knot got a bit bigger, enough to feel her lips as he moved through them, but not much more than that. She started pressing down harder, driving him deeper into her, moaning loudly. "Oh! Ohhh!" He thought she was done, but she kept thrusting and the moaning kept going on, until he almost wanted to giggle. The whole situation seemed very comical to him.

Finally, her moans trailed off into little whimpers, and she looked down at him with a smile. "That was very nice. Very nice!"

He brushed her hip. "I'm glad."

She moved off of him, and sighed. "You didn't, though."

"How—oh." Of course. If he'd finished, he'd be tied to her. He hadn't thought about that aspect of it.

"Do you think you could?"

"Maybe." He nodded. "You surprised me, is all."

"I'm sorry." Now that she'd finished, her demeanor was different. She was no longer being driven by lust. "I just thought it would be nice to get some practice in."

"You seemed to enjoy it," he said. "That's enough for me." The small lie seemed to make her happy.

"You are sweet." She leaned over to kiss him, and lifted herself off him in the same motion. "We'll try again. Maybe when I'm in season, you'll be more interested."

"Maybe," he agreed. "Um. We can't really go back to the dance."

"No," she said, giggling. "Not with all those canids there. There's a bathroom down the hall where I'll clean up, but I think just my family's waiting for me. Probably everyone else has left by now. You can go if you want."

He nodded, fastening up his pants even though his member wasn't fully back in his sheath yet. "I think I'll say my goodbyes to Tish and Tika if they're still here, and your family, and then go home. It's been a long day."

"It's been a wonderful day."

"Yes, it has." They kissed again, and he helped her off the bed. "Now, where's this bathroom?"

He waited outside while she cleaned up, even though she said, "We don't have anything to hide." The awkwardness of their furtive lovemaking in the bedroom made him want to distance himself from it, and going in with her would only reinforce that it was really part of their experience. Besides that, he still felt shy about undressing in front of her. She cleaned up, and when she came out again, he couldn't smell any of her musk about her.

"Here, use this." She handed him a small cup of cream. "The lavender is pretty strong and it'll cover any smell. It's what I use, but that's okay. People will assume we were close anyway."

"Thanks." He went into the bathroom, where there was a cold cup of water. That got his shaft back into his sheath in a hurry; he almost yelped as he splashed it on himself. He rubbed the water into his fur, and when his teeth were chattering and he couldn't stand it any more, he rubbed his sheath dry. Even the rubbing couldn't coax his shivering member back out into the open. He added a bit of the lavender cream once he was mostly dry, and then pulled his pants back up and joined Ilyana in the hall.

She sniffed him experimentally. "You smell fine."

"Thank you." Because it seemed like the right thing to do, he offered her his arm, and she took it, beaming. They walked downstairs slowly.

Tish, Tika, and the Rodions were standing in the hallway. They all turned as the foxes approached them. "Ah, here they are. Interesting statuary up there?" Tish said with a grin.

"Fascinating," Volle replied blandly, tail twitching just a bit.

"Everyone had a wonderful time, darling," Katiana said to her daughter. "You're a woman now. And you're almost part of the family." She hugged Volle and nuzzled him.

He returned her embrace with a smile and a wag of his tail. "I'm delighted to be so close to both of you." Marcel was waiting nearby, and reached out a paw, which Volle shook. "You've a delightful vixen, and I consider it an honor to be courting her."

"We're honored to have you," Marcel said. He released Volle's paw and took his wife's arm. "Lord and Lady Tistunish, thank you again for everything you've done for our daughter. We are in your debt."

"Nonsense." Tika said. "Your daughter is delightful and we're happy to help."

"Thank you both," Volle said.

"You're very welcome." Tish bowed to him. "And now, I think we will take our leave of you."

"Good night!" The wolves linked arms and walked out into the snow, where a servant scurried to fetch their carriage.

"I think I'll return to the palace as well," Volle said. "I'll see you soon, Ilyana." He bent and kissed her paw.

She smiled at him, and touched her nose to his. "Until next time, Lord Vinton."

He bid goodnight to her parents and walked out into the snow. The servant was riding up on his carriage, and hopped off to open the door for him. Volle thanked him, stepped inside, and the driver whipped up the horses.

Before the first creak of the wheels, Volle had smelled wet fur in his carriage. He thought at first it was the servant, but then his eyes discerned a shape sitting on the bench in the corner. Xiller! was his first thought, but he saw immediately that it was far too small to be the cougar. The smell was wrong too: weasel, not cat. It took him a moment to identify, with his head still dizzy from the smells of the cotillion and the amorous vixen.

"Tella?"

"You stink," she said.

"What?" He thought that maybe she meant that she could smell the vixen on him, but she didn't elaborate. Her voice was rough and cracking. "Tella?"

"Your cougar's dead."

Chapter 17

The words slammed into him, unexpected and devastating. It was a full minute before he could work his throat open enough to croak, "What?" A million thoughts and hopes ran through his head. *She's mistaken. She's playing a horrible joke on me. He set this all up so I'd be grateful when he got back. She thinks she's telling the truth, but she's wrong.*

"They executed him. Last week. We just heard."

No. "The southerners?"

"The Ferrenians. Us."

He was breathing harder now. His hopes were fading, and the more he grasped at them, the more they eluded him. "Why? Why?"

He could see her eyes glittering at him, gathering all the light diffused by the snow and focusing it on him. She made an inarticulate noise, then ripped the words from her throat. "He killed Prince Gennic."

The Prince? Volle couldn't make his throat form words.

Tella had no such trouble anymore, her voice spilling over him as though her declaration had been the stopper in a bottle of vitriol. "Your lover, Volle, ripped his throat out. Slept with you for a few days and then walked into the castle at Caril and killed the Prince. Nearly killed Prince Murron too. Did he mention any of that when he was sticking you in the ass? Or didn't it come *up?*"

She yelled the last word, and the driver stopped the carriage. "Everything okay in there?" They could hear him dismounting on the right hand side.

"Don't bother coming to the meeting next week," Tella hissed at him. "Nobody wants to see you." She skittered across the carriage and disappeared out the left hand door in a flash, seconds before the driver opened the right hand side.

"You okay in here?" His broad muzzle, striped black and white and flecked with snow, looked in with concern.

"Home," Volle croaked. "Please." Tella's words had torn through him until he felt that only a few scraps of fur and muscle were holding him together. His throat was almost painfully constricted, and he was afraid that if he tried to say another word, he'd break down in tears.

The badger nodded. "All right. Home it is."

The trip home was interminable. The carriage bounced over the streets, but Volle barely noticed. The air was cold, but he was colder inside. *She had to be lying*, he thought, *but the emotion had been so forceful coming out of her that he couldn't believe that. So it must be true*, and in a stroke, he'd lost everything: Xiller, his prince, and his job.

Maybe even his life. There was no chance they'd let him stay here after a mistake of this magnitude. And the Duke would get his mouthful of fox.

But he barely considered that past his first realization. He kept picturing Xiller, and he couldn't reconcile the image he had of the happy, smiling cougar with the death he'd caused and suffered. He'd wanted to be a hero: how was assassinating a prince heroic? Or a cub? It didn't fit.

Then he remembered that he'd been talking about how much he hated the Ferrenians, in an attempt to get into the anti-Ferrenian group, the one that had no doubt hired Xiller. Had he done any of that talking in front of the cougar? Had he helped him believe that his mission was heroic? His thoughts made him complicit in the horror. No wonder nobody wanted to talk to him. He barely wanted to talk to himself.

He started to sob, quietly, letting the thoughts melt away from him and just giving voice to his anguish. He called up his memories of the Prince, that noble and gentle cougar, and of Xiller, the sweet and lithe one, neither of whom he would ever see again. He wept for his country, losing a beloved prince in his prime, and he wept for Xiller's family, who would never know what had become of their heroic son. He wept for Xiller, tricked into committing an atrocity, and he wept for himself, because his heart felt as though it had fallen to pieces in his chest.

When he looked up, the carriage was approaching the palace. He caught a glimpse of the snowy street down which the Lonely Cock was situated, and suddenly banged on the roof. "Stop!"

The driver pulled up, and Volle threw the door open before he could get down. "Hey!" he called, but Volle was already running down the street through the snow. Two inches had accumulated and more was falling still, but he paid no attention to it.

The bar was more than half full when he got there. Everyone stared as he walked in, dressed in his fine clothes and dusted with snow, ears back, tail down, and a wild look in his eyes. He looked around, but didn't see the weasel anywhere. He was about to shout for him, but then caught the bartender's eye.

"Helfer," he gasped. "Lord Ikling. I need to find him."

The bartender's ears flicked with concern. "He went home half an hour ago. But Lord Vinton, you're soaked. Stay and have something to warm you up before you go back. On the house."

Volle shook his head violently, spraying the counter with snow. "No, I…have to go…" He backed away from the bar and then ran out the door.

His carriage was still at the gate. The driver was conferring with the guard, and both looked up as Volle approached.

"Lord Vinton, what's the matter? You go off in the snow like that, you'll get soaked."

"Back." Volle panted, gesturing towards the castle.

"Sir, your papers?" Volle had already climbed into the carriage, but the guard prevented him from closing the door. Blindly, he rummaged in his purse and thrust the papers at the guard. The guard, a deer he'd seen a few times before, scrutinized the papers and then handed them back. "Everything okay, Lord Vinton?"

Not trusting himself to talk, Volle just nodded and pulled the door shut. A moment later, the driver pulled through the gates and toward the palace. Volle pushed the door open as soon as the carriage had stopped and ran up the stairs, ignoring the startled foot-marten who only had time to reach out before Volle was through the door.

It was good that he knew the way to Helfer's rooms so well, because he could barely see. His eyes were misted with tears and snow, and his nose was clogged as well. He didn't clearly know why he sought out Helfer rather than Tish, but Helfer had met Xiller and Helfer knew him better, and it was Helfer he first thought of and ran to when he needed someone.

He opened Helfer's door without knocking and walked into the parlor. "Hef! HEF!" He stood in the middle of the parlor, melted snow dripping off him, suddenly wondering whether he should go further into the rooms. "Hef!" he called again, starting to pant from the exertion and the emotions that threatened to overtake him again.

Caresh came into the room at almost the same time as Helfer, the latter with a short skirt on, the former in a robe, both looking very rumpled. "It's okay, Caresh," Helfer said, waving the fox away with a paw. "Volle, what in Gaia's name is wrong? You look horrible."

"He's dead, Hef. They killed him."

For a moment all he heard was his own harsh breath, on the edge of tears again. Then Helfer put an arm around his waist. "Come on in," he said gently. "Caresh, some tea? And maybe a bit of something stronger." He guided Volle into the sitting room to the couch.

Volle stopped before the couch. "I'm all wet."

"Shh. Don't worry about that. Sit." He sat, and Helfer sat beside him. "Who's dead?"

"X-Xiller." Volle felt his body shaking again. "Oh, Hef, I could've stopped him if I'd just asked what he was doing, I could've kept him here and he'd still be alive. It's my fault." He felt the sobs welling up in his throat. "And he'd still be alive..." He had the sense not to mention Prince Gennic's name, but that was the muzzle and scent in his mind as he said that last part.

"It's okay, just shhh..." Helfer put his arms around him, and Volle leaned into the weasel's shoulder and let go, soaking his fur with tears.

He sobbed until he couldn't muster any more energy. Drained, he slumped against Helfer, rubbing his eyes and nose with a paw.

Helfer rubbed his shoulder. "Come on. Have a shot of this, then some tea."

Volle lifted his muzzle as the acrid alcolohic smell filtered through his nose. He nodded and took the small cup from Helfer, and gulped the contents. Fire shot down his throat and into his stomach, making him cough, but the warmth was just what he needed, and it settled him somewhat. He leaned back against the wall, panting.

"Better? Okay, drink some of this." Helfer handed him a cup of warm tea, and he lapped obediently at it. "Now, what happened?"

Volle took a deep, shuddering breath. He looked into the cup, where the tea swirled gently, breaking his reflection into many pieces. "Coming back from the cotillion...a friend told me...Xiller was killed on his mission."

"Who told you?"

He hated the walls that went up immediately, preventing him from telling Helfer everything. While one part of him screamed to just say it, that it wouldn't matter when he was recalled and his friend deserved the truth, part of him was already calculating how to stop the weasel from questioning further, and the latter won out. "Just a friend, Hef. Politics. I shouldn't involve you."

It worked. "All right. But do you know the information was accurate?"

"Pretty sure." He steadied his paws around the cup as they started to tremble. "If I'd only done more..."

Helfer put his paws around Volle's. "Listen, Volle. I...did I ever tell you what happened to my father?"

Volle shook his head, looking up at the weasel's wide eyes. "What?" Then he recalled. "Tish said he was killed by bandits? I'm sorry..."

"It was two years ago. But...I was supposed to be with him on that trip. He was grooming me to take over in a few years. He was worn out from all the work he'd done here, and the people trying to get around him and through him. He wanted me to come with him so he could take me around Vellenland. But I refused. I liked it here, hated it at home, and didn't want any part of it. And after I heard, I always wondered if maybe, if I'd been with him, we could've fought off the bandits. Maybe he'd still be alive."

Volle blinked. "I'm so sorry."

Helfer shook his head. "It's done with. The point is, Volle, there's no way I could have known. And there's no way you could have known either. He was all grown up, he took his own risks, and you couldn't always be there to save him."

Volle nodded. "I know. But that doesn't help me convince myself that I couldn't have tried." It's my job to find out things, he wanted to say. I should have gotten from him that he was part of a plot against Ferrenis, I should have figured it out and stopped it.

But he couldn't tell Helfer that, any more than he could tell anyone else in the palace. He lapped at his tea and leaned back, closing his eyes.

"Are you tired?" Helfer asked. "Want to stay here tonight?"

"No. No, I'll go back to bed. I...thank you, Hef. I'm sorry to have bothered you."

The weasel shook his head. "Don't be silly. I wish I could do more to help you. I'm sorry for you. I liked him a lot."

"Yeah," Volle whispered. "I did too." Both cougars danced in front of his eyes then, so he opened them. "Actually, maybe I would like to stay tonight. Thanks, Hef."

"You're more than welcome." The weasel smiled. "Let me get a sheet for you. You can get those clothes off in the bathroom. There's a light robe in there that probably won't fit, but will at least cover you."

"Thanks," he repeated, and stumbled to the bathroom, closing the door behind him. Helfer's tub was currently filled with jasmine-scented powder, and suddenly Volle felt the need to be clean. He stripped his clothes off and then rolled in the talcum, sighing as he felt the powder work into his fur. He shook himself and brushed his fur off, then put on one of the short robes that was hanging on the wall. It fastened just below his ribcage and barely covered his sheath, but he was past caring.

Helfer had spread a sheet out on the couch when he returned to the sitting room. He slumped down on it gratefully, exhausted.

"Just call Caresh if you want anything. I'll be right in there. You going to be okay?"

"Yeah." Volle sighed and rested his head on the small pillow. "Thanks again, Hef. I'm glad you didn't go."

The weasel patted his shoulder. "Me too, fox. Sleep well."

He fell asleep almost instantly. He didn't dream at all, but when he woke in the morning, his pillow and muzzle were damp.

Light streamed in through the window. The snow had stopped overnight, and when he went to look, he could see the houses and streets carpeted in bright white. The street was already brown, dirtied by thousands of paws walking through it, and the snow there was wet and slushy. He looked at the people walking along the street and wondered how many of them knew, and how many would care if they did know. He wondered if he could see the inn where Xiller had been staying that last night. He wondered what he was going to do next.

He had to talk to Seir, despite Tella's warning. She was the only one who knew the whole situation, and she might be angry, but she would listen to him, too. He would go and drop a note with her name in it, and see her tomorrow. He would have to see Tish, too, but he could do that maybe later today.

He gathered up his clothes and knocked lightly on Caresh's door. The fox opened it and peered out.

"Caresh, Hef isn't up yet. I need to go out, so I won't be running today. Can I wear this robe down and send Welcis up with it later?"

"If his lordship would like, it might be more expedient to bring his lordship's clothes here. That robe is rather risqué, and even though the palace is quiet at this time, his lordship might prefer not to risk an embarrassment."

"I don't care…" he started to say, then sighed. "No, you're right. Can you fetch Welcis, or at least have him pick out clothes for me?"

"Consider it done." Caresh stepped out and into the hallway before Volle could thank him. He returned to the parlor and sat, brooding, until Caresh returned a few minutes later with a stack of clothes.

"Your lordship." He bowed, placing them on the side table.

"Thank you, Caresh."

"It is a pleasure to serve your lordship. Will there be anything else?"

Volle shook his head. "No. But thank Helfer again for his hospitality."

"Yes, sir." He turned on his paw and left.

Volle slipped the pants on, then shed the robe and shrugged on the yellow linen shirt Welcis had picked out for him. He folded the robe and laid it on the couch, then slipped out and went downstairs to his own chambers.

Welcis was waiting for him. "Your lordship, Caresh said there was some problem…?"

"Xiller is dead." Volle had thought himself numb to the words, but he felt a stabbing in his heart and had to stop for a moment before sitting down at his desk.

Welcis maintained a respectful silence for several minutes while Volle got out two pieces of paper and scribbled "Seir" on both. When Volle stood and turned to face him, the skunk spoke. "I am most terribly sorry to hear that, sir."

Volle was about to retort that Welcis had never liked him, but he saw the genuine pity in the skunk's eyes, and bit back his tongue. "Thank you." He walked through the room, and then a thought occurred to him. "Please, Welcis, don't discuss this with any of the other servants. I would greatly appreciate it."

"Yes, sir. Again, my deepest sympathies. And, sir?" He cleared his throat as Volle stopped and looked at him. "I would like to…apologize for my behavior during said person's visit. It is true that I did not approve of his lordship having a guest, but that in no way should be taken to mean that I disliked the guest. I found him charming and …" He stopped. "He will be missed."

"Yes," Volle said softly. "Yes, he will." He took a cloak from near the door, pinned it around his shoulders, and left the room.

He stepped through the gardens, his paws adjusting quickly to the chill of the snow. He went to the nearest drop site and stuffed the note into it, then went to the next one and placed the other note in there, just to be sure. He hoped that no matter how she felt, she would come and meet him.

On his way back to the palace, he realized there was one other person he could talk to. The cathedral stood silent, snow-shrouded in the bright morning light, and he headed towards it as though by instinct.

Even if the Felid Cantor weren't there, someone would be who could give him comfort, if not guidance.

He walked through fresh snow in the front garden and around the side to the door he'd used before. Cautiously, he pushed on it, and found it open. He slipped inside and closed the door behind him.

It was warmer inside--not much, but he wasn't cold today. His fur and the cloak kept him warm enough. The light through the stained glass was bright, and he felt the familiar sense of comfort mixed with awe that he associated with the cathedral now. There were only a few people praying in the pews, and he didn't see any Cantors walking around, but after a few minutes, the Felid Cantor was at his side.

"Good morning, son of my brother," he said softly. "How may we assist you?"

"Brother of my father," Volle said weakly, "I need comfort. I need an ear and a shoulder."

"Come this way." He thought the bobcat was leading him to the chapel they'd used with Xiller, but he turned to the adjacent door and opened it. There was a small room inside with two seats, a copy of the Word of Gaia, and very little else. "This room is quiet," the bobcat said as he closed the door behind them. "We cannot be heard outside. Now tell me, son of my brother, what trouble weighs on your soul?"

"Brother of my father," Volle said, "Do you remember the cougar I came with last time?"

"Of course. Something's happened to him." The priest looked at him astutely.

"He died. I should have figured out what he was doing and stopped him. He was only seventeen." He paused to get his voice under control again. "He went on a dangerous mission. He wouldn't tell me about it. And he wasn't doing good, as he thought he was, he was being tricked into doing something...something evil. So I have his death and his deed on my conscience, brother of my father. I can't..." He panted heavily. "How can I make amends?"

The priest put a paw gently on his head, considering. He picked up the Word and flipped through it. "There is a passage from the Story of Canis that I believe you should listen to. But first, I am very sorry for your loss. Your friend is with Felis in Gaia now, as are all called before their time."

"Is he?" Volle asked roughly. "Even if he killed?"

"If he was pure in heart and believed he was doing the work of Gaia, then perhaps, yes, even that sin can be forgiven. As long as he did not eat of the flesh of another of Gaia's children, he can be redeemed."

Volle nodded, and the priest opened the book and read.

"Saith Canis to his litter, 'For so much as you may follow me, I leave you my scent, I show you my tail, I am the Finder and Trailmaker. And you may find the path easy to see or hard to see, and easy to follow or hard to follow. But know this: always it is there, and even though you stray from the path, always you may find it again.

"'But know, too, that I will not place your paws on the path. Hear my voice, mark my scent, and make your way, but your way is your own. Gaia loves you, and I love you, and even should you leave my path, we will always love you, and it is through that love that you may find the path again. Look for my scent, o my children, and mark it well, and always you will find it if you seek it.'"

Volle remembered that story from the Life of Wolf in his own church, but the words still resonated with him, and he felt tears building behind his eyes as he listened to the priest read them. "Thank you, brother of my father," he said softly.

"Do you understand?"

"I think so."

"There are two messages there for you, son of my brother. The first is that your friend chose his own path. You did not place his paws upon it; you failed to see and therefore failed to save. And that is sad, but only he can choose to be saved. It is not your sin to atone for. And for yourself, should you stray from Canis's path, remember that it is through his love that you can find your way back. You can make your penance by finding the path again if you have lost it."

Volle nodded. "What penance would you have me say?"

"Say the Devotional to Canis five times, and then if you wish, you may light a candle for your friend." The priest reached out and took his paw gently, and Volle looked up to see tears shining in the bobcat's eyes as well. "I share your grief. I saw the joy in his soul, and I hoped I would get to know him better. He shone brightly, though not for long, and if you tell me his name, I will treasure his memory with you."

Volle swallowed the lump in his throat. "Xiller," he said hoarsely. "Only I can't pronounce it right. It was K-ziller."

"Xiller?" The priest said it flawlessly.

"Yes, that." Volle met the bobcat's gaze. "He was so passionate. He wanted to do wonderful things, and he loved and fought fiercely."

The priest sighed. "Passion is a two-edged sword. It gives us great potential, and also blinds us. In the young, especially, it is dangerous, because they have not the wisdom to temper the passion." Volle nodded. "And it is a great tragedy to lose a passionate soul to blindness. Come, let us pray for him."

They bowed their heads. Volle said a quick prayer to Cougar, and then to Felis, praying that Xiller would find peace, and that Prince Gennic would find peace as well, and that the royal family and his country would heal.

When he looked up, the priest placed a paw on his shoulder. "Go now, son of my brother, and say your penance, and light your candle. Canis and Gaia go with you; yes, and Felis too." He smiled. "The ancestors look after each other's kin from time to time, when the bond connecting families is a strong one."

"Thank you, brother of my father," Volle said softly. "You have been a great help."

The priest escorted him out of the small room and showed him the rack of candles. Volle thanked him again and knelt down at a pew. He said the Devotional to Fox rather than the Devotional to Canis; it was essentially similar, only closer to his heart.He'd been embracing the Orthodox church since his arrival in Tephos, but now he felt the need to return to something familiar.

When he'd said it five times, he bowed his head, stood, and made his way over to the candles. He lit two: one for each cougar, and he said their names to himself as the flames caught. He said another short prayer, and then left the cathedral.

He felt better, though not healed. He'd hoped for instant healing, but of course that was silly. He would be grieving for a long time, both for his prince and for his lover. The double loss still resonated in his heart, and as he looked at the stark grey walls of the palace, he realized he didn't feel like returning there yet. He'd been wrenched out of his life, and he wasn't quite ready to resume it.

So he walked through the city, stopped in a pub for lunch, and didn't talk to anyone. The clouds had gone and the day remained dazzlingly clear, though cold enough for the snow to stay on the ground. Volle marched through the snow, hardly caring where he went, thinking of Xiller and Prince Gennic. It seemed incredible that two individuals so far away from him could affect his life so much, could make him think that he'd never laugh again. And yet, he didn't see how he could.

It was only once he found himself across the river from the palace, on the opposite side from the main entrance, that he began to think about who had sent Xiller on his mission. He looked up at the windows of the palace and immediately thought of the Secretary. Prewitt, who had so disingenuously admitted and disavowed knowledge of Xiller. Xiller had definitely met the "golden bear." And Dereath was tied into it somehow.

Grief was augmented by a sense of urgency. He had to talk to Tish. He didn't care whether the knowledge was public yet, or if Tish asked him where he'd heard this. It was important, and the feeling that grew in him as he hurried around the palace was that there were people in the palace responsible for Xiller's death, and Prince Gennic's, and there might yet be a way to avenge them. Anger impelled his paws to the entrance, and back to his chambers to drop off his cloak, and there he received a nasty shock.

Sitting in his parlor, smirking, was Dereath Talison.

Chapter 18

He looked relaxed, sprawled in a chair with his pink tail laying behind him on the floor. He had been looking out the window and turned to see Volle enter. He was wearing the same outfit he always did: black vest and pants, and a silver belt, though now he also wore a white linen shirt beneath the vest.

"What are you doing here?" Volle spat roughly. He felt his paws clench into fists and forced them to uncurl.

Dereath sneered at him. "What, no 'welcome back'? No 'nice to see you again'? Not even curious about where I've been?"

"I don't care. I'm more interested in where you're going." He gestured to the open door. "Don't make me throw you out."

Welcis appeared at the entrance to the sitting room. "I am sorry, sir. He was most insistent, and he says he has something important to tell you." He gave the rat a disparaging look. "I did lock your desk, sir."

"Thank you, Welcis." Volle folded his arms. "Say your piece and get out."

"I had a very nice trip," Dereath said. "Thank you for asking. I decided to see the south, since I'd never been there. You know, the Mittan Forest when the leaves are changing color is beautiful. I highly recommend it."

"I'll remember that. Now, out."

"Oh, I'm not done, silly fox. I had plenty of time, thanks to your interference," here the first trace of anger appeared on his muzzle, then smoothed over again, "so I decided to visit your people in Vinton. It's such a lovely little backwater, and the people were very friendly, especially when I told them what good friends we are."

Volle clenched his teeth and took a step towards the rat, then restrained himself. Dereath gave him an amused look. "Oh, yes. Don't worry, you came off very well in all of it. I wanted to hear what they had to say about you, so I couldn't exactly tell them the *truth* about you. Much as I wanted to. Who knows what archaic concepts of loyalty those hicks have down there? In any event, they were very cooperative. They told me, among other things, that you arrived with a hare and a mouse. Which is interesting, because you arrived in the city with a marmot and a hare. What happened to the mouse? Or the badger, who they said drove the carriage? No, no, don't answer now. I'm sure you have a perfectly reasonable explanation for all of it. But that's not even the most interesting part.

"I followed the road back over the mountains. It was a cold trip, but your people very thoughtfully equipped me with provisions for the journey. What do you think I found at the other end of the road? Well, of course you know what I found. There's an inn at the border, with a very friendly bartender. In fact, most of the people down south are very friendly. I may decide to move there."

He paused, waiting to see if Volle would react to the teasing, and then went on. "The innkeeper remembered a hare and a mouse, driven by a badger, but he didn't remember them with a red fox. He remembered them with a black fox, and he said they were a merchant group returning from Ferrenis. Now, that is some ways north of where you are supposed to have come from. In fact, it's almost closer to Caril than it is to Merinland."

Volle caught a scent, and turned. Two bears stood in the hallway just outside his door. He recognized Prewitt's scent, and assumed the other was one of his assistants. "I thought it odd," Dereath went on, "that you would have disguised yourself, and entered the country further north than you claimed you did, in the company of two Ferrenians. And Secretary Prewitt and Minister Fardew thought it odd, too."

Prewitt stepped into the room. "Lord Vinton, what do you say about all this?"

Volle unclenched his fists again, and relaxed as best he could. Looking at Prewitt, he tried to forget what he'd been thinking about him just an hour ago. "I think the rat here is very clever. He's trying yet another trick to get back at me, this time taking advantage of my humble origins to cast doubt on my parentage." The speech became easier as he went on. "I did enter the country from Merinland, and as Dereath would have learned had he followed one of the other paths through the mountains, there is a trail that leads from Merinland to the road. I walked along the road for a while, and the merchants picked me up. They did mention that they'd picked up a black fox but he'd left them. Coincidence, I guess."

"A very fortunate one," Dereath sneered. "And what happened to them in Vinton?"

Volle shrugged. "I spent most of my time there going out with the governor. I didn't ask the merchants their business. The hare wanted to travel with me to Divalia, so we shared the carriage. I suppose he had business here."

Prewitt addressed the rat. "Did you find a trail to Merinland?"

"No."

"Did you follow all the trails?"

"Prewitt, he's lying!"

"That's not what I asked, Dereath."

"Why are you interrogating me? No, okay, I didn't follow all the trails. Do you know how many of them there are?"

"So he could be telling the truth."

"But he isn't!"

"All right, that's enough. Dereath, get back to Minister Fardew's office." The rat glared at Volle, not moving. "Now."

The bear's tone had enough force in it that it drew Dereath's gaze away from Volle, back to the bear. Reluctantly, he got up out of the chair, straightened his vest, and walked haughtily past Volle. He turned at the door and looked back at the fox. "So sorry I couldn't make it back in time for your little tramp's cotillion. I'd have liked to have you stuck here for it. But maybe while you're under guard, I'll go see your little wolf. I imagine he'll be lonely."

"Stay away from him!" Volle yelled, but Dereath's laughter as he walked down the hall was his only answer.

He growled and turned to Prewitt. "What did he mean, stuck here?"

The bear flicked his ears apologetically. "I'm sorry, Lord Vinton, but we are going to have to ask you to stay here in the palace while we check this out."

"What? But he's just trying..." Volle broke off, fuming.

"I know, I know," Prewitt said soothingly. "And I'm sure that's how it will turn out. But this is a pretty serious allegation, you know. I'd really appreciate it if you'd cooperate with us. I'll try to make this go as fast as I can."

Volle tried to relax and slow his breathing. "How long?"

Prewitt shook his head. "A couple weeks? We'd like to send someone down to Vinton to verify your story. If we could find that black fox or the merchant, that would be ideal, but I don't know how much chance there is of that. Do you have any clues that might help us? Do you remember the merchant's name?"

"Yes, it was..." Volle paused. "Senom, I think. Marik Senom." Immediately he regretted giving them the name. He didn't know what would have happened to Reese's alias once he arrived in Divalia, and a merchant who'd disappeared would only add credence to Dereath's story. "But I could be wrong about that."

"Well, it's something to go on, anyway. I'm sure we'll have this resolved quickly." He held out a paw. "I just need your papers."

"My...why?"

"Not that we don't trust you, you understand. Just to be sure." He flicked his ears again. "I do sincerely regret this inconvenience, Lord Vinton."

Volle reached into his purse and took his papers out, and placed them in Prewitt's paws. "Work fast," he said.

"Thank you, Lord Vinton. We will."

"Oh, and one more thing." Prewitt turned in the doorway to listen. "When you're done, can I skin that rat and hang his hide on my wall?"

Prewitt laughed. "I don't think it would go with your décor. Take care, Volle."

"Thanks, Prewitt." He closed the door and stalked to the window. Welcis, who had watched the whole proceedings from the sitting room doorway, approached him from behind.

"Sir, is there anything I can do?"

Volle considered, then shook his head. "Not unless you can…wait, yes there is. Do you know the Jackal's Staff?"

"I am familiar with the location of the establishment, yes."

"Could you take a message to Tally for me? You'll know him immediately. White cougar, painted some garish color, dressed like a female."

"The person sounds immediately recognizable, sir. I am sure I will have no trouble. What message would you like me to deliver?"

"I'll write it down. I just want to warn him not to let Dereath near Richy. Fox knows what he'd do." He unlocked the desk with the key Welcis handed him, scrawled the note quickly on a sheet of paper, and folded it around a gold coin. "Here. If you could take that, I'd be very much obliged."

"I am happy to help, sir." Welcis pulled a cloak around himself and left.

Volle paced the parlor for several minutes after he left, chewing his claws. Anger was a welcome alternative to the grief he'd been feeling, but he wasn't sure how long he could sustain it. Before it evaporated, maybe he should go see Tish. At least if he could remain angry, he wouldn't end up bawling in front of the big wolf.

His stomach growled at the smells in the main hall, and he realized that the palace was having dinner. He didn't feel like joining the nobles in the main dining hall, so he continued upward to Tish's chambers. If they'd finished dinner, then he would wait and have his when Welcis returned.

They hadn't, as it turned out, and welcomed him in. One of the servants set another place while Volle sat there, unable to keep his tail from lashing or his ears from folding back. When the servants had left the room, Tika leaned forward. "What's the matter, Volle?"

He looked from one wolf to the other, and suddenly couldn't figure out where to begin. He crammed a bite of food into his muzzle and chewed, to gain some time.

"Come on, it can't be that bad." Tika smiled playfully, but Tish's expression was more wary.

When Volle swallowed, the black wolf put a paw on his and said quietly, "You heard, didn't you?"

Volle stared back into his eyes, and saw grief and sympathy there. He just nodded.

"I'm sorry. I should have seen."

"Seen what?" Tika asked, her smile gone, looking from one to the other.

Tish took a breath. "Volle's friend was killed on his mission."

"Oh. I'm so sorry." She sat back and put a paw to her muzzle. "How terrible."

"Prewitt," Volle said. "He's the one. He sent him off."

Tish nodded. "I think you're right. He's very clever about it. I must say I never thought he was involved in any of that."

"That's not all." Volle briefly told them of Dereath's visit and his imprisonment inside the palace. He felt his fur bristle with renewed anger as he told the story.

Tish looked sternly at him. "Is it true?"

"Of course not." Volle felt a bit of uneasiness in his stomach at lying to Tish. He felt as though somehow the wolf would be able to tell, but he just nodded.

"All right. Then I'm sure they'll find the merchant. That should be enough to clear your name. What did you say his name was?"

"Marik Senom." He'd given the name out to Prewitt, so Tish might as well have it too.

"I'll ask around for him and see what we can turn up."

"Thanks." Volle felt his fur start to settle down, and he took another bite.

"Worry about eating now," Tish said with a smile. "Looks like you need it."

"Mmm." Volle nodded, and set to his dinner.

"I'm certainly glad this didn't happen two days ago," Tika said. "Imagine not being able to go to Ilyana's cotillion! We couldn't have moved it here on such short notice."

"He said he wanted to get back by then," Volle said around a muzzle full of food.

"Who?"

He swallowed. "Dereath. He said he'd hoped to ruin that for me." Though actually he'd have been doing me a favor, Volle thought. Even when he screws up, it turns out badly for me.

"He's certainly making a nuisance of himself." Tish tapped a claw thoughtfully on the table.

"Nuisance?!" Volle said it louder than he'd intended to, and then lowered his voice. "Sorry. He threatened Richy, too."

"Richy?" Tika asked.

"Er, a wolf friend of mine."

Tish nodded. "I can go warn him if you like."

"I already sent Welcis over. I think he'll be fine."

"I didn't realize you were that attached to him."

Volle's ears flicked. "I'd be upset if something happened to him because of me." He struggled to keep his emotions in check. Picturing the things Dereath might do to Richy, the poor innocent wolf, brought back the grief and anger in force. He picked up his glass and took a drink of wine, and focused on the taste on his tongue, trying to let the emotions subside.

"I see. Very charitable."

Volle sighed and put down the wine. It wasn't working. "I should go."

Tish covered his paw with his own. "We're always here if you need us."

"I know," Volle said. "Thank you both." He stood, waited awkwardly for a moment, though he wasn't sure for what, and then walked out.

Welcis greeted him when he returned to his room, telling him that the message had been delivered, and that Tally had thanked him. Volle nodded, told Welcis he'd already had dinner, and dismissed him for the night. Closing the door of his bedroom behind him, he looked at the bed. It looked the same as it had for the last month. So why did it seem so much emptier?

He stripped and climbed between the sheets. Sliding his paw under the pillow to pull it closer to him, he touched a leather pouch and froze for a moment when he remembered what it was. Slowly, he pulled it out and held it up to the faint starlight. It jingled softly as he held it up.

"You promised," he whispered. "You *promised*." He held the pouch to his nose, but it had lost any scent except for its natural leathery smell. He held it to his chest and curled up around it. Though he didn't cry, nor did he sleep; his thoughts spun with could-haves and should-haves, images of both the cougars, their scents and smiles, their paws on his chest, and the holes that were left in his life and the lives of others by their passing.

Sometime during the night he resolved to take the gold to Xiller's relatives in Villutian. He opened the pouch to count the gold, but he couldn't seem to count it properly and the gold pieces looked different to him, not like the Tephossian Royals. There were either fourteen or fifteen of them, or maybe sixteen, and they seemed to have pictures of Xiller in his jaguar makeup on them. Frustrated, he put them back in the pouch and went back to his attempts at sleep.

Chapter 19

In the morning, he woke tired and bleary, the pouch still clutched in his paw. Helfer was sitting beside the bed.

"Morning," he said cheerfully. Volle grunted something. "I came to drag you out for a run."

Volle shook his head. "Not today, Hef. Tomorrow. I promise." His paw curled around the pouch as he said those words.

"You sure?" Volle nodded. "All right. If you promise…"

"I do. Honestly. I feel a bit better. I just need one more day."

"All right." The weasel got up and put a paw on Volle's shoulder. "Mind if I have lunch with you?"

"No. I'd like that."

"All right. See you then."

"Thanks, Hef." Helfer smiled and left, closing the bedroom door as he went.

Volle settled back in the bed. In the battle between sorrow and anger that had raged in him since yesterday, sorrow now had the upper paw. His immediate world was no different, but knowing that Xiller wasn't going to return to share his bed again had changed everything. Knowing that Prince Gennic would not take over the crown, as they'd always assumed he would, changed everything. How was King Rachlas taking it? Was the royal family devastated? No, they would be brave and vengeful.

He supposed he would see the towers of the palace at Caril himself before long. In all the excitement surrounding Dereath's surprise appearance yesterday, he'd forgotten that he would likely be removed from Tephos before Prewitt's investigation amounted to anything. Seir would let him know when he saw her today…

He sat up suddenly. How was he to meet Seir if he couldn't leave the palace?

He chewed his lip and pondered that. He could take the secret passage by the baths, but in the middle of the day that area would be dangerous and discovery was likely. If only he could get a set of papers— Arrin! The fox worked with the Steward and could get him forged papers, just for a day. It wouldn't be too difficult, and no one would be the wiser.

He threw on a shirt and pants, and hurried upstairs to the Steward's office. Alister's inner door was closed, and thank Gaia, the office was empty except for Arrin. He looked up as Volle entered, and his initial smile faded a bit.

"Volle, they said you're under arrest! What are you doing here?"

"I'm just confined to the palace." He lowered his voice, sitting next to Arrin's desk. "I need to ask you a huge favor."

The fox looked distinctly uneasy, and Volle suddenly knew what his answer would be, but he pressed ahead and asked the question anyway. "I need to get out of the palace today to keep an appointment. Can you get me a set of papers?"

Arrin's ears folded all the way back. "I can't."

Volle tapped the desk softly. "Can't or won't?"

"Volle, you're—they say you're a spy or something, and that you had something to do with some foreign prince getting killed…"

Guilt triggered anger, bringing an involuntary growl from Volle. "Do you believe that?"

Arrin recoiled. "I don't know. Is it true?"

Volle stared at him. "Not entirely," he said grudgingly.

"But some of it? Which parts?"

"I'm not a spy. I heard that the cougar who was here was the one who killed Prince—that prince. But I didn't know anything about that."

Arrin chewed his lip. "I'm sorry," he whispered. "I can't…"

He got up and turned away. "Thanks," he said brusquely. Volle knew he was being unreasonable, but he couldn't understand why Arrin wouldn't at least try to help him. His anger was compounded by his underlying guilt at knowing that Arrin's reservations were justified: he was a spy, and he did want the papers to go meet with another spy. Arrin should still have trusted him, he told himself as he stalked out of the office.

Every little thing that could go wrong was going to go wrong, he felt. Nobody was really trying to help him. He felt, in that moment, utterly alone.

The feeling lasted all of ten minutes, until Helfer joined him for lunch. The weasel's attempts to cheer him up didn't exactly work, but they did make him feel less persecuted.

"It was a nice run through the snow. You should've been there. Nobody's been in the garden since the snow fell, even the gardeners, and it's beautiful, all white and clean." He grabbed a roll off the tray Welcis brought in and stuffed it in his muzzle, continuing to talk muffledly through it. "Cold, but you get used to it. Mmf. And you get nice cool breezes up the skirt. Wow!"

Volle pushed food around the table and gave Helfer a weak grin. "I'll come out tomorrow."

"That's the spirit! And we'll go to the Lonely Cock tonight, and you'll feel better. You'll see. You just need to get—what?"

Volle was shaking his head. "I can't. I'm confined to the palace."

"What?!"

"Dereath. He used his vacation to go digging up stories about me coming into the country from somewhere else and insinuating that I'm not who I say I am. So Prewitt confined me to the palace until he can check some of the stories."

Helfer regarded Volle closely for a moment, but when he spoke, his words were not at all what Volle expected. "You know, being confined to the palace isn't such a big deal." He winked.

Volle stared at him, and then remembered. "Hef, you'd…"

"Shh." He indicated the parlor door, behind which Welcis had retired. "I was just thinking that instead of going out, you could come have dinner with me tonight and we could have a quiet evening together."

"That sounds great. Could I come by earlier, though? I really don't have anything to do since I can't take my walk through town."

Helfer grinned and nodded. "Sure. I'm not doing much this afternoon anyway."

"Thanks, Hef." He managed a better smile. "Seems like I'm saying that a lot lately."

"Sorry you have to. You're having a rough couple of days. At least the cotillion seemed to go so well."

Volle chuckled without much humor. "Everything started to go bad there. Ilyana decided to get in a practice session. It was pretty bad. Then I got home, and…" He stopped talking and looked down at his plate.

"I know." Helfer sighed.

Volle hadn't really had the time to think about what his night with Ilyana had meant. That had been pushed back to a remote corner of his mind, to deal with at some future time. At the moment, he wasn't sure it was something he would have to deal with at all. He found himself almost looking forward to the order to return home. At least he would be out of this morass.

But he would miss Helfer. He looked fondly at the weasel. "I'll get over it eventually, Hef. I really appreciate your help."

"Hey, whatever I can do. I know what it's like to lose someone close to you."

Volle shook his head. "What you went through is far worse. I might have loved him, I'm not sure. But you lost your father. That's horrible."

Helfer was silent, and then sighed and picked up a piece of meat. He looked at it before popping it into his muzzle. "Losing anyone is terrible, especially when it happens so suddenly. But you just have to move on. That's what I learned. Death is a part of life." He looked up. "Did you go to the Cantor? That helped me, back when…you know."

Volle nodded. "It helped me remember that Gaia and Canis are looking out for me. And that Felis is looking out for him. Easy to lose sight of that. Though I wouldn't have thought you'd pay much attention to the church."

Helfer chuckled. "Weasel is a nice ancestor to have. He likes you to do whatever makes you happy. For some it means serving others." He indicated Welcis again, behind the door. "For others, it means sampling all of life's pleasures to the fullest."

"Isn't it 'Mustelis'?"

"Oh, properly it is, but we like to call him 'Weasel' because everyone knows who his favorites are." He grinned and leaned forward, lowering his voice. "Besides, it really annoys the skunks and badgers when we do that."

Volle smiled, and Helfer clapped his paws together. "Well, finally I got a real, honest-to-goodness smile out of you, fox. You'll see—a quiet dinner with me will have your spirits back up in no time."

"Oh, that's just the rumor the servants want to hear," Volle said. "You know that they already think we're lovers?"

"Sure." Helfer shrugged. "Kind of nice not to live up to their expectations, I think."

"Yeah." Volle flicked his ears. "I don't know if I want my spirits lifted just yet, Hef. I think I want some time to grieve."

"I understand. We can do that too, if you want."

"Maybe. I don't know what I want just now." Except to talk to Seir and get this over with.

Helfer nodded. "Come on up whenever you're ready."

When Volle did come up to his chambers, a couple hours later, he showed him the door in his wardrobe. "There's a ladder behind it, here, and careful, it's missing one rung. You go down a passage and come out in a smelly basement that's a storage area for the palace, which by a coincidence, I happen to own." He grinned. "A lot of my mead and wine is stored there. The key is hanging just inside the passage. Just wait until it's deserted and then go out into the alley. And for Gaia's sake, don't be seen. Questions about how you got out would be very awkward."

"I have this cloak and I put on plain clothes," Volle said. He was wearing the linens he'd worn upon arriving at the palace, both because they didn't identify him as a noble, and because he fully expected not to be one by the end of the day. "Maybe I should leave the cloak."

Helfer eyed him critically. "If you don't mind being cold, I think it works better without the cloak."

Volle nodded and hung the cloak on a nearby peg. "All right. And…thanks again."

Helfer patted his shoulder. "Anything to help you out. Just be careful."

As Volle walked through the low, dank tunnel, he realized that Helfer hadn't once asked him why he wanted to go out. The weasel's trust in him made him smile tightly, and vow inwardly to repay him if it were at all possible.

As promised, the key hung just inside the door at the other end of the long tunnel. Volle took it and pushed the door open carefully.

The storage area was dark, lit only by the light of a grimy window in one corner. His eyes were already adjusted to the dark of the tunnel, so he saw the stacks of crates and barrels easily. He listened, but caught no sound other than his own breathing, and no living scent other than his own and that of a couple small rats. Quickly, he eased out into the room and closed the door behind him.

He navigated his way easily through the storeroom and found the door out. The key unlocked it smoothly. He eased it open, checking the alley for movement before sliding out, closing and locking the door, and pocketing the key. It was done so quickly that anyone glancing into the alley, away, and back again might reasonably have thought the fox had appeared out of thin air.

Anxious to avoid attention, Volle stayed to some of the smaller streets he knew and got to the park without seeing anyone he knew. The park was crowded with children playing in the snow and adults enjoying the crisp winter air, but he found an empty bench that had already been cleared of snow and sat down. He could just see the corner of the park where the lion statue stood, and the statue's head stood above a row of bushes. From this distance, against the bright snow, it was hard to make out the details of the head, and he had little trouble substituting Xiller's head in its place.

He didn't know how long he stared at the statue, but when he turned his head, Seir was beside him on the bench. Her head was bowed and her paws were clasped in her lap. She wore a plain woolen cloak that was pulled tightly around her shoulders, and grey linen pants. Her paws were bare even though they had much less fur than Volle's. Some mice wore boots in the winter, but others hated the restrictive feel, and Volle knew without asking that that was why Seir went barefoot.

"He didn't know what he was doing," he said in a low voice.

"It's pretty hard to tear out someone's throat by accident."

Volle felt the sick feeling in his stomach again. "He thought he was being heroic. They told him the Ferrenians were evil."

"That doesn't help very much."

"It's all I have."

Seir looked at him then, and put a paw on his knee. "I know," she said softly. "I'm sorry for all of us."

"He was set up, Seir. They used him like a weapon. But he had feelings, and dreams. He wasn't just a sword, made to kill. But that's how they used him. He didn't realize it, and neither did I, but I should have seen it. He wasn't that clever—he admitted that himself—how could he be on an intelligence mission alone?"

"It doesn't make much sense for him to be an assassin, either," Seir pointed out.

"Maybe that's why I didn't see it." Volle sighed and looked at his paws. "I'm ready to go home. Even if it means Duke Avery gets a shot at me. I imagine he's slavering at the prospect."

Seir kicked a little pile of snow with her paws, which were just long enough to reach the top of the drift that had gathered at the base of the bench. "I'm sure he would be if he knew the whole situation."

For such a small creature, her embrace seemed impossibly large.

"I don't want another week's respite before you tell him. I just want this over with. I failed, I'm sorry. I'm sorry for more things than you can imagine."

Seir gave him a quirky smile. "If you're in such a hurry to see him, I'm sure we can arrange a visit, but not all of us think you've failed." He met her eyes and saw the warmth in them, the softness that she so often disguised beneath her hard manner. "Your failure to gather information did not cause the death of Prince Gennic. It merely failed to prevent it. And you are not the only one at fault."

"I'm the main one. I had the assassin in my bed." He spoke the words emptily, so used to the flood of emotions that the statement had little impact on him.

"And who's to say you could have prevented him from leaving? Perhaps he would have killed you if you'd confronted him, and then we'd have lost you and the Prince. Perhaps the people who sent him had a backup—we know there was at least one other working with him in Caril, who slipped through our paws. The point is, Volle, it was tragic, but holding you solely to blame for it is not only counterproductive, but inaccurate. You didn't bare your teeth to the Prince, nor did you send the weapon who did."

Volle blinked, as the import of her words crept over him. "I'm staying?"

"You're staying."

He felt a constriction loosen in his chest, and he let out a long breath. "I promise I'll do better."

"Under the circumstances," Seir said drily, "it would be hard for you to do worse."

Stung, he searched her eyes, and saw the depths of her pity and sympathy there, hidden only slightly by the sarcastic remark. "It would, wouldn't it?" he said, and then his voice broke and he leaned onto her shoulder, and found that he still had some tears left to be shed.

She got to her knees on the bench and put her arms around him, and for such a small creature, her embrace seemed impossibly large. "They used him, Seir. He was so naive, all he wanted was to be a hero."

"I know," she whispered, and rubbed his back. When he lifted his tear-streaked muzzle some moments later, he saw to his surprise that her eyes were glistening too.

"You didn't even know him."

She cleaned his muzzle with a paw, and sniffed. "I know him through you, Volle. You have a tender heart, and I don't think you could feel that way about someone who wasn't good at his core. I can't reconcile that with the assassin who tore out the throat of our prince, but if I view them separately, I can hate the assassin, but cry for your lover."

"I guess that's what I'm doing." He sniffed, too, and wiped his nose. "And Prince Gennic...I never knew him, really, but..."

Seir nodded. "He would have been a good king. Young Likrash will be a good king too. He just needs a few more years to grow into it. But losing Gennic is a blow. From what I hear, the kingdom was in an uproar." Volle remained silent, bowing his head again. Seir touched his arm. "But Volle, without your information, they might very well have attacked the southern kingdoms. He looked like a jaguar, and probably nobody would have taken off his armor to check for a smeared spot if our message hadn't gotten through. And there wasn't any other clue to his identity. All he had on him was a bit of Ferrenian currency. Thanks to you, we know where the attack came from. And we also know that it probably did not have the sanction of the king."

Volle shook his head. "I don't think it did. This is a separate group. I'm working with Tish—Lord Tistunish—on figuring out who they are."

"When you find out, let us know. Tella is especially anxious to know."

Volle nearly gave her Prewitt's name then, but restrained himself. He didn't have any direct evidence, just a hunch. He didn't see immediately how he could get direct evidence other than by asking the bear directly, and he didn't think that would be very fruitful, but he could try it. For Tella, he wanted to be sure. He knew what she would do once she knew.

Thinking of Prewitt made him remember Dereath. "There's another problem, too." Briefly he outlined Dereath's allegations and his current plight.

Seir nodded thoughtfully. "How much of a risk are you taking being here right now?"

Volle shook his head. "Nobody saw me."

"All right. We've kept Reese in his identity here, so producing him won't be too much of a problem. He's become fairly well known in the market. He bought a spice booth and goes by to monitor it every now and then. Do you think we should get the black fox, too?"

"What, you mean me?"

Seir smiled. "Do you think we just picked black because we had the color lying around? There's a black fox in Vinton right now who will swear he was picked up in Ferrenis by merchants, but left them in the mountains because they were going too fast and he wanted to live the mountain life."

Volle nodded, and thought. "I think they'll find him, then. Prewitt said they were going to send some people there."

"All right. I'll tell Reese to be more visible in the market the next few days so they can find him easily. Don't worry, Volle, this won't be a problem. We still have confidence in you."

"Who has confidence in me?" he asked harshly. "You?"

"More than just me. I didn't make the decision to withhold the full story from Duke Avery alone."

"Who else? Sherr? I know Tella hates me now, and Reese doesn't have the authority."

Seir smiled. "You always were good at figuring things out. That's what we're counting on."

He gave her a long look. "I'm figuring out a lot of things."

"Good boy." She patted his knee. "We shouldn't stay here long. We'll keep the regular meeting schedule. If you're still confined to the palace, send word with someone."

"I'll tell Helfer to tell Tally," he said. "I already had to warn him about Dereath."

"The rat?"

"That's right. He made a vague threat to Richy—the wolf I see there. I just don't want him to have the chance to do any damage."

"Sounds reasonable. Tally will keep him safe. He won't risk his boys, not for as much gold as that rat could carry."

"Well, Dereath probably can't carry all that much, but…" He trailed off, staring at the snow. An idea was taking shape in his head.

Seir didn't seem to notice. "Good. I'll see you later, Volle." She nuzzled him and he nuzzled back distractedly. "What is it?"

"They set him up," he said softly.

"Who?"

"Xiller. The cougar. They paid him—he got a purse full of gold. And he left it with me." He left out the reason; he didn't want his voice to break down again. "I didn't look at it until last night. It wasn't Tephossian Royals. It was some other gold coin with a jaguar head on it. I thought I was dreaming, but I wasn't, was I? Those were southern coins. They paid him in southern coins."

"I don't follow you." Seir had sat back down and was watching him worriedly.

"They paid him in southern coins!" he repeated. "He was Tephossian, from Villutian. He was going to Ferrenis. What did he need with southern coins?"

Seir shook her head, and then her muzzle made a small "o." Volle saw the expression and nodded. "You said it yourself: *he wasn't carrying anything but some Ferrenian currency*. What if he'd been carrying a purse full of southern gold? And none of his spots were smeared?"

"There'd have been no doubt." Seir rubbed her front incisors, staring through the snow rather than at it. "So…"

"So they meant for him to be caught and killed. They never meant for him to come back alive." Volle focused on the head of the lion statue. The noble warrior was still roaring at an unseen foe, but Volle now thought the foe was not just an enemy, but a betrayer who had previously been a friend. A different kind of roaring filled his head, the angry rush of understanding.

Seir sighed deeply. "This is a filthy business. There's little room for compassion, and it so often gets crushed. I'm sorry, Volle."

He felt pain in his paws and realized that his claws were digging into his pads. He unclenched his fists and tried to regulate his breathing. "The gold...that's it." Abruptly, he stood up. "Thank you, Seir. I'll see you soon, I hope."

"Take care of yourself, Volle." Her paws slipped off his cloak as he strode away.

He felt like running, but he controlled his pace. The gold wasn't going anywhere, and neither were the records Ullik kept—meticulous records, he'd been told, about every financial transaction that took place in the palace. Including the person who had changed a sum of Tephossian Royals for a stack of southern gold to plant on an unsuspecting cougar so that when he was caught, the Ferrenians would assume he'd come from the south. Turning their hostile eye to the south, they would...what? Forget about the Reysfields? Perhaps.

The important thing was that Ullik would have a record. And there, at last, would be concrete proof. He could guess pretty well which name he would find in the book. As for how to get Ullik to show that record, well, he had a pretty good idea of how to do that, too, if he had to. His jaw was set grimly as he marched back through the snow to Helfer's storeroom. Carefully, he locked the door behind him, as well as the door to the tunnel.

Helfer was in the wardrobe pacing when he came back. He looked up at the click of the door, and his shoulders sagged in relief. "Weasel's teeth, but you were gone a long time. Welcis came looking for you and I had to have Caresh get rid of him." He chuckled. "I could only think of one thing to tell them we'd been doing, I'm afraid."

Volle nodded curtly. "It's okay. I need to go see Ullik."

Helfer stopped him as he made for the door. "It's almost dinnertime. Ullik won't be in his office."

"Then I'll find him in his chambers."

Helfer eyed him. "It's that urgent?"

Volle sighed. "Yes. And no. I need to get something from him, Hef. Something to prove..." He stopped. "Sorry. Politics."

Helfer grinned. "And if you get it, can you use it tonight?"

"I...guess not."

"So why not stay here for a while? I don't think you should go out again, but I can go and maybe bring back some entertainment to relax you a bit." Volle hesitated. "Oh, come on. Have dinner with me, at least."

"Hef..."

"Please?" The weasel smiled entreatingly.

"Oh, all right."

Volle didn't taste much of the meal. He had the vague impression of vegetables, but it all tasted the same in his muzzle. Helfer chattered throughout most of the meal about his upcoming trip to Vellenland, and by the end of it, with the help of a little wine, Volle was able to relax a bit.

That still left him rather wound up. Helfer caught him drumming his fingers on the table and poured him another glass of wine.

"I'll go to sleep," Volle objected, lapping at the wine anyway.

"So take a nap while I'm gone." Helfer shrugged. "Just stick around. You really do need to relax. I'll be back soon, I promise."

"All right." Volle stretched out on the couch and watched the weasel slip through the wardrobe door.

His paws twitched with the need to check the gold in the pouch. He was sure his vision of them hadn't been a dream, but he wanted to hold the coins in his paws, to see them again, to be absolutely certain. Part of him just wanted to do something, anything, and part of him wanted to see the coins because they would feed his rage, made mellow by the wine.

He actually got up and walked to the door, but was stopped by Caresh. "Sir," the valet said smoothly, "Of course his lordship may do as he pleases, but Lord Ikling's desires were that his lordship remain here."

"I know, Caresh. I just need to check something and then I'll come right back."

"His lordship may wish to consider that such a course of action might be detrimental to his lordship's relaxation."

"I can relax just fine," he snapped. "I want to check something."

Caresh's expression softened and he laid a paw on Volle's shoulder. "Would his lordship please reconsider?"

Volle stared into his eyes. He knew that if he insisted, the servant would step aside and let him pass, but he also knew that Caresh was trying to help. Part of him resisted the help, the part that had gotten used to being a lord. But underneath, he was still a young fox, and the words of the older Caresh had a soothing quality to them. He trusted the servant in a way he never could have if he'd been brought up a lord; that is, he trusted him to make judgments. The bond of their species also lay between them, and he found the scent of the older fox to be reassuring and calming. Slowly, he lowered his muzzle.

"All right," he said. "You're right, I don't need to go right now."

"Thank you, sir," Caresh said slowly, bowing.

Volle waved a paw. "Thank you."

"There is one message for his lordship. His lordship's valet requested that his lordship be informed that the king requested a brief informal audience tomorrow morning."

"The king?" Volle's ears shot up. "What about?"

Caresh shook his head. "That information was not, unfortunately, included as part of the message."

"Now I have to go ask him." Caresh looked at him without speaking for several seconds, until Volle nodded. "Ah. You didn't tell me until I'd promised to stay."

"His Majesty's request was an informal one," Caresh said with an apologetic tilt to his ears. "His lordship is not likely to require any preparation for it. And it is unlikely that his lordship's valet has any more information than has already been conveyed."

"All right. Thank you."

"Good night, sir."

Volle pushed the sitting room curtain aside and pulled it closed behind him. He sank down on the couch and turned over things in his mind. There was no longer much mystery about what had gone on, at least to his thinking; what he wondered was what could be done about it. He wanted badly to take his revenge personally, but even if he thought himself a match for Prewitt, he wouldn't be doing himself or his country any favors by putting himself in that sort of position. Possibly, he could tell the King and let him handle it. But that would ruin any chance he had of getting into their group, or whatever would be left of it when Prewitt was arrested, and for all he knew, the King was aware of what had gone on and wouldn't arrest the bear anyway. Besides, telling the King would bring up all sorts of sticky questions about how he knew what had happened to Xiller—questions he had so far managed to avoid in his discussions with everyone at the palace. He wasn't sure how to demonstrate his loyalty, nor even who to demonstrate it to.

Loyalty brought Canis to his mind, and the text the Cantor had read to him. Canis preached loyalty to the pack, to the family, and to the church. Growing up, Volle had followed Fox, whose teachings were similar but included only family and church. The royal family was part of everyone's family regardless of species, and so revenging himself for Prince Gennic's death would be doing honor to Fox and Canis. But, he thought, it was not that simple. He worried at the question, wondering what more he needed to do.

He had never been terribly religious, but now he worried about following the right path. He had always honored his family, up until his mother's death, and he had always honored the royal family, and otherwise he'd lived his life as he pleased. Was his current plight meant to teach him that he had strayed? He felt uncomfortable assigning so much personal meaning to Xiller's mission and death, much less Prince Gennic's death—was all of Ferrenis paying because he had misstepped? He thought that might be expected of the more capricious Mouse (Rodenta, to the Orthodox Church) or the stricter herbivores, but not of Fox. Fox loved his children but allowed them to make mistakes and learn from them. So he was meant to learn from this, he supposed.

He had fallen into a half-dream in which Fox and Canis were arguing over which one of them was really his father's brother when the wardrobe door clicked, and Helfer's familiar scent drifted to him, along with another, almost indetectable.

"Asleep?" Helfer's voice was amused.

Volle cracked his eyes open and identified the scent before the wolf came around the corner. "Richy?"

"Hi." He was wearing a robe and smiling shyly, looking around the opulent room as he stepped through the doorway. Helfer closed the door behind him, grinning widely.

"I thought you weren't allowed to meet clients outside the Jackal's..." Volle trailed off as Helfer's grin widened and Richy's tail wagged from side to side.

"Tally agreed that these were special circumstances," the weasel said. "Since you can't come to him, it seems he must come to you. So you can come in him," he giggled. "Or on him. Whichever you like."

Richy slipped off his robe, beneath which he was wearing only his loincloth. He brushed a paw down his front and smiled alluringly. His paw lingered on the fastener of his loincloth and his gaze met Volle's with a question.

Volle felt a familiar stirring in his sheath. He sat up on the couch and covered Richy's paw with his own. Slowly, he undid the fastener and held the loincloth as it fell away from the wolf's sheath. He reached up and touched the white fur with a gentle black paw, then cupped the white sac that hung below them. He looked up and saw the wolf smiling down at him.

Helfer was sidling towards his bedroom. Volle saw Richy's eyes flick quickly in that direction, and without looking over he said, "Hef. You can stay. If you want to."

The weasel paused, but Volle didn't see his expression. He only saw Richy's smile widen slightly. "You sure?"

"Yeah. It's okay. I don't think I'm up for very much tonight, and I'd hate for Richy to have wasted a trip." He grinned, and only then did he look at the weasel. "Besides, you owe me a show."

Helfer smiled back at him, and folded his arms. "All right," he said. "If it will help you relax."

Volle nodded. "Oh, it will." Truthfully, he couldn't have said at that moment exactly why he had offered to let Helfer join in. He only knew that his bond with Richy had been altered, and not just by the location. When he'd touched the wolf's sheath, he'd waited for the mental release that would let him forget about his problems and his other life, and it hadn't come. He was prepared to enjoy Richy's company, but he didn't know if he would be able to give himself to the wolf as fully as he had in the past. And maybe it was for that reason that Helfer's company didn't matter. Or maybe he was just being a polite and considerate guest.

Richy's paw caressed his ear, and the wolf spoke gently. "Want to get those clothes off?"

"In a minute," Volle said with a smile. He brushed his black nose up the soft white fur of Richy's sheath and inhaled the musk through the fur. Slowly, he rubbed his muzzle up and down both sides, letting his whiskers trace the shape of the wolf's sex and feel the warmth radiating from it. Richy breathed out happily, and his tail began to wag.

All for a bigger tip, Volle noted cynically to himself, and then smiled as the pink tip of Richy's member chose that moment to appear at the opening of his sheath. Well, maybe he's enjoying it just a little, he thought, and let his tongue curl up under the wolf's sac and then dragged it up the long sheath, dampening the fur and letting the musk roll through his tongue and nose. He could hear Helfer's breathing quicken, and heard the rustling of the weasel fiddling with his clothing. He slid his paw around the wolf to hold his rump, and slowly licked up the long sheath and the few pink inches that were showing again. On the next lick, his tongue encountered still more of the long member, and it only took him four more licks to bring the full, hard length out into the air.

Richy whined softly as Volle slid his lips over the firm erection, teasing it with his tongue. Out of the corner of his eye, he saw that Helfer had discarded much of his clothing and had one paw stuck inside his pants, watching the two of them.He lowered his muzzle, taking as much of the wolf into it as he could, and when he felt his lips against the fur of Richy's sheath, he took a moment to suck gently on the stiffness in his muzzle. The sensation did relax him somewhat, letting him focus on the feel and scent of the wolf and the long erection that filled his muzzle. He explored it with his tongue, letting his other thoughts drain away as much as they could, and he felt as though the wolf in his muzzle was spreading warmth throughout his body, driving back his worries and letting the natural response of his body fill him.

A tingling sensation rippled through his fur, especially at his own sheath, which felt full and warm itself. He imagined a connection between it and his tongue, and drew his tongue along Richy's length one last time before letting it slowly slide out of his muzzle. Glancing at Helfer, he slid his muzzle down over the wolf's erection again, letting it slowly disappear into his russet-and-white muzzle, curling his warm tongue around it as it entered, sucking gently on it, pressing his palate against the tip, and then slowly sliding his muzzle backwards, finishing with a lick to the gleaming tip.

Helfer was panting at this point, and Volle was worried that he would come just from watching. He beckoned to Helfer and grinned, sliding his paws down to remove his own pants, though he left his shirt on.

The weasel followed suit quickly, revealing a large sheath and an erection that was already dripping fluid down its length. He grinned back at Volle and posed, showing off for the fox while casting an appreciative glance down at Volle's lap. Though he wasn't fully erect, Volle had become aroused enough to be showing quite a bit of his own member. He brushed a black paw along it, smiling for Helfer and Richy, and then scooted back to the corner of the couch, sweeping his tail out of the way.

Richy took a step forward. Volle reached out for his paw and held it warmly, pulling him down to the couch. "Just the muzzle tonight," he said, touching his nose to the wolf's. He still felt guarded, not ready for full intimacy, but his body ached for release.

Richy nodded with a smile and settled himself on the couch between Volle's legs, his large black nose an inch from the fox's sheath, tail wagging slowly over his raised rump. He didn't look back at Helfer, but Volle knew the wolf was aware of him, and Helfer did too. "If you're not going to use that nice ass, Volle," he said, panting, "I sure will."

Volle grinned, and so did Richy, wagging his tail harder and lifting it slightly. Helfer padded over to one of his chests and rummaged in it, finding a small ceramic pot. He dipped two fingers into it and rubbed the cream on his erection while walking back to the couch, where his paw disappeared under Richy's tail. The wolf had been brushing his nose up and down Volle's sheath, and he jumped slightly at the touch, then settled back again.

Helfer positioned himself behind the wolf and smiled at Volle, then pressed forward. Volle saw Richy tense slightly, then relax, and he rubbed behind the wolf's ears. When Helfer started to thrust his hips forward and back, Volle could feel the motions in Richy's body as it lay against him. The sight, as well as Richy's soft brushings, had brought him fully erect, and now Richy was teasing his pink member with a soft tongue, timing the licks with the weasel's thrusts from behind.

It was only a few minutes before Helfer started to pant and moan, and thrust faster, and then he pressed himself against the wolf with a loud moan, hips working fast. Volle felt the thrusts through Richy, who kept licking, unruffled, and Volle was amazed at how easily Richy was able to keep his focus. He was caught in the middle, as it were, but performing admirably and satisfying both ends.

It mirrored what Volle had been trying to do for the past few months: satisfy himself as well as the various people who were depending on him. He didn't feel that comparing himself to a prostitute who was having things shoved into every available orifice was that bad a comparison, when it came right down to it. He only wished he'd been able to do his job half as well as Richy was doing his.

The wolf's tongue was more insistent now, and Volle abandoned his introspection to focus on its warm licks. Despite his body's need, his arousal was building slowly, partially because of his distraction, and partially because Richy was taking his time. Helfer had pulled out of the wolf and sat back on the couch, panting, his glistening member still erect against his stomach. Volle eyed it again and then looked self-consciously down at his own, which seemed small by comparison, especially given the difference in body size.

He grinned, looked back at Helfer, and figured that was a rather silly thing to worry about. Helfer had noticed his glance and grinned back, then slid off the couch and padded around to where Volle was sitting.

He leaned in, placing his erection alongside the fox's. "See? Almost the same size."

Volle grinned at him. "Yours is longer."

"Yours is thicker. Plus you've got that neat canid knot there." He indicated the base of Volle's member, where his knot was just starting to swell. "Hmm, Looks like you've still got a little time left, so..." He stepped back and picked up the jar again, this time rubbing some cream under his own tail.

Volle watched as Richy's licks became firmer, setting his fur a-tingle again. Panting, he rubbed his paws harder through the fur behind the wolf's cute dark ears. Helfer knelt beside the couch and slipped his muzzle under the wolf's hips, licking and then taking Richy's member into his muzzle. Again, Richy continued to lick at Volle without showing much reaction, though he did squirm and lift his hips.

He had just been teasing at Volle's tip and sliding his lips over it when Helfer squirmed his whole body under the wolf, his head between Volle's legs. He grinned up at the fox. "Nice view."

"What...oh," Volle grinned as the weasel started to wriggle his way backwards, and he saw Richy's hips press downward. Helfer sighed deeply and closed his eyes, and Volle's body shivered as he imagined the wolf's long member sliding into the weasel, the half-swollen knot pressing through his tight tail hole.

Richy began to rock his whole body back and forth, sliding his muzzle down Volle as he worked his shaft in and out of Helfer. Volle tuned out the weasel's squeaks and pants and concentrated on his own arousal. Physically, he was ready, his member shivering in almost painful delight at every lick, but he couldn't get over the mental part.

Was he afraid of letting go? He dismissed that thought as soon as it came to mind. More likely, he thought, was that he was still grieving, and it just didn't feel right. His paw tightened on Richy's head.

The wolf stopped and looked up at him, tongue hanging out. His hips didn't stop moving, and Helfer's cries were getting louder as his paws clutched the couch.

He was about to tell Richy to stop, and then he hesitated. Xiller wouldn't tell him to be chaste. He'd be urging Volle on, telling him that he needed the release. The thought made him smile, and he petted Richy's ears in response to the wolf's questioning gaze. "Just needed a short break," he said.

Helfer moaned, eyes squeezed shut, and his leg pressed back against the couch as his paws grabbed the fabric. His whole body seemed to be shuddering under Richy, and then he relaxed, panting.

"Wow, without your paws? Just rubbing into the sofa?" Volle grinned down at Helfer, and even Richy looked a bit curious.

Helfer nodded, still panting. "Soft...fabric..." he said, and then looked up at Volle. "You're falling behind."

Volle smiled, caressing Richy's head. "You've been behind most of the night. I'll be done soon. I'll just let you get out of there."

"Oh, if that's what you're waiting for…" Helfer squirmed, and Volle heard a slick sound as Richy's member slid out of him. The weasel dropped to the floor and sat there, turning his head to watch Volle, giving him a "go ahead" nod.

Volle noticed that there was indeed a large wet spot on the couch beneath Richy's stomach. The wolf kept himself off the couch, on his paws and knees as he lowered his muzzle over Volle's erection. This time, his tongue did its work quickly and insistently. Volle clutched the couch back and seat with his paws, his body shivering all over, and he even imagined for a moment that it was Xiller whose muzzle was caressing him so wonderfully. He let himself enjoy that fantasy for only a moment, then wrenched his eyes open and forced himself to watch Richy's lupine muzzle sliding up and down along his length.

His knot was already so tight he thought it might burst, and his breath was coming in short pants. Richy's muzzle and tongue brought him to the edge and held him there for several seconds, while his body tensed and gathered energy, and finally he couldn't hold back any longer. His climax arched his back, pressed his hips up into Richy, forced his sheath into the wolf's muzzle and his member almost back against the wolf's throat. He came in shuddering spurts, feeling as though a spring he hadn't realized was inside him was being released all at once. His muscles unwound and relaxed as he moaned loudly, bucking up into Richy less each time, until finally he settled back into the couch.

Helfer got up and stretched, grinning. "Hope you didn't wake up Caresh. That felt good, huh?"

Volle nodded, panting. He kept scratching behind Richy's ears as the wolf swallowed and opened his muzzle, giving Volle an affectionate lick along his sensitive length. Volle squirmed, pushing the wolf's muzzle away good-naturedly.

"Oh, you're not done yet," Helfer called. He was digging in his chest and came back holding something behind his back. "Turn around and lie on your back," he told Richy, gesturing with his paw.

The wolf obeyed, with a half-smile on his muzzle. His erection was still full and his knot was about half-swollen. Volle reached out and brushed a paw along his soft white sac while he watched Helfer. The weasel had turned with his back to Volle, so Volle could see that what he held was some sort of ridged, polished wooden thing.

He waved it at Volle. "Take that, and slide it into him when I tell you."

Volle reached out and took it, turning it over in his paw. It was shaped like a wolf's penis, with a small knot at the end and a handle behind that. Rather than being an exact copy of the shape, however, it had six small ridges in it, each one circling the shaft, evenly spaced from the tip to the knot. Volle ran his fingers over the ridges, which were only raised about half an inch, and rolled smoothly into the main surface. "Where did you get this?" he asked as Helfer straddled the wolf.

"Oh, around," Helfer said with a grin. Volle saw Richy's head crane up, trying to see what he held, so he put it down quickly and hid it with the wolf's tail. Richy lay back down with a smile, but his tail twitched a bit anxiously.

Helfer handed Volle the jar of cream after applying a bit more to himself, then guided Richy's erection up under his tail, settling down on it with a sigh. Volle watched the length disappear and felt a brief stirring in his sheath, but his energy for the evening was mostly spent. He couldn't imagine how Helfer could still be erect, much less bouncing up and down on the wolf as he was, but he supposed it came with being a weasel. Or a rabbit.

"Oh, Volle," Helfer panted, "Now, now!"

Volle quickly smeared some cream on the wooden dildo and pressed it carefully against the small hole between Richy's legs, moving his sac out of the way. Helfer's bouncing didn't help things, but he finally found the right spot and pressed, working it further in. He heard Richy's gasp as the first ridge slid into him, felt the tension at the second, and then each of the next three was met with a soft "Oh" of pleasure.

Helfer was thrusting himself down quite hard now, muttering, "Come on, I want to feel that knot…come on, wolf…" and Richy was squirming as Volle pulled the toy out and thrust it back in. "There it is, it's starting…yes, like that…oh! Push it all the way in, Volle, all the way!"

He was forcing himself down now on Richy's very large knot, and squeaked as it popped into him, panting and moaning very fast, his little body shuddering violently. Volle pushed, and pushed a little harder, and with a little wriggling, the wooden knot slid into Richy, sending the wolf into similar shudders, though his moans were much lower-pitched and softer.

Volle watched the two writhe together, holding on to Richy by the toy's handle and wriggling it until the wolf yelped for him to stop. "Please!" Volle relented, and the wolf lay back on the couch, panting hard, tail thumping the fabric.

Helfer was slumped against the back of the couch, panting too. He turned to see the handle and Volle's grip on it, and nodded. "Good. Don't want to…lose that in there." He winked at Volle.

Richy lifted his head. "Lose it?"

"Don't worry," Volle said. "I've got a good hold on it. See?" He wriggled it again, making Richy whine.

"Oh, don't tease him," Helfer said. "He's done a good night's work."

"And then some." Volle smiled. "I'll pay for it."

"I can take care of it."

"You went out and got him. It's okay, Hef. I feel better. Really."
And he did, though mostly physically. He'd managed to forget about
his problems—almost—for a short time. Watching Helfer with Richy
had been arousing, but Helfer's casual ordering about of the wolf had
also reminded him that people use other people all the time to get what
they want. Sometimes, in rare cases, they pay for it, or make it enjoyable
for the person being used, or both. But that couldn't happen all the time.
If he was going to be successful, then he was going to have to use people, and he wouldn't always be able to make it pleasant for them.

Not Richy, though, if he could help it, and never Helfer. He swore
that to himself. The weasel was apolitical and a good friend, which
made him at the same time useless and inestimably valuable. He felt
bad enough having taken advantage of his secret passage to go meet
Seir, and he promised Helfer silently that he would never again put
him in danger if he could at all help it. He reached out and squeezed
the weasel's shoulder with his free paw, sealing his silent promise to
himself.

Helfer smiled back at him, panting. "Well, I could go another
round...in a bit...but I think our wolf is all worn out."

"Looks like it." Volle grinned affectionately at Richy. "Maybe you
should put him back."

Helfer nodded. "I think I will, in a bit."

Volle stood. "And I think I'll go to bed." He let Helfer slip his
paw into the toy's handle, then tugged his pants on. Leaning over, he
touched his nose to Helfer's, then bent over to give Richy's nose a lick.
The wolf licked back and smiled. "Thank you both. I needed this."

Helfer patted him. "Thanks for staying. And for sharing."

"See you soon," Richy said.

A thought occurred to Volle, and he stopped on his way out.
"Richy? I think you should watch out for a rat from the palace, named
Dereath. He said something about trying to get at you."

"I can defend myself," Richy said. "Anyway, he came by already.
Tally threw him out when he started yelling."

Volle sighed, uneasiness creeping into his stomach. Dereath wasn't
going to leave him alone, but at least he couldn't get at Richy or Ilyana. And Arrin...Volle didn't think Arrin would be an issue. "All right.
Good. Just take care, okay?"

"I will."

"See you tomorrow," Helfer said.

"Maybe not. I have an appointment."

The weasel looked at him questioningly, then nodded. "All right.
Good night."

"Good night, you two." He slipped past the curtain and out the
door.

Chapter 20

Welcis was asleep when he got back. He put the appointment with the king out of his mind for the moment, and went back to his bedroom, closing the door behind him. Going immediately to his bed, he reached under the pillow and drew out the small pouch of coins. The starlight was bright enough for him to see the stitching on the pouch. He teased open the drawstring with a claw, and hesitated, then reached in and drew out a coin.

The face of a jaguar stared back at him.

He turned the coin over and read with some difficulty the name of the southern kingdom: Terrialis. The relaxation he'd achieved over the last hour began to dissipate. He shook the pouch out into his paw. All the coins were the same. Southern coins: evidence, not reward.

He closed his paw around them and growled softly before replacing them in the pouch. He slid the pouch under the pillow, undressed, and lay in bed wondering what he would say to the king. The anger roiling in him again kept him awake for close to an hour before he finally succumbed to sleep.

Welcis woke him in the morning by laying out clothes on the bed. "Good morning, sir," he said with a bit of cheer. "Your appointment with the king is in just over half an hour. Just enough time to get dressed and prepared."

Volle rubbed his eyes and yawned. "What am I supposed to be prepared for?"

"His Majesty's messenger did not say. The meeting is informal, so I suspect no preparation is needed. But his lordship must be dressed appropriately."

"Yes, I suppose so." Volle flicked his ears, which felt muzzy from sleep, and yawned again. He let Welcis dress him in a semi-formal outfit, with a nicely ruffled yellow shirt and matching pants. The skunk smoothed the front of the shirt out several times, then brushed off the short black hairs that had clung to the fabric.

"Your lordship knows the way?"

"It's the audience chamber, right?"

"No, sir. The informal audience is in the King's chambers, in the receiving room. Shall I accompany you?"

"Yes, thank you, Welcis."

"My pleasure, sir." The valet inclined his head, and led Volle out of the chambers and into the corridor. They walked to the Bear staircase and up all three flights of it, then down to a richly painted door detailed with reliefs of bears. Two guards stood in front of the door, both bears with impressive-looking swords at their sides.

Welcis walked up to them. "Lord Vinton to see his Majesty."

One bear held out a large paw. "Wait here." He opened the door and walked inside, closing it behind him. A moment later, he reappeared, gesturing to Volle with a paw. "You can go in. You wait outside," he said to Welcis.

Volle walked through the door, which the bear closed behind him, remaining outside. He had walked into a large room, decorated with velvet curtains and tapestries, with four windows on the far wall. Between the second and third window stood a round table with five chairs around it. Two of the high-backed wooden chairs were occupied, but with the bright windows on either side of them, Volle couldn't discern any details about the figures other than a general bear shape.

"Come in, Lord Vinton," one of the figures said as he paused, trying to catch scents on the air. The King was the one on the left, he was almost sure, but it was the other who'd spoken. His scent was only vaguely familiar. He guessed at the identity.

"Thank you, Lord Alacris." He bowed, and then bowed more deeply to the figure on the left. "Good morning, your Majesty."

He heard the King's deep chuckle. "The noses of the children of Canis are rightly praised. Come forward."

Volle walked over a thick carpet until he was standing at the table. Alacris gestured for him to have a seat, so he pulled back one of the chairs and did so.

"We were most saddened to hear of the charges brought against you by Talison," the King rumbled. "Secretary Prewitt assures me that they will be disproven soon. I hope they have not been too much of an inconvenience for you."

Volle shook his head. "No, thank you, your Majesty. I only regret the circumstances that led to their appearance."

"Most diplomatic. We will have words with Talison regarding his personal grudges. When the charges have been disproven, of course. It is a serious thing, to accuse a Lord of treason."

"Treason?" Volle kept his tail from twitching. Surely he'd only been accused of fraud.

"You presented yourself to us as Lord Vinton and swore fealty to this throne. If you did so without meaning it, the crime is treason. But this is not the place to discuss pointless semantics. Alacris?"

The other bear shifted. "You have possibly heard about the unfortunate happenings recently in Ferrenis."

"I heard the prince was..." Murdered. "Killed. By someone pretending to be what he was not."

"Someone you knew, we think." Alacris fixed him with dark eyes. "The assailant was described to the court as 'a very large cougar painted to look like a jaguar.' They said, in fact, that he was as large or larger than a bear. You were seen with a cougar matching that description around the palace a month ago, and it came to our attention recently that one of the footservants saw that same cougar painted to look like a jaguar."

Volle sighed and nodded. "His name was Xiller." He focused on his grief, not his anger. He didn't have enough proof to tell the king about the setup yet, and he wanted to wait to hear what the king thought about the incident. It sounded like he hadn't known about it. "I didn't know anything about what he was doing. He didn't tell me. I only know that he was originally here with Dereath Talison." That last sentence had come to him as he was wondering what he could tell the king, and he congratulated himself on finding a bit of information that was not only true, but might get Dereath in trouble.

The king and Lord Alacris glanced at each other. "The same Talison who...?"

"Yes." Volle shrugged. "He seemed very upset when Xiller left his chambers to stay with me. Perhaps..." He let the sentence trail off, allowing them to draw the very clear conclusion from it.

The bears shifted in their chairs. "We will have to have a talk with young Talison about several issues, I think," the king said. "Is there anything else you can tell us, Vinton?"

Volle searched his thoughts. That he was a gentle, innocent cougar? They didn't want to hear it, and he didn't want to say it again. He shook his head. "No, your Majesty."

"If you do think of something, you will let us know." Alacris said that, and it was not a question.

"Of course." Volle said, and then, taking advantage of the fact that they were slow to dismiss him, said, "Who would have sent him on such a mission?"

They exchanged glances again. "That is what we're trying to find out," Alacris said. "The King would never condone such an attack, but until we can find the originator, there will be suspicion that it was approved by his Majesty."

"Do the Ferrenians think that?"

"They are not certain enough to take any action." The King shifted, and leaned forward, his massive upper body resting on the solid wooden table. Volle could smell him clearly now, and caught some of his underlying mood: he smelled and sounded cautious and a little worried. "But they are suspicious. They do not know that he came from this palace, but it is only a matter of time before their spies find out."

Volle tapped the table. "So it is imperative that you find out quickly."

"That we find out quickly, yes." Alacris's sentence gently included Volle in the 'we.'

"It was a horrible thing to do."

"Yes," the king said, cutting off Alacris's answer. "It was a strike against the family, and now the country will be united as one family against the aggressor. That is why we must know who it is. If we can help punish...then there will be less danger to us."

"They probably thought that painting him as a jaguar would make the Ferrenians think he was from the south. Then they'd be angry at the south."

Again, the king looked at Alacris for a long time, and this time it was Alacris who replied, slowly. "That is what we believe, yes."

"I didn't know there was fur paint that could disguise a cougar as a jaguar." Volle felt emboldened and looked innocently at them as he posed the implicit question.

Alacris coughed. "Yes, it is something we've been working on. Experimental. Wasn't supposed to be used, just for cosmetics, you understand...a bit more permanent than the fur dyes we've been using."

He doesn't lie very well, Volle noted. Outwardly he just nodded. "Shouldn't you have Lord Fardew looking into this?"

"We do. And we will ask him about Talison's involvement next time we see him." Alacris set his paw down on the table. "Thank you for your time, Lord Vinton. We look forward to seeing you cleared of these charges."

"As do I." Volle rose and bowed once to each, then turned and walked quickly to the door.

"Welcis," he said as they walked back to his chambers, "did you see Xiller that last morning?"

The skunk looked distinctly uncomfortable. "I did, sir."

"So you noticed the paint."

"Yes, sir."

"Did you tell anyone about it?"

"I...fear I did, sir." He hung his head. "I hope I have not caused his lordship any trouble."

"Not more than I deserve, Welcis." He sighed. "Where is Lord Ullik's office? It was by the stairs, that way..."

"Yes, sir. Over here and down this corridor." He seemed relieved not to be talking about the cougar any more.

"Thank you, Welcis." He strode ahead, intending to leave the skunk behind.

"Sir?"

He spun on one paw and turned. "Yes?"

"Sir, Lord Ullik is not likely to be in at this hour. He is most likely taking his lunch."

"Lunch. So I've missed the run with Helfer."

"Yes, sir."

"And I have the tribunal this afternoon."

"Yes, sir."

"All right. I'll see Ullik tomorrow." He set off back the way they'd come, and Welcis followed him.

At lunch, he realized that it was the first time he'd taken lunch with the other lords in several days. Out of habit, he sat next to Oncit, though ingratiating himself with the wolf was the last thing on his mind.

"Been celebrating?" the wolf said sourly.

"Pardon?"

"You heard about the Ferrenian prince, right? Assassinated. You couldn't be happier, could you? Your enemies getting their comeuppance."

"Comeuppance?" Volle saw bitterness in the angle of the wolf's ears, and heard it in his voice. Clearly, he wasn't happy about the assassination either. Could he have been wrong? Was Oncit not involved? In any case, he was still feeling too raw to hide his emotions. "A cowardly act like that, a comeuppance? I wouldn't wish that on my worst enemy. Yes, I wanted to defeat them; yes, I wanted to win our glory back, but in honorable combat, on the field of battle, not sneaking in the night like thieves and bandits. All that act accomplished was to unite their country in grief, and from what I hear, possibly turn their eyes to us in anger. I ask you, why would I be happy about that?" Some of his raw grief leaked into his voice despite himself; he tried to tune it out by improvising. "How do I want them? Divided, quarreling amongst themselves, and unready to meet us in battle. I want to beat them in combat, not with craven tactics like this."

Oncit was staring at him, and the lords who had turned their ears or heads to listen to him applauded briefly. He noticed Ikinna among them, and the weasel raised a paw. "Hear, hear! Couldn't have said it better. We'll beat those heathens in a fair fight—no need to go sneaking in the night."

Volle gave the weasel a comradely nod, as his cronies cheered his words. Oncit was still staring at him, and as the other lords turned away, their talk a little more animated, Volle said quietly to Oncit. "So, tell me. What should I have been celebrating?"

"I stand corrected," said the wolf quietly, and he said not another word through the whole lunch.

They only dealt with one case on the tribunal, a simple matter of inheritance that they ruled on unanimously. After that, the rest of the afternoon was passed quietly. Volle sat apart from Oncit and Boursin while they played a dice game, brooding over his own thoughts. Ullik would have to wait until tomorrow, and tomorrow was Gaiaday; there were the services, and Ullik didn't usually do business after that. Perhaps he could corner him on the way back from services and take him to his office. He hoped he would be allowed to attend services. Since the whole palace went en masse, papers weren't checked. He would ask Welcis when he got back.

Thinking about the services brought him back to Fox and Canis. He still felt that he was meant to learn a lesson from the past events. Not to let attachments obscure his purpose? Seir had already made it clear that he needed to learn that, and he was sure it would be a long time before the memory of Xiller let him give himself to anyone else. He could think of the big cat now without the throat-closing grief of the first day after he'd heard the news, but the name still elicited a sadness that wouldn't pass for a long time, if ever.

To defend and honor his family? He had been doing that. He supposed he could consider Seir, Reese, Tella, and Sherr as part of his family, but they hadn't been betrayed by him any more than his real family had. The royal family had suffered much more, but what else could he do for them?

Or perhaps he could think along the lines the king had been talking earlier: All of Ferrenis was one family, his family. He was representing all of them here, not just the royal family. Honoring his family meant doing whatever he had to do to keep them safe, and he hadn't been doing that. He'd been acceding to his own principles, trying to walk the line between the fox he wanted to be and the job he had to do. And while he felt slightly uncomfortable lying about his hatred of Ferrenis, he found that much easier than potentially ruining the life of a vixen and her cub or cubs just to secure his position as a noble.

Ilyana, he realized, lay at the heart of his problem. If he continued to reject potential mates, there would be talk and it would become a distraction, just as the courtship itself had been a distraction. This would not necessarily endanger his mission, but by sparing her, he was setting a precedent for himself that might ultimately lead him to a bad decision in the future. His ability to make sacrifices, not just of himself, but also of others, was at stake here.

This dovetailed with his thoughts from the previous night, his revelation that he would have to use people. He couldn't ask others to make sacrifices just for him, nor could he always use them just for his own ends. But he could require those sacrifices to protect his family. He would never be as ruthless as the ones who had sent a gentle cougar to kill and be killed, but where his family was concerned, he would have to be willing to risk not only his own life, but also that of others. His family was his country, and his mission was to keep them safe. That was how he was to honor Fox and Canis.

The more he thought about it, the more right it felt. They'd never told it to him in those terms. His mission had always been given to him in dry, abstract, nationalistic terms. There was a plot against the country, there would be troop movements in the Reysfields, he was just supposed to gather information. If he thought about his mission in those terms, it was hard for him to get passionate about it.

Whatever else would come out of this incident, he would no longer lack passion.

Chapter 21

By the end of the tribunal, he was heartened enough by his new resolve that he flashed Oncit a tight smile when he caught the wolf examining him. Startled, Oncit looked about to say something, but then he turned and walked in the opposite direction.

"Maybe I got to him," Volle said to himself as he walked quickly back to his rooms. He would look for Oncit at lunch on Ursiday and try this new tack. At the very least, it seemed to have rekindled the wolf's interest in him, which had faded since their dinner together.

"Welcis," he said as he entered his parlor, "will I be allowed to go to services tomorrow with the rest of the palace?"

"Yes, sir."

"Good. Thank you."

"Sir? Lord Ikling requested your company at dinner tonight if you have no other plans."

"Oh? No, I haven't. I'll go see Helfer."

"Very good, sir. Might I suggest a change of clothes?"

"Of course." Volle changed into a less formal linen shirt and walked upstairs, reaching Helfer's chambers just as Caresh and a footservant were returning with trays of food. Caresh showed him into the parlor, where Helfer was sitting with a mug of apricot mead, which Volle could smell from the doorway.

"Come in, sit down." The weasel waved him to a chair. "Caresh, get him some mead."

"Thanks for the invitation." Volle took the chair, sweeping his tail through the back, as Caresh went to fulfill Helfer's order.

"You missed the run, so I thought I might as well share dinner." Helfer grinned. "So who was your 'appointment' with?"

"King Barris."

Helfer blinked, the mug halfway to his muzzle. "Really? But it's not his day."

"I know. It was informal. He just wanted to ask about Xiller. He's not very happy about what happened."

Helfer looked closely at Volle. "He's not the only one. He thought you knew something?"

Caresh had returned with a mug, which he handed to Volle. Volle sipped the pungent brew from it. "I did live with him for three days. It's not unreasonable. But I couldn't tell him anything."

"Could he tell you anything?" the weasel asked astutely.

Volle licked his lips, getting the apricot taste from them. "No. Except that he didn't know about it and didn't order it."

"That's good to know. Some appetizer?"

"Sure." They ate the small fish cakes that were being kept warm under a metal lid, one by one. The cakes were just the right size for Helfer's muzzle, but Volle found himself eating two at a time. They were salty but otherwise delicious.

"I wanted to thank you for last night, too, Hef." Volle wiped his paws off on a napkin as he swallowed the last cake.

"Oh, you're welcome." The weasel was sniffing at the main course as Caresh lifted the lid from the tureen to reveal a thick beef stew. "Mm. So you didn't mind me staying? You felt better afterwards?"

"Yes, I felt better, and no, I didn't mind." Volle smiled as Caresh ladled some stew into a bowl. "I was glad I finally got to see you in action."

Helfer chuckled. "Sorry it was one of my less inspired nights. Normally I could've gotten at least one more, but, you know, I didn't want to wear out poor Richy."

"Very considerate of you." Volle started on the stew, which was delicious, and the conversation ended there for a while.

After the apricot tarts ("made from Vellenland apricots," Helfer said), they relaxed, Helfer with more mead and Volle with some wine. They were quiet for a time, until Volle noticed Helfer's wide grin and said, "What?"

The weasel grinned into his mead. "You're pretty cute."

Volle flicked his ears. "Thanks. You are too. Impressive, too." He grinned back at the weasel.

Helfer lapped his mead and settled back. "That's another reason I like rabbits. They're usually really impressed with me." He winked.

"I bet." Volle took a sip of wine.

There was a long pause. Helfer looked up and said, "We don't have to do that again."

"I know," Volle said. "But I am glad we did."

"Me too." A pause, punctuated by the lapping of mead. "We could do it again. If you wanted. But we don't have to."

Volle grinned. "I might want to sometime. But last night was special. I needed both of you. I hope you're never in that kind of position. Again," he added hastily, remembering Helfer's father.

"I do too. It is nice to know there's someone you can trust...anywhere."

"Thank Canis for that."

"Thank Weasel." Helfer raised his mug and Volle raised his glass, and they emptied them together.

"Services in the morning," Volle said, getting up. "I should get to bed. Didn't sleep much last night."

"Same here." Helfer put his mug aside and stifled a yawn.

"When do you leave?"

"Day after tomorrow."

Volle nodded. "I'll see you off."

"Course you will," the weasel said cheerfully. "And I'll come find you when I get back."

Volle grinned and hugged Helfer tightly. "Thanks."

"Aww, I told you, it was my pleasure. In more ways than one." Helfer hugged him back.

"For that, and for just being my friend when I really needed it."

"Well, that's my pleasure too." Helfer smiled.

Volle leaned over and nuzzled his ears. "Mine too. Goodnight, Hef."

"Goodnight, Volle."

His mood the following morning was lighter than it had been in days, though he was not at all cheerful. He was looking forward to the services and to the interview with Ullik afterwards, and in anticipation of the latter, he slipped one of the southern coins into his purse. His grief and anger were already fading after only a few days, but his resolve remained strong.

The services were the same as always. Volle didn't know if he expected a special prayer for Prince Gennic, but the Gaiavox didn't lead one, so he said his own during a moment of silence. The Canid Cantor had chosen a responsorial prayer for the Canids called "To The Life Of The Pack," in which the congregation dedicated various parts of their bodies and lives to the Life of the Pack, and the priest, representing Canis, did the same. In light of his new resolve, Volle took this as a good sign, and he was even more heartened when he looked up at the stained glass window depicting Canis and saw the sun shining through it.

He managed to slip away to the candles. He lit two candles, saying quick prayers for Prince Gennic and Xiller as he did so, and when he placed the candles in their holders, he noticed another pair, burned almost all the way down, in the row just above them. He was examining them curiously when the Felid Cantor passed by and gave him a warm smile, which he returned.

"I hope you have found peace," the Cantor said quietly.

Volle made sure nobody else was within earshot, and replied in a low voice, "I think I have, brother of my father. Thank you."

The bobcat's smile grew. "Thank Canis, and thank Gaia, son of my brother. From them comes all peace and love." He reached out a paw and plucked the burned-down candles from the rack. "I was just about to light two more."

"Oh. For whom?"

"For you, son of my brother. For the two souls you pray for. I have lit two candles every day since your visit, when you did not return."

Volle felt a weakness in his chest and a pressure behind his eyes. "I haven't been able to…I've been restricted to the palace."

The Cantor nodded and smiled. "It is our duty. The candles should properly be lit every day for a month, and often people are too busy to come every day."

"Thank you," Volle whispered. "I promise, as soon as I can…"

"Do not fret, son of my brother. I am happy to do it." The Cantor dropped the candle ends into a box near the rack, and made a brief sign towards Volle. "Gaia and Canis's blessings be with you."

"And with you, brother of my father," Volle said softly. "Go in peace."

His eyes were still misty as he hurried out with the last of the congregation, hoping to catch Ullik before he disappeared into the palace. His effort was only half-hearted, as he no longer really felt like confronting the squirrel, but he reminded himself of his duty.

The person he did not expect to see was Sherr. The porcupine was standing along the ropes separating the commoners from the nobles, watching the procession go by as though he were just another gawker. The others were giving him a wide berth, though they huddled against each other in the chilly morning air. He caught Volle's eye and briefly nodded, making a sign with one paw near the ropes.

The sign was a general "okay" sign. Volle nodded to show he'd gotten it, and immediately broke eye contact. The sign had to mean that Reese's impersonation of the merchant had taken place and gone well. Otherwise, he assumed, Sherr would have signaled to him to hang behind, and they might have made an attempt to rescue him.

He wasn't sure he'd want to be rescued in that case, because rescue would mean being sent home, and being sent home meant facing the Duke's formidable teeth. But he would do whatever they deemed best, and the sign from Sherr gave him a good deal of relief.

Ullik was hard to miss in the crowd, and the fact that Volle couldn't see him meant that the extravagantly dressed squirrel had already gone into the palace. Volle hurried through the crowd and up the nearest stair, heading towards Ullik's office in the hope that his chambers were in the same wing.

Luck was with him. He turned a corner and saw Ullik and his wife strolling down the corridor, just about to stop in front of a door that was decorated in gold leaf. The Exchequer's head came up as he heard Volle's claws click on the stone floor, and his eyes narrowed.

"Lord Vinton."

"Exchequer Ullik," Volle said evenly. "And Madame… I don't believe I've had the pleasure."

"My wife, Lady Ullik," the squirrel said stiffly. His wife extended her paw with a smile.

Volle brushed his muzzle against it cursorily. "Lord Ullik, I have some business to discuss with you."

"I will be in my office tomorrow." The squirrel put a paw on his door.

"I would be most obliged if we could discuss it immediately." Volle spaced his words out just enough to give them weight, he hoped.

"Will it take long?" His wife had a very screechy voice. Volle tried not to fold his ears over.

Volle shook his head. "About five minutes, I should think."

Ullik's eyes gleamed as they met Volle's. He coughed into one paw. "Of course I will be happy to be of service. Dear, have Furtina put on some tea. I will be back shortly."

"What do you want?" he said as Volle followed him down the corridor to his office.

"Just to look at some records," Volle said.

The squirrel gave him a look. "The palace financial records are private." He slowed.

Volle could see his office now, and kept going. "This isn't anything important," he said, placing a paw on the office door handle. He reached into his pouch with the other. "I found this strange coin, and I wanted to know who it belonged to so I could return it."

Ullik waddled up to the door and examined the coin. He looked at Volle. "Give it to me, I'll return it." He reached for the coin.

Volle pulled his paw back. "I hope you won't be offended if I don't trust you."

"What makes you think I would know who it belongs to?"

"It's new. It hasn't traveled much. I'm guessing it was not dropped by a foreign dignitary—of which there have been none since I've arrived here—but was requested through your office." He dropped the coin into his purse. "Am I right?"

Ullik hesitated, then opened the door. "Inside."

He waddled through and went immediately to his office, gesturing Volle in and locking the door behind him. "Now," he said, "even if you are right, what makes you think I'll just let you go nosing through my books?" His beady eyes glinted.

"I don't expect you to. I expect you'll show me exactly which entry I need to see." Volle wrinkled his nose. The smell in here was as bad as he remembered.

"And why would I do that?"

Volle licked his lips slowly, letting his tongue travel visibly around his muzzle. "Because I have something you want."

He'd entertained the vague hope that Ullik would let him see the book without him having to do anything unpleasant, but the slow smile that met his remark told him that Ullik had only let him into the office because he expected Volle to make this offer. He walked over to the shelves of dusty books and selected one, then brought it over to Volle so the fox could read the title: "Foreign Currency Transactions under King Barris."

Volle reached for it, but Ullik held it behind his back. He leaned against the desk. "I think I will require your part of the bargain first." With his other paw, he unfastened his pants and slid them down.

His sheath, Volle saw, was already engorged, and he was partially erect, getting more so as Volle looked at him. He steeled himself, and knelt in front of the squirrel.

Without preamble, he took the short member into his muzzle and started to bob up and down, reminding himself that he was in control. Ullik moaned at the first touch of his tongue, then coughed wetly and started to breathe heavily.

The taste was bad: squirrel musk, dirty fur, and a smell that Volle identified as a goat. The thought that Ullik hadn't cleaned himself since his last encounter nearly made him throw up, and then the thought of vomiting on the squirrel's groin almost made him laugh out loud. He settled for wagging his tail and kept at his unpleasant task until he felt the squirrel shiver and heard his wet panting deepen. Abruptly, he lifted his muzzle and looked up.

"Keep going!" Ullik said harshly.

"The book. Now."

"Finish!"

"Once I've seen what I want to."

Ullik glared at him, panting, then said, "Fine!" and opened the book and thrust it towards Volle.

"Thank you." Volle needed only a couple seconds to read the last entry: 10 Tephossian Royals to 15 Terrialis guilders. For Secretary Prewitt. The confirmation of his suspicions, set out before him in Ullik's neat handwriting, sickened him nearly as much as the foul taste in his muzzle.

"Done?" Volle nodded, and Ullik threw the book back on his desk. "Then finish!"

For a moment, Volle considered leaving the Exchequer in his current state, but he might need his good graces in the future, he reminded himself. He bent over and took the foul-tasting shaft into his muzzle again, bobbing and licking until the squirrel uttered a series of short grunts and thrust his wide hips against the fox's muzzle. Volle felt the warm splash and foul taste on his tongue, and when he drew back, he saw the squirrel's eyes on him.

Ullik wanted him to swallow, and when he saw Volle hesitate, reached out a paw. Volle twisted his muzzle away to one side and deliberately spat onto the floor. Standing, he looked Ullik in the eye. "You really should get a pot in here," he said. "Thank you, Ullik." Without waiting for a reply, he turned, unlocked the door, and left the office.

He spent the afternoon in the garden, wrapped in his cloak. The chilly air didn't bother him as he paced around the rear garden, near the spot where he'd first met Xiller. The nearest bench was about fifty feet down the path, but he didn't feel like sitting down anyway. The snow had blanketed the spot, making it difficult to distinguish details and smoothing the whole garden into a soft white sculpture. Volle didn't need to see the bushes or smell the particular trees; he knew the spot by heart and paced up and down in front of it.

He walked around for nearly an hour, his paws chilling slowly in the snow, not thinking about much of anything. He didn't want to think about Prewitt. He would tell Seir, of course—*Tella is especially anxious to know*—and then it would rest in their paws. He wasn't thinking about Xiller, except peripherally. He wasn't thinking about Ilyana. Mostly, he just wanted to be outside, breathing the fresh, cold air, alone.

He smelled the fox before he saw him, a hint carried on the breeze. He didn't stop his pacing until he heard the crunch of snow, and then he turned. "Hello, Arrin."

The fox was bundled up in a cloak, carrying something in his left paw. "Hi, Volle." He stopped, tail swishing over the snow, about five feet away. "I hope I'm not interrupting."

Volle shook his head. "What is it?"

"Here." He held out his paw and uncurled it. Inside was a wrinkled set of papers. "You've been cleared. I asked to return your papers tonight. Prewitt is going to give you the official notification tomorrow and was going to do it then, but…" He shuffled his paws. "I asked to."

Volle took them and checked them quickly, then stuffed them in his purse. "Thanks." He looked away, but still caught the lowering of Arrin's ears out of the corner of his eye.

"Listen, Volle, I've been thinking about…I don't think you were right to ask what you did, but I didn't answer properly either. I should have been there for you and I wasn't. I mean, I should have supported you. So I think, maybe, we shouldn't…shouldn't go on. I don't think it would work."

Volle shook his head, still looking away from Arrin, his ears flicking at the sadness in the fox's voice. "No, I don't think so either."

"I'm not trying to accuse you, or say you were wrong. Well, I think you were, but so was I. I don't know what I'm trying to say." He sighed, his breath a puff of white in the air that hung for a moment before fading.

Volle folded his arms. He would not allow himself to feel guilty that he'd tried to take advantage of Arrin, because as a good spy, according to his newfound resolve, he had to live the role to himself as well as to others. Lying to Arrin in the name of his country was no sin. He did, however, want to mend fences. He genuinely liked the fox and didn't want to make him more miserable than he had to. Being aloof and self-righteous now that he had been cleared had made enough of his point by now.

"I'd still like you to teach me music, if you have the time." He favored the fox with a smile. "No reason we can't be friends."

"Yeah." Arrin's tail wagged and he smiled. "It's just…you have this rat after you, and all these complications. I was thinking about that too.

I don't mind being your friend, though. I do think you're a pretty nice fox."

"Thanks," Volle said drily. "I'm sorry about Dereath. That does make things more complicated. But you're nice, too. And you probably deserve a less...exciting fox."

Arrin grinned abashedly. "Maybe."

"Has Dereath been to see you this week at all?"

"No. Should he have?"

"You know he brought those charges, right?"

"Oh. No, I didn't." His ears flicked. After a long pause, he said, "If I'd known..."

"You'd still have done the same thing."

Arrin sighed. "Probably. I really don't like that rat, though."

"I don't either. I think Prewitt's going to have a long talk with him about bringing charges against a noble."

Arrin's ears came back up and his eyes glinted. "He won't enjoy that."

"I sincerely hope not. Maybe he'll leave me alone now."

"I hope so." Arrin put a paw on his shoulder and then sighed. "I need to go. I promised my mother I'd come visit her. And anyway, it's cold out here. How long have you been standing here?"

"A while. I like it." Volle grinned toothily at him. "Go on, take care of your mother. I'll be fine."

"I'll see you for dinner sometime." Arrin leaned close to brush his muzzle against Volle's but he didn't offer a kiss.

Volle brushed perfunctorily back and nodded. "Talk to Welcis." He waved as the other fox retreated along the path. He felt only a touch of sadness; any chance at a relationship had vanished the other day in Arrin's office. Mostly he felt relieved. Another complication had straightened itself out, and his life was a little bit simpler and easier. He took a deep breath of cold air and felt it spread into his lungs, and then walked quickly to the front gate and down to the park, simply because he could.

The next morning, clouds filled the sky and the air was warmer. The snow had melted enough to leave puddles of slush all through the garden, but the bushes still had white crowns. The stairs had been swept clean, so Volle's paws remained dry as he watched Caresh load Helfer's bags into the carriage. Helfer stood alongside him.

"Think it'll all fit?" Volle asked as they watched Caresh secure a bag to the roof. "How much stuff do you need, anyway?"

"You've no idea what the laundry is like back there. I can't wash anything or it will be completely ruined. They have no idea how to treat linen, let alone cotton. And then I have to dress differently to meet with the governor than I do to see my mother, or my potential brides, or my farmers. Really, packing is quite an ordeal. I'm more worried that I didn't leave anything behind."

"I don't see how you could have," Volle said. "I suspect if I went up to your chambers, I'd find them stripped bare."

"You might find someone stripped bare, at least." Helfer grinned and pressed a key into Volle's paw. "Speaking of which, here. The door is locked while I'm gone, but if you need to use the chambers for some reason, you can."

"Oh, I wouldn't—"

"You would, and you can. Just be careful about it, okay?"

"Sure. Thanks, Hef." Privately he resolved that he wouldn't bring anyone in through Helfer's entrance, because he had no idea who knew about it and who didn't, and giving away secrets like that was abhorrent to him, though Helfer seemed to do it on a weekly basis.

Caresh had managed to fit the last of the bags into the carriage itself, and approached them. "The carriage is ready, sir. An early start would ensure us safe passage across the Otrine before nightfall."

"Yes, yes." Helfer turned to Volle. "If we get to the river at night, it's dangerous. The other side is not so bad. Where's that purse you wanted me to take?"

"Oh, here." He handed Xiller's purse to the weasel. "Ten gold Royals. Thanks a lot for doing this, Helfer."

"It's not a problem. Villutian's right on my way. I'll put the purse in their paws myself. The commander of the army should know where to find them, eh?"

Volle nodded. "I'm sure he'll remember Xiller."

Helfer gave him a warm, sad smile. "It's a nice thing you're doing."

"It's the right thing. Thanks for helping. I'd offer you money, but I think I'll just find a nice rabbit for you when you get back."

"You do that and I'll not only deliver this myself, I'll go back next year to make sure they spent it wisely."

Volle laughed. "It's a deal." He hugged Helfer warmly. "Stay safe. See you in two weeks."

Helfer nuzzled him and hugged back. "And you stay out of trouble."

"I'll do the best I can." He waved as the weasel walked down the stairs and jumped into the carriage. Caresh bowed to Volle, then stepped in after his master. The door closed, and with a snap of his whip, the driver started the horses on their way.

Volle watched until the carriage had passed the front gate, and then followed it on foot. He walked down the street, which was busier than it had been for the past few days. The warmer weather and vanishing snow was bringing out some of the less cold-tolerant species, like the rabbits and weasels.

He made his way slowly to the cathedral, whose grey bulk loomed darkly against the light grey of the sky. Inside, it seemed slightly colder than outside, perhaps because there was no sun to warm the stone. He walked to the candle rack and lit two candles to replace the ones from the previous day, then knelt and said two prayers. He did see the Felid Cantor, but he appeared busy, and Volle didn't really need to speak with him anyway.

For nearly an hour, he prayed, and then he left the cathedral. He walked around the palace and to the north, to some of the areas he hadn't visited the previous day, again simply reveling in his freedom. When he finally returned to his chambers, Welcis told him that Prewitt had been by to see him in the morning and would call again the following morning. So Volle stayed in the next morning and waited, and about mid-morning, Welcis showed in the large golden bear, with a wolf trailing behind him.

"Secretary Prewitt and Lord Oncit," Welcis announced as he closed the door.

Prewitt turned to the skunk when he walked in. "Welcis, I would like to speak to your master in private. Would you mind terribly waiting in the main hallway until we're done?"

Volle nodded to Welcis's inquiring glance. "Yes, sir," the skunk said. He left immediately, closing the door behind him.

Volle flicked his ears. He was mildly surprised to see Oncit there with Prewitt. Seeing the bear stirred dark emotions in him; he couldn't keep his ears from folding back, but he did lift them again quickly. If they noticed, they didn't say anything. He watched them walk toward the chairs, the smaller wolf staying behind the bear, and he flexed his paws, fighting the urge to leap on Prewitt with claws and fangs bared. With some effort, he forced down the hatred and gestured to two nearby chairs. Neither offered any explanation for Oncit's presence as they sat, and when he spoke, Prewitt started with the charges.

"We contacted the merchant, Lord Vinton, and I have word from Vinton that they did see a black fox pass through there some months ago. I am satisfied for the moment that the charges are groundless. I've dismissed them, and yesterday I had quite a long session with Lord Fardew and his clerk Dereath. I told him in no uncertain terms that to accuse a noble of treachery is a serious matter, and that if Fardew weren't standing up for him, he would have been expelled from the palace."

"Why is Fardew standing up for him?"

Prewitt shook his head. "I don't know. I trust Fardew enough that I don't want to get rid of his clerk without strong reason. But I let both of them know that one more transgression like this would be sufficient reason. I don't think you'll have any trouble from Talison for quite a while."

"Thank you." Volle felt relieved, though a part of him warned that Dereath wouldn't give up, having come this far. He would resent this victory as he had the previous ones, and he might be less obvious about it, but he would keep looking for chinks in Volle's armor.

Calm down, he told himself. Maybe he'll just give up and go back to chasing guys who want nothing to do with him. But he couldn't quite make himself believe that.

"So this is your official notification that the charges have been dropped. I believe your papers have already been returned to you." Volle nodded. "Then that concludes the official portion of my visit."

Volle waited, knowing that Prewitt wanted him to ask what the unofficial portion was. He met the bear's level gaze and waited quietly while Oncit fidgeted in his seat.

After a minute, Prewitt smiled. "Exchequer Ullik told me that you found a southern gold piece of mine and were going to return it. I suspect it was dropped by your visitor from a month back."

"I found all fifteen of them," Volle said. "He left them behind." He didn't trust himself to say any more than that.

Prewitt's smile didn't waver. "Ullik said you exchanged all but one of them for Tephossian Royals. I wonder when I might expect the Royals, and the last one back."

"You might not," Volle said coolly. "The Royals are on their way to Xiller's family. As he carried out your mission, I was certain you would wish his family to have his payment."

"No messenger left for—his home province yesterday." Prewitt had been about to say the province's name, Volle noted, and had stopped himself in case Volle didn't actually know it.

"Lord Ikling was passing close by Villutian on his way home," Volle said. "He kindly agreed to deliver the payment for me."

The bear nodded slowly. "And the last Terralian gold?"

"I will keep it. As a souvenir. I did send his family the entire ten Tephossian Royals, you know. I figure that means I bought the coin."

"I don't mind you keeping the coin," Prewitt rumbled, "just so long as you don't show it to anyone who might understand its significance."

Volle wondered why Prewitt seemed so unruffled at having his secret found out. Obviously Oncit already knew it; the wolf was leaning back in his chair behind Prewitt, eyes half-closed, but ears perked and alert. Volle glanced at him briefly but got no sign.

"I don't intend to show it around," he said.

"I do appreciate that," Prewitt said. "And I know you had an audience with the King recently, and as soldiers have not come to my chambers, I assume you did not share any of this with him."

"It was rather careless to put your name in the financial books."

The bear spread his large paws. "Nobody else who knew had the authority to order foreign currency. Any other name would have aroused more immediate suspicion. And if all had gone as planned, the gold would have been considered evidence by the Ferrenians, and nobody in the palace here would even have heard of its existence, much less had a reason to suspect that someone here had originated the plot." He shook his head. "I don't mind telling you that it could only have gone more wrong if that idiot had failed to kill the prince." Volle gritted his teeth as Prewitt went on. "Instead of them being distracted away from us, their attention is squarely focused on us. It'll be four or five years before we can even think about proceeding."

"We?" He forced the word out through clenched teeth, but Prewitt didn't seem to notice.

"Ah, yes, I'm getting ahead of myself. There is a small group I have organized that is attempting to reclaim the Reysfields, and maybe, in the long term, more."

"More?"

"We feel that with the right strategy, we can win a war with Ferrenis and actually take over the country. Weakening the royal family was part of that long-range plan. But that's far off in the future. The Reysfields are strategically important from a standpoint of terrain as well as supplies...but we don't need to go into that now. Oncit tells me that your sympathies are firmly in line with our goals, and that you would be a good addition to the group. You haven't gone to the King with your information, so I'm forced to conclude that either you want to join us, or you're hoping to blackmail me. If it's the latter, then I will be very disappointed, and I might add that your chances of success are very small. So you'll join us, and maybe with your help, the next mission won't be such a disaster, eh?" He leaned forward, smiling, eyes bright.

Volle opened his muzzle angrily, but a small motion caught his eye. He saw Oncit shaking his head minutely, just for a moment. He stopped. "I certainly think the last mission had some flaws," he said stiffly. "I would be honored to help with the next one."

"Splendid!" Prewitt reached forward and slapped him on the knee, and it took all his restraint to keep from slapping the huge paw away. "Oncit here will be your contact. No discussions in public now, remember."

Volle nodded. "Of course not."

The bear rose, and Volle and Oncit followed suit. "I think that is all. Please save any questions for our first meeting, if you would be so kind."

"Secretary, I would like to discuss our contact system with Lord Vinton, if you can carry on without me," said Oncit, the first words he'd spoken since entering.

"Certainly. I will see you both within a couple weeks. I'm sure we're all anxious to hear your views, Lord Vinton. Good day."

When he was gone, Volle offered Oncit a seat again, but the wolf shook his head. "I want to make this quick," he said in a low voice. "You're probably wondering why I only recommended you recently when you've been spouting off against Ferrenians for weeks. I was the only one who thought that this assassination was going too far, and even though Prewitt had ordered me to check you out, the last thing I wanted was to bring on another young firebrand who would agree to any crazy scheme as long as it harmed Ferrenis. But when you said it disgusted you...well, I could see the sincerity in that. So you hate them, but you are still bound by the rules of war and dignity. I like that. I want someone like you at my side, so I won't be...so afraid to stand up for the things I believe in." His tail wagged slowly and he looked at Volle hopefully.

Volle smiled and patted him on the shoulder. "Don't worry about that. I think we have the same ideas about what's decent. I've served alongside you on the tribunal for a couple months now."

Oncit nodded, wagging his tail a little faster. "I thought so. That's all I wanted to say, Lord Vinton. I'm glad you're joining. You seem decent."

"I like to think so," Volle said. "Would you like to stay and talk? Lord Black left me a whole jar of candied locusts. They're pretty good." He offered only out of politeness, and because he'd found he couldn't eat more than one a day himself. He didn't really want to stay and talk to Oncit; his anger at Prewitt was still burning in him.

Oncit waved his paw. "No, thank you. I need to get back upstairs. I think my wife will be returning soon."

The way he said it caught Volle's ear. "Returning from where?"

The wolf turned a sad look on him. "I think you know. I think everybody knows. They don't think I do, but I do. She doesn't think I do either. It's okay. It makes her happy. I don't know if I could any more."

Volle bit his lip and nodded. He suddenly felt no anger, just pity for the old wolf. "I'll see you at tribunal," he said quietly.

Oncit just nodded, looking embarrassed to have admitted so much, and left quickly.

And so there it was, as easy as that. Perhaps 'easy' wasn't the right word, but still: He knew who was involved and they had welcomed him into their circle. It had only taken three or four months and the death of a lover and a prince. He took one of the locusts and crunched it thoughtfully, letting the sweet and smoky flavor fill his muzzle as he looked out his window, surveying the gardens, for the first time, with a feeling of accomplishment.

Chapter 22

The note he'd been expecting came a week later, while he was in the middle of writing up some notes for the Agricultural Council. Welcis brought it to him, and he smoothed out the paper on his desk. The message was short and to the point: "I'm ready. Please come tonight. –Ilyana."

He folded it back up and returned it to Welcis. "Thank you. I will be visiting Madame Rodion tonight."

"Very good, sir. Semi-formal clothes?"

"No. I don't expect she'll really look at my clothes much."

"I see, sir."

"And Welcis?"

"Sir?"

He rested his elbows on his desk and his muzzle in his paws. "Can you get me two or three bottles of some kind of mead?"

He drank the last bottle of blackberry mead in the carriage on the way over. Snow had fallen again the previous day, and was falling again, but the two bottles he'd already drunk kept him warm even in the chilly carriage. As he gulped from the last one, he noticed that his tongue was numb to the sting of the alcohol, and that the ghostly snow-covered buildings were dancing before his eyes. He opened the door and stuck his nose out into the cold air to see if he could smell the ghosts. He felt the searing cold on the inside of his nostrils, but no smell of ghosts. Perfect, he thought muddledly.

When he stepped out of the carriage, the ground rushed up to meet him rather sooner than he expected, but he kept his balance. If he walked slowly and planted his feet, he could walk through the swaying yard without much trouble. The door seemed a long ways away, so he was relieved when the driver clambered down and helped him find it. The driver's weight seemed to steady the yard, and Volle was able to walk more quickly with his help.

He vaguely heard the muffled conversation the driver and Katiana Rodion had at the door — "Was drinking mead on the way over" "as long as he can walk" — but didn't interpret any of it. The door closed, and someone started to help him up a flight of stairs. He smelled Marcel and tried to say, "Good evening," only it came out rather slurred, like "G'v'ing." He blinked and was surprised to see only Katiana beside him, her scent clearer now though still he thought Marcel had met him at the door. "How did you get here so fast?" he tried to ask, but Katiana stopped him in the middle of whatever he actually was saying.

"Ilyana's in my brother's room. Do you understand? They're staying with us. You go in here, and I'll go upstairs. Do you understand?"

Volle nodded his head and pointed at the door. "Ilyana…in there."

She sighed and nodded. "I wish you weren't drunk."

"I am not…well. Maybe a little."

The door was open and he was inside a strange apartment, and then the door was closed. He seemed to hear the sound of the door closing before it actually happened.

"Volle?"

It was Ilyana's voice, but different. He couldn't pinpoint how. "Here," he said, and walked towards it, a little more steadily than he had outside.

On the second try, he found the right room, the scent of her heat strong enough to penetrate even his mead-induced fog. She was lying on the bed on her side, nude, one leg crossed over the other as she watched the doorway. Her tail thumped against the bed when she saw him.

"After last time, I was worried you might not…Oh, I'm glad you're here. Come here!"

He lurched toward the bed, vaguely aware of his paws as they carried him across the room. Her scent was all over, and though he didn't find it exciting, it definitely caused a reaction in his body. Between his legs, he could feel a warm throbbing, and the more he breathed, the warmer it got. He was already fumbling with his shirt when she said, "Oh, I can smell you…take your clothes off!"

She dug at his pants while he wrestled the shirt over his head, dropping it to the floor. His head was clearing, he noticed, but not by a lot. It was just enough to keep him on his feet as his pants dropped to the floor.

Her paws were all over his sheath and erection, and then her muzzle was too, licking at it while he tried to get the shirt off. When he finally did, she pulled him down to the bed. "Please, I need…" her eyes begged him as she lay on her back, legs spread.

He needed it too, now. He made a wavering motion with his paw. "Turn…turn over."

"Oh, okay. I like that." She giggled and rolled onto her stomach, then got up on her paws and knees, waving her tail at him.

He suspected he could have finished however she was lying, but at least in this view it looked more familiar, and he felt his mental arousal growing. She had a nice rear that reminded him of…of… He couldn't remember. He got up behind her, leaning over her back and pressing against that rear. She guided him into her, panting with satisfaction.

Automatically, he started thrusting back and forth, his head giddy with mead and her thick, lustful scent. The familiar feelings building up in him seemed tinged with nausea as he kept moving, smelling her and listening to her squeaks and pants. He panted harder himself, almost unable to stop even if he'd wanted to, his knot growing quickly, though it still slid into and out of her easily.

He slid one arm around her, and now his thrusts were less easy, his knot spreading her lips as it pushed through them, and her squeaks were taking on a higher pitch. He felt it coming and braced, pressing harder and faster, and then he was no longer able to pull back. He shuddered against her hips, felt the climax surround him, and distantly heard her cries as well. It seemed much more diffuse this time, a warm wash of pleasure spread out over minutes instead of a sharp peak of ecstasy. He rode it happily, resting his muzzle on her back.

"Oh, Volle…" he heard her say breathlessly. "Volle…"

He wanted to reply, but his muzzle didn't seem to want to open. He felt so very heavy, all he wanted to do was lie down. It didn't seem considerate to have her bear all his weight, so he slid to one side, dragging her with him, and ended up on his side. He remembered only her saying his name one more time before the weight became too much for him and his eyelids drifted shut.

Pain was creeping around the edges of his head. Bright lights flashed even though his eyes were shut. A horrible mix of smells assaulted his nostrils: vixen in heat, the musk of sex, and …rancid blackberry mead? No, not rancid, just…vomited. He groaned and put a paw to his head.

"Awake?" A familiar voice greeted him.

The room took some time to resolve once he finally opened his eyes. Blurry patches of light and dark settled into the shapes of the chair and dresser he'd barely noticed upon entering. He was lying in a bed, naked, covered by a blanket, and in the chair…

"Tish?"

The black wolf grinned at him. "I'm surprised you're awake so soon."

"That smell…" He closed his eyes and fought to keep his stomach quiet, as the vomit smell encouraged it to rebellion.

"I don't know what possessed you to get drunk on blackberry mead."

"Helfer said…"

The wolf waited for him to finish, and when he didn't, shook his head. "I told you Lord Ikling wasn't a good influence on you."

"Had to…for a female." He tried to sit up. His stomach protested and he froze.

"Don't try to sit up too fast. You had to get drunk for a female in heat?"

"I'm okay." He sat up a little more. The blanket slid down his shoulders but kept him modest. "Didn't think…about the heat part. Did I really throw up?"

"A couple hours ago." Tish laughed at Volle's wince, and the boom of his laugh made Volle wince more. "Don't worry. Ilyana was long gone by then. She got worried when you fell asleep and her parents sent a messenger to fetch Tika. I came along."

"Is she okay?"

"She's fine, she's fine. Being in heat is a little like being drunk when there's a male around. At least, that's what Tika tells me. Tika explained that you'd had some tough times at the palace and that was probably why you were drinking, and Ilyana was perfectly happy after that. She's very excited about the cub. She feels the mating was a success."

Volle flattened his ears and stayed silent. Tish tilted his muzzle, then said quietly, "I'm glad you went through with this. It will be good for you."

He was too tired and too sick to censor his thoughts. They spilled out of his muzzle before he could stop them. "It's as much your fault as mine if their lives are ruined." He looked straight at Tish as he said it.

He didn't know what reaction he expected, but the wolf just nodded, not smiling or frowning, ears up. "I suppose it's about time we had this talk. If you're caught, you mean."

Volle nodded, taking a moment to relish the fact that he'd been right. "They'd be ruined. She'd have no more prospects, the wife of a traitor."

"I suppose you'll just have to make sure you don't get caught, then. You've done an admirable job of it so far."

"I've come close, though."

"Volle, in your line of work, you have to make sacrifices. Ilyana is strong. I won't pretend that her life will be ideal if you're disgraced, but she won't be broken. It's a risk I took when I encouraged Tika to choose her for you."

"Does Tika know?"

"About what? About why I pressed her to choose Ilyana? Yes. The depth to which I'm involved? She guesses. We've not talked about it. But nobody is as good at concealing a single secret as one who talks incessantly about a number of others, wouldn't you say?" He winked. "I know I can trust her, and maybe one day I will tell her everything."

"How did you get involved?"

The wolf settled back. "That's a very long story. I don't know that I'll ever have the time to tell you all about it. It spans twenty-some years and I was a very different wolf when it began. I was young and idealistic, and, like you, I thought I could perform a dishonorable task honorably."

"You're not so different."

"Thank you. I am older, though, and no longer under the illusion that what I do has some honor to it. When I was young, though—ah, I thought about nothing but honor then. I studied the history of Bucher and determined that it must never happen again. Full peace with Ferrenis, I thought, was the only guarantor of future stability. Our countries share much, you know. The southlands are full of jungle cats, the western plains are full of grazers, and the northern countries all keep to themselves. Ferrenis and Tephos lie in the cradle of the Panbestian church, the only two countries where carnivores and herbivores live side by side, and yet they squabble like littermates rather than working together as packmates..." He grinned at Volle's pained expression. "Sorry. I will skip the history lesson for today. At any rate, I believed in that, and I still do. My grandfather had been a friend of the Ferrenian Ambassador, back when such a position still existed, and my father still knew some people in town who had connections. Through them I got in touch with the Ferrenian intelligence, and offered to do some small tasks.

"It took them many years before they trusted me to do anything of significance. I helped three agents gain positions in the palace over the years, including you. Under their orders, I never did any spying directly after the first few years of our association. I was too valuable to risk. That is why we're having this conversation here, and why we will never discuss this anywhere inside the palace walls." He looked at Volle sternly, and the fox nodded.

"So that is my story. I suppose Seir told you?"

Volle bristled. "No. I figured it out. Well, she did hint. But I already suspected then."

"Oh? What gave me away?" The wolf wagged his tail, grinning.

"One thing that nobody else in the palace knows."

"Which is...?"

"That Derrik, the investigator who 'found' me, is a Ferrenian agent."

Tish nodded quietly. "I wondered if you'd catch that."

"Even then, I wasn't sure, but Dewanne made that offhanded comment about you knowing everyone. He said something like 'I wouldn't plan a trip to the bathroom without consulting Tish for the best attendant.' I don't remember exactly what it was, but suddenly I realized: you referred Derrik to him. You probably put Dewanne up to finding Lord Vinton, too."

"Just a hint here and there." Tish looked pleased. "It worked admirably. He's very insecure about the place of foxes in the nobility."

"And that's why you wrote me a letter of recommendation, which allowed me to slide into the nobility despite the fact that nobody had even met me before I arrived at the palace. I didn't think that odd at first. They fed me some line about you being a sympathizer but not realizing I was an agent, and I realized that had to be false. You wouldn't put your reputation on the line without knowing what you were getting into. You're careful and deliberate, and—ow." He put a paw to his head. He'd talked too long, and a short stabbing pain in his temples cut him off.

"Here." Tish walked over to him and handed him a small bowl of water. Volle lapped at it gratefully while Tish went back to his chair. "You're right. I'm sure Prewitt thought it odd that I wrote that letter too, but he probably thought I'd met you at least once."

"Prewitt..." Volle rubbed his eyes. "I left his name and chamber location with Tella on the way over here. They'll be killing him tonight."

Tish nodded. "I wondered when it would be. Good thing we're here, isn't it?"

Volle's paws worked. "I wish I could be doing it myself."

"You'd best leave those thoughts behind." Tish growled softly. "If there were a way to satisfy the Ferrenians and leave Prewitt alive, I would have found it. They demanded a death in return for Prince Gennic's. This has nothing to do with your cougar, as much as his death might be worthy of vengeance as well. All right?"

Volle nodded grudgingly. Tish went on. "I believe the king will have little difficulty figuring out why Prewitt was killed. Security at the palace will be a little tighter for a while, but I think we can all live with that in exchange for some safety, don't you?"

"I don't want him to be forgotten."

Tish tilted his muzzle again. "Do you have something in mind?"

"No. Yes. How...how would I buy a statue from the park and move it into the garden?"

Tish shrugged. "Ask the King. If he requests the statue from the city, they'll give it to him. It's just a matter of whether he'll want to go to the trouble of moving it."

"I'll handle all that." The statue would be enough. He relaxed, felt his paws unclench.

"He'll probably allow it, then. If you need me to, I'll put in a good word for you."

Volle smiled. "Thanks."

"Anything else, before I go tell the Rodions that you are alive and well?"

Volle paused. "Why didn't you tell me right away?"

"Standard procedure. If you were caught early on, or proved to be unsuitable for the job, you couldn't give me away if you didn't know I was working with you."

The mention of his inexperience and unsuitability now raised no more annoyance than the bite of a stinging fly. He brushed it off, secure in the confidence that he had done his job. "Wouldn't it have been easier to keep me from getting caught if I knew I could work with you?"

Tish smiled. "Perhaps. But I won't be here forever. In perhaps another ten years, I would like to retire and leave the Tistunish duties to my son, the governor. And I needed to be sure that my replacement could handle himself without my help."

Volle blinked. "Your what?"

"You don't think Avery would let me retire without a successor in place, do you?" He smiled. "He'd chew my tail off first."

Volle laughed nervously. "He threatened other parts of me."

"I bet he did."

"I don't think I could ever replace you, though, Tish."

The wolf got up and put a paw on his shoulder. "We would not be having this conversation if I didn't think you can, and will." He smiled. "Now get up and get dressed. We have a wedding to arrange."

Volle winced. "I'd rather sit here hung over in my own vomit, thank you."

Tish roared with laughter and clapped Volle on the back, lightly. Volle held his ears in pain. "Come on, boy. It won't be as bad as the cotillion, I promise. And you'll never have to sleep with her again, if you're lucky. Good Canis, did I really just say that?" He chuckled and extended a paw.

Forcing a smile, Volle took the paw, and stood, holding the blanket around him. He eyed the pool of vomit on the floor. "I suppose it would be polite for me to clean that up."

"Think like a noble, boy. That's what servants are for."

Volle tilted his muzzle. "Welcis isn't here."

"They have servants upstairs. We'll give the Rodions a gold Royal for the trouble, and they'll be happy to have their servants clean up here."

"Okay." Volle stood, hesitating, the blanket held to his midsection.

Tish looked at the blanket and then down at Volle's pants, on the floor. "Why don't I wait outside for you?"

"Thanks. And, Tish…thanks."

The wolf smiled. "It's entirely selfish, I assure you." His eyes twinkled. "I look forward to an early and indolent retirement."

"I'll do my best," Volle said softly. Tish waved, and then left quickly, closing the door behind him.

Volle skirted the mess on the floor and picked up his pants. He dressed quickly, but stood in thought for a moment by the dresser, massaging his head. Then he looked up at the ceiling, toward the room where his future wife waited for him. With a sigh, he squared his shoulders and went outside, to fulfill his duties.

Chapter 23

The Lonely Cock was about half full. Volle sat in a shadowy corner, nursing an ale, watching a sandy-furred wolf at the bar. He was cute, and he'd been sitting there for twenty minutes waiting for someone. For the last ten minutes he'd been looking more and more agitated, and now he just looked resigned. his ears and tail drooping. He was awfully cute; Volle saw several other patrons trying to catch his eye, without much success.

He wasn't sure whether he wanted to start anything. He wished Helfer were here; then there wouldn't be any doubt. But Helfer wouldn't be back for another day or two, probably, and Lord Black hadn't come with him this time, and he was feeling lonely. He studied the wolf's shirt and well-worn cloak. Probably a young farmer in town, or an artisan's apprentice. His fur looked scruffy and there was dirt on his clothes.

In the course of looking around, he caught Volle's eye and stared. Volle blinked, and then supposed that there must be some reflection off his eyes. He smiled, showing white teeth, and the wolf lowered his muzzle with a grin. He knew how to play the game, Volle saw. In fact, he wasn't sure that the whole act of waiting for someone hadn't been a charade.

After five more minutes of pouting, the wolf gathered his drink and walked shyly over to Volle's table. He stopped and looked a bit startled when he saw Volle's fine clothes, but gathered his confidence and took another step towards the table. "May I...?"

Volle widened his smile and gestured to the opposite side of the table. He breathed in the wolf's scent: light, young, and musky. Curiosity and desire. He knew he wasn't fooling Volle, but he enjoyed putting on the act. "Your friend stood you up?"

The wolf smiled and flicked an ear. "Yeah. Pretty rude, huh? My name's Lenny."

"I'm Volle." He glanced around the pub and saw that the others who'd been looking at the wolf had apparently given up. None of them were looking his way anymore.

"So you live in the palace?"

Volle nodded. "That's right."

The wolf tilted his muzzle. Volle estimated that they were about the same age. His sandy-colored muzzle darkened to brown on his ears and the top of his head, and Volle could see a patch of creamy white at his throat. "So I guess we can't go back to your place."

Volle shook his head. He'd left Helfer's key in his chambers, even if he hadn't resolved not to use the secret door.

"Well, my 'room' is a small closet in back of my master's shop, so we can't go there. Maybe there's a room here?" His ears perked hopefully.

Volle grinned. Lenny probably didn't have the money to pay for a room himself. "No rooms left."

"How do you know?"

Volle indicated the bartender with his muzzle. "While you were sitting at the bar, two couples went up to ask the bartender something. He shook his head and they walked away."

"Oh." The wolf fidgeted and lapped at his drink. "Maybe if we wait…" He started eying the other patrons, clearly wondering if one of them had a place with a suitable room.

"Why wait?" Volle grinned. Lenny looked back at him, tilting his muzzle again curiously. Volle dipped his muzzle to indicate the table and the dark space beneath it.

"Wha—here? Right here?" Lenny whispered, but Volle could hear the excitement beneath the surprise in his voice. He nodded, and a moment later, the wolf's scent changed, desire increasing sharply. Volle grinned at the wolf, and got a grin back in return. "Well…okay."

Volle leaned back. "You go first." The wolf looked warily at him as he casually unfastened his pants. "Don't worry. I'll make sure you get your turn. I promise."

Lenny considered for a moment, then nodded. He glanced quickly around the bar, but nobody was looking at them. With a grace that surprised Volle, he slipped under the table.

A moment later, Volle felt a tug at his pants, and warm breath on his sheath. He smiled, leaned back, and closed his eyes.

Epilogue

In the city of Divalia, the capital of Tephos, the palace sits in the center beside the river Inside the walls, the palace is surrounded by three gardens on the north and south. The main garden, in the front, is where all of the most beautiful flowerbeds are placed. The rear gardens consist mostly of hedges, bushes, and trees, simple and unadorned.

If you were to wander through the western rear garden, you might eventually come across an old statue of a lion warrior. He stands boldly facing the outer wall of the palace, sword raised, lips curled in a fierce snarl. His mane is richly detailed, though much of the detail has been lost to time. There are nicks and blemishes in the bronze, and it has turned mostly green with age. There is no plaque to identify the origin of the statue, nor any dedication to explain its presence.

If you were to take the palace's residents through the rear garden and point the statue out to them, probably one in ten would remember having seen it before. Not one in a hundred would be able to say from where it came, and of those who could, none would admit to knowing why.

But if you watched the garden closely, once in a while you might see a figure approach the statue. He stands before it silently, head bowed, and remains there for several moments. And sometimes when he leaves, a flower remains at the base of the statue, an enigmatic remembrance whose softness seems curiously out of place beneath the fierce statue, in that austere secluded corner of the garden of the palace.

www.ingramcontent.com/pod-product-compliance
Lightning Source LLC
Chambersburg PA
CBHW051636050726
47502CB00011B/553